Polaris: The Demon General & the General Practitioner

Book Three of the Series

Bai Hu

白
虎

Dui

对

Polaris: The Demon General and the General Practitioner

ISBN-13: 978-0-9966338-2-6

Titles in the Series:
Polaris: Emperor of Nan Rong
Polaris: Empress of Ning
Polaris: The Demon General and the General Practitioner
Polaris Special: Dui's True Ending
Polaris: The Curse of Ice Blue Eyes

Polaris:
The Demon General
&
The General Practitioner

By Lenne Penry

Polaris: The Demon General and the General Practitioner

Polaris: The Demon General & the General Practitioner

Chapter 1: A Missing Monarch

Chapter 1: A Missing Monarch

Chapter 1: A Missing Monarch

"To the east, the elder star lies." A familiar tune bursts as I walk down the dirt road. It is late afternoon and the sun's vigor isn't as oppressive as it had been earlier so, I decided to return home. What a great day it was for fishing! I caught three large catfish! This should last for the rest of the week.

"The younger's name is Bao Lai! Pft! Ha-ha! What was that? That was way too shrill!"

Singing at the top of my lungs to test my terrible skills for the sheer fun has become a habit of sort, to stave off silence. It's a good thing no one's around to witness my embarrassment, or so I thought.

Without warning, the ground begins shaking and a few stones beside my feet jump as though scattered on a beating drum. When I look up, two horses are galloping hither at full speed. The men atop are clad in heavy armors decorated with unmistakable colors of the imperial army. What could soldiers possibly be doing in this secluded little area? Every succeeding, rapid thump of horses' hoofs peppering the road gives evidence that the fleeting thought is inconsequential. The men see me, I know they do, but there is no sign of them yielding. This little road is barely enough for them to ride side-by-side as they are. There is no room for me, too. They are going to run over me!

Every second they near, panic escalates. Without thinking, I dart for a gully to be out of their way. As luck would have it, my foot slips and I fall onto a thick thornbush. My precious fish are covered in dirt and my clothes and flesh are cut by the jagged thorns. Small amounts of blood begin trickling from my arms and back. Such as it is, I at least had my life.

The horses fly by where I previously stood on the road. Those men undoubtedly would have trampled me without a second thought. There is no remorse from them; not even a slight apology. But then, what could anyone expect from imperial soldiers? They cower before their lords and treat everyone else their doormats.

Naturally, temper gives into fury. Climbing out from the gully, words begin gushing without discretion. "I'm so sorry to be in your ways, my lords! I just thought men wearing imperial colors are supposed to protect the people, not run them over!"

The horse on the right comes to a halt, followed by the one on the left. The men whip around their steeds. I can feel blood draining from my face. I never speak when I should and always do when I shouldn't, I realize that, but it is too late. Retreat seems an obvious choice. Yet, they have horses, how can I outrun them? Then again, why should I run? I've done nothing wrong.

The two mumble a few words to one another and then advance. The one on the right, the man who stopped after having heard my charges, dismounts and approaches first. He is tall and his eyes are sharp and cold. Even so, I can't help but notice the hazel colors of his irises and the long majestic silver hair. What an unnatural combination! He appears more of a demon from an old silk scroll than a man; and maybe, he is. That scowl on his face is sending chills down my spine. I'm not inclined to believe myself a coward. Still, it takes clenching both hands just to keep from shaking.

The odd man scans me over, every inch from the top of my head down to my toes. Then, like a beast, sniffs the air around me as if searching for something. His strange actions fill me with dread, but also restlessness. The sun is on the verge of setting. I need to go home. Whatever fear overtaking me is pushed back by sheer obstinacy. My lips part; yet, I do not have the chance. The galloping of another horse down the dirt road startles me to turn as another armored man rides forthwith. Unlike the others, his light suit is common and bland, without their intricate, expensive embellishments. I assume he must be of lower ranking. The brown mare stops abruptly and the rider jumps off.

"I'm sorry, Generals! I got lost! You both were riding so fast, I couldn't keep up!" The young man gasps for air, though I wonder why, since the mare had been sprinting and not him.

"If you can't keep up, then you shouldn't have come." The sinister, demon-like man replies. "And, if you are going to be a burden, I will kill you."

The young man winces, before embarrassment sweeps over. I don't think that was an empty threat considering the feral expression crossing the older man.

"I'm sorry, General Hu. I'll try harder." The young man mutters through a low bow.

Since his arrival, I've been gawking at the newcomer. He appears particularly childish. I didn't think the army is so desperate that it needed such young recruits. Then again, what do I know about warfare? When the young man finally notices my silent intrusion, he flusters, kneels down, and then bows deeply onto the ground.

"Your Highness! I didn't see you there! I'm so sorry! Generals, you've found our lord at last! Thank goodness!"

"He is? Where?" I spin around, only to meet my shadow. The phantom he addressed isn't there, but a demon suddenly flies past me.

"Get up, you idiot!" General Hu growls furiously.

"I don't under—" The young man is forcibly pulled to his feet before he can finish.

"Do you have any idea what you've just done? Give me a reason not to kill you right here and now!" Immediately upon his outburst, Hu unsheathes the sword latched to his hip. Gold engravings on the blade reflect the setting sun, turning the fearsome thing blood red.

Chapter 1: A Missing Monarch

"Hold on there! What's your problem?" Jerking the young man back, I step in between the confrontation. "He didn't do anything. What's wrong with you?"

"Stay out of this!"

"How is anyone supposed to stand idle when you threaten a boy for no reason? Bully someone your own size!"

"You've got a big mouth for a little girl."

"And you've got a pretty big skull for someone with no brain."

Where did that come from? Insulting strangers isn't a habit of mine. That slipped out naturally as if I were bickering with an old friend. My master often said trouble followed my temper.

"Why you—!"

Resentment boils within his gaze. I have no doubt that if he were inclined, would cut through me to slay the young man. General Hu's grip around the sword tightens and the surrounding heavy feeling heightens. I really thought he would strike. Just as the end seems near, a hard voice terminates the scene.

"That's enough, Bai Hu. Qing Hai meant no harm. Anyone could have made such an easy mistake. Had you let insults go, we wouldn't be in this mess." The man who rode on the left horse had watched the event without interest, but now he thinks it's necessary to intervene.

As he comes closer, his tall figure and broad shoulders tower over me. Black raven-colored hair, encompassing the strong face and stern jaw, flutters in the gentle wind. Kind eyes, as blue as night skies, though distant as they are, seem to study me with great care. Never in my life have I met men such as these. The capital must be another world comprised of fantastic people so very different from commoners elsewhere.

"Qing Hai, don't be so impulsive," continues he.

Qing Hai smiles weakly and bows to both men. By the by, he glances at me from the corners of his eyes, though I don't understand why.

"You, girl. Why are you dressed as a man?" The one with blue eyes inquires.

"What do you mean, *'girl?!'*" Qing Hai flusters terribly while turning completely to face me.

"Answer!" General Hu pushes on.

Well, that's a silly question. "It's none of your business," is how I want to rebut. Actually, there are a number of reasons, but I won't be bullied into admission.

"Because men's clothes are more comfortable," is my indolent reply.

Chapter 1: A Missing Monarch

"Sarcasm, is it? Or, do you think you're funny, girl?" General Hu growls. "Maybe, you are. I see a complete fool standing before me and the only usefulness for a fool is to die and make room for others."

"I expected as much from imperial soldiers. You want to harass the common—to boast whatever little power you have? Go for it, but do it in your own time! I've got places to go and things to do."

Turning around, I start away when Hu grabs my collar. "Where do you think you're going? Do you think we'd let you leave after this?"

"She's a woman, General! You can't just manhandle her that way!"

"A woman who knows too damn much! We have to kill her! There is no choice! Don't you agree, Yue?" Hu turns to the other man, but the one with blue eyes I thought to be kind, simply shrugs.

"I don't know anything!"

As I attempt to pull away, Hu's grip tightens. A hefty jerk from his meaty paw slams me against the heavy armor. It feels nothing short of hitting a wall. My back is now bruised and bloodied.

"Leave her alone!" Hai reaches for me but Hu knocks him to the ground.

"I told you, I don't know what you're talking about!" Turning around for one final effort, a fist slams across

Hu's face with every bit of strength I can muster. Slowly, the hold on my collar loosens. The General rubs his face absently.

"That really hurts," Hu remarks flatly.

I can't tell whether he is mocking me. That doesn't matter. I've backed far enough from him that another escape could be attempted. Should I fail, he'll kill me for sure. Then again, could I reason with him instead? Maybe an act of faith by not running would be more prudent. My mind races but I only have seconds to decide.

Before resolve can form, my feet decide for me. Hu reaches out and misses by a hair's breadth. Wind whips across my cheek and tousles unkempt hair, drowning Hu's incessant cursing and the surge of voices trailing behind. After an indeterminable span of time, I stumble and fall to the ground. My chest and legs are burning in tandem. Quickly, I crawl over to a nearby bush and lie still to recover.

Soon as the thought of escape resumes, Hai suddenly picks me up from the shrub. I never heard him approached.

"Ack! C-Calm down! Please, Miss! Stop flailing!"

"Let go!"

Despite my voice and body trembling erratically, his pleading, apologetic stare hold more anxiety. The rounded eyes and boyish face peering down remind me that he's just a child. Hai has no interest in my death. He's in as much trouble as I am, if not more. My reply is a short nod and then, he puts me down.

"Are you going to let me go?"

"I-I can't do that. I'm good at tracking. He'll know I'm lying if I say otherwise. Listen, I won't let him harm you. You have to believe in me. General Yue won't allow him to kill you in cold blood."

Hope rising in my chest is dashed away sorely; replaced by exasperation. "Are you kidding me? General Yue couldn't care less what happens to me! He just shrugged when Hu said he'd kill me! And you... Hu would have killed you if it hadn't been for him! You can't even protect yourself. How can you protect me?"

Hai's gaze lowers. Though I didn't mean to, it's obvious I wounded his pride. A short pause ensues and then Hai looks up and gives a brief smile.

"General Hu's not all that bad. It's just... it was my fault. I said something I shouldn't have and he's only trying to protect the country."

"How is killing me going to protect the country? I'm not the emperor of Ning!"

"There's no time to explain. You'll just have to believe me. I won't let him hurt you." Hai extends a friendly hand. By the ardent expression of kindness in his eyes, it's palpable that he will do everything to protect me; though, his ambitions may be too much for his skills.

Running is pointless. He's found me after all and he can do so again. Even if Hai were to let me go, General Hu might slay him for failing and I don't want that on my conscience.

Chapter 1 – 2

"Took you long enough, kid." General Hu mutters gruffly as he sees us emerging from the woods. As we come near the two men, Qing Hai moves in front of me whilst keeping the right hand cradling mine behind his back. He squeezes tightly to reassure everything is well. When he speaks, the hardened tone is completely unexpected.

"She is willing to cooperate. There is no need for violence. I will not stand by and allow you to harm a civilian when no crimes have been committed."

"You dare speak to me like that, Recruit? Pass basic training and you think you're tough? You're lucky you're Minister San An's nephew or I'd take your head."

Qing Hai does not respond. Even though his back is to me, I can feel strong defiance in his stance. Following a long pause, Hu lets out a sarcastic laugh. "All this for a woman you thought was a man a moment ago? Fine. Whatever. Yue and I decided not to kill her after all. She could be useful to us; at least, she better be if she wants to live."

"Useful how?!" Hai's grip tautens.

"Don't be such a pervert. I wasn't implying anything depraved. I like my women to look like women and I definitely don't need to coerce anyone. Bring her along. We'll let San An deal with her."

"My-My uncle? What does he have to do with this?"

"The sun is setting. Don't waste any more time." Hu turns around and remounts the ironclad steed. Yue does the same. They start for the road ahead at a slow trot. Hai gradually lets out a heavy sigh. It's obvious he was more frightened than I was during the exchange.

"Let's go. My uncle won't let anything happen to you. I promise." Hai throws a smile over his shoulder. I'm inclined to believe him, simply because I don't have a choice.

Chapter 1 – 3

Well into the dark night, hoofs steadily pound against the ground, stopping only a time shortly before daybreak, and then continue again. My body and mind are exhausted; mostly, I'm anxious of what lies ahead. Why must I meet Minister San An in the capital and how can I be a threat to our country's security for dressing as a man? I want to ask, but Hai had said nothing of import for both of us to be in trouble. If he does tell me something useful, I am certain General Hu will end us.

In the late afternoon, we finally reach An's massive gates. The bustling capital is beyond anything my imaginations can dream. Beautiful buildings, beautiful people, and beautiful things all crowd together in this magnificent place of commerce. Each wondrous sight, exotic scent, and cheerful tone sends my heart fluttering from elation. At the same time, fatigue wreaks havoc and all I want to do is collapse.

"Just a little farther," Qing Hai whispers encouragingly. If it weren't for him sitting behind keeping me upright, I would have fallen off the horse long ago. His amiability is greatly appreciated. All the same, I hate these imperial soldiers. They brought me into this chaos, of which I don't want any part.

Eventually, we near the massive palace jutting above every surrounding structure. The wealth of a nation is clearly displayed for all to see. The breathtaking scene seems surreal. Charmed by magnificence, a smile begins curling over my lips, which then abruptly dissipates when General Hu turns about.

"We're going through the back entrance," he snaps. His eyes are as sharp as knives. For whatever reason, he is vexed again.

After a while, the back entrance comes into view. General Yue goes inside to fetch the Minister while the remaining two stand guard. I don't know why they bother. I have nowhere to go. At least, I have no way of returning home. I don't even know which way home is. My sense of direction has always been terrible.

Feet shuffle and sway to keep awake while stress and lack of sleep are slowly pulling away consciousness. Qing Hai pats my shoulder and smiles. I do my best to return the gesture. All the same, my vision is reeling. I can barely see straight. In time, another man dressed in beautiful silk exits with General Yue. As he sees me, charming brown eyes grow wide. His face is the last thing I remember before losing all consciousness.

Chapter 1 – 4

A large decorated room finely furnished with polished, dark-colored wood furniture. Windowpanes, wall panels, and arched doorways are exquisitely embellished by unmatched intricate patterns. Surrounding me on this massive bed are silk sheets the color of honey so luxuriously soft that by comparison, rose petals are no less than jagged thorns.

Sitting up, I rub my head absently but fatigue suddenly surges, and then I fall back, caught by two large, fluffy feather pillows. For a moment, I thought I must be dreaming, until *his* voice shakes me to be on alert.

"Boo!" He's glaring at me from the sofa by the closed windows. What madness is this? His hair is no longer silver. It is dark brown. The long locks hang loosely toward his waist. Upon construing my confusion, Hu laughs.

"I'm not a hundred years old. There's no reason why my hair should all be grey. Makes me look like a demon though, doesn't it?" He grins and his fangs can clearly be seen.

"You are a demon." I roll my eyes.

He returns another laugh. "Glad you liked my costume. It makes people in battle so very afraid of me. Anyway, after all I did to frighten you, it was the

Minister who made you faint? That's a big insult to the Demon General."

He sounds like he's joking around but that seems out of character for him. If he had held a sword over the bed and tried to stab me, it would be more believable.

"Is that why you're here? Do you want an apology?"

He smirks, though there is something strange in the response I can't quite understand.

"Our guest needs sustenance and rest after the previous ordeal. Would you mind sending Jin in here for me, Demon General?"

The voice that abruptly enters our conversation belongs to Minister San An. For a quick moment, he turns to me with a slight smile, before refocusing attention to Hu. The younger man grumbles incoherently; though, ultimately complies and leaves the room.

Wasting no time, Minister San An sits on the edge of the bed and raises the back of his hand to examine my forehead. He is in his thirties, I surmise, rather too young and handsome than I had imagined a minister would be. Dark coal black hair draping down his shoulders swing gently when he reaches for my wrist. "Remain still and let me check your pulse."

I figure, I have no choice. Since the Demon General takes orders from him, then Minister San An is not a man to be reckoned with. After a minute or so, he frowns.

"I'm afraid your pulse is rather weak. Please, allow Jin to tend to you. Inform him should you need anything. I know you must be very confused but I—no, your country—needs a great favor from you. Later, I will explain everything and I hope you will consider the matter. For now, I must return to court for the assembly. Please, excuse me."

I haven't the chance to say anything when he parts from the room as swiftly as he had entered. I will not lie, I am enjoying the pampering and attention of such handsome men; the Demon General included. Whatever it is the Minister will ask of me, I don't think I will deny him, especially since I am, after all, being held hostage. Going against the wishes of the imperial court could easily be viewed as treason.

As I ponder San An's unspoken request, a young man in his twenties enters the room with a tray of food and tea.

"Oh, hello."

He ignores me until the tray is on the side table. The young man, knitting his brows, carefully studies my face. "I can't believe it. You look just like him."

"Just like who?"

"His Highness," he replies.

The answer to the ordeal is so obvious; I can't believe how slow I am. Qing Hai mistook me for our emperor when he thought the Generals had found him. It must be that His Highness is missing. This is not something known throughout the land. Why should it? Once Ning become aware of the situation, war would come to our borders immediately. This is the reason Hu wanted my demise and also the reason I was brought to the capital.

"Do you understand now?"

I bite my lip and nod.

"Good. I advise that you agree to this, but I also want you to know that this is not something to be taken lightly. This is not a chance to be pampered. This is an opportunity to protect your country. If you do not play the part wholeheartedly and are exposed, you will be executed for impersonating His Highness. Even though the idea was not yours, no one will stand behind you. The council will deny all connections to this plot. Worse, if it is discovered that His Highness is missing, our land will suffer not only from external political strife, but internal. The vast number of nobles vying for his authority is endless. They will stop at nothing until one is left to claim the throne. I know this is a lot of pressure. That is why I am here to assist you in any way I can. My name is Shu Jin. I go by Jin. I am His Highness's personal attendant."

"I am... Bao Lai. I-It's nice to meet you."

Chapter 1: A Missing Monarch

This is not news I want to hear. I need to flawlessly impersonate the most important person in the country or everyone could die? What nonsense! Aggravation surges but it only makes me lightheaded. I fall back onto the bed.

"Are you all right?" Jin rushes over and puts his arms around me. This is a little friendlier than expected from someone I'd just met.

"Isn't it inappropriate for you to touch His Highness this way?"

A startled expression bursts in exchange for my weak laughter. Then, he smiles. "Yes. I'm sorry, Your Highness."

Jin moves away, fetches the tray of food, and places it in front of me. Before exiting, he turns around once more. "Oh, I had forgotten. General Bai Hu and Qing Hai asked for permission to visit you. I advise only speaking to one of them since you need rest and they tend to draw out conversations whenever they are together."

"What would His Highness do?"

"He would not meet with either. His Highness He Pi is selective of his acquaintances. Should I send them both away?"

It would be rude to turn away Qing Hai. After all, if it weren't for him, Hu would have finished me. On the other hand, I've not forgiven Hu's rough behaviors.

Polaris: The Demon General and the General Practitioner

There are more than a few choice words left unspoken between us. Mainly, by me.

Chapter 1 – 5

"No. Please send Hu in."

Jin makes a slight bow and then leaves. Moments later, the Demon General bursts through the doors.

"Why'd you call me in here?"

He shouts irately as if I had forced upon him the visit. Worse, he seems entirely serious. I fluster, not knowing what to say. As my fingers nervously fumble together while formulating a response, Hu bursts into laughter.

"Pft! Ha! The look on your face is priceless."

"You...! What do you want?!" Colors burn my cheeks. He acts like such a bratty child; completely different from the serious man I met on the road. The only response I receive is a smirk. If he merely came to mock me, I might as well ignore him.

Looking down, a small puncture wound on the back of my left thumb catches my eyes. The blood that pooled has dried to a dark scab. I'm inclined to pick at it.

"I thought I cleaned all that up."

Having forgotten that he is still here, his sudden voice causes me to jolt. Barely do I look up, he's already kneeled next to the bed. Hu grabs my hand and turns it every which way to look for more specks of blood. His touch is so rough; his hand feels like one large callus. He frowns when my hand jerks away.

"Don't flatter yourself." Hu ruffles my hair with a large palm.

"What are you talking about?" I knock his hand away and attempt to smooth out the locks to no avail. My hair is a large messy tangle.

"I'm not flirting with you. I just thought I cleaned all of your wounds."

"I never thought you were flirting with me! Wait, my wounds?"

I stretch out both arms and realize the robe is brand new and made of fine silk. My hands reach behind to touch my back. Bandages run rampant across my body.

"You-You bandaged me?"

Hu grins mischievously. "I cleaned and bandaged your wounds. Even changed your clothes for you. Aren't I a nice guy?"

"You did what?!"

I start off the bed making fists but he'd already moved toward the door. Hu sticks out his tongue and then disappears down the hall.

That jerk! The more his face comes to mind, the more I want to hit him again!

Chapter 2: Someone Special

When the moon is high overhead, the door creaks open and Minister San An enters. He smiles sweetly whilst giving an amiable glance. Unintentionally, slight color creeps over my face.

"I did not mean to disturb at such late hours, but I've received word that you've considered the task."

"I don't truly have a choice."

"Perhaps, not *truly*, but there are other choices. By that, I mean if you appear a fool at court, the truth will be known and you will not have to pretend very long."

"Of course not, I would just be executed." My sardonic answer is accompanied by a tepid wave into the air.

The Minister smiles again and then I become embarrassed for my brash response.

"I know you feel trapped but I am not cruel. I cannot permit you to leave because you know the truth and yet, I don't think an unwilling person would be of use to us. We can always continue the ruse we have been using for some time now, while our men search for His Majesty. After careful deliberation, I've come to a single conclusion that will relieve you from this deception and also preserve your life."

My posture stiffens. The Minister draws close and leans down to face level. "The only way is to have you watched over by one of us."

"I don't understand. You're all watching me."

"Yes, well, perhaps at a closer level." He looks away for a quick moment. A delicate hint of uncertainty enters the expression; dissipating as quickly as it comes. Turning back, he smiles. "You may enter the Circle at the Peony Palace or you can simply wed one of us and become the responsibility of whomever you choose."

He has to be joking. Become a consort to the missing emperor or marry a random person? Either path would certainly keep me from having to impersonate His Highness and allow my life to be spared, but they are far from what I'd expected. I stand frozen in place; my face as crimson as the sash around San An's waist. The reaction must amuse him, because the Minister laughs.

"Was that too sudden? I will permit you some time to think things over. There's no need for an immediate answer. One is required come sunrise. I hope you will consider these alternatives if truly, you do not wish to take part in our political ploy."

"I don't understand. Why must these be the alternatives? I could stay as a servant to one of you or just tend to the gardens. I am not very bad at tending to gardens."

"I'm afraid these boys won't take their duties seriously were they to watch over a servant. But a wife... a man will be inclined to give all his attention to his wife and therefore, will ensure both your safety and honesty from allowing another soul to know our secret."

So, it is all a matter of trust and I am not viewed as trustworthy, is that it?

"It's not that I do not trust you," San An answers my mental inquiry. "I cannot say the same of the others. Once you leave these grounds, one or more might attempt to take your life."

There's truth to his reasonings—bizarre as they are. I have no idea which path to take. As I contemplate the choices, he continues.

"And, should you choose me, I will ensure for you a life without hardship. You will never be in want of anything. I am not your first choice, perhaps. I am not young and handsome, but as I am not as young as these boys, I am also not as foolhardy. They can love and hate on a whim. I will undoubtedly love you with every part of me until I draw my last breath. So please, do consider things carefully."

If I flush any deeper, my head would turn into a tomato! What is he talking about? He's gorgeous! And yes, he is older than the others, but there is something dignified and mature with this age. Ack! What am I saying? I have no interest in this! I just want to go home and eat my fish and water my garden.

I turn elsewhere and try to think of anything and everything to distract from the moment. When San An places a hand on my shoulder, I jump back.

"Do I frighten you?" Slight pain crosses within the tone.

"N-No! I... just... I don't understand! Yesterday, your boys thought I was a man and I know I'm not half as pretty compared to the women I saw strolling around the markets. I can't even imagine how beautiful the women in the Circle are! You, sir, can do a lot better!" I fold my arms and keep my head down, embarrassed by my own outburst.

"Conceivably, you are not the most beautiful woman, but beauty is only part of the equation. You have all of our attentions and that makes you special. Everyone wants to claim someone special."

Inexplicable resentment begins creeping over my psyche. My eyes dart to his face. "A prize, is that it? Because I resemble His Highness, that makes me special? You want to win me because it inflates your ego? If that's the case, then I'm sorry to say you don't understand what love is, Minister!"

Taking a seat near the window, I scratch my head irritably. I thought he would be angry. Instead, San An laughs. A smile reappears.

"No, I'm afraid you don't understand what love is." He replies. "To find someone special is ordinary inclination. It is natural to be able to discern between beauty and ugliness, intelligence and stupidity, and yes, even common and rare. Love simply means to care for, so how can caring for someone I find special means that my love is less than any man who loves for beauty, intellect, or even money? Love is love, no matter the reason. If love needs to be based on any particular reason, then I think that is too mechanical."

My head tilts due confusion. I don't know how to argue with that and my own ignorance just draws me deeper into a void. I want to reply but nothing will come. Following the painful ensuing silence, San An relieves a sigh.

"Forgive me, I did not mean to grieve you. I only wanted to speak my mind, for I fear regret will consume me if I did not at least try. You are entitled to your opinions. I merely hope you will not think too poorly of me for having caused your anxiety."

"N-No. I don't think poorly of you at all! It's just that you don't even know me. I could very well drive you mad." My attempt to chuckle off the tension is met with his simple smile.

"What if I say that you already have?" The sheepish tone comes forth and then, he quickly glances away.

"I don't understand."

"That you don't understand makes me admire you even more."

San An reaches out; though, before his fingers graze my cheek, he withdraws. My heart immediately flutters and my face feels warm. Following a span of silent contemplation, a soft chuckle breaks from his pale rose lips.

"It's late and you need rest. Let us end here for now. I look forward to speaking with you again. Please, don't hesitate to call for me should you require anything. It is my desire to fulfill all your wishes." The Minister bows gracefully before taking his leave.

My eyes widened during our exchange and even now that he's left, I can't seem to force them back to the original position. I'm so confused! What was all that about? Did he just seriously propose to me? The image of his smiling face is engraved into my mind. The more I struggle to push it away, the more it comes flooding back.

Around him, I feel inferior in every way, and for some reason, it makes my heart race. The intellect and guidance of an older man, is that what I need most? What am I thinking?!

Vigorously shaking my head, I stuff my face in my hands. Sometime later, I fall asleep in distress and before I know it, Jin comes into the room and wakes me to prepare for the dreadful event.

Chapter 3: The Path to my Future

Around noon, the men assemble in the chamber. Following a brief conversation, my decision is requested. Before me stand the Generals Zhen Yue and Bai Hu, Qing Hai, and Minister San An. Yue is indifferent, so he looks off elsewhere, while Hai is terribly embarrassed with his eyes to the ground. Hu smirks at me but I don't understand why. Finally, San An smiles sweetly with hope in his eyes.

Even though the Minister made a tempting offer, I can't imagine that I deserve his good nature. I shuffle and twiddle my thumbs nervously with my head down. They are waiting for an answer but I'm uncertain which one to give. Shyly, I look up and scan the room once more. The instant my eyes fall on Hu, the Demon General reaches out and snatches my arm.

"Well, it doesn't look like anyone here wants a tomboy, cross-dressing, violent woman. I guess I'll have to take one for the team."

"Are you proposing to make her your charge, Bai Hu? There are more qualified men amongst us." San Nan frowns.

"Hai is inexperienced; he wouldn't know what to do with her. Yue probably won't even talk to her. She'll die from boredom. And you, Prime Minister, have better things to do. I can use a woman to clean my house. I'll take her."

"You're so damn insulting!" Hai frets. "You better be nice to her!"

"Don't tell me how to treat my wife." With those parting words, Hu starts for door, dragging me along. I don't even have the chance to protest.

Before I know it, we are outside. He leaves me by the gate and then returns with a horse.

"Get on," a large palm extends down.

"What if I don't want to go with you?"

"Not even married for ten minutes and you want to fight me?"

"We're not married, you idiot!" I back away from him and start inside. I'd rather join the Circle at this rate.

Barely do I take three steps, he's already jumped off the horse and grabbed my hand. My attempts to shake him off prove futile.

"Why are you obstinate? I'm your only chance for survival."

"You're the one who dragged me into this in the first place!"

"I know! Let me make it up to you!"

A strange expression of guilt rushes toward his face. Is that why he keeps bothering me? He actually feels bad for what he did?

"You don't have to do this. You can just let me go. I won't tell anyone."

"Sorry, I can't do that." Hu's firm grip around my hand slightly loosens and then he takes the lead. I don't know why I choose to go with him. Maybe, I don't really have a choice after all.

Chapter 4: The Demon General

We ride down several streets, passing stalls after stalls filled with enticing aromas from delectable foods. The streets are lively. Every sight, scent, and sound elevates the senses. I've never seen anything like this in my life! Just swinging my head from side to side in order to record a fraction of the wondrous sight is making me dizzy.

After ten minutes or so, Hu stops and dismounts from the steed. He extends a hand to me but I don't take it. I'm still mad at him. I climb down by my own accord. Hu ties the reins to a nearby post and proceeds to take me inside one of the shops nearby. The shopkeeper, upon realizing he's not an ordinary customer, rushes forward to offer her services. He ignores her and walks farther inside. I scuttle along, unsure why we're here.

"Wife, pick what you want." He sudden blurts cheerfully.

"Don't call me that!"

Although his back is to me, I can tell he is grinning.

"Wife, I don't have all day. Pick something already."

From one side of the store to the other are wall after wall of fabrics and silks stacked high to the ceiling. Beautiful robes, dresses, and coats are laid on every table. Hairpins, hats, purses, and decorated clogs line the entire back partition. I doubt the emperor's closet is even this impressive.

Without receiving a response, he casts a glance over his shoulder. "Don't you like anything in here?"

I shake my head. "I don't want anything."

"I didn't ask if you want anything. I asked if you like anything."

"You don't have to do this." For a moment, I turn away, sighing angrily, until his big palm is on my head again, messing my tangled hair even more.

"Do you think you can just wear that dingy robe for the rest of your life?"

"When I find a job and make my own money, I'll buy a new one!"

I fold my arms like a child in tantrum. His jaw clenches.

"No one likes a stubborn woman," he ruffles my hair. "Shopkeeper, my wife likes pink. Bring me one of everything pink in her size."

"What? I hate pink!"

"Well, if you don't pick something, you'll be wearing pink every day."

Why my face suddenly burns from his obnoxious laughter, I'll never know. If I don't play along, he'll drag this out just to irritate me. I might as well shut him up once and for all by pointing to the cheapest looking robe.

"Fine, I want that one."

Hu walks over and surveys the grey article. A frown appears on his mouth. "This is a man's robe."

"Oh, I can wear that. I don't mind."

"I do. I mind it very much. Pick something else."

The shopkeeper abruptly comes running over with a pile of pink robes. She'd taken Hu seriously.

"She'll look so pretty in this one, sir. And this one too. This one's for temple... this one's for dinners at your parents' house... this one's for daily wear... this one's for festivals." On and on she goes about the luxurious differences and special appeal of each piece. Frankly, they all look the same to me. Her attempts to exploit Hu's loosened purse strings are irritating to say the least.

"Which one is the cheapest?"

The shopkeeper frowns at my curt interruption, and after a discreet sneer, tersely holds up a cotton robe. I pass the robe to Hu. "This one. I want this one."

"I thought you hate pink."

"I don't care! I just want to leave!"

He surveys me from a sidelong glance during the following awkward pause. Embarrassment keeps my attention elsewhere. Slowly, Hu hands the robe back to the shopkeeper.

"Wrap this one up."

Chapter 4 – 2

Hu is silent as we leave the shop and increasingly distant thereafter. I didn't mean to come off as ungrateful or even to have offended him. I know he is trying to take the situation with humor but my obstinacy can't adapt to this abrupt change. A conflicting feeling is boiling inside.

"Hey, I'm-I'm sorry."

The surrounding crowded streets are bustling with so much life, I barely heard my own whispered apology. I doubt he did. At least, I thought so, until we stop in front of another building. Jumping off the horse, he grins with an extended hand.

"I'm not mad at you, Wife."

"Will you stop calling me that?"

"Nope."

The irritating grin on his face widens in exchange for my grumbling. Once we pass through the restaurant's threshold, Hu seizes my hand and pushes through the heavy crowd toward an empty table in the far back. Customers are teeming; the servers must be functioning on luck alone to avoid toppling trays at every step.

"What are we doing here?" I look around nervously.

"Don't ask stupid questions, Wife. It's a restaurant. People eat here."

"That's not what I meant!"

"Don't make such a fuss, Wife. I'm hungry. Unless you're willing to cook for me, we're eating here."

A belligerent quip is on the tip of my tongue. However, I am promptly denied the satisfaction when a pretty young woman comes running over with a pot of tea. The crimson crystal on her gold hairpin dangles vigorously from the high-spirited sprint.

"Hi there, General! Do you want the usual? Oh, who's this?" She is startled when she notices me. I can imagine why.

"This is my—"

"Sister. I'm his sister!"

"Oh, I didn't know you have a sister. It's nice to meet you. I'm Kai."

Kai smiles sweetly. I begin to feel nervous. I always feel nervous around women. Her hair is so pretty, same as her face and clothes. She's absolutely charming. For my disheveled hair and unfeminine structure, I can't keep from feeling self-conscious.

Hu grins, and by the by, inferiority begins to take me. From my lowered head escapes a soft reply. "It's nice to meet you too. I'm Bao Lai."

"Bao Lai? That's a pretty name."

It was Hu who said this. My widened eyes meet his curious stare.

"I thought she's your sister. You don't even know your own sister's name?" Kai bursts into laughter. She glances at me, then at Hu, and although she understands, doesn't prod further. "What do you want to eat, Bao Lai?"

I scarcely glance up and shake my head. "I'm not hungry. Thank you."

"Just bring her some dumplings. She's *shy* about spending my money. Did I find a good one or what?"

"Definitely!"

The two exchange meaningful laughs. I can't keep from flushing thoroughly. I thought to say something but can't think of anything. Kai swiftly leaves the table, leaving my distraught behind. As a last resort, I cast my full attention out the nearby window to be taken by the hectic scene of shoppers and vendors flying up and down the busy street. Just when I'd forgotten my predicament, Hu reaches over and ruffles my hair.

"Don't bother falling for Kai. She doesn't swing that way."

"Excuse me?"

"You were all nerves around her and then there's the whole cross-dressing business. Makes me wonder..."

"That was not why!"

"No? Sure seems that way to me."

"How else am I supposed feel when she's... ten times the woman I'll ever be?"

My response trails off into mumbles. It's embarrassing to admit my irrational fear of women. It's not as though I wish to contend. I've just cross-dressed my entire life. I certainly don't think of myself as a man but I don't ever think I am what a woman should be either. How can I ever feel equal next to the real thing?

The large palm lands on my head again. "Then, don't be jealous. She's an old friend."

"I'm not. Your business is your business, not mine. And stop messing up my hair!"

"Your hair's already messy. I want to make it worse, so when I take you to a hairdresser, the transformation will be that much more exciting."

"Hairdresser? I don't want to go to a hairdresser."

"Yes, you do. You just don't know it yet. Yi Ci can make any ugly duckling into a swan. You'll want to look a lady after you know you can pass for one."

"I am not your doll! No matter what you do, I won't look like any of these girls you're accustomed to!"

His rough hand withdraws. A streak of rouge crosses his face. I am not going to apologize this time. This is the truth. He should just deal with it.

Following our meals, which was finished in awkward silence, Hu grabs my hand traverses back outside. I thought he would take me to this Yi Ci but the route he follows moves away from the bustling markets toward a quiet residential area. Eventually, Hu dismounts in front of an average-sized house with a red-shingled roof, a plain yard of few trees, and paved stone walkway leading to a door decorated by an ornate tiger head knob. He does not offer his hand.

I follow him through the entryway and as I move inside, can't believe my eyes. His house is spotless. Everything has its place. With his personality, I was expecting clothes on the floor, dirt everywhere, and trash piling in the corners. There's not one speck of dust to be seen. In fact, the only thing that doesn't belong in this perfect scene is me. Instantly, my hands fly to my hair in order to smooth out the mess. A few strands become loose and fall to the floor. I kneel down to pick them up when regret come over me for not having met the hairdresser.

"What are you doing?" Hu leans down, his voice distant.

"Sorry, I didn't mean to dirty your floors."

Chapter 4: The Demon General

"They're your floors too, you know."

My vision instantly blurs. This isn't a joke. I'm to stay here with him for the rest of my days. This is to be my house. These perfect floors—my floors. And, this man—my husband. I can't breathe. What am I supposed to do? I can't be in here!

As quickly as my feet can move, I dart back outside. Hu manages to seize my collar just as I pass the threshold.

"Where do you think you're going?"

"I can't go in your house! It's not right! I don't belong here!"

"Look, I'm not going to bite your head off or anything! Just get inside!"

"I can't!"

With his free hand, Hu tugs at my flailing arm and forces me to face him. "Why? Do you find me that revolting?"

"No!"

"Then, what's the problem?"

"You're too perfect!"

I don't know why I said that. My cheeks are burning and I've lost the will to struggle. He stares at me, reflecting my confusion in full. Slowly, the frown twists into a smile, and then he bursts into laughter.

"I've been rejected for a lot of things in my life but never because of that! How dare you accuse me of being too perfect? You're a horrible, *horrible* wife!" The delirious laughter, though to my embarrassment, somehow lightens the tepid air. He pulls me inside. I tread carefully on his pristine floors, afraid my dirty shoes would scuff the polished wood.

"What's wrong? Why are you still tense?" Hu pats my downturned head.

"General, do you think I could... I could meet with Yi Ci?"

"General? I'm not your general. You may call me... Handsome Husband Hu or Sexy Demon Husband."

I don't respond to his nonsense. Hu frowns. "Why do you want to meet Yi Ci?"

"Because my hair's a mess."

"I can tell. That's why I'm not taking you."

"Why not?"

"You're right. You can't look like any girl I'm accustomed to. Why bother? Besides, if your hair stays a mess, I can keep on doing this!" He covers my head with his palm and tersely ruffles my hair into a complete knot.

Chapter 4: The Demon General

"Stop that!"

The obnoxious laughter continues as if it were his only capability.

"I'm going to take a nap. The Prime Minister said whoever takes you as his charge can have the day off. That's the only reason I volunteered."

Hu waves at me while walking into one of the rooms. I remain in the middle of the floor not knowing what to do next. In due time, his head, covered by a sulking glare, pokes through the doorway.

"Aren't you coming, Wife?"

"Where?"

"It's like talking to a child!" Hu mutters under his breath. Coming hither, strong arms scoop me into the air. The brazen general then waltzes into the room.

"What the hell are you doing?!"

"Stop thrashing. I'm sleepy but I need to watch you. That means you have to go to sleep too."

"I'm not sleepy!"

Hu shrugs. He drops me on the bed and then lies down adjacent. The bed is a corner. The only way to leave is to climb down the foot or climb over him. I can't do either. His heavy arms feel like chains around me.

"Go to sleep," he mutters wearily.

"I told you, I'm not tired!"

"Stop being so loud. You're hurting my ears."

With that flippant remark, Hu's embrace tightens. The warmth of his body ironically makes me quiver. He's fallen asleep. No matter how hard I try, I can't break free. Fighting with him eventually wears me out. I lie still and glance around the room though not much can be observed. His broad shoulders are obstructing my view. In time, the obnoxious man begins muttering in his sleep. I stare at that sleeping face but nothing can be discerned.

What a face he has! When he's not running his mouth, I think he's rather handsome. His long hair drapes lovingly over beautiful features. The cascade is covering parts of my hand. They feel like strands of silk.

So far, I'm at a loss. He's completely different from the man I'd met yesterday. I wonder if this is the real him or if the so-called Demon General is his true side. Or maybe, he's just a complete idiot. That sounds more fitting.

A heavy sigh can't help but escape. As I contemplate my next move once he wakes, a soft seductive scent overcomes the senses. His cologne is intoxicating. I can't control myself from leaning in closer to sniff his shirt.

"I fall asleep for two minutes and you're already trying to take advantage of me?"

I snatch back in terror only to find him grinning.

"I was doing no such thing!"

"No? You're hurting my feelings."

"I thought you were tired."

"Can't sleep next a woman who's trying to rub her face in my chest. You're such a pervert."

He lets out a bark of laughter and ruffles my hair. I'm too embarrassed to answer and so, I just close my eyes.

"Hmm? Asleep already? Good night, Wife." He gives a peck on my forehead and resumes the nap. It is nowhere close to night but engaging him any more than necessary would be futile.

Chapter 4 – 3

The warmth which lulled me into slumber slowly dissipates. Upon opening my eyes, the Demon General with threatening silver mane is buckling a belt around heavy armors. I fall back and pretend to still be asleep.

"I know you're awake." His tone is taut and slightly savage, just as I remember from the road. "Don't even think of escaping while I'm away. If I have to kill you, then I will."

He turns toward me with a piercing icy gaze exuding from unfeeling eyes. A chill runs down my spine, freezing my entirety into an inexplicable numbness. I can't keep from trembling in the presence of the murderous aura, as though locked in the attention of a real demon. Memories from that moment we first met come back to me. My breath is caught inside my throat.

On the other hand, he's done this to me before. The moment I take him seriously, that obnoxious guffaw will bray in my ears. If he's only putting on an act to stay in character, he's certainly convincing. Maybe, I should extend an act of my own.

Descending from the foot of the bed, I make a flaunting march toward the door. "I'm not afraid of you, *Demon General*. I'll come and go as I please."

Soon as the words leave my mouth, a massive force slams my body violently against the closed door. My arm is twisted behind my back by grips so severe, the ligaments in my elbow begin to tear. In the next moment following my inadvertent cry, a sharp blade presses against my throat. A slight trickle of blood begins to pool on the cold steel.

"I won't tell you again!"

The inhuman growl drilling into my ear signals more so a promise than a threat of what's to come. That is not a man I feel behind me, but a beast. Every hair is standing on ends. All my muscles are shaking so terribly, I can barely stand.

Is this the real him? The man who called me 'Wife' earlier isn't capable of this assault. Was that easygoing, teasing, flippant man truly the Demon's mask? Without knowing why, light tears mist over my eyes.

"Kill me then." They come out in a soft whisper, the unthinkable words that are forming. I'm terrified and yet, something in me resents this feeling. I continue to forgo common sense and challenge him. "If you're going to keep me as a prisoner for the rest of my life, I'd rather die!"

His grip on the sword tightens; the blade cuts a little deeper. I close my eyes to accept my fate when he suddenly withdraws. Falling to the floor, my hand immediately reaches for my neck. Blood is laced over the open palm. A petrified stare arches to meet his. There is no remorse on the grave face that peers down. All I can see is apathy.

Hu sheathes the blade and exits the room. I hear the door closes as he leaves the house and at once, my mind begins to race. Should I run away? I can't stay with a man who's so willing to take my life. And, if my life is already lost by staying here, what's the worst that can happen if I leave?

My heart is beating furiously at the prospects of freedom. If I escape now, there is a good chance he won't find me. What should I do?

Run (Continue to page 59)

Stay (Continue to page 60)

Chapter 4 – 4

I wait a moment longer until I'm certain he's out of sight before pulling back the curtains to take a quick glimpse. The streets are mostly empty except for a few drunks wandering around and couples walking hand-in-hand. How I envy their freedom. I can't live my life cooped up in this house. It's no different from a slow death. I may as well take my chances. I have to leave. It's now or never.

When the coast seems clear, I open the door and then sneak quietly down the streets. Thank goodness his house is located close to the city gates. After a few turns, I reach my target. In the dark of night, the guards are oblivious of my position below a large wagon on its way out.

The heavy wheels turn. The oxen cart moves forward. Five minutes later and then finally, I am free! I roll from underneath the wagon, running for dear life until my legs burn and chest heaves. What sweet sensations, these feelings of freedom!

After another hour of traversing under soft moonlight, sudden clamor from behind shakes me to turn. As I do, a sword pierces my chest straight through the heart. The last thing I see is silver hair waving in the wind.

The End.

Chapter 4 – 5

I can't run away. I know he'll find me. My life was already over the moment I opened my mouth on that road. This delayed death is all that I can hope.

For a long time, my body would not stop shaking. Yet, when it does, fatigue overcomes my senses. The room suddenly spins and then I lose all consciousness.

Chapter 5: Rumble in the Red Light District

Warm afternoon sunlight seeps into the room, softly nudging me. When I can no longer fight off the nuisance, grudgingly, I leave slumber behind. My body feels like lead; mostly, I just find it difficult to breathe. Something is constricting my throat. I reach up to find a wad of bandages wrapped around the wound and immediately recognize the terrible bandaging as belonging to a certain jerk.

Slowly, I lift off the bed. With the covers removed, the pink robe Hu had purchased the day prior is fitted perfectly on my body. The cotton fabric is soft and light. Though I hate to admit it, I feel a bit girlish, and I don't dislike this feeling. The other bandages around my body have been removed. When I reach up to touch my hair, it is completely untangled. My hair was a mess. Even trying to straighten one strand should have jolted me to wake. Who knew his rough hands could be so gentle? But then, gentle he hardly is. He nearly slit my throat!

My fingers finally find the end of the massive wad of bandages. After unwrapping about ten circles of the constricting thing, one long strip falls off, but there is still a massive amount of cloth around my neck. I find the ends of another, and then another, and another. By the time I begin to see blood on one of the pieces, the blanket is covered with white strips.

"He's such an idiot!"

Speak of the devil! As though on cue, the door creaks open and a nervous Hu, forcing a smile, peeks his head inside the room. Having perceived my wrath, Hu fully opens the door and enters with a tray of food and tea. The dumplings are clearly from the restaurant we visited yesterday.

"You like to sleep late, don't you, Wife?"

Hu places the tray on the side table and then shyly sits on a corner of the bed. I glare at him angrily while he does the very least to acknowledge me. His eyes dart all over the room, searching for something to say. However, there is no need to beat around the bush. We have to talk about it sooner or later.

While undoing the last layer of bandages, I begin. "Why didn't you kill me?"

The Demon General jolts, before chuckling nervously. "I never meant to hurt you, Wife."

"My name is Bao Lai!"

Aside from anger, confusion takes over me. He seems sad and contrite; completely benign from the general in the silver mane. How can wearing a costume change a man that much, or is he acting now?

A sudden surge of cool air flooding through the window brushes against my throat, causing the cut to sting. On impulse, I push a hand against the wound, involuntarily wincing.

"Are you—are you okay?" Hu starts to reach over; stopping once met with my enraged stare.

"You shoved a sword at my throat! You tell me!"

Hu withdraws. He looks so apologetic that I feel guilty for having shouted at this seemingly overgrown ignorant child.

"I'm sorry..."

"I doubt that. Your other persona didn't seem too bothered. What is it with you? Do you have multiple personalities or something?"

I was being facetious; all the same, I seem to have touched a nerve. His jaw furiously grinds, then standing up, Hu promptly leaves the room.

It's not possible though, is it? Otherwise, he wouldn't have stopped himself and I'd be dead. If it were true, somewhere inside, this Hu must have a small level of awareness and control over the other. That's assuming I'm not getting ahead of myself. It could always be another mean joke.

I realize there's no point in sitting here contemplating what ifs when the one person who knows the truth won't reveal his secret. Exhaling a sigh, I start from the room and is again met with those nerve-wracking pristine floors. I tiptoe across until I come upon the powder room. When I exit, Hu, who's been waiting with his back against the wall, startles me through the irritated tone.

"I hope you don't plan to do anything foolish."

Frowning, I turn to meet him. "If you want to kill me then do it already."

He scoffs and looks away. "You're a disobedient woman. I get it. I'll let you have every liberty with me but I can't let you leave. I need your word that you won't run away."

"Why?"

He thinks things over for a moment, still unsure of his choices. In time, an agitated groan escapes. Hu furiously scratches his head. "What if I say... I will let you go outside if you promise me, you'll return?"

"Are you serious? You'll let me go?"

"Go outside, not leave permanently. I know this house is no palace; you'll get bored after a few hours. Anyway, I have soldiers to train and rounds to make, I can't always watch you. The fact that you didn't leave last night makes me think I can trust you. Don't prove me wrong. So, what do you say?"

"I promise!"

"You promise what exactly?"

"I promise that if you'll let me leave, I'll come back."

Maybe can I live freely after all! I'm so elated I unknowingly smile at the big jerk. He returns a smirk and then heads back toward the bedroom.

"Are you going to sleep?"

"Yeah. I have to leave at sundown."

"Do you work every night?"

"No. I'm not working tonight. Just going to visit my girlfriend. Wake me up before sunset, will you?"

He said it so casually, I don't know how to react. While there's nothing between Hu and I, his girlfriend can't possibly be complacent about our living arrangements. Unless she doesn't know or... he's a big fat liar. In the end, it's none of my business.

Chapter 5 – 2

Although he told me to wake him, I didn't need to. Right before sunset, Hu sluggishly comes out of the bedroom, yawning loudly while rough fingers scratch his head. The long brown hair is messy and puffed, resembling a lion's mane.

"I hope you don't intend to go to your girlfriend's house looking like that."

Lifting his half-asleep gaze in my direction, his fangs suddenly make an appearance under a wide grin. "She doesn't mind. What about you? Are you still bleeding?"

"I bandaged myself. I'm fine now. You did a half-ass job, Demon General. Couldn't kill me and couldn't bandage me properly."

"I'm sorry I tried to slit your throat," he sighs sarcastically. "Will you forgive me?"

"Not a chance. I'll hold it over you for the rest of your life. Anyway, you might as well eat before going out. I scrounged up whatever you had in the kitchen, which wasn't much, so don't expect miracles."

I point to the table in the kitchen. A frown falls over his mouth.

"You cooked, Wife?"

"I told you stop calling me that."

Running long fingers through his hair, Hu cautiously approaches the table to look into the soup bowl. The speed with which he employs to pick up a spoon and taste the food is so agonizingly slow, I feel as though time stood still. If he's afraid it's poisoned, he might as well just say so.

"Blech! What is this? It's so bland!"

"What do you mean bland?" I run over to the table to taste the food again. It tastes fine to me. "Are you just being a jerk?"

"No, Wife, your cooking is terrible. Who'd want to eat this except monks? Where are the savory meats and aromatic broth? There's hardly anything in there!"

"Oh! Yeah, I guess you're right. Sorry. The monks taught me how to cook. This is pretty much a decent meal for them."

"You're not a... nun, are you?" He peers suspiciously from a sidelong glance.

"No. An old priest took me in when I was an infant and I grew up as a student in a temple to the south."

"Is that why you cross-dressed? Can't imagine the monks would want a girl running around distracting them."

"Yes, well, most of them ignored me anyway. I just..."

I manage to hold my tongue before revealing too much. Why I wanted to tell him everything is a mystery. He sends over a curious glance, almost prying, and then suddenly loses interest. Shrugging, Hu drops the spoon onto the table.

"Well, good first attempt, Wife. You still need some cooking lessons."

"I only cooked thrice a week for the monks. We had a rotation system. It's your turn next. Let's see if you do any better."

"Cook? Me? That's what restaurants are for." He stands up and lazily scratches his chest. Then, walking over to a drawer, takes a few coins and places them in my hand. "There's a vendor down the street. Go get something to eat. I need to head out."

A little while after disappearing into the bedroom, Hu exits the house in civilian clothing. He's going to visit his girlfriend which means I have plenty of time before he returns. I might as well see the markets. I've heard nice things about night markets. I can't imagine how exciting the ones in the capital must be.

Back when I was studying at the temple, the old priest never let me wandered off at night, except during the Spring and Harvest Festivals, but then all the students had to go together and I was never allowed to roam about freely. He was always overprotective of me. I often forced myself to behave more of a brute so that he'd see me as another temple boy and permit the freedom I desperately wanted. Now that I'm alone, I miss his lectures. Well, that's not entirely true. I'm not alone. While I'm not any more partial toward Hu, having someone to talk to isn't a terrible thing. Aside for the obvious reasons why I despise him, he has been kinder than I expected.

The few coins jingle in my hand. I have no intention of taking more from him than I already have and I still plan to pay him for this robe, somehow. For now, the coins are placed on the table and then I start outside.

Even though the house is located far away from the palace, bright lights coming from the markets surrounding the massive edifice can clearly be seen and may in fact, partially illuminate this part of the neighborhood that otherwise would feel drab. It's almost a festival; certainly a feast for the eyes. Anticipation beckons. I run toward the commotion. The scents of roasted meats and nuts wafts heavily near the entrance and intensifies as I near the center. I thought this place was beautiful during the day. It's ten times better at night!

Stalls upon stalls of specialties and delicacies pour forth tempting aromas. The lanterns above light cheerful, glowing tones, drowning out the darkness and obscuring the moon above with their indescribable brilliance. The streets are brimming with excitement and fanfare. Men, women, and children huddle together in long lines at the steamed bun carts giving off such tantalizing smells that my stomach starts to growl. A part of me wonders if maybe I should have just taken the coins. Ah! I'm letting my belly command my conscience! His hard-earned money should be spent on himself and otherwise, his girlfriend.

An hour or two of endless wandering sates desire for sightseeing. It's getting late. While I haven't explored the other three fourths of the markets, I best wait until tomorrow. Enjoying too much of the sights will leave me wanting once I grow bored. And so, I turn back toward the direction from whence I came.

Thirty minutes after my departure from the markets, exhilaration grows dull and then sometime after, the notion of fear begins to take over. When I came in, there was an orange carp on one of the businesses near the entrance. Following that marker, I had walked here believing I saw that same orange light, but now that I take a closer look, these lanterns are all red and that is definitely not a carp. Oh, dear Heavens! Please tell me I'm not that stupid!

I'd mistakenly follow this light above by taking so many turns that when I look to leave the Red Light District, the glowing warmth of the night market is nowhere in sight. Anxiety is snuffing out composure; it's becoming hard to breathe. I reel about looking for any familiar pointer in the distance but all I see are dark alleys, red lanterns, and women calling to men from the windows. The sight is so unnerving, rationality is wavering. While my chest heaves dry breaths from panic, my feet flee down a random path.

Chapter 5 – 3

Just my luck! A dead-end! I whip around to search for another route and instead, find three men blocking the narrow alley behind this abandoned house. This must be some sort of joke; a nightmare come to life. I can't hide because they'd already seen me or maybe, they'd followed me. Slowly, like predators stalking a prey, the men close in. Their long shadows encroach, overtaking mine and whittling down what little composure I had. Backed into a corner, my heart beats out of my chest, my blood run cold, and my body shakes violently.

A few days ago, I was worried for my freedom. At this moment, I fear a fate worse than death. I may have been sheltered most of my life but even I know what is to be expected by the hands of these beasts. Despite my predicament, a greater worry nags at my conscience. A certain stupid grinning face suddenly surfaces in the back of my mind. If I don't return home, he'll be worried. I promised. I promised Hu.

"What the hell do you want?!"

The words spew out my mouth without discretion. Whatever fear I felt moments ago are drowning under the rage burning in my chest.

"Shut your mouth girl, you'll wake the neighbors," the ugly one in the middle chuckles. His heavyset stature overshadows his beady eyes and smoked-stained teeth. I can smell opium from this distance; mixed with body odor so toxic, it's amazing his associates haven't suffocated. The other two aren't any better. One lanky fellow is lurking behind the fat one like a shadow ready to pounce. The other lout, though handsome, seems the type to bait unsuspecting victims. His effeminate countenance can't hide the perverse disposition which in this moment, he makes no attempt to suppress.

"Now, now, Ben." The effeminate man laughs in an almost sweet manner. "It's impolite to tell a lady to keep her voice down. I like a woman who screams; the louder the better. When it's my turn, don't hold back, okay, sweetheart?"

How vile. I'd thought my cross-dressing made it difficult to fit into society but being seen as a woman is so much more exasperating. I never had this problem when I dressed as a man.

And, as a man, I studied with the monks at the temple. Even if most of the other students disliked me for what I was, the old priest always pushed me to learn everything I could. To him, knowledge was the path to enlightenment. Yet, why am I reminiscing about the old priest now? If these brutes murder me after doing whatever sordid things they have in mind, it won't be long until my master and I are reunited. As much as I wish to see Master Tai Hung again, I still owe Hu for this robe. Yes, that must be why I desperately want to see his stupid grinning face.

My eyes dart deliriously for a route to escape. There isn't any. Like a fool, I keep moving back while the brutes leisurely advance as though they are enjoying this game of watching their victim squirm, a game that has grown far too common for them, I imagine.

In the pale moonlight, a sharp glimmer catches the corners of my eyes. A rusted shovel left behind, worn and half-rotted. The speckled metal reflects the lantern hanging overhead from a nearby wall. Yet, it's not the blade of the shovel that instincts called me to but the wooden handle that resembles the staff I used to spar with the other students. Then, it was just practice. Perhaps now is as good as any to put those lessons to good use.

I grab the shovel and kick off the rusted blade with the bottom of my shoe. Taking the stance Master Zhuang taught me, I dare them to come closer.

"Well, aren't you adorable? You think a stick is going to save you, little girl?"

"At least I'm not a little bitch like you! Does it always take two dumbasses and a fat ass to threaten one girl?"

They weren't expecting that! The old priest, Tai Hung, used to wear his hands out from smacking my head for constant use of profanity. I do become profane when I'm angry. Apparently, I'm not the only one who's offended by this confrontation. As Master Zhuang taught us students, an enraged opponent without skill is the easiest to put down. By the look of these men, I doubt they're truly skilled. That look of confidence and intimidation is one I remember well from the lackluster students who couldn't hold their weapons properly. Besides, it's not a matter of how hard I hit them; it's a matter of where I hit them.

Infuriated by my sudden, albeit false, smugness, the fat one in the middle growls and then lunges forward. The narrow alleyway is to my advantage as his large figure keeps the other two at bay. I jab the pole forward. The blunt end lands squarely against his throat. He immediately leans down and grabs onto his gullet. Exploiting the momentum, I slam the pole across the back of his head and neck, breaking a part of the rotted wood.

The remaining two follow suit and I continue to swing wildly every which way, not able to recall what exactly I had hoped to accomplish. At first, I just wanted a route to escape but now, I wonder if I should punish these men for their crimes. I can't possibly be the first woman they've ever cornered, nor will I be the last, unless I end them now and do the world a favor.

What am I saying? Master Zhuang did not teach the students to kill. He taught us self-defense.

One man groans and then another man screams. I think I must have jammed the pole into his eye. His pain unexpectedly sends a sensation of satisfaction to overwhelm me, pushing me to take vengeance for all the victims who couldn't find justice for themselves. My grip around the wooden pole tautens. Maybe, justice is right. I'm not fighting against another student. I'm fighting for my life! It's okay to not hold back.

"Bao Lai!"

When I hear his voice calling to me from the other end of the narrow alley, my senses jolt back to reality. One of the assailants starts on his feet and then attempts to run past Hu. His efforts are in vain. The General's gauntlets break across his pretty face. The man falls backward to the ground, groaning in pain, but Hu does not let up. He continues to beat the man savagely. The sight sends a terrifying chill down my back. That retribution was the very thing I sought to do. For the lives that man's undoubtedly taken, this is the least he deserves. However, passing judgment in this way isn't right. He should first answer for his crimes.

I say that, but the rage in me won't subside. Ultimately, I...

Stop him (Continue to page 76)

Let Hu punish the criminal (Continue to page 88)

Chapter 5 – 4

"Hu! Stop!" I jump over the other two and try to pry him off the third but his strength is too immense. "Stop! You're going to kill him!"

"He put his hands on you then he deserves to die!"

"He didn't! He couldn't! I can defend myself!" Another attempt to pull Hu away proves futile.

"What the hell are you doing here anyway? I thought you promised not to run away!"

His frustration is more so toward me than the man who is already unconscious beneath the heavy blows. I make one last attempt to stop his fist. In his state of fury, Hu knocks me hard against the stone wall by mistake. Fortunately, the shock is enough to cease his madness. I can hear his breathing grow more ragged. His broad shoulders tremble. Hu turns to me; the expression on his countenance is pure shame and remorse.

"Hu... Bai Hu, enough is enough."

He moves away from the unconscious man, his chest heaving. The air between us grows stagnant for a long while until, from afar, the sounds of whistles break the silence. Soon enough, a handful of guards come upon the scene. Amongst them is General Yue, who scans the wounded men, then me, and then Hu. Without much consideration, he places a hand on Hu's shoulders.

"Take your wife home. We'll take things from here."

Scoffing, Hu grabs my arm and starts from the Red Light District toward the markets and the direction of the city's main gates where our house resides. He's walking so fast, I have to run to keep up.

"Hu, I'm sorry! I got lost. I wasn't trying to run away."

He doesn't answer. Anger and boiling resentment are exuding from the darkened atmosphere around him, growing ever darker.

I jerk back my arm. "Hu! Listen to me! I apologize! I made a mistake! Say something!"

He stops but doesn't look back. I walk to the front of him, hoping to force a reply, but when I arch to meet his gaze, see small tears well in the corners of his eyes.

Caught between confusion and guilt, my lips part in an attempt to utter another apology; he would not allow the chance. The course is resumed until we reach the front of the house.

"Go inside. Lock the doors. Clean up and go to sleep." He relinquishes me and then whips around.

"Where are you going?"

"I might have killed a civilian. I'm going to accept my punishment."

"He's a criminal! More than likely a slave trader! He's no ordinary civilian!"

"That's not for you decide. Go in the house."

He leaves abruptly, giving me no room for protest. I watch him march toward the market districts; every step an assault against the conscience. Letting him pay for my poor decision is impermissible.

Hu looks down, wide-eyed, and flusters when our arms are suddenly tightly latched.

"Didn't I tell you to go inside the house?"

"This was my fault. I'm coming with you. Whatever happens, I won't let you take the blame."

"I don't care for disobedient women." Despite his words, the tone sounds teasing. For a moment I thought his usual upbeat self has returned until I look up. His expression is distant and taut. "You're not doing me any favors by coming."

"If I could speak to Minister San An, I'm sure we can sort this out."

"The Minister couldn't care less for anyone else's opinion. Just because you finally look like a woman doesn't mean you can charm him. Hell, you can't even charm me and my standards aren't very high."

"Really? I'll have you know the Minister proposed to me. You dragged me from the room before I could say anything."

He scoffs. Slight color crawls over his cheeks. "Even if you are telling the truth, it wasn't my fault you didn't speak up. What the hell were you waiting for anyway, an invitation?"

"I didn't want to cause trouble for the Minister. He deserves much better than me."

"Huh. And what about me?"

"You? If we get out of this mess, I'm going to cause you as much trouble as I can. I'll torment you, Bai Hu, like an enraged ex-girlfriend."

"Better get in line." He scoffs again.

I can't keep from smiling. The silly banter suddenly dispels the tension between us. Leaning closer, my hands wrap a little tighter around his arm. The scent of his cologne lightly lifts into my nose every step he takes. Even if it is the gallows I am walking toward, I feel no regret.

"Is this how you treat all the men at the temple?"

"What do you mean?"

"I offered you my hand yesterday and you wouldn't take it. Now, you can't keep your hands off me. Who knew all it took was a change of clothes to girly you up?"

Oh, dear Heavens, he's right! I fly off him, unsure why I've clung to his arm in the first place. As illogical as it is, I feel an inexplicable comfort in his company, as though we've known each other for years. Even so, I've never been the touchy-feely type and I definitely shouldn't be so close to a man who has a girlfriend.

"I-I'm sorry!"

The moment distance increases between us, his hand seizes mine. I'm embarrassed from having advanced on him so casually, that I can't say a thing. Neither does he. Our march to the palace continues with the same prior silence plaguing the atmosphere, except now, I'm glad that to be the case.

Chapter 5 – 5

Upon reaching the entrance of the barracks, Hu goes in alone, leaving me by the gates. I shuffle uneasily not knowing his intent. It was my fault. While I'm not sorry for having resorted to violence, I am sorry Hu had to be involved. He overreacted because of me, to protect me. And, what if he intends to continue doing just that, by taking all the blame? He's certainly stupid enough to do that! I don't know why I keep trusting anything he says!

With my hands balled into fists, I run into the barracks, inadvertently slamming into someone coming in the opposite direction. The force knocks me back a few steps while my counterpart falls to the ground. I know that wincing face!

"Qing Hai!"

"Oh! It's you. Hey there. I almost didn't recognize you, Miss Bao Lai. What are you doing here?"

"I'm sorry! Are you all right?"

"More or less," he chuckles nervously while reaching for my extended hand.

"Thank goodness. I'm sorry for cutting this short. Do you know where Hu is?"

"Sure. I saw him enter General Yue's tent."

"Which one is that?"

"The one with his name on it," Qing Hai chortles. After dusting off his clothes, Hai reaches for my hand and takes the lead inside until we come upon a large tent with the massive characters *'Zhen Yue'* painted on one side of the white canvas.

"See? Not hard to find at all. On a side note, the General doesn't like people touching his things so… don't. People kept coming in his tent by mistake. He finally painted his name on the outside. That tells you how particular he is, doesn't it?" The last part Hai whispers; laughing mischievously to himself.

"Definitely a unique approach. Thank you, Qing Hai."

"Sure. No problem. It was nice seeing you again." Smiling boyishly, Hai waves a friendly farewell and goes on his way.

I rush through the tent just as Hu comes out, nearly smashing my face against his heavy armor. The Demon General frowns. "You can't even follow the simplest of directions can you? Even a dog knows how to stay."

"A dog stays, that's what makes it a dog!" On impulse, I clench my hands in preparation of another row. However, the smile on his face is rather sweet. "What's happened? Where are you going?"

"I was going to take you home but since you came bursting in here, I guess I have to also escort you out too. So the torture begins, does it?"

"Torture begins?   Does that mean everything is okay?"

"If by 'okay' you mean that ugly asshole is scarred for life, sure. He's not dead. I'm being suspended for two weeks without pay. Might as well call it a vacation." Scoffing, Hu walks past me and out of the tent.

I glare after him, to then realize General Yue's been staring at me since I came in. The usual stonewall look on his face is now accompanied by half-furrowed brows. I can only surmise his dislike of me has deepened. Still, Hu had gotten off with barely a slap on the wrist and I feel as though Yue had no small part in that. I make a short obeisance in his direction and succinctly follow Hu out.

Chapter 5 – 6

"What? Now that you know I won't be executed, you're going to act cold?"

We're making our way home. I'm following a short distance behind Hu, careful not to repeat my earlier mistake. Apparently keeping my hands to myself also provokes displeasure from the General. He stops and turns to engage me.

"How am I acting cold?"

"On the way to the barracks, you latched onto me like a possessive girlfriend and now you're scuttling behind me like a little sister. Make up your mind. How should I treat you?"

"Isn't that for you to decide?"

"Huh. Let's see. Girlfriend, walk next to me! Nope. Sister, hurry up! Definitely not. Wife, come along! That sounds about right." Hu's pace resumes and then his arm extends to the side.

"Come along, Wife!" He calls out sharply.

The marching pace increases until we're adjacent. "I've told you my name is Bao Lai."

"I already have enough women hounding me. Trying to remember another name is too much trouble."

"I see. And, how did you end up in the Red Light District? I thought you were visiting your girlfriend. Does she work down there?"

"Me? Dating a prostitute? You've got some nerve making that kind of accusation. I'm a soldier of the imperial army. We're supposed to keep stupid girls who get lost wandering alone at night out of trouble. Tends to be a lot of that type down in the Red Light District."

The sarcastic glare directed at me makes swinging at him the first option to come to mind; except, retaliation is no longer a compelling reaction. Instead, my pace quickens and then I leave him trailing behind. Only a short moment passes before, once more, we're abreast.

"Don't scare me like that again." He mumbles the words ever so softly. They were barely audible. The look on his face is enough for me to realize the anxiety I've caused.

"I'm sorry."

Lowering my head, I reach out and grab his still extended hand. He squeezes tightly in return.

"Whatever. I knew you were trouble the moment I laid eyes on you. Anyhow, want to tell me where you learned to fight like that?"

"Wasn't really fighting; more like friendly sparring. At the temple to the south, Master Zhuang Gu used to take the students out in the fields for training."

"Zhuang Gu, that famous general from Ji?"

"Yes. The very same. Although, not a general anymore, he said. I don't know why he joined our temple but he never stayed very long. He'd leave and come back from time to time. After the old man... my master, passed away, I heard the General left permanently."

"Why did you leave?"

"I didn't have a choice. I was thrown out around the same time. The old priest was the only reason the senior members permitted my stay."

"How long ago was that?"

"A bit over a year."

"I see. That's pretty recent, which explains a whole lot."

"What is that supposed to mean?"

"I've been wondering why you make such a terrible woman. It's all coming together now!" He guffaws like a moron but I don't hate him for it. I prefer this happy version of him more than anything.

"Yes, well, I've never even worn women's clothing until you bought this." I hold out my arm and examine the pattern of the robe. Although I've never liked the color pink, I am fond of this robe. "I'll pay you back for this, I promise."

"Oh, please! Don't insult me. The least a man can do is afford his wife a new robe."

"I am not your wife!'

"You said this was my decision, Wife. Don't go back on your words now."

He has a point and I don't have a rebuttal. With nothing else to say, we continue home hand-in-hand down the desolate streets.

Continue to page 90

Chapter 5 – 7

Bad people should be punished. The satisfaction of watching a wrong righted is more thrilling than I imagined. I stare at the relentless beating and yet can't bring myself to stop Hu. His gauntlets are turning red. Blood splatters over his armor and then trickles toward the ground. The rage coming over him, the savage expression, and maddening eyes, all mount to one effect: the world has one less criminal.

From afar, the sounds of whistles break the silence. Soon enough, a handful of guards come upon the scene. Amongst them is General Yue who scans the dead man, then me, and then Hu. Without much consideration, he places a hand on Hu's shoulders.

"Take your wife home. We'll take things from here."

Without responding, Hu grabs my arm and then drags me out of the Red Light District toward the markets. Once the city's main gates become visible, he moves away.

"Go. Get out of here." His gaze averts. Hu's low tone is shaken by an emotion I can't decipher.

"You're... letting me go?"

"Isn't that what I said? Go!"

"Hu, I'm sorry. I got lost. I wasn't trying to run away."

"I didn't ask for an explanation. Frankly, you're a pain and I won't be able to watch over you from now on. Do me a favor and just leave. Isn't this what you wanted?"

"But..."

I did ask to leave and I should feel ecstatic; except, I'm not. This strange ache in my chest deepens every second we are closer to parting. I can't keep from panicking and no matter what I wish to say, words can't be conveyed. For a moment, I thought his wavering eyes meant he'd changed his mind but Bai Hu abruptly turns on his heel and marches back toward the market district. I stand still, dumfounded by this unexpected release.

In time, the moon above begins to wane. An indiscernible loneliness creeps over my chest, rendering all my expectations moot. I turn to the gates and do as Hu commanded by taking to the main road leading out of the capital. I don't know where I'm going and worse, won't know what to do once I arrive. The path ahead is obscured. For now, all I can do is continue on.

The End.

Chapter 6: A Date to Remember

Something is poking my face. The agitating staccato beats sweep away a nice dream which I can no longer remember.

"Stop that!"

I knock his hand away. Hu is sitting on the bed poking my cheeks and forehead with his rough forefingers. Although I am finally awake, he refuses to quit.

"Do you always oversleep? I thought monks are supposed to wake up early for prayers."

"I am not a monk!" Turning on my stomach, I shove my face into the pillow. "Go away. Go talk to your girlfriend. Let me sleep."

"No can do, Wife. She has to work."

"Then go to the restaurant and talk to her."

"Restaurant?" The revealing accusation gives pause to his poking barrage. "I told you, she's an old friend."

"I may be a little naïve but I'm not *that* stupid. I know what men actually mean when they say 'old friend.'"

A few of the monks at the temple also had *old friends* who came to visit from time to time. After such friends left, the monks were chewed out by the seniors.

"Sorry to say you don't know anything about men."

I feel him lie down so I lift my head and look over my shoulder. Last night, he wouldn't let me out of his sight once we arrived home. We slept beside each other. Stranger even, he woke me by mistake during the night, though I feigned to have still been asleep, when his big arms wrapped around me and his face buried into the nape of my neck. While he drifted to sleep soon after, I couldn't have been more awake, burning from embarrassment. My heart finally gave out near daybreak before I fell back to slumber; also the reason for why I've overslept. The memory of his touch is rushing blood to my head. I feel faint again.

"You're being too quiet, Wife. What's wrong?"

"You... like me, don't you?"

His cheeks are suddenly ablaze. Hu rolls his eyes to the corners and returns a cautious stare.

"You think so? You think I prefer a woman who's stuck in limbo between genders?"

"I think you like a woman who knows next to nothing about men and nothing about being a woman. The attraction will eventually fade, you know, when you realize how dull I really am."

"You're jumping to conceited conclusions, Wife."

"Sooner or later you'll grow weary of that too, this pretense we play. Eventually you'll meet the woman you'll really love and come to resent me for keeping you from those ambitions. And I probably will. I'm the jealous type. I don't easily let go of what's mine. So, now that you know, what are you going to do about it?"

His eyes return to the ceiling; his lips sealed. I can't read what he's thinking. Maybe, he now understands not to become attached to me. He shouldn't be wasting time making fun of his fake wife; he should be looking for a real one. Minutes pass by and his position remains unchanged. I roll my eyes and then push off the bed. As I attempt to move off, big arms wrap around my body. Before I can get a word out, he's crouched over me. Hu wears a blank expression, touching my face carefully with his rough hands.

"You're just that stubborn, aren't you?" I reach up and poke his left cheek with my index finger.

He seizes my hand in a trembling grasp. "I don't easily let go of what's mine either."

The instant my lips part to question his motive, a quivering kiss presses on my mouth. Shock and confusion render defenses moot. All I can see are his face turning bright red, the long lashes of his eyes fluttering, and his silky brown hair draping over our faces. His shy kiss grows with more fervor as time passes. I can feel his heart beating out of his chest, no different from my own. I don't understand what's happening but once I could give more thought to the idea, he's moved away.

"It's only polite when someone's kissing you, to kiss back." The silly tone is there but his attention is to the wall.

"That's terrible logic." I reply, looking in the opposite direction.

"Yeah, you're right. It's only polite when I kiss you, for you to kiss back."

"Really? And where would I have learned how to do such things? From practicing with the monks?" My finger jams severely against his cheek and then I start off the bed.

"It's like talking to a child!" He grumbles.

"I haven't been here a week and you're already this audacious. I'm telling your girlfriend."

"Says the woman who rubbed her face in my chest."

"Don't flatter yourself. I was just wiping my nose on your shirt."

I walk into the living room to hide my flushed face. I should be infuriated by his advances and yet, I'm not. Being near him... with him, feels so familiar and comfortable. Our close predicament hardly feels a change to me, but resumption.

He comes forthwith, patting my head once near. "So, where to today, Wife?"

"My head is not your arm rest, Husband! And, I don't know. What do you mean, 'where to?'"

"Didn't I tell you I'm suspended from work for two weeks? Let's go somewhere nice. Where do you want to go?"

"As I recall, it was two weeks without pay. You probably shouldn't have too much fun."

Hu pats my head again. "Pay, no pay, whatever. Life's too short to worry over money."

"Are you serious? Is this how you live? How do you plan to retire?"

"I'm a soldier, dear. I'll more than likely die from battle than old age."

Despite his casual reply, my chest turns cold at the notion of his death. He's chosen a dangerous occupation, just how dangerous, I can't even begin to imagine. Last night, I fought three weaklings and it took everything in me just to do that. In his lifetime, he'll battle hordes of men within his superior league more often than not. Whatever skill or luck have kept him alive all this time has a chance to fail, and once is all it takes for me to never see him again. My throat suddenly becomes constricted and my nose is burning.

"Hey, hey. No crying in this house! What's wrong?"

Hu rushes to provide a comforting embrace. I bury my face in his chest, grasping his robe tightly. "You dumb jerk! Don't even say something that stupid!"

"I said a lot of stupid things. What are you mad about?"

I can't bring myself to repeat the horrible thought. Raining tears drown out my voice while I clutch him tighter. In time, a small sigh falls from above.

"Oh... Well, there's always that chance. I won't lie and say I'll always come home but I do plan to."

"That's your answer?!" I squeeze tighter, tilting my head up toward his face.

More than anything, he just looks sad. "I lied, you know. I don't have a girlfriend. Never had one."

"What does that have to do with anything? You can have as many as you want! Don't change the subject!"

"I never had one because I didn't want anyone crying over me!" He pauses. With greater force, his arms draw us closer. "I'm sorry. You just looked so troubled standing there in that room. I forgot my reservations, so I volunteered."

"Do you regret it?"

His lips thin into a line. His head gently shakes. "I don't want you to be sad but now that you're mine, I'm not giving you to anyone. You'll just have to bear with me. I promise to come home no matter what."

"You promise? Well, that's not good enough!"

"I'm trying to be romantic here! Why are you yelling?"

"I don't know what's romantic and what isn't. It doesn't sit well with me for you to run off to face who-knows-what while I sit here and wait. I'm not that feeble. Let me help."

"Help how?"

"Either leave your post or I'll join you."

"What?" He raises an eyebrow.

"You heard me."

"Don't you know women aren't allowed? Even if you could join, I wouldn't let you."

"And you'd never consider leaving?"

"No," he shakes his head adamantly. "It's been our childhood dream. I promised and that promise won't be broken."

The words naturally flowing from Bai Hu hits directly into my heart. A thin veil of reluctance in the back of my mind is on the verge of shattering to a new revelation. I'm so close but can't reach it. "*Our* dream? How did you know that was my childhood dream?"

"Er... I-I meant *our* as in m-my promise to a friend. My friend and I—we—our dream! Right? I mean, my friend couldn't join so I promised myself to join for him. Don't get me wrong, I would have on my own accord but it was also for him. What's with the suspicious look? Is that so strange?"

"No. It's just that I, too, made promises with a friend. We would have joined together but he left temple a long time ago."

"Hm. Just as well. Like I said, women aren't permitted and I don't have any intention to leave."

"Fine. Since you've made your choice, I'll make mine." Pushing away from him, I walk back into the bedroom to find my hair tie. He follows forthwith and leans against the doorway.

"All right, impulsive woman, what are you thinking?"

"I'm thinking if I can't join as a woman then I'll arrive at the recruitment office as a man. Where did you put my other robe?"

"I hate it when you tie your hair like that!" Hu walks over to take down my hair. "This is not a joke. It's a serious crime for a woman to infiltrate the military. Instead of fighting me on this, why can't we just make the most of our time together, however long that may be? H-Hey, I told you, no crying in this house. What's your deal anyway? Are you suddenly in love with me? Sure you won't just *grow bored* of me eventually?"

"Don't make fun of me!"

Hu laughs when my face presses into his chest. I don't know what love is, so I can't say, but I know I've grown attached to him enough that I don't ever want to let him go. Maybe I am his possessive girlfriend.

Suddenly, I've floated off the ground. Hu scooped me into his arms and is walking over to the bed. He gently lays me down and then moves atop.

"Brazen bastard. What do you think you're doing?"

"Life's too short to be so damn formal all the time. Yesterday, when I thought those men had... I was ready to kill them, no matter the consequences." A visible surge of rage enters his expression, causing his shoulders to tremble. His breathing grows shallow from fighting hard to keep the overwhelming emotions at bay. "One thing's for sure, I don't want another man to ever lay hands on you. I don't know why I'm so damn obsessed or why I feel as though my heart will burst if you reject me. All I know is that I have a reason to come home now instead of wandering outside every night like a lost fool and I'm not going to let anything keep me from you. Do you understand? Maybe it's too sudden and it doesn't make any sense. I don't understand it myself but I want you to believe me."

The more he talks, the faster my heart races. It's no secret that even though I am confused too, I still reflect his sentiment fully.

Reaching up to touch his loving face, I return a short nod. "I believe you. Go where you must but always come back to me. Else, I'll hunt you down."

He frowns at my grin. "You're the most unromantic person ever!"

"What's that?"

"Nothing, dear."

Slowly, he leans down until our quivering lips touch. His arms wrap tightly around my body and I hold him in turn. Such strange sensations overwhelm me; I lose my strength in his embrace. His rough hands, trembling, run over my body. I don't have the slightest idea why his touch feels so natural, why I've no inclination to reject his advances, or why I've fallen out of character. We've only just met. We barely know anything about each other. He nearly killed me. And I... don't seem to care. All my reason melts away.

Gently, Hu undoes my robe and then by the by, he claims me as his own.

Chapter 6 – 2

The sun is setting, and already in the distance, glowing lantern lights prepare to take its place. In the early twilight, we stroll toward the night market. A lovely wind flutters by, playfully picking our robes and hair. His hand, around my waist, pulls me in closer toward his warm body.

A sweet whisper flows from under the loving gaze. "Are you cold?"

"No. The wind feels nice."

"Yes. I suppose after all those hot and heavy things we did at home, the cool breezes are a nice change."

Every inch of me erupts in flames. "Stop making fun of me!"

"So temperamental, Wife! I can't wait to tell all the guys that temple girls aren't as innocent as they seem. What would the monks say if they knew!"

"You started it!" I clench my hands into fists and look away. It's a poor defense but it's all I have.

"I also ended it too. If it were up to you, we'd still be at it."

I punch the jerk on the arm and leave him behind. He runs to catch up.

"That really hurts! You're a lot stronger than you look."

"If you think I'm strong then let me join. I'll go along as your personal attendant if I have to."

"This again? I've told you it's not possible."

"Then maybe I should speak to the Minister."

"I don't think you'll have much influence on San An once he finds out how naughty you've been."

"Will you stop it already?!"

Slapping Hu's arm, I run forward. He reaches out and pulls us back together.

"I'm sorry!" He laughs loudly. "I'll stop. I promise. At least, until next time."

"There won't be a next time!"

"Liar. You looked like you had fun. I can see you lusting after me already."

"Bastard!" I shove him away and then run into the crowd. Hu's obnoxious burst of laughter clearly resonates from behind. I hate him so much I can't even describe it! I hate him so much, I never want to part from him!

In time, Hu catches me, smiling an apologetic, boyish smile. Then, hand-in-hand, we walk toward his favorite restaurant. He leisurely bypasses the crowd to the table in the far back, the only empty one on this floor, as though it were permanently reserved for him. On cue, a beat after we sit down, Kai comes over. She's startled to see me.

"Bao Lai! You look so different!"

"Oh, uh. Thank you."

"She's a real cutie, huh?" Bai Hu grins.

"Sure is! You've changed too, General! I don't think I've seen you this happy since Feng You."

My eyes grow wide from her brash declaration. Kai catches her mistake and immediately forces a change of subject.

"S-So, the usual, General? What will you have, Bao Lai?"

I couldn't hear anything after Feng You. My eyes are stuck to his face. Hu is blushing, which means it can't be good.

"Yeah, the usual." Hu mutters softly. "Bring her some mushroom dumplings and soy pudding. They're her favorite."

"How do you know that?" My widened eyes grow wider. The last time we came, he also ordered dumplings for me, and that was only minutes after I became his 'wife.' Come to think of it, he asked the shopkeeper to bring all the pink robes as a mean to provoke me to choose a new outfit. Meaning, he knew I hate pink. Maybe this familiarity between us isn't coincidental.

I give him a dubious look. In turn, his eyes race about until finally setting on Kai. "T-That's what most girls like, right Kai? Anyway, also a pot of your black guava tea."

"That's also my favorite," I frown.

"Green tea it is! You hate that, right?"

"And how would you also know *that*?"

Hu's incoherent rambling worsens. At length, Kai's giggles silence his flustering.

"You sure know your *sister* well, General!"

She pats his shoulder and then saunters away toward the kitchen, leaving behind an increasingly nervous Hu. He's definitely keeping secrets from me; the most irritating one being Feng You. I avert my gaze out the window. Once he's worked up the nerves, his hand reaches across the table.

"Don't you want to ask me?"

"Nope." I yank my hand back.

"So, you're just going to sit over there and be angry with me?"

"Yup."

"Typical jealous girlfriend," he mutters.

"How would you know? You said you've never had a girlfriend but I'm sure that's just nonsense to make stupid girls like me fall for your whims, right?"

"Hey, hey! I don't have to lie to get what I want. Besides, you're the one who seduced me with all your tears. What's a man supposed to do?"

"Excuse me? A gentleman would just hand over a handkerchief, not his entire body!"

Our angry staring contest begins and then ends just as swiftly through laughter erupting without reason.

"Do you want to know who she is or not?"

"No, but tell me anyway."

"I didn't lie. Never had a girlfriend. Feng You was just a lover."

"Just a lover? You think that sounds better?"

"Hear me out! That was a long time ago. Back then, you were probably still a flat-chested little girl. I would have gotten arrested for even talking to you."

"Really? How old were you back then? And... how old are you now?"

"I was seventeen. I'm twenty-eight now."

"We're almost the same age, you moron!"

Hu squints, peering carefully, while scratching his face. "Are you serious? I wanted a young innocent wife, not an old woman."

The spoon from my side of the table flies at his face. He puts his hands up defensively, laughing all the while.

"Get to the point!"

"Okay, okay! It was a long time ago, it didn't mean anything."

"If she made you happy, then why didn't you marry her?"

"A man can be happy in any moment when he's with a woman. That doesn't mean he's in love. Feng You and I made each other happy but we didn't love each other. She thought I was too serious and I thought she was fickle."

"She thought *you* were too serious? Is she daft?"

"I told you, that was a long time ago."

"And I suppose you've changed into a sarcastic jerk because of her, believing if you'd stop being serious, she'd take you back?"

"Stop overanalyzing everything. That's not why I'm..."

Suddenly frowning, Hu's gaze thrusts toward the ceiling. A rush of colors stains his cheeks. "Look, I won't tell you not to be jealous. I like it that you are.

Just, don't think for a moment I would ever look at any woman except you in that way. Understand?"

"Hmm, have you ever noticed how handsome General Yue and the Minister are?"

"What are you doing?"

"Nothing. I don't know why I suddenly realize how handsome they are. Would you mind if I think of them the next time we're together?"

Hu picks up a spoon and gently taps my forehead. "You are the *meanest* woman I've ever met in my life!"

The moment a grin appears over my face, a piercing scream erupts from the streets. In seconds, Hu jumps onto the table and then climbs out the window.

"Stay there!"

The panicked warning comes as his feet land flat on the ground. I barely have the chance to grasp what's happened and he's already running down the streets. Immediately, a group of soldiers push through the crowds with General Yue and Qing Hai leading the pack. The two do their best to maneuver around the patrons but most of their men are less tactful. Civilians are practically shoved down and trampled on while carts are flung to the side, spilling everything the vendors had to sell for the night. Screams of fright are followed in succession by shouts of frustration.

"Bao Lai, where's Hu?"

Chapter 6: A Date to Remember

I turn to meet Kai coming with our orders. She's been so nice. I can't believe I have to do this to her.

"I'm sorry, Kai. I'll come back later and pay for the food, I promise."

Without giving her the chance to reply, I climb out the window and run after the soldiers. Hu is unarmed and he has a head start. Anything could happen should he meet danger before the other soldiers have a chance to close in.

Instead of clearing the streets, the chaos brought large groups to crowd together, making it difficult to push through. I can't reach them at this rate. In my futile attempt, someone knocks me against the side of a large shop, and then I see in front of me, a wooden beam extending toward the roof. Using the opportunity, I climb up the beam onto the shop's shingled roof.

A dark green robe flickers in the distance followed by men in red armors. I run after them, jumping from rooftop to rooftop. The fact that this marketplace is overly crowded with shops makes the ordeal rather easy. The roofs are so close together, I barely have to hop to make it across.

The familiar green robe suddenly lunges forward, tackling someone to the ground, before punches are exchanged. The imperial soldiers reach the scene and surround the culprit who doesn't show any inclination of yielding. I keep running until I'm finally on the roof above the encounter.

"Give up! There's no escape!" Qing Hai gives the signal to his fellow archers while aiming his crossbow at the masked man.

Bai Hu is strong but his opponent is slightly more agile. They scuffle for a time and then at length, comes apart when their stalemate becomes painfully obvious. Hu joins the imperial ranks and takes a sword from another soldier. Together, they close in on the man. The culprit, however, seems little perturbed. A normal person in such an overpowered situation would panic and prepare for melee but all he does is survey the area. His weapon is not even drawn.

In one quick turn, the culprit knocks down a guard on his right and then climbs up the side of a shop. Qing Hai immediately launches an arrow but the man twists his body just so at the last moment to barely avoid contact. The other archers following suit are too late. Once the culprit pulls himself onto the rooftop, comes face-to-face with me. We look at each other, wide-eyed and bewildered. I am not sure what I should do.

Lunge at him (Continue to page 109)

Do nothing (Continue to page 110)

Chapter 6 – 3

An enemy of Hu is no friend of mine. I don't know what he's done but this man can't be allowed to go free. I want Hu to be proud of me. Mostly, I want Hu to be safe. The ordeal won't end until this man is captured.

His body twitches, prepared to run past me. In turn, I lunge forward. He evades swiftly and marginally, so that I fall on my face inches away from him. However, an arrow hurls at the position he's moved into, causing his retreat to momentarily stalls and giving me a chance to redeem my mistake. Quickly, I grab onto his ankles and attempt to drag the assailant down.

His footing is lost, a blue light flickers in the night, and then the dreaded feeling of cold steel pierces my chest. Everything turns dark.

The End.

Chapter 6 – 4

We stand frozen from shock; though, the standoff is short-lived. The noises below pull back his senses. Suddenly, the man rushes forward, pushing me aside. I grab onto his arm steadfastly without thinking. In one quick movement, he turns on his heel and draws something from his hip. A blue glimmer in the pale moonlight and then a cold stream flows down my arm. Everything around drowns out in muffles. A rush of wind blows past my hair toward the rooftop, whose flickering lights are growing ever distant. I'm falling, I think. I must be. The hazy moment ends when I land on something firm and warm. My vision reels as I try to make sense of what's happened but until he calls to me, I could make neither heads nor tails.

"Bao Lai! Bao Lai!"

It is Hu who calls my name and it was also he who has broken my fall. I try to respond but nothing will come.

"Damn it! I'll kill him! I'll kill that bastard!" His deadly roar is no mere threat. The same rage I'd seen in him yesterday when he came for me in the Red Light District is now tenfold. When I attempt to sit up, he embraces me with such ardent fervor, as though to suppress hidden sobs, that his shoulders tremble.

"Hu. Bai Hu." I finally manage to regain little control of my body.

"Idiot! I told you not to come! Why don't you ever listen?!"

His arms tighten, slightly crushing me under their protection. I didn't mean to be in his way but an apology just doesn't seem to suffice. Words are stuck in my throat. The moment I reach for his face, Hu cuts off my attempt.

"Qing Hai, take her to Master Dui!"

I look around and none of the clad imperial soldiers are present except for Qing Hai. Everyone else must have run after that man.

"Where are you going, General?" Hai kneels down to take me into his arms.

"Don't ask stupid questions! I'm going to kill that asshole!"

The anger from inside radiates to the surface. I can feel the magnitude of his rage burning like a thousand suns. I squirm in Hai's arms while reaching out to Hu, only to manage a pathetic whimper. "Don't go."

He whips around; his face twisted like that of a beast ready to pounce. Upon noticing my startled gaze, his fury suppresses. Hu's attention averts to the ground. "This is my job. You know that. If you can't understand and support me, then just leave."

His hard tone makes me turn cold. The sight of him walking away twists my heart into a knot. Though I can't place it, I know this pain. This pain of abandonment he's somehow induced in me before. I struggle in Hai's arms but that only makes his hold tighten.

"Stop! Please! We have to get to Master Dui's before your bleeding worsens."

"No. Put me down, Hai!"

Hai takes off running when I attempt to squirm out of his grip. Away from the bustling market, he makes haste down several streets toward a poorer district where shabby houses scrunch together in tight rows. Compared to the luxury I'm used to seeing in An, this entire area appears foreign. Many of these structures are as rundown as my old house, if not worse, and mine was acquired for free. That is, the house I'd lived in near the village of Kou was abandoned before I made it my own. I never imagined that hovel could best any living quarters in the capital.

Once we arrive at the clinic. Hai kicks open the door. "Master Dui! Master Dui! Where are you?"

Frantically, Hai turns every which way in the empty room. I thought the master isn't here, so I begin to protest. However, slowly, a bundle on the floor starts budging and then a head pokes out from what looks like a rug. A man with messy hair then emerges from underneath, yawning loudly.

"What do you people want? Unless you're dying, come back tomorrow."

"Master Dui!" Hai snaps crossly.

He looks over at us for a short moment before a large smile appears. "Well, you've got a pretty girl with you. Why didn't you say so?"

Immediately, the physician jumps to his feet, rushes over, and scoops me from Hai's arms. He makes haste into the back room and then pulls bandages and tools from a cabinet drawer.

"What did you do to her?" Master Dui, drawing water from the reserve tank into a bowl, glares at the young soldier.

"An assassin injured Miss Bao Lai. You best check to be sure she wasn't poisoned."

The word 'assassin' makes both the doctor and I freeze. Hu is going to fight the assassin—no, kill the assassin—in his enraged state. He loses control when he's angry and he can be so reckless! If this assassin manages to poison him, Hu won't retreat to find help. He'll continue to fight until either he or his opponent falters.

On impulse, I make for the door, but the doctor pulls back. "Calm down. I don't know what you're fretting about but it can wait."

"I have to find him! I have to make sure he's okay!" This time, my attempt to make a run for the exit is blocked by Qing Hai.

"The General is worried enough as it is. If he sees you, he'll just lose concentration. I'll go look for him and make sure he comes back to you."

Hai makes a quick nod and then runs out the door. Despite his assurance, my knees buckle under those familiar words, sending me to the floor. 'Comes back to me.' Hu promised to come home to me. I can only pray that he'll keep his words. I don't know what I'd do if he... I can't even think it!

"Don't worry, dove, I'll take good care of you." The sudden lecherous tone shakes me from depression. I turn to meet the doctor who's winking seductively.

"Treat my damn wounds so I can get out of here!"

"Whoa, whoa, whoa! No need to bite my head off! Sit over there and remove your robe."

"Why? It's a flesh wound, dumb pervert!"

"Pervert?" He sulks defensively. "I'm a doctor. I've seen everything I need to see about the human body. Although, if you're going to be shy about it, I'm tempted to give you a free physical."

"I'll give you a free broken arm if you do anything stupid. Bandage me already!"

Once settled into position by the basket of bandages, I pull down a part of the collar, exposing my arm and shoulder. There is a long cut where the blade met my flesh but it doesn't appear very deep. The good doctor smiles and attempts to pull down the robe a bit more. When I threaten him, he draws back and grins. As lecherous as he is, Master Dui seems to know what he's doing. In no time, the bleeding stops, as does the pain.

"So, your boyfriend's a general? Sure you don't want to date a doctor instead? We're known for our gentle hands."

"Really? I'm known for breaking gentle hands. So, let's just say I'm doing you a favor by saying, 'no.' Anyway, Hai mentioned something about poison. Do you see anything?"

"If that guy's really an assassin and you were poisoned, it'd be pretty obvious by now." He responds in the most condescending manner ever imagined.

"I see. Then, thanks. I've got to go."

"What about my payment?"

"I'll come by tomorrow and pay you. I don't have money right now."

"Money? Who said anything about money? You can just pay me with whatever you have on you. Or, you can just pay me with you, if you'd like."

"I'd like to stay and pay you with my fist but I have better things to do so, you'll get money and you'll get it tomorrow!"

Chapter 6 – 5

Once outside, I close my eyes, expecting to catch any notion of weapons clashing in the distance. However, by now, the streets are silent. Out of fear, everyone has returned home. If Hu is still after the culprit then he's too far away for me to find. And, if they've caught the assassin, then the soldiers would be at the palace. Otherwise, I don't even know what to think. Whether optimism or expectation urges my feet, I start walking home. Maybe he'll be there waiting for me. Maybe he returned home, just as he'd promised.

"Bao Lai!"

Barely have I reached the end of the street, her anxious voice calls out to me. Kai's small feet make great haste down the dusty pavements. Her jeweled hairpin swings wildly. When she stops, the lady is completely out of breath.

"Kai, are you all right?"

"Y-Yes. I'm fine." She stoops over to catch several more breaths until her reddened cheeks resume their former pallid hue. "Thank goodness! I heard a woman was injured in the scuffle at the markets. I was so scared that it was you. I ran here to Master Dui's but, you are here. Was it you?"

"Yes, it was just a flesh wound though. I'm fine. I can't believe you ran all the way here to check on me. That's so kind. Thank you, Kai."

"Of course! What are friends for? I'm just glad you're safe."

She smiles enchantingly in that familiar manner I've come to expect. Kai really is a nice person. I've never had any female friends due to my predicament. I often thought women to be intimidating, but she's very personable. Besides, Hu is her friend and I want to be friends with all of his friends too.

"Thanks. Has everything calmed down in the markets?"

"For the most part. A large group of soldiers came a short while ago to disperse the crowds. That clash was probably the most exciting and terrifying thing to have happened in years! People will be talking about it for weeks and I... will have to pretend everything each customer tells me is new and feign to be *shocked*!" Pausing, she giggles. "By the way, Bao Lai, where is Bai Hu? Shouldn't he be with you?"

"He's... needed elsewhere. Duty calls. You didn't by chance catch a glimpse of a dark green robe running after the soldiers, did you?"

"No, I didn't. Or, maybe I did but didn't notice. I was worried about you. You don't look happy. Is everything all right? You can tell me anything, you know that."

Chapter 6: A Date to Remember

"I, um, I'm not sure."

She must be worried about Hu too. A part of me wants to exhale my troubles in a quick breath and alleviate this heavy feeling over my chest; another wants to keep my personal plight hidden. Somewhere in the midst of my idleness, a comforting hand lands on my shoulder.

"I know what you're going through, Bao Lai."

"You do?"

"Of course! I think most women at one time or other are fallible to men in uniform. The problem with men in uniform is that they can't ever truly take them off. He'll always put duty first."

"That's not what's bothering me. It's just that I... have caused him so much trouble. I thought I was strong but I'm nothing compared to real warriors and instead of helping him, I ended up making stupid mistakes and putting him in danger. I don't know how to become stronger, to stand as his equal. More than anything, I just want to protect Bai Hu."

"I see." Kai glances into the distance, pondering quietly for a time. Her light brown eyes carry forlorn when they return to me. "I'm sorry, Bao Lai, but it won't do. Women aren't meant to play warriors. You can't protect him, and the more you try, the more danger Hu will expose himself to for your sake. You're both my dear friends. I'm telling you this for your own good."

I disagree with the notion that women can't be warriors. Still, that doesn't change my weakness. I feel useless because she's right. The more I try to prove myself, the more trouble I cause for Bai Hu.

"Then, what should I do, Kai? I can't watch him run toward danger and do nothing. I know it's what he wants and it's what I've told myself to accept but in the end, I couldn't stop impulse."

"Two people who aren't right for each other shouldn't be in a relationship."

"What?"

Kai's direct stare puts my nerves on guard. Just days ago, the thought of leaving crossed my mind but I stayed out of obligations and mainly, because I didn't have a choice. Now, I freely choose to stay with Bai Hu. The very idea of parting from him drills a deeper pain into my heart than I ever thought imaginable. I warned him from becoming attached. That warning was more suited for me.

My head shakes a silent rebuttal, causing the awkward atmosphere to turn tense. At the same time, Kai's warm smile suddenly appears to change everything back to serenity.

"I think you misunderstood my intentions, Bao Lai. I meant that in relationships, partners shouldn't have conflicting goals. You want him to be safe and he wants to run into battle. What happens when you wish to raise a family and he'd prefer to raise an army? In order to make you happy, he would have to forfeit his ambitions—his happiness. That also goes for you. The right decision isn't always the easiest but in the long run, less painful. Make that selfless decision before he decides for you both."

"Hu wouldn't—I mean, I don't think he would."

"How well do you know Bai Hu?"

Kai is fully aware of my ignorance. I can't admit it and for that reason, a seed of doubt is present in my mind. She may be right but another indescribable feeling has taken over all logic. Nothing else matters to me when I'm with him. Surrendering my newfound happiness would be no less than ripping out my own heart. It's unthinkable.

"I know that Hu is a kind man. He's taken it upon himself to guard me despite the troubles I've caused. That's more than I can ever ask for."

"I'm sorry. I didn't mean to make you uncomfortable. You're right! Hu is a kind person and you are a good girl. I'm sure everything will be fine! He's not likely to repeat the fiasco with Feng You, right?"

"What about Feng You?"

"Well, how about that? It's getting late. I had better return to the restaurant and clean up before Mrs. Lim comes by for inspection. I'm glad you're all right! Say hi to the General for me!"

"Wait, Kai! Hold on a second! What about Feng You?"

She waves farewell and retreats into distant shadows. I can't say I'm not in the least agitated by her crass suggestion but I understand she must have a reason. Besides, Kai was thoughtful to have come a long way to see me. If only she hadn't left after placing me in this obscurity.

Chapter 6 – 6

My speed picks up to a full run toward the bright lights of the night market and then to the road that eventually leads home. When I arrive at the house, the lights are not on. He's still out there. Coming home to an empty house; the thought was painful and reality is worse. I can't stand this dreadful feeling; except, I've no one to blame but myself. That assassin was practically in my hands and I couldn't stop him. Once more, Hu's in trouble because of me. If I had stayed put then maybe, he would be here now instead of who knows where exacting vengeance.

I look back toward the market, hoping for him to walk up the street. The darkened horizon laced with sparkling diamond stars is somehow melancholy. The neighbors' houses are lighted by large beautiful lanterns and still my soul is frozen by quiet dread. I didn't know I could feel this way. If we continue on, is this the feeling I'll be forced to endure each day? Fear shall be my new companion and anxiety my new friend. It's inconceivable. I can't accept not knowing how he fares. It's a selfish thought, but his duty should not come before me.

Maybe he's right. Unless I can support his decision, I should leave. His position is difficult enough; Hu doesn't need a clouded mind caused by a troublesome woman. Besides, I was made Hu's ward merely to protect His Highness's predicament and that secret is

123

safe with me. If ever I could leave in peace, now is the time.

Despite the thought, I've already turned on my heels and making my way back to the markets. He'll hate me for this but I need to know that he's safe. However, I'm barely two blocks from the house when a black horse rushes hither, kicking both forelegs into the air as the beast abruptly jerks to a halt in front of me.

"Get on." The hand that extends down from the commanding officer belongs to General Yue; his expression as flat as ever. Though his brash orders leave me wanting, I know he would never waste unnecessary words. I reach for his hand. With one quick motion, he pulls me atop and then takes off before I barely have enough time settle onto the saddle.

"Are you taking me to Hu?"

"Yes."

"Where is he?"

"Far from here."

"Why aren't you with him?"

General Yue's response is to quicken the pace of the steed. I jolt forward, grabbing onto his waist to keep from falling. His body unexpectedly stiffens at my touch. This must be uncomfortable for him but I can't help it. Maybe he's ascertained the same; and so, he remains quiet and unnaturally rigid. We ride past the eastern gate and then onto the main road. With each passing second, moving farther away from the capital.

"I need you to stop him," Yue resumes giving orders when the steed reaches full speed under the hazy moonlight.

"Stop who?"

"Your husband."

"Is that why you came to fetch me? What is he doing out this far? Where are you taking me? Why didn't you stop him?"

Too many questions rush through my head. I mindlessly blurt them out. Yue has no interests in my ramblings. He continues.

"Bai Hu loses himself when he adorns the silver mane helmet and becomes the Demon General. I cannot stop his madness when the Demon's rage reaches this level. It is not my intent to place you in danger but I must ask for your help."

"His mane?" My thoughts race back to the night when he held the sword against my throat. He was wearing that silver mane and the dizzying coldness from his eyes as he considered taking my life then, haunts me still. "How can a helmet turn a man into a beast? It doesn't make any sense!"

"That is a conversation for husband and wife. It is not my place. I do ask that once we arrive, you'll attempt to remove that helmet. Take every caution. In his state, I do not know if your persuasion will be enough. If he appears hostile, retreat and I'll try another method."

Though I push more questions, Yue will not answer. He's busy contemplating the best option should I happen to fail.

Screams and blood-curdling snarls abruptly pierce the night air. We've yet to happen on the scene and already I can sense his rage oppressing the area like a thick dark veil. The closer we come to the din, the more I feel as though we are descending into the underworld.

The steed immediately jolts, kicking both forequarters into the air, refusing to budge one fraction forward. I would have fallen off had Yue not quickly reached out and fastened our bodies together. Under his soothing, the beast eventually calms. The reverse is happening in me. Shaking from strained courage, I climb down the steed and slowly make way toward the vortex of frenzied darkness.

The clouds above part slightly. Blue steel glistens in the night. Streams of seemingly endless blood flow down the blade. Deathly quiet. The reaper of those lifeless bodies is the only man left standing. His head tilts in my direction. His silver mane ruffles gently in the wind while chilly hazel eyes gawking apathetically seem to push my soul into the brink of oblivion. His face and armor are drenched in blood and gore of his fallen foes. And how many there are! I can't imagine twenty men having the strength to do as he had done single-handedly. Never in my life have I ever witnessed such brute force!

The merciless scene robs the last bit of composure. My chest is heaving violently to catch fleeting breaths. My legs won't budge. For a long time, we stare at one another until the clouds above completely disperse from around the moon. Hu shakes the blood from his weapon, and upon sheathing his blade, starts in the opposite direction.

"Wait! Stop!"

The fear of losing him breaks composure free from the fear of him, bringing back control to my body. He pauses and then slowly turns back. The bloodstained gauntlets start for the blade latched to his hip. Yue moves in front of me.

"Bai Hu. What are you doing? She is your wife."

Hu peers at Yue and then again at me; ultimately, deciding that he isn't interested in either of us. An overwhelming feeling of despair rises within. I can't bear to watch him walk away. A part of me knows that should I let him go, we'll never meet again. Tears blur him from my vision. In a rush of panic, I stumble into a sprint after Hu and immediately tumble back from Yue's firm grip.

"What are you doing? Let me go!"

"No. He'll strike if you come close."

"Then what am I supposed to do? He's walking toward Ning! No matter how strong he is, Hu can't defeat an entire army by himself!"

"If you run after him, he'll kill you first and then walk into Ning. How is that better?" Yue's voice is stern but calm. He's considered the most appropriate path. It's not one I can follow.

"He's my husband! It's my choice! Either let go of me or help me call him back!"

"Your husband is also my friend. The man inside that beast would want me to keep you safe."

More and more, the distance between us grows. Every step takes away another piece of my composure. I can't take it anymore!

Yue's grip tautens like iron chains in anticipation of my escape. I'm so sick of being weak and dependent on these men. It wasn't that long ago when I dressed and lived as a man myself. I know I can't ever hope to be in their league. They are so amazingly strong! Still, if my encounter with the slavers has proven anything, it's that strength isn't everything. Yue is a man, a somewhat reserved, I'm guessing, very shy man. When I last grasped onto him, he turned into a stone statue.

Ceasing to struggle, I turn to Yue and overlay his hand with a sensual touch. "Since you're his friend and comrade, it makes sense that if he can't fulfill his duties, you're now my guardian. Right, General Yue?"

Chapter 6: A Date to Remember

He stumbles back a step, quickly regaining control thereafter. As though seeing through my devise, the iron grip resumes. Apparently, he's just that stubborn. I press our bodies together, wrapping my arms around his waist and arching my face upward puckering for a kiss. Yue's calm eyes grow wide while his face twists in disgust. For every step he stumbles backward, I follow suit, until desperation forces down his guard and Yue tumbles onto the dusty road. Once his grip loosens, I take off like the wind.

Thumping footsteps giving chase draw his attention. Hu instinctively whips around. The look of apathy on his brows is now replaced by agitation, turning my feet to lead. We're not standing that far apart and still, he feels a world away.

"Hu... Handsome Husband Hu, I know you can hear me." The more my voice quivers, the deeper his brows furrow. "I'm sorry for doing another stupid thing but you need to stop this. You were angry because that man injured me, right? I'm all bandaged up, see?"

A small smile curls over his mouth when I hold up my arm.

"All better! I'm all better! So, come back home! You promised you'd always come home to me, didn't you? Take off that helmet so we can go."

His eyes are glued to my arm while the ambiguous smile widens. Smiles can't be bad. Growing confident, I move a little closer, freezing in my tracks when his eyes dart to my face with the familiar beastly glare.

"Please, take off your helmet, Hu. I want to go home. Take me home."

I extend a hand in the same welcoming manner he'd shown me yesterday. His eyes hold a steady gaze to my own, as though looking through every thought I dare to hide, while I struggle hard to keep from blinking lest he believes I'm deceptive. Slowly, with one foot in front of the other, I move a little closer until he's within my reach. All I have to do is take his helmet off. His hands are to his side and his weapon is still sheathed. Now's my chance. I can attempt for the helmet; though, it would be too optimistic to believe that won't come without a price. Otherwise, I can attempt to coax him into removing the helmet on his own accord.

Do it myself (Continue to page 131)

Coax him (Continue to page 135)

Chapter 6 – 7

Those eyes couldn't be any colder. My words won't reach him. All they can do is hold him still for a moment until his interest is lost. I best chance it.

One pace at a time, I continue, until my fingers come into contact with his armor. "Don't withdraw. It's me. It's 'Wife' or 'obsessive jealousy-prone girlfriend,' whichever you'd like."

There is no reaction to my weak smile. More and more, I move in until we're close enough that I can embrace him. Even though that is all I want at this moment, I can't imagine he'll accept me. Carefully, my hand glides from his armor toward his face and then fractions of an inch away from his helmet. I stop to gauge his reaction, which remains unchanged, and continues until the tips of my fingers graze the Demon General's silver mane.

Considering how close my fingers were to his helmet and how far he'd have to reach across for the blade, logic dictates that my attempt to draw off the helmet should have been successful. I never even saw his hand move when blood suddenly erupts from my arm. On impulse, I withdraw, but he's caught hold of my wrist; his sharp claws dig deeply into the flesh until more blood flows.

"Hu, stop it!"

He ignores all else except for the blood on my arm. Hu sniffs at the warm scent, smiling an unsettling smile that grows wider with every inhale. The bloodlust in him makes me cringe though that reaction is short lived. He glides the blade across another part of my arm to watch another stream drips. Pure excitement rises into his expression at the sound of my sharp cries. Grinning from anticipation, he lifts my arm toward his mouth. My vision is hazy from the burning tears. I can't see else except for his silver mane fluttering in the night wind. Hu's so close to me. I would do anything to have him back!

The red tongue strokes a corner of his mouth, running happily over one of the sharp fangs aching for sustenance. Until his lips touch the wound, I choke back the surging tears and let the Demon close his eyes to enjoy whatever pleasure my blood can bring.

The oppressive chill of the netherworld that threatened to consume my soul disperses in an instant when the helmet is ripped off his head. Hu suddenly freezes. His eyes spring open to confusion and utter bewilderment; the look of which reminds me of a child awoken from a bad dream. He looks at me and then at the blade in his hand before realizing the mass amount blood on his armor. His body quakes and he collapses to his knees.

"Bao Lai... Bao Lai, did I...?" The voice is soft and strained. His breathing grows shallow and then tears well in those remorseful hazel eyes. The pleading, confused darting eyes twist my heart into a knot, but I when lean down to provide comfort from an embrace, he pushes me away.

"What's wrong?"

"*What's wrong*?! How can you ask me that? Don't you know what's wrong?! I did that to you, didn't I? What the hell are you doing here?! Why don't you ever listen to me?!"

"I'm sorry!"

I reach out again but he moves farther back, screaming so deliriously that I don't know what to do.

"Don't apologize! I hurt you and you want to apologize? Are you stupid? Yue, what the hell were you thinking?!"

Yue, who has been watching the event from afar, is now beside me. "I thought she was the only person who could persuade you to remove the helmet. Had I known she would be this brash, I would have reconsidered. However, she has proven herself capable of reaching you one way or another. That is why I did not interfere."

"Look at her arm! How you can stand by and let that happen? I could have killed her!"

"No, you couldn't have. Had she been anyone else, she would already be dead. You gave her an opening to remove the helmet. Even if you deny it, we both know it's the truth. This woman is special to you. The Demon General couldn't bear to see her die."

"No, he wouldn't have let her die! He'd just cut her up and drain her dry! *Son of a bitch*, Yue! I told you to protect my wife! Look at her! I'll send you straight to hell!" Hu's grip on the blade tightens. Without another word, he lunges forward.

"That's enough! I can't take anymore bickering!" Hu pauses when I shuffle in front of Yue. That look of despair is all left in him. I need to take him home and let him sleep off the burden that is slowly eating away at his conscience. "Bai Hu, let's go home. You can scold me later. This was my fault. Don't blame General Yue."

Hu grits his teeth. He wants to protest but the sight of blood still flowing down my arm makes him shivers. From under his chest plate, Hu retrieves a handkerchief and desperately ties it around the wound but blood simply soaks through. I begin to feel light-headed and then somewhat numb. Tremors are becoming worse. Everything goes dark.

Continue to page 137

Chapter 6 – 8

"Please, Bai Hu, let's go home. It's been a long night. Aren't you tired? That helmet must be heavy, let me carry it for you."

The upturned lips curve into a frown. Hu looks to his right, fingers locked onto the hilt of the sheathed blade.

"You don't need to draw your sword anymore. That man was punished. There's nothing else here."

The mangled bodies of the Demon's victims are jumbled into heaps of flesh. There's no telling who's who. If it were only that assassin I wouldn't shed a tear but I can't tell whether or not he was slain. The fallen are all dressed in similar colors, and while their worn weapons vary, they're definitely not standard-issued. These men aren't soldiers. My guess is highwaymen.

The gruesome scene is difficult to ignore. Unknowingly, my absent-minded stare keeps to his victims and the glistening pools of blood reflecting the moonlight's glow. In the midst of the disturbing observation, one revelation resonates: that assassin wore black. His suit should stand out amongst these dull yellow fabrics stained red. He isn't here.

A heavy boot kicks up dirt. Hu's impeccable timing seemingly synchronizes with my realization. Once more, he moves down the road leading east toward the Dong Bing Garrison.

"Wait! Bai Hu! Come back!"

His single-minded mission won't permit anyone's interference. I rush after him on impulse, extending my hand to reclaim whichever part of him that I can reach. My fingers graze the silver mane. In the same moment that I catch sight of fiery golden eyes, a flicker momentarily passes through my field of vision and takes me to the next world.

The End.

Chapter 7: In Want of Forgiveness

My back hurts. It feels like I'm lying on a rock. No matter which way I turn, there isn't a comfortable spot to settle. The room is nearly pitch-black. Slivers of sunlight ever so slightly enter from around the heavy drapes that cover all the windows. This definitely isn't our house but something about this odd arrangement is familiar.

I scuttle into the main room where one chair and one table are the only furniture present. A teapot is placed next to exactly one teacup and one little ornament of a glass puppy smiling as he looks up. The endearing scene tugs at my heart. I can't keep from walking over to examine the glass figurine. However, the instant my finger reaches out to poke the mutt, an unexpected interruption turns every muscle rigid.

"Don't touch that." His tone matches the usual expressionless face. Before I could get a word out, Yue moves to reorganize the ornament which hadn't even connected with my finger.

"Your husband is at the palace reporting to Prime Minister San An. He asked for me to watch over you."

"Oh. Is he... is Hu doing okay?"

Yue shrugs. When he's finally satisfied with everything on the table in its proper place, turns to stare at me. Although a slight frown is present, his gaze is as empty as ever. I remember now. Qing Hai had mentioned that he's very particular and I must have upset him.

"I'm sorry, General, I did not mean to disturb your... toy."

"It's not a toy," he replies without relinquishing the awkward stare.

"Right, of course not." I look away for fear of not knowing how to respond. As my gaze averts down, blue sleeves hanging off my arms catch my eyes. My wounds no longer hurt. The bandages are just right. I can barely feel them. The one wrapped around the slit on my neck is neatly tucked under the collar, so that any notion of it is obscured. This is definitely not Hu's sloppy handiwork.

"You bandaged me. Thank you for all your help, General. May I have my pink robe back? I want to go home and wait for Hu."

"No."

"No?"

"No. He said to keep you here until he returns. I don't permit any other color of robes in my house."

Is he serious? Here I thought he was the normal one but compared to him, Hu is the sanest man on earth. Why does he keep staring at me? Is he literally taking

Hu's command to *watch* me? Unless... Yue is waiting for an invitation.

"General, is something the matter?"

"No."

"You keep staring at me and it's making me uncomfortable."

"Oh." He looks away. "I suppose I do have one question."

"What is it?"

"I thought Bai Hu and I were long time comrades. Is there a reason I wasn't invited to the wedding?"

"Wedding? That's what's bothering you? General, we aren't married."

"What?" Yue returns that lifeless stare to my face, which now carries a faint notion of panic. "But he calls you his wife and he's taken you."

What a thing to say to a woman! I fold my arms defensively and downturn my scorched cheeks. "Did that bastard tell you that?!"

"Tell me what?"

"That he's... claimed me?"

"He didn't have to say it. I can tell when something has been sullied."

What the hell is that supposed to mean? I am sorry I even bothered speaking to him at all!

Chapter 7 – 2

There comes a knock at the door, relieving Yue from my side. Finally, I can relieve an exhale. In time, Hu enters the house, yielding by the doorway. His expression is taut.

"Hu!" I rush to him with open arms, so overflowing with joy that I nearly burst into happy tears. In response, he turns away. "What's wrong?"

"The Prime Minister wants to see you. Come with me."

He opens the door and darts outside. I grab my shoes, hobbling on one foot at a time while pulling them on, and follow forthwith.

"Hu! Wait! Are you okay?"

He's already walking so fast that I can hardly keep up and still, the moment I close the distance between us, the quicker his pace becomes.

"Bai Hu! If you're not going answer me, I won't take one step more!"

He turns around, fuming from my brash threat. The disdain in those sharp eyes seeks to tear holes through me. His fangs grind and then he spits out a hard response. "Are you disobeying me again?"

The bitter accusation rips into my conscience. I've caused him so much trouble already. I know he's angry because he was worried about me. The least I can do is show Hu a bit of consideration. The Minister, with his near-resolute authority, is ten times more dangerous than any assassin. He shouldn't be kept waiting; else, my incivility will reflect poorly on my overseer.

Hanging my head in shame, I run forward to keep with Hu's pace. Soon after, we arrive at the palace where San An comes to receive us in the gardens.

"Always a pleasure to have you in company, Bao Lai. I hope the General is treating you well." San An's sweet smile slowly dissolves pieces of my angst. I wonder if he's this nice to everyone or just me, since I happen to share His Highness's face.

"Yes. He's been very kind and protective of me. I couldn't ask for anyone better." I want Hu to know how I feel even if that means he has to hear it from my conversation with the Minister.

"I see. That is surprising but I am glad to hear it." San An's curious eyes glide from Hu and then back to me. Another smile appears. "You're probably wondering why I've called you to this garden. As you know, there was an incident last night. This is where the assassin attempted to take my life."

"*Your* life?"

"Yes. Attempts on my life haven't been endeavored for a very long time. I don't know if I should feel nostalgic or afraid." He pauses for a moment to gaze lovingly at the beautiful peaches above as though they hold deep memories.

"In any case," San An continues. "I was told that General Hu tackled the culprit, who then shortly after, had a run-in with you on the roof of a shop. Quite a fantastic story. What were you doing up there?"

"Are you trying to accuse her, Minister? She was with me the entire day!"

I didn't perceive the Minister's accusations until Hu shirked away his former silence and places himself between San An and me. Those searching eyes of his reach over Hu's enraged, trembling shoulders, to burrow into mine. The more I look into San An's gaze, the more I realize the smile on his face is hardly just that. I knew he was a dangerous man but it was difficult to fully understand the danger hidden under the genial demeanor and sweet smile. In this moment of exposure, coldness exuding from his eyes makes my breath stalls. Once more, my mistakes are causing trouble for Bai Hu. The least I can do is stand on my own two feet and discharge San An's doubts.

"Hu, it's okay. I have nothing to hide." When I tug at his shirt, Hu looks over his shoulders, glaring agitatedly, until he understands that this ordeal won't end until I've faced San An. In time, his fury resigns and then he steps aside.

"Minister, I ran after Hu because I was worried. There were so many people blocking the streets that I thought to scale the rooftops instead. It was a random act in a moment of caprice, but what else could I have done when my husband was in danger, except to blindly follow and... cause him even more trouble." Useless tears try to peak. While I fight hard to push them back, Hu's fidgeting worsens.

"I see. Thank you for your honesty." Unlike his dubious demeanor moments ago, San Nan replies warmly. "Now, I must insist on one more question. While you came face-to-face with this man, did you notice anything particular about him? Any scars on his face, distinct colorations or markings?"

Our encounter was brief and confusing. However, now that I think about it, there was something. "Maybe... he had different colored eyes."

San An moves closer. A gentle hand lands on my shoulder. "Tell me."

"I don't know if it was because of the lights reflecting from the lanterns or the hazy moonlight, but I thought I saw one eye being brown and the other blue."

"Blue? Who the hell around here has blue eyes except Yue? I know he didn't do it."

Hu's outburst goes unanswered. San An thanks me and then pushes for our departure. With the Minister's word as law in His Highness's absence, we had no choice but to walk home side by side in depressing silence.

After stepping into the house, Hu marches to the bedroom and closes the door. As childish as I thought he is naturally, this stern silence is evermore juvenile. Agitated, I throw open the doors only for my face to turn red for another reason. He's standing there half-naked.

"You should learn to knock," he shoots over a hard glare.

"Where are you going?"

"I'm dressing for work. Unless you want to watch me strip, kindly leave."

"I thought you were on suspension."

"Things changed. They need my help. I probably won't come home for a while; so, don't go looking for me. I left some money in the drawer. You know the one. Take care of yourself. I'll send Hai over to check on you once in a while."

"So, that's it? You don't want to talk about it? You'd rather just ignore me for the rest of our lives?"

His eyes narrow. When he finally replies, the tone is noticeably strained. "I have nothing to say to you."

His disregard cuts deeply. He must know I was only worried about him. I can't understand why he's so repulsed over one stupid mistake. Is this the extent of his attachment? Kai's warnings suddenly resonate in my mind. Two people who aren't right for each other shouldn't be together. I should make the selfless decision before Hu decides for us both, before I share the same forgotten place in his heart as Feng You.

We barely know each other, that's a given, and yet I don't want to ever be away from him. On the other hand, if he has grown tired of me and the troubles I've inflicted, then maybe the least I can do to ease his distress is to part ways here. Easier said than done. I can't find the will to move away from the door, and while I hope that to him this was more than a short fling, his demeanor is tearing down all prospect that resentment will fade.

"Bai Hu, do you... Should I leave?" I mumble the terrifying idea, hoping that he wouldn't truly hear me.

"Do whatever you want," he replies succinctly, not even bothering to look over. Hu reaches for the belt buckle on the bed and continues changing into uniform without a single notion of alarm.

The unexpected indifference ripples an excruciating pain across my chest. I feel as if someone's ripped my heart out. Yesterday, he said he cared about me, he didn't want anyone else to have me, and now he couldn't care less if I leave. Aside from me, was Feng You his only lover? What if he's had others and these practiced tender words come too easy, same as his goodbyes?

What am I saying? I can't think poorly of Bai Hu! I believe him. I believe everything he said and I still do! He's pushing me away out of guilt. That must be all it is. I must have misunderstood.

"Hu. Last night, I was worried when you ran off. I thought... all consequences be damned! It was reckless. I'm really sorry! Things aren't over between us, right?"

He quickly turns away and snatches the sword hanging from one of the bedposts, giving an even quicker reply. "It's over. I don't want to talk about it anymore."

Chapter 8: Master Dui

Following one last glance toward the man who means the world to me, the bedroom door closes and then I take to the streets. I don't know where home is anymore but it isn't in that perfect house with those perfect floors and the perfect man whose spirit I've crushed in four short days. And yes, it has only been four days since I became his *wife*. There isn't a reason for me to feel this miserable. I hope he'll draw the same conclusion and in the days to come, return to the good-natured man I've come to adore.

The tiger door handle, red-shingled roof, and simple yard fall behind, blurring into one with everything else in my collapsing world. Heavy feet lead the way through an unplanned path. Yet, somehow, I'm suddenly standing in the markets. What a despicable thing, returning to the last place we were happy together. What good is it? I can't change the past, though if I could, it's doubtful that I would have kept from running after Bai Hu.

I turn back toward the eastern market entrance, nearly falling on my face when a soft hand takes hold of mine.

"Hey there, pretty lady, how's your arm?"

I know that voice. It makes me cringe. Master Dui, the physician from last night, is fondling my palm between his fingers. Scowling, I jerk back my hand.

"What do you want?"

"So cold, my dove? Were you coming to see me for the payments due?"

"No, I don't have any money."

"Well, you know my offer. I'll happily accept that robe of yours as payment if you'll take it off right now."

"Does that work on anyone?"

"Does what, love?"

"Your perversion. Does it actually work on anyone or does every woman just laugh at you for being a moron?"

"Sometimes," he grins.

I don't quite know what that means. His lustful smile makes my skin crawl. I would fulfill my threat to pay him with my fist had Master Tai Hung not taught me better than to leave a debt unpaid. Besides that, I naturally hate feeling obligated to anyone for anything.

"Look, I don't have any money but I do owe you, so if there's anything I can do to pay off the debt, that *isn't perverse*, just say the word."

He frowns while scratching the messy hair. With a shrug, Dui sighs, turns his back to me, and then starts away. A third of the way down the block, the physician throws a proposition over his shoulder. "Fine, fine.

Have it your way. If you want to clean up the clinic for me, we'll call it even."

Chapter 8 – 2

Master Dui strolls into the clinic and immediately collapses underneath the large pile of rugs in the middle of the room. I can't believe he's going to sleep again. It must have been a miracle for this lazy bum to have mastered such a difficult trade.

"What do you want me to do exactly?"

"Come lie down next to me," he casually replies.

I ignore him and walk to the backroom. There is a pile of dirty bowls caked with dried herb mixtures next to bandages strewn haphazardly nearby. Most of the small drawers of the apothecary cabinet are either open or on the floor. He's a pervert and a slob.

Once I begin to gather the bowls, he's suddenly by the doorway. "You really want to clean this mess?"

"Yes, then we're even. Got it?"

"Fine, fine. Those bandages are clean so just roll them up and stick them back in the basket. Those bowls should be washed separately; I don't want mismatched concoctions seeping into the wood. When you're done, sweep the floors, dust the shutters, and clean my bed sheets."

"Bed sheets? I don't see a bed in here."

He points to the pile of rugs in the reception area.

"Why do you sleep underneath dirty rugs?"

"It's warm, dove. Feels like being covered by multiple women all at once!"

I can't take him seriously when he laughs that way. Whatever. Years ago, Master Tai Hung used to provide medicine for the temple and villages nearby. I had to sit with him long hours grinding herbs and pretending to listen to his rant about medicinal properties. He'd make a mess and then expected me to wash up afterwards. This is hardly new. Instead, the irksomely nostalgic feeling makes my tasks nearly enjoyable. At least back then, Master Tai Hung was alive and I wasn't alone.

Late evening, after my chores were finished, I enter the reception area when the little bell on the door unexpectedly jingles. An elderly woman hobbles in, a bit shy of a snail's pace. Master Dui sluggishly sits up from the floor where he'd been sleeping and rubs his fuzzy head of hair.

"Mrs. Zhang, I was wondering when you'd stop by." In saying so, he moves to one of the shelves and takes down a packet of medicine. "Twice a day, same as usual. You know the drill."

"Yes, thank you, Master Dui. I haven't had many sales this week. Can I pay you next week?"

"Don't sweat it. Just send your daughter over to spend the night with me later and we'll call it off."

The nerve of him speaking to an old woman like that! I clench my hands into fists, ready to swing at him, when Mrs. Zhang bursts into laughter.

"You're so *bad*, Doctor! If I were thirty years younger, you'd be in trouble."

What did she just say? I involuntarily twitch from such lewd conversations.

"I'm sure I would be," Dui chuckles. "Anyway, best get home before it becomes too dark."

Her wrinkled smile is as bright as the sun. After thanking him, the lady hobbles back out the door. He just gave away that medicine for free; a week's worth, if I'm not mistaken. I thought he was an ass but maybe...

The moment I foolishly permit a pleasant opinion of him to take form, Dui swings around and fondles my hands between his nimble fingers. "Don't be jealous, love. I'm only into young women."

"Then you're sorely mistaken. I'm far from one."

I pull back my hands. He frowns. "Really? That's a shame. You sure look young. Well, whatever. You can go now if you want but my bed's always open."

I can go. My debt has been paid. And yet, one look at the darkened streets and dread springs into my chest. We're far from the markets where all the lights are and I, as embarrassing as it is to admit, have not fully gotten over my childhood fear of the dark. If I had a home, the trek wouldn't be a bother. To wander aimlessly down dimly lit streets without purpose is a thought that makes me cringe.

"Well? Which is it, dove?"

"I... I don't really have a place to go. Could I sleep in the backroom for the night? I'll do a few more chores tomorrow before I leave."

He raises an eyebrow. A small, calculating smile curls over his moistened lips. "Finally broke up with your general boyfriend, have you? Sure, you can stay as long as you want, so long as I get what I want."

This idiot doesn't give up. His house, his rules. Since I can't follow those rules, I best retreat. However, the moment I reach for the door, his warm hand covers mine.

"I meant you could organize my herb drawers. Is that too much to ask? Why the frown, love? Were you expecting something more... laborious?"

Dui raises defensive hands into the air in response to my threatening glare. I start for the backroom, locking the door behind. The moment my back hits the cold floors, a light stream of tears swells and then overflows. It's been half a day since I've seen his face. Already, I miss Hu so much. This pain, deep and piercing, somehow doesn't seem new to me but a repeating nightmare.

Chapter 8: Master Dui

'We barely know each other!' I keep telling myself that and then soon after, wonder where Hu is at the moment. I shouldn't, but can't stop this irrational obsession, until the lines between consciousness blurs into wistful slumber.

Chapter 9: The Physician's Assistant

"Mullein. Where was that other box of mullein?"

These shelves are a mess. Some herbs are stored in three separate boxes while others are sitting bare on counters, dusty bowls, or lodged behind the cabinets. How he finds anything is beyond me!

I was still fumbling about for the other box of mullein when the little bell on the door flies against the wall in a loud crash. A flood of people swarms into the clinic. Dui rises from beneath the rugs, running his fingers through his messy hair, while letting out an exaggerated yawn.

"Master Dui! You have to save her! Please don't let her die!"

The frantic woman clutching a child in her arms runs toward Dui and lays the unconscious girl on the floor. Her desperate pleas and hysterical cries are immediately overshadowed by others following suit, carrying in new patients, all of whom are adults. Not one is without bruises or open wounds. A few are a mangled mess with internal organs exposed and covered in mud. The sight of so many bloodied bodies is a sore reminder of the Demon General's wrath.

"What happened?!" Dui jumps up and stumbles forward to examine the girl and the other adults.

"The beast went wild, I couldn't stop it!" A man making his way toward the front of the irate crowd cries out bitterly. He's shaking violently, more so due fear than guilt. From the atmosphere taking over the room, it's possible that if one life is lost amongst these patients, he'll be forced to join the victim. "I told everyone to move out of the way! I did! I tried! Didn't anyone hear me?!"

"The cart tipped and fell on her! My little girl!" The poor mother cries in anguish. She couldn't care less for the man's excuses; neither does Dui.

"And the others?" Dui's tone suddenly turns hard to match his demeanor.

"They were either injured by the horse or the cart. There was so much commotion, I can't even remember what happened!" The driver blurts defensively though that only serves to lessen the already limited sympathy from the others.

"All right. I need three people to stay. The rest of you, get out. You included, madam." The last part Dui remarks to the girl's mother.

"No! I won't leave little Xiao! You can't—"

"You brought her to my care so please, trust me."

"B-But, she's in pain. She must be!"

"I will do everything I can to save your daughter. I promise. Please, wait outside."

"Well, let me hold her hand and make her comfortable. Here, let me wrap this scarf so she won't be cold."

"Madam, I will have to remove her clothes to check for injuries. That is not necessary."

Despite Dui's urging, the woman remains obstinate, rambling more useless things as a mean to comfort herself. I can feel his agitation rising along with those in the room, but before I could assist, he kindly repeats the request.

"How can I leave her? Her father will be worried sick. What could I possibly say to him? She's our only daughter. He named her after his mother. Did you know her favorite candy is taffy? We had some just today—"

"Oh, my god! Will you please *shut up*?! There are too many people on the brink of life and death, your daughter included, for me to humor your nonsense!"

Her hands fly to her hips, ready to lecture the master, when others in the crowd forcibly pull the screeching woman outside. Dui lets out an angry grunt as a mean to brush off irritation and then moves to further examine the patients. Determination burns brightly in his eyes. I didn't know the lackluster doctor could be this passionate when it comes to his craft.

"I need your help." He suddenly calls over his shoulder.

"Yes, of course! I'll do whatever I can."

"Fetch all the bandages from the drawers and then boil some water. I'll probably have to perform a few surgeries; not sure yet until I have a better look. If I do, I'll need the tools sterilized."

"I understand."

While I start for the tools, he digs into the herb drawers.

"What are you looking for? I moved things around earlier. Just tell me what you need."

"More antiseptic. I don't have enough on hand."

He's fumbling about the drawers but his eyes keep darting back toward the injured. The more time the good doctor wastes on the little things, the more his patients are slipping away.

"I'll take care of it. I know a little about medicine. Go on, do what you must and I'll bring it right out."

He glances over curiously but then decides now isn't the time to question my claims. Dui runs back into the reception area and barks orders to the three remaining helpers. Hours pass by and all I can do is watch the master at work. The only assistance I provided during the surgeries was emptying bloodied water buckets and boiling fresh batches to sterilize the tools. Out of the three helpers, one had to leave. The young man couldn't stand the stench of blood and gore; the sight was even worse.

Never before have I fully appreciated what it means to save a life. At heart, I've always respected those who could effectively wield a sword but it seems to keep one life is a thousand times more arduous than taking one away. Despite his lechery, all I feel for Dui in this moment is admiration.

Chapter 9 – 2

Once the brutal, agonizing procedures were completed, Dui makes another round. For the time, everyone appears to be stable. I can't believe he was able to accomplish in this little clinic what many doctors couldn't in large hospitals. Even patients, who were mangled messes, who otherwise would surely have been lost, now have a chance for survival. The methods he used were unconventional, that is, I have never seen such procedures before. They couldn't have been learned in this country.

"There isn't much more to be done. You might as well get some sleep. Thanks for roughing it out." This, he says to the two remaining helpers, who are visibly relieved to finally be released.

The doctor falls back and lets out a weary exhale. The messy bird's nest that is his hair is drenched in sweat. Dui suddenly arches from a ripple of pain spreading down his cramped back. "Dove, can you help me clean this up?"

"Yes. What do we do about the patients?"

"Let them sleep. It's too painful for them to wake. The draught I gave them won't wear off until tomorrow anyway. Might as well clean up while we can. Their families will come soon and I don't need to hear any screams just because there's blood on the floor."

"I understand. I'll boil more water and prepare the cleaning agents. You best go wash up. You're covered in blood."

"Right. Can't have that or they will *definitely* scream bloody murder."

By the time everything settled, it is night again. The patients' families either went home or are sleeping in the reception area. Dui is lying in the backroom, staring at the ceiling, his eyes glazed over by uncertainty. I've resumed my original task of organizing the herb drawers.

"I'm guessing you'll be spending the night again?"

I turn in anticipation of rebuking his perversion. There is none. "Yes, if you don't mind."

"I don't mind." Dui pauses. "So, let's hear it. I know it's been eating away at you. Might as well vent. It'll make you feel better."

"What do you mean?"

"You left your boyfriend, right? I get jealous just thinking how lucky he is to have someone to run after. Doesn't make any sense why he'd ever let you out of his sight. I know I wouldn't."

"It's... a long story. Let's just leave it at that."

"Sorry, dove. I didn't mean to dredge up bad memories."

Chapter 9: The Physician's Assistant

For a long time, the room falls silent, and even though there's another person next to me, I feel utter loneliness. I miss Hu. I know I shouldn't think about him anymore, especially when I chose to leave, but the more I push the thoughts away, the more they come rushing forth until wavering composure yields and eyes overflow with tears.

"What's wrong?" Dui puts a hand on my shoulder and pats gently. "Oh. Sorry. Should have just kept my mouth shut."

"No. I'm an old woman, I shouldn't act like this."

"Old woman? What makes you think that? Ah, I see. The Demon General has a way with the ladies, doesn't he? By that, I mean he can be a complete idiot. What? You didn't think I know him? I know almost all of the soldiers. They've each come for treatment at least once or twice. Anyway, don't cry or I'll start crying too."

"Why would you cry?"

"I'm easily influenced," he shrugs. "Tell you what, since you helped me a great deal today, if you want to stay for a while, I can use the help. Most days, it's nothing hectic, but then days like these come around and then I don't know which way is up. I can't pay you much. So, if money's not an issue... free room and board, and on my honor, I'll keep my hands to myself. What do you say?"

For whatever reason, the gallantry in his absurdity forces a smile to my face. He's more than tolerable when his perversion is contained. Nevertheless, I shouldn't stay in the same city as Hu. We'll undoubtedly run into each other. And maybe, that's also why I want to stay. I have no resolve.

"What do you say, dove?"

Accompanying the repeat, light ticklish fingers travel up and down the length of my waist. I turn around with a fist but Dui's already moved away.

"I thought you said you'd keep your hands to yourself!"

"Yes, if you would agree to stay, but you haven't answered."

"Fine, I'll stay! And while I'm at it, I'm going to clean you up and find for you a decent girlfriend, so you can stop acting like such a moron!"

His smirk morphs into a pouting frown. Dui sighs in exasperated concession and collapses onto the floor; his face is to the wall. "Yes, Mother!"

"My name is Bao Lai!"

There is no response.

Chapter 10: Matchmaker

For the next two weeks, my time was spent cleaning Dui's messes and occasionally, endeavoring to clean him up. The fuzzy ball on his head has gotten worse. I bet he hasn't brushed his hair in ten years. Every time I attempt to undo the tangles, he'd yell and knock the comb away. Despite his insolence, most days, he'll at least humor me by washing his face and bathing. In exchange for my forced improvements, Dui taught me how to make basic draughts and more notably, how to cook.

A loud crack resonates from the other side of the door, followed by an irate groan. I chuckle to myself because the routine has become so common. There's bound to be another rebuke.

"Ah! Was that necessary, love?"

"I told you to keep your hands to yourself!"

That voice definitely belongs to Miss Liu Guan.

"Then how could I have mended your wounds, dove? It'd be a shame to leave scars on those milky thighs."

"Are you quite finished?!"

"Just one more thing."

A lecherous chuckle, a loud shriek, and then another slap breaks across his face. Miss Liu storms out of the clinic, slamming the door behind. I'm amazed the door hasn't collapsed from the repetitious abuse by every woman under sixty who has set one foot inside the clinic.

The perverted doctor sighs dejectedly. A hand flies over my mouth to keep back chortles just as he opens the door to the backroom.

"Keep it down in here, love. You're driving away all my customers."

"Oh, yeah, it's my fault! Right. Nice going, Doctor. Should I prepare a balm for your cheeks?"

"Only if you'll rub it on me." He points to his behind and smiles. Thereupon, realizing our agreement to keep me from his lechery, the doctor returns to indifference. "Forget it."

"Oh, sorry, I was ignoring you. Did you say something? Hey, by the way, I found this in the back of your closet. It's nice. Why don't you wear it?" I hold up the brown robe with red trims and pretty etchings held together by an obsidian belt buckle. The fashion is a bit outdated. The material looks brand new.

Dui frowns. "It's itchy."

"Then why did you buy it?"

"I didn't. It was a gift from..."

"From?"

"Nobody."

"Liar. There are only two reasons why you'd blush. It's either from a former paramour or from your mother. Otherwise, you'd tell me."

"Well, you're wrong, Mother!"

"Stop calling me 'Mother!' You've been doing it all week!"

"Going through my things without permission, snooping into my personal life, making me clean up so I can find a nice girl. If you're not acting like my mother, what are you doing?"

"If you had a nice girl then maybe you can stop flirting with everyone and actually get somewhere. No one likes a pervert."

"Ouch, Mother! That really hurts!"

Despite his opposition, he grumbles and takes the robe from me.

"Fine, I'll wear it if it'll make you happy, Mother!"

"You stubborn so and so. Go put it on and then come back here. I'm untangling your hair one way or another!"

"I told you, I hate it! You'll yank all my hair out!"

"Don't talk back to your mother!"

Dui rolls his eyes and drag his feet behind the dressing screen. How fast life goes. Two weeks ago, I was 'Wife,' and now, I'm 'Mother.' These men are going to drive me into an early grave.

Moments later, the physician emerges, sulking. He's actually quite handsome when not in his usual rags. I can't wait to see the full transformation once I manage to fix his hair! Dui rolls his eyes at my excited smile and then grudgingly plops down with his back to me.

"What are you pouring on my hair?"

"Oil."

"That smells like... cooking oil?"

"What else?"

"Are you crazy?!"

"Sit still!"

He growls angrily and yet still falls back into position. Once the oil is worked through the fuzzy knot on his head, I attempt to part his hair wherever I could and begin to run a comb through the mess, tangle by tangle. He continues complaining and I continue to ignore his protests until they concede to irate grumbles. After two hours, his messy blob of hair now has potential. I slide to the front of him to have a good look. To my surprise, he appears a different person.

"Why are you making that face, Mother?"

"You just look so handsome. I feel proud."

Colors creep over his face. He turns away, seemingly disgusted.

"Now that we've straightened out your hair, found for you a nice pair of clothing, there's one thing left to do. Once we've contained that lecherous attitude of yours, you'll finally be ready for your debut!"

"You make me sound like a prostitute!" Dui brings up both hands to dishevel his untangled hair.

"I just finished combing that! Knock it off!"

He continues to fuss, ruining a day of planning and two hours of work. I grab his wrists in the attempt to subdue his sabotage but the doctor is rather fragile and has poor balance. He falls backward, taking me with him. My cheeks are scorched from lying atop; his are ten times more crimson. Caught in the spur of the moment, our eyes meet and then soon after, avert in opposing directions. I push away while he recoils to one side.

"That's very inappropriate, Mother."

He whispers the words so bashfully that I can't keep from laughing. Despite his casual perversion, he can be very childish sometimes. It's rather endearing. I wonder if this was how Bai Hu saw me when we first met, unkempt and juvenile.

Burdened sadness suddenly bears down by the careless thought. Even though our time together was short, the attachment won't leave me. My heart is hurting in a manner I can't describe and the pain is one I'm unable to fully grasp.

"What's wrong, Mother?"

"N-Nothing."

"Uh-huh. Say, do you want to go out for dinner? I don't feel like cooking and you can't cook to save your life."

I can't bring myself to speak. Words are choked up inside. Dui sweeps an arm around my shoulders to draw us closer. "Come, Mother. Let's go out for dinner."

He tugs at my arm. Without knowing else to do, I drag my feet and follow him out.

Chapter 10 – 2

"Mother, why are people staring at us?" Dui, who's been glancing every which way like a nervous child, leans over and whispers softly into my ear.

I fell prey to egocentric dejection and haven't noticed how far we've walked. The area around is filled with beautiful lanterns, happy patrons going about their merriment, and the scents of a thousand delicacies wafting from every direction. We're at the night markets. An antsy Dui tugs at my arm, tilting his head cautiously toward a group of unexpected spectators. I'd wondered if his usual obnoxious *charms* had ever earned anything aside from a palm across the face. From the nervousness encroaching over his reddened cheeks, I've deduced the master must be inexperienced.

"They're not looking at *us*. Those girls are looking at you! Why don't you go over and exercise your charms?"

"I'm not ready for debut. We haven't fixed my personality yet."

"There's nothing wrong with your personality. Your perversion is the imposition. So long as you keep acting as you do now, you'll be fine."

Dui flushes deep red from ear to ear while gripping my arm tighter like that of a child clinging to his mother. I don't know any of these girls; therefore, I can't just approach and ask on his behalf. That would be weird.

On the other hand, I suppose there is one woman I know around here, but going inside to find her means chancing to meet *him*. Ah, well, Dui's been kind to have taken me in these past two weeks, it's the least I can do.

I sprint toward the window near the back of the Ping Ming Restaurant, which is adjacent to Hu's usual table, and then peer inside. The table is empty. Hu said he would be away for work. Everyone at the palace must be busy searching for the assassin. There's not much chance for an unexpected encounter.

The restaurant is as crowded as ever, if not even more crowded than I remember. Given Dui's thin stature, I walk in front of the doctor and push our way through, while pulling him along to the only available table on the ground floor permanently reserved for the Demon General. Moments after we sit down, Kai runs over.

"Bao Lai? It is you! Where have you been? I can't believe you're so inconsiderate! Don't you know how worried I was?! Um... Who's this?"

I'm surprised she's worried when it was her suggestion for me to leave Bai Hu before causing him more grief. Then again, I did forget to pay her for the food last time. Working at Dui's clinic has provided a mean to clear my debt. She looks down at the coins I've pressed into her hand, befuddled.

"Sorry, I know I should have came back and paid you earlier but I'd forgotten. Kai, this is Dui. He's a friend."

172

Chapter 10: Matchmaker

"Dui?" Kai inches closer, peering suspiciously. "Oh, *Master* Dui! The physician, of course! You look so different, sir."

"Sir? Him?"

Dui's gaze averts. Embarrassment is leaking from him in torrents.

"Have you been with Master Dui all this time, Bao Lai?"

"Yes. Please don't say anything to Bai Hu."

"Well, sure I won't, but when did you and Master Dui become... close?"

"What? No! I work at his clinic!" My cheeks are boiling. I fear they may explode. He kept calling me 'Mother.' I didn't consider the obvious insinuating consequences when others see us together. "I brought him here to, well, introduce you two—of course, you already know each other. Dui knows just about everyone though, doesn't he?"

"Yes, knows him and his gentle hands very well." Kai giggles. Her eyes roll upward, seemingly recalling incidents of her prior encounters with a lecherous Dui.

"Dui's really not like that, Kai. He's just shy and before now, it has come out in a very stupid manner."

"Oh? Is this the real Master Dui? It's nice to finally meet you."

Kai brushes his arm flirtatiously. Dui winces. I think he might burst into tears.

"You women are so cruel," he finally manages a feeble whisper.

When the cruel women laugh at his expense, Dui further withdraws. The shy doctor's furrowed brows, filled with unexpressed exasperation, are on me. Therefore, he does not notice Kai's curious gawking. I do. I see his dilemma. It would be impossible for him to be forward with Kai when his mother is nearby. I start up and make an excuse to leave. He initially flusters at my sudden departure but when I turn back over my shoulder, see that Kai had already taken my seat across the table. She's chatting noisily and the doctor's posture is more relaxed.

Success!

Chapter 10 – 3

The cool night air is a nice change from the muggy dungeon that is the restaurant. Despite the unpleasant memories the markets hold for me, I can't help from falling hopelessly astounded by the sheer throng of excitement. On a regular night, it can still best any festival elsewhere.

Up and down the streets, the number of vendors seems to have doubled since my last visit and for that same reason, more temptations to be had. Drugged by sumptuous scents flooding my nostrils, my stomach growls deliriously. There aren't many coins left in my pouch but I can certainly afford a steamed lotus bun.

The last elusive coin retreats below the lining of the old brown pouch. My not-so-thin fingers are having a hard time coaxing it to surface. While I change strategy from enabling to fighting the elusive copper, the sound of his strident cry turns my posture rigid.

"Bao Lai!"

He's standing a distance away to my left. The startled expression, widened eyes, and flushed cheeks on that familiar face must reflect my own. The torture in his eyes is unbearable. I want nothing more than to run into his arms, but as pulse thumps in my ears and my heart swells, I impulsively turn on my heels and run in the opposite direction. Coward. I'm a coward and I don't know why. Seeing him again was all I wanted.

Why am I running away? I'm screaming for my legs to stop but they won't obey.

Faces pass by in rapid blurs. The heat rising from my chest spreads a dull pain throughout. The more I call for him inside my mind, the faster my pace becomes. Suddenly, a strong grip, a sharp tug, and then I fall into his embrace.

Burning tears consume dulling vision. My head buries into his chest to keep him from seeing the insipid weakness. His body is shaking or maybe it's mine, I'm not sure.

"Where have you been? I've been going out of mind! What the hell were you thinking?! Why did you leave me? You said you'd always be at home waiting for me!"

His irate shouts are overflowing from another passion that I lose all reservations. The embrace between us is long and vigorous, as though seeking to validate each other's existence. I breathe him in. Every nostalgic trace is evoking something deeper in me.

Once I muster enough courage to face the frustration I've caused, my face lifts off his chest. Hu nudges up my chin, running his rough fingers over my jaw.

"You said that if I can't support what you do then I should... and then... when I asked if I should leave, if things were over, you..."

I can't get the words out. Any excuse would be just that. I don't need excuses. He can be angry. As long as I can feel his warmth, that is enough for me to be happy.

"I thought you meant you were leaving the house for a while. I didn't think... I'm sorry. I'm such an idiot! I'm so sorry!"

There isn't any reason to apologize. Time together is precious. We shouldn't waste it worrying over childish mistakes. I clutch his shirt and shake my head. As though having read my thoughts, Hu's embrace grows tighter. Then, taking my hand within his own, we walk home together.

Chapter 10 – 4

The moment we pass through the door, he sweeps me off my feet and then enters the bedroom. Gently, he crouches over me from atop the bed, pressing deep passionate kisses that shed away all my lingering anxieties. His burning large palms run my up arms and then back down toward my waist. Naturally writhing from the sensation, my arms are thrown around his back, pleading for more of his touch.

"Don't you dare leave me again," he whispers hoarsely. The warm breath burns again my skin and yet also sends shivers down my spine. "I don't care what stupid things I say or do, I want you to promise that you won't leave again."

"Are you certain this is what you want? I'll keep on causing trouble for you."

"Yes, you're a cruel woman sent to torment me. I accept the torment with open arms. Tell me, where have you been?"

"I've been working at Dui's clinic."

"Dui? Did that pervert put his hands on you?" His lovely seductive voice is suddenly replaced by a fretful tone. The former sultry eyes are now those of a petulant child.

"It's not what you think. You've completely ruined the moment!"

Chapter 10: Matchmaker

I slap his hands to push him off.

Hu scratches his head huffily. "You are the most unromantic person in the world!"

We sit there glaring at one another. I'm just so happy to be near him.

"So, you won't leave again, right?"

I shrug. "Maybe I won't if you'll compromise."

"I can't leave the military. It's my life." He looks down at his calloused hands, honed from years of dedication that can't be undone.

"I know. I never should have suggested for you to give up who you are. The military to you is as medicine is to Dui, I see that now. I'm sorry for being selfish. Still, so far, our troubles have been stemmed from secrets. I want you to be honest with me. Who are you really, Demon General?"

His eyes narrow from recalling an unpleasant memory. Hu grabs my arm and pulls up the sleeve. Light bandages are wrapped nearly the entire length of my arm. His eyes shimmer from shame. "I did this to you!"

"Yes, you did. But also, you didn't. I know *you* would never hurt me, so tell me the truth, who is this other person?"

"You won't want to be with me if I told you."

"Does it matter? I can't seem to escape you. Not for long, anyway."

"It's not a joke, Bao Lai. I'm not proud of this. It's not a part of me I want you to know."

"If it's a part of you then I do want to know. You shouldn't keep secrets from your wife."

At the mention of 'wife,' his smile reappears. He leans over and gives a peck on my forehead. "Okay, I'll tell you, but not right now. Right now, I want you to tell me everything that's happened at the clinic. Tell me which hands and which fingers Dui used to touch you so I can break them tomorrow."

"Hmm, I like this jealous side of you. Maybe I should leave more often."

"Don't you dare, Wife! Do you know how much it hurts to walk into this house without you here? I've been alone most of my life but I was never lonely... not until you left. I feel like we've been apart for a lifetime."

"I-I'm sorry. And yes, I feel the same. There's not been one day since we parted that I didn't think of you. I've missed you."

Embarrassment floods me. We sound like long-time lovers or maybe an old married couple when neither is true. I lose all reason when I'm with him and somehow it feels right.

Hu's smile carries a hint of bashfulness when reaching for me. Wasting no time, I push down my general and kiss him vigorously. Once his lips begin to travel down my body, I start to undo his robe.

"You're so impatient, Wife." He chuckles softly. "I never would have guessed that impertinent cross-dresser I met not long ago would have me wrapped around her little finger like this. Temple girls are dangerously naughty."

"Yes. I'm going to have my way with you, Bai Hu, while you're feeling vulnerable. What do you say to that?"

Embarrassment keeps him from responding. His cheeks are boiling. If anything, it just makes me want him more. True to my words, I repeatedly take advantage of him.

Chapter 11: A Misunderstanding

Light creeps in through the windows. Hu and I lazily stretch our tangled limbs as we welcome the new day. I've never been as happy as I am now, to see his face next to mine when I wake. I wish that we can have this happiness forever.

His arms tighten. I snuggle in a little closer.

"You hurt me last night," he whispers. "Taking advantage of poor me so many times, I'm sore all over."

"You're welcome!" I tap his forehead. He frowns at my grin. "Are you going to work today?"

"I'm supposed to, but if I don't show up, Yue will cover for me."

"He will? That's surprising. He strikes me more as the type to come over and drag you to work."

"Well, normally, he might, but he's been a little distant toward me recently."

"Because you threatened him?"

"I threaten him every week. He doesn't care. No, it's something else. After you stayed the night at his house, he'd frown whenever he sees me. Did something happen between you two?"

"General Yue is not as brash as you to pull strange women into bed."

"Guess you're right. I've never seen him with a woman in my life. He also hates people touching him so, never mind."

"Maybe... I do recall he was a bit miffed we didn't invite him to our wedding and visibly disturbed that you weren't honorable enough to have done so after having *taken* me."

The calm, cozy atmosphere suddenly erupts into frenzy by Hu's loud bursts of projecting laughter. His big arms constrict. *"Really?* Oh, that is good! That *prude!* I'll have a fun time giving him hell later. Now, I actually want to go to work!"

His mischievous expression is simply precious. However, his joy is somewhat disheartening. I can't return the humor.

"Hu, does that mean you would never... consider marriage?"

"Wh-What's with this, suddenly? You're already 'Wife.'"

"Just 'Wife' but not your wife?"

He gives an uncomfortable glance before flushed cheeks turn away completely. "Is that something you want? I've never... planned on marriage."

"You also didn't plan to have a *girlfriend* either, only lovers, right?"

"I'm not a dishonorable guy—!"

"I know. It's fine." The words flying out of my mouth surprise both Hu and me. "I didn't mean to imply that I expected a proposal or that I'm ready for such a commitment. I'm happy for what we have between us. If we can remain this way, it's good enough for me."

He stares over dubiously at the same time those thoughts settle in my heart. I never imagined a normal woman's life could be mine nor did I know what that was before my time with Hu. Maybe meeting the right person changes everything. It certainly has for me. Here in this house where I've learned to call home, is where I want to remain. I shouldn't ask for more.

"I'll... think about it." He mumbles hesitantly.

"That's not necessary."

"You say that but you're pouting."

"I am not!"

"Okay! Don't shout at me, Wife. I don't want you to run off again. If you're unhappy, tell me."

"I'm not unhappy."

"That's still far cry from being happy, isn't it?"

"I said I'm fine. Why are you making a big deal out of this?"

"Because I promised myself a long time ago that I'd ensure your happiness."

Chapter 11: A Misunderstanding

"What... are you talking about? We've known each other less than a month."

There goes that awkward stammering again. He's not making any sense and then Hu attempts to laugh off the discomfiture. I'm onto him. He's definitely hiding something.

"Just how did you know my favorite food, my favorite tea, and my most hated color?"

"I-I didn't! I don't! I guessed them! You're a cross-dressing temple girl. Naturally, you'd hate girly colors and love vegetarian foods, right? Well, look at the time! Yue will come and drag me to the barracks if I slack off again!"

His endeavor to escape me is futile. I've grabbed a hold of his long hair. Wincing, Hu falls back in a heavy thud. The flustered general is pinned under my weight.

"We've met before, haven't we? Long before that day on the road."

"W-What makes you say that?"

"Because you're panicking and because you're not denying it. Besides that, a gut feeling. Tell me, where did we first meet?"

"It's not like that! I grew up in Bi Xi!"

"Bi Xi is... to the north of our capital of An."

"That's right! *Far* north, near Mount Chou."

"And you've never been to Tian Mao Yi near Pa Xu Village in Hong Long Province?"

"Never. The first time I came south was for recruitment in the capital."

He's certainly not the best liar. Those answers came swiftly. There must be truth to them.

"Oh. I see."

"Are you disappointed?"

"Not as much as I am confused. I really thought..."

"What? That it'd be romantic if we knew each other as children? That we didn't meet on the road by chance? That this is fate?"

"I didn't say all that!"

"Of course not. I can't leave it up to the most unromantic woman in the world to say anything so sweet."

How does he turn the table on me just like that? Now he's sulking and I feel bad!

In the still room, we sit apart, staring into space while silence grows. I wonder... am I unromantic? That is, does he prefer someone more passionate? Someone like Feng You, perhaps.

"I should get ready for work."

Chapter 11: A Misunderstanding

Hu, moving to the edge of the bed, finally breaks the drawn pause and pulls back my wandering mind. Despite our pasts, I want to relish our present. The night was long but somehow didn't seem long enough. Even now that we are close, I still miss him.

"Wait," I grab onto his arm which tenses at my touch. "It's still early. I'm lusting after you already, General Hu. Can I take advantage of you one more time?"

"Didn't I tell you I'm sore all over? You're such a slave driver."

Although he begins to move away as if to reject me, Hu eventually turns and pushes my shoulders down. His kisses are even more passionate than I remember and he takes time tending to my every need.

"You're a bad person," he whispers fretfully in that tantalizing hoarse tone I only ever hear when his guard is down.

"And you're a good boy." I whisper back, grasping his broad shoulders more strongly to convey my increasing desires.

Each moment is as beautiful as the last. His feverish hazel eyes pierce mine to gauge my reactions, sending exhilarated chills through me. There's something so alluring about them that I begin to lose all my senses and yield to his every whim while he finds new ways to invoke my desires.

Though superficially, our engagement seems purely lustful, at heart, I feel that we have both become enslaved to something much deeper. That idea in itself, is both more thrilling and frightening than anything we've ever experienced.

Chapter 11 – 2

I arrive at the clinic to find the door still locked. After banging a few raps, it's still dead silent on the other side. Dui's not the type to miss a good night sleep nor is he the type to stray away from the clinic for very long. Unless, he never came home last night after his time with Kai and that means...

"Bao Lai!"

The panic-stricken voice demands my attention, forcing the stupid smirk off my face. I turn to find Dui, clothes and hair both a mess. His eyes are red, his face pale, and he seems on the verge of collapse. I guess he *was* up all night.

"There you are. Way to go, Doctor!"

Soon as the words leave my mouth, his arms fly around my shoulders and Dui crumples onto me. If he weren't so light, we both would have landed on the pavement.

"Wh-hey! You're burning up, Dui!"

He doesn't respond. The limp body falters. He's excessively tall, it's difficult for me to keep him hoisted. I press him against the wall for support and then rummage through his pockets for the keys.

Chapter 11 – 3

"Hey, wake up."

For the fifth time, I nudge Dui's arm. The doctor mumbles incoherently and then succumbs to slumber's lull, showing no sign of coming to. What was he thinking, running about in the early morning cold air? His body was drenched in sweat which only made his condition worse. I changed his clothes and made certain he was comfortable but the fever doesn't seem to dampen under the many wet cloths placed on his forehead.

Despite my unwillingness to have paid attention during Master Tai Hung's medicinal lectures, this recipe is one of several he managed to beat into my head. The draught is my last resort but it won't serve any purpose if he won't drink it.

"Dui! Wake up! Listen to your mother!"

I shake him more forcefully. His flailing arms retaliate by brushing me away, one of which smacks against my face. More incoherent mumbles and then his already feverish cheeks grow hotter. My head lowers to eavesdrop in this dream of his which seems to be keeping him from reality. It must be fantastic, marvelous...! I should have known, lecherous.

The mumbles gradually grow louder and more exuberant into strident declarations. From what I gather, his wish to be swarmed by a crowd of women has finally come true. No wonder he won't wake. Still, I know one aspect to be true. There are some things so tantalizing that dreams just can't replace, because a glimpse of the real version is a thousand times more shocking.

One hand crawls over his chest. The other runs through his hair. I lean close to Dui's ear and whisper a hot breathy semi-lewd confession of desire, the way Bai Hu managed to ignite my passion during our times together.

Dui's hot cheeks rupture into raptures. Blood-shot eyes fly wide open and then he trembles while attempting to retreat.

"Calm down. It's just me. Drink this before you—"

Those tremulous arms are suddenly around my shoulders. Dui strains to breathe or maybe, he's straining to keep from crying.

"Dui—"

"Where did you go?"

The half-concerned, half-angry whisper hits me with a wall of guilt. Was that why he ran about all night?

"I-I went home."

"I came back and you weren't here! If Mrs. Zhang hadn't noticed you earlier, I don't know what I'd do!"

"Dui, I'm sorry. I left with Bai Hu. I wasn't thinking. I thought you were preoccupied with Kai. That's no excuse though, is it? I'm so sorry!"

His fingers dig deeper into my shirt, though feebly. I don't know else to do except return his embrace to keep the crumpling figure upright. There are many people in this town dependent on the good doctor, including me, and yet I can't do anything for him. Worse, I've put him in this position through my carelessness.

Once his shoulders calm, Dui lifts off. Air is caught in my throat when I perceive his countenance. That expression is too hard for his usual disinterested face. Even the imposing tone coming from his mouth is as stiff as his eyes.

"You've gone back to him?"

"Hu and I... yes, we've gotten over our misunderstanding."

"Then why are you here?"

"I... work here?"

"Your lover is a well-to-do officer. This job pays next to nothing because the doctor has nothing. Don't waste your time."

The meaningful stare accompanying his urging renders me speechless. He's right. I have a home. I don't need this job; except, I like working here. I've learned much from the skilled physician who could be the richest man in town if he didn't keep giving away free treatments, even to those who can more than afford them. For that very reason, his reputation with the common is that he's a genius; the other physicians consider him a fool. I didn't think he cared either way. In this instance, a hint of self-deprecation he's hidden all this time is exposed. I sought to give my opinion of his kind heart when Dui brushes me off and falls back onto the futon.

"Dui, drink this before falling asleep again."

"I'm fine. It's just a cold."

"You give medicine to everyone who comes by with a cold. When it's you, why hesitate?"

"I said I'm fine! Leave me alone!"

"Stop being a brat! Your mother commands it!"

"You're not my mother!"

He turns his back to me. As much as I want to continue badgering him, quarreling can't be good for his health. I may not be his mother but he's certainly childish. If that's the way he chooses to be then I'll accommodate. Softly, my fingers stroke his hair.

"Dui, be a good boy and drink this for me. You can't see Kai when you're sick like this. I bet she's worried about you too."

"Oh please! I am not interested in Kai! Stop using me to bait her away from your boyfriend!"

"What is that supposed to mean? Kai and Hu aren't..."

"Not yet. Not since you interfered. Do you know how many times he's had to carry her over here for a *sprained ankle*? She's always jumping up and down the moment he leaves. I thought to tell you last night when you darted off and left me with that vixen. When you didn't come back to the clinic, I was sure you'd done something rash because of the rumors she'd spread."

"What... rumors?"

"Ones to secure her position with your boyfriend."

Having relayed the burden he's carried all night, Dui falls silent. I can't believe what I'd just heard nor can I imagine Dui's claims to be false. He doesn't have a reason to lie. His illness is proof of sacrifice. He's run around all night to protect me from foolishness while I left him with a woman less than trustworthy. I thought Kai liked Bai Hu, but the kindness she'd shown me obscured the idea of trickery. Then again, maybe that isn't true. Once Hu and I were together, she purposefully inserted Feng You as a mean to cause a rift between us and urged me to end our relationship.

I don't know what to believe, but at the moment, I couldn't care less what type of woman Kai may be. Dui is sick and I am responsible.

"Dui," I nudge him again without success. "I'm sorry. Thank you for thinking of me but please don't be careless like that again. There are hundreds of patients depending on you, kind doctor, so you have to look after yourself first. Please, drink this. It'll lower your fever and boost your immunity."

"I haven't taught you that recipe yet," the physician, rebuffing my seemingly bluffed efforts, mumbles sleepily into the pillow.

"You didn't. This is the official Tian Mao Yi Elixir of Healing created by one Master Tai Hung. He said it's patented. I think he lied."

Dui slowly turns back, showing little to no interest in my forced grin. The concoction, on the other hand, he sniffs and taste in several pensive sips.

"Eh... the draught is effective but it's also the most revolting thing in the world. Best to down the bowl in one breath."

"You've actually replicated it!"

"It's not that difficult. The old man made me prepared several hundred batches of the nasty brew before Master Peng usurped his post."

"The old man is... Master Tai Hung?"

"*Was*. He died a little bit over a year ago."

The thought of my master surges a wave of regret to my chest. I fight hard to keep them back though a few tears manage to escape. Master Tai Hung was like a grandfather to me; the old codger certainly lectured my ears off as though I were his blood. I was, for the most part, ungrateful for his teachings, until I find myself lost without them. Even now, I still rely on the things he's taught me in order to muddle through this maze called life.

"Did you study medicine under Tai Hung?"

My body jolts when Dui's thumb spreads across my cheek to brush off the rogue tears. His former hard expression has softened.

"Ah, not so much medicine; more so, everything. I was Master Tai Hung's ward."

"That's impossible. The temple didn't accept women and the master never mentioned you. He had a pup with him, I remember, but the pup was always quarreling with another student in the training fields to mind me."

"You were at the temple? How did you know Master Tai Hung? I was his pup! They called me Little Hung, cross-dressed and all!"

I'm so happy to meet another person who knew my master's greatness that I smile unrestrained. Dui returns a dubious stare, sniffing the brew again.

"Tai Hung was my mentor for a short time and this brew was my test. Until I could replicate his masterpiece, he refused to continue my training. But, he taught you."

Chapter 11: A Misunderstanding

"You're offended?"

"Aggravated! I left Pa Xu Village to better my skills and while I've developed my own methods and brews, I still can't determine what's in this. It's been almost two decades and here you are, reminding me of my failure. "

"The old man was rarely straightforward with his ambitions. Maybe he planned your failure so you'd find your own methods."

"Perhaps. That doesn't lessen my aggravation, Pup."

"Spare me the nicknames. Now finish that and go to sleep! Your entire body is trembling!"

"No can do, Pup. This failure must be rectified."

"I'll tell you what's in it."

"And let Tai Hung win? I won't forgive you."

Against my continued urging, Dui stumbles off the futon. However, the draught's effects had set in. Along with lack of sleep and exhaustion already plaguing him, Dui tips over. I manage to catch his limp body but his grip loosens and the bowl is spilled onto my face. Through a momentary distraction, my support is weakened and in the next moment, I'm staring at the ceiling with Dui resting atop. My lips part but he cuts off the attempt.

"Shhh! Don't speak!"

He's behaving strangely though I do wonder if I'm the one imagining this odd sensation. Something flat is pressing against my chest. The pressure then tightens into light squeezes moving in circular motion with increasing intensity.

"Dui—!"

The indecency! I can't believe he's fondling me!

My irate cries drown under his feverish lips and piercing hot tongue. I push him off, but his arms are latched around my waist. When Dui rolls to the side, I'm pulled on top. The unexpected tussle stuns my senses and I lose the strength in my arms, collapsing flat onto his chest. Dui's lips quickly move to my cheek and chin, sucking vigorously against my skin in a disorderly fashion. It is then that I realize his tongue is chasing the remainder of the draught from my face before they dry. He's not willing to give up Master Tai Hung's challenge. Even so, this is unacceptable! There's nothing to explain the fondling aside from his lechery. I ready my fist to wake him once and for all!

Chapter 11 – 4

"Dui! Dui, come out here!"

Of all the bad timing! My heart stops the moment that voice resounds through the small clinic. Hu bursts through the door, the force of which sends the little bell atop to the floor. In his arms is Kai, wincing, though that wince is short-lived. One look at our predicament and then her frown turns to a short half-smile before fully reverting to a false flabbergast.

"Bao Lai? Master Dui? I don't believe this! I thought you were a good girl! How could you go on like this behind Hu's back?" Kai's tone falters to the verge of tears. Her keen eyes are of another opinion.

I didn't want to believe that Kai was calculating. A part of me had hoped that Dui's charges were stemmed from delusions. Yet, there she is in Hu's arms, probably claiming her ankle is sprained again, while her melodramatic goading is turning Hu's already distraught expression to pure outrage.

Jumping off Dui, a sleeve runs over my face to clear the brew. The physician sits up but doesn't provide any rejoinder. He's turned away.

"It was an accident." I look Hu square in the eyes to convey the truth. I know he wants to believe me, and he would, if she weren't pushing otherwise.

"Bao Lai, is this why you didn't want me to tell the General that you'd been spending every waking moment with Master Dui? I'm sorry, I didn't know."

There goes that apologetic and distraught tone. It's difficult for anyone to disbelieve her concern. Hu's doubting stare is growing more somber. I could lash out but there isn't any proof aside from Dui's opinion of her envy, and as we are, that won't carry any merit. Instead, I choose the more obvious route.

"Is your ankle sprained again, Kai?"

Her eyes grow wide from my hard tone, having perceived that I now see through the former false pleasantries. Her pretty face sneers in my direction before upturning wounded eyes to Hu.

"General, I-I'll be fine. Really! Seems our friends need some time alone. Why don't you take me home instead?" Her sweet voice begs for Hu's retreat. Once Kai manages to bind his attention, a pained whisper is submitted. "I can't bear to see you suffer like this."

Her heartbreaking pleas not only tug at my paramour's resolve, they are turning his perception of me further away from the truth. I don't hate Kai for loving Hu but to win him in this manner is absurd. She's known him for years. There were plenty of opportunities to express her affections instead of waiting for this moment when Hu is vulnerable to reel him into her embrace.

Chapter 11: A Misunderstanding

I can't stand the unforgivable deception! My hands are shaking fists but there's nothing to be done.

Hu's tortured eyes look away from me while Kai's quickly cast down a victorious smirk. When he begins to turn back, I can't control myself anymore. Just as I jump to my feet, Dui tugs at my sleeve and then forces a loud, hacking, wet cough. Hu's pace ceases.

"Ah, what's all this ruckus?" Dui puts on his casual, irate tone. "I was sick after coming home early this morning from your house, Kai. You were happy and satisfied when I left. What happened?"

"W-What?" Kai's frantic eyes grow wide and so do mine. She's stuttering for a comeback which seems to elude her usual grace.

I appreciate Dui's continual self-sacrifice to protect me but this is wholly unfair to the one person in the middle of these lies: Bai Hu.

"Dui—"

The physician cuts off my interjection. His fingertips brush against my cheek to remove the last bit of dried herb. "You're really something, Mother. I never imagined you'd be that eager to shove medicine down my throat. Do control yourself. I might choke to death next time."

Shrugging, Dui drags his tired, nearly limp body off the floor and approaches the door. Against her insistence, he usurps the lively Kai from Hu and then

201

waltz into the backroom, posing that lecherous smile every woman in town knows too well. I'm caught between wanting to protect Dui from exhaustion and protecting Hu from misunderstanding. The debate is settled when Hu chooses for me. The front door snaps shut. On impulse, I rush after the person most important to me.

Chapter 11 - 5

"Bai Hu!"

At the sound of my voice, his pace quickens before something inside suddenly holds him back. Hu stops, then grudgingly stare over his shoulder. I rush to take hold of his arm.

"Bai Hu. Don't leave angry. It was an accident."

"I'm not angry, Wife."

He's said those words to me before. This time, I know he is. The expression on his face clearly displays the betrayal he feels. I grasp his hand, not knowing where to start. The warm hand which usually clasps mine whenever they touch, remains limp. Hu stares toward the direction of the palace and then shyly moves away.

"I have work to do. I might not be home tonight. Remember to lock up."

"Wait! Why won't you believe me? Did someone... did someone alluded that Dui and I are together?"

"Not at all, but since you've brought it up, are you confessing?"

"No! There's nothing to confess! It was a misunderstanding!"

"One that took my intrusion to correct. If I hadn't barged in, how long were you planning to continue that misunderstanding?"

"You...! Bai Hu, that's not fair!" My hands are shaking violently. I don't know what to do. Tears are threatening to fall. I push them back as hard as I can until, to compensate for the pain, another emotion rises to clear them once and for all.

"What were you doing with Kai? I thought you had to work."

Hu's eyes narrow. He scoffs and then glances away, perturbed. "You're turning this on me? It's my duty to save damsels in distress and she was in distress."

"Sprained her ankle again?"

"Yes. She works hard in a thankless job. It's bound to take a toll on her fragile figure. My friend was in trouble. I did what was necessary."

"Right... *friend*."

Hu frowns at my glowering. I trust him, so I shouldn't be jealous, but the thought of her stealing him away using such dirty tactics makes my blood boils. Resentment is becoming more difficult to suppress.

"Don't give me that," Hu sneers. "She's looked after me all these years, like a sister. I'd appreciate it if you won't accuse Kai to cover your own shortcomings. You lack experience with men so you did a stupid thing.

Fine. I'll forgive you. Resign from the clinic and don't bother with that foolishness anymore. I'll see you at home."

"Wh—Excuse me?! I don't need your forgiveness because *nothing happened*!"

"Don't make a scene," he replies flatly.

There are numerous patrons occupying the streets, many of whom don't mind stopping to gossip over our shameful public display. I'm more than embarrassed; however, embarrassment can't erase my agitation.

"I'm returning to the clinic. For the same reason that you can't quit the military, I won't give up medicine."

Master Tai Hung would have wanted this for me. While I spent my youth focused on the art of combat, he pushed me toward medicine—his specialty. I am his pup; his successor. I was the closest thing he had to family. The reverse was also true. The least I can do for my master after the ungrateful way I've treated him in life, is to in death, follow in his path. Not only that, I finally realize this is my calling. I want to save lives.

Hu remained silent during my retreat. By the time I entered the clinic, Kai and her weak ankles have long escaped Dui's busy hands.

Chapter 12: The Minister's Proposal

"Is there arrowroot in this?"

Dui sniffs the batch of Master Tai Hung's secret draught which I've prepared. He's adamant to defeat the Master's test one way or another.

"That's cheating, Dui. You can't go down a list of ingredients and ask me that; otherwise, I might as well give you the recipe."

"You really are his pup. He said the same thing to me. By the way, I clearly remember you now, Little Hung. Whenever we studied herbalism together, you'd swap my ingredients with kitchen spices and replace my tonics with mud water. And, on three different occasions when I came to the temple, you hurled those water bombs laced with shredded flower petals. You and that short brat with the fangs, whatever his name was. It took me forever to remove all the flower bits from my clothes."

"Oh... that's right. We did. To be fair, it was his idea. I just added flower petals. I didn't think you knew it was us."

"Who else would have been that jealous because I had her master's constant praises and undivided attention? It was not my fault I was studious and you were a lost cause. I said I'd pay you back for that someday."

He casts a sly grin over his shoulder. My face grows hot from the embarrassing memories. I really was a brat. At the time, Dui's genius irritated me. I was more suited to be a brute so that I could fit in with the temple boys. For a while, I tormented him with an old friend whose name I can't recall, the boy with fangs as Dui mentioned. He was my best friend and worst enemy. We constantly fought, made up, and then caused trouble together which usually ended with Master Tai Hung flogging us both. He visited Tian Mao Yi for about two years, and then out of the blue, disappeared. Shortly after, Dui also left to further his studies and I was alone without friend and rival.

"I'm sorry, Dui, for harassing you back then."

"Now there's something you don't hear every day!" Dui stretches his arms into the air and chuckles. "Hmm! Well, that's enough. I'm not getting any closer. Want to have lunch at the Red Koi?"

"No, I'm not hungry. You go on."

The room falls deafly silent. I was too engrossed in grinding the medicine for Mrs. Zhang to notice and thus, when a warm hand overlays mine, I knock over the basket of dried ingredients.

"Are you all right?"

"Isn't that something I should ask you? How are things... at home?"

"Fine."

Though I attempt to brush off the prodding by continuing to grind the mixture, my counterpart remains adamant.

"If that were true, you'd come to lunch. You're afraid Hu might be on patrol and get the wrong idea if he sees us together, isn't that right? Didn't you tell him the truth?"

"And which truth is that? That despite his refusal to believe it, his friend is in love with him? Or, that I didn't wale on you fast enough when you kissed me?"

"I was close to an epiphany. It couldn't be helped when most of the brew was on your lips."

"You could have used your fingers, but then, they were too busy rubbing my chest!"

"I was delirious!" The defensive cry sends deep stains to Dui's cheeks. His gaze averts toward the wall.

"You're just a pervert."

"If you had left me alone like I'd asked, this wouldn't have happened."

"I couldn't. You were ill."

Frowning, the physician moves away and then ducks under the pile of rugs in the corner.

"Ugh. Will you please throw those nasty things away?"

Chapter 12: The Minister's Proposal

"No can do, dove. Like many women crowding at once, I tell you!"

There goes that lecherous tone I haven't heard in a while. I can't tell if he's really a pervert or just pretending. Who am I kidding? A false pervert wouldn't have fondled me casually when he could barely sit. On the other hand, he doesn't appear that superficial. There are in fact, many things I don't know about this so-called prodigy. While he's not busy, I should satiate my curiosity. What should I ask?

"Why are you such a pervert?" (Continue to page 210)

"Why did you want to study medicine?" (Continue to page 211)

"How old are you?" (Continue to page 212)

Chapter 12 – 2

"Hey, Dui?"

"Yes, love?"

"Why are you such a pervert?"

"What's... with that question?" His head pokes out from under the pile of rugs. Dui runs a hand over his hair, which is beginning to billow into the former fuzzy mat of tangled knots.

"I mean, you're handsome, talented, and kind. It's not as though you can't find someone special. So why act like a pervert to drive good women away? Unless... you want to drive women away. Oh! I see now. You prefer men. That makes sense. Never mind."

"Come again? Don't go about making that kind of judgment without facts."

"It's nothing to be embarrassed about."

"I'm not embarrassed!"

"So you admit it?"

"When did I say that?!"

Continue to page 213

Chapter 12 – 3

"Hey, Dui?"

"Yes, love?"

"Why did you study medicine?"

"Because my mother told me to." His muffled voice flows out from under the pile of rugs.

"It's that simple?"

"Not everything needs a complicated answer."

"Right... fair enough."

"How about you?" His head pokes out from underneath the covers. Dui runs a hand over his hair, which is beginning to billow into the former fuzzy mat of tangled knots.

"Because Master Tai Hung forced me to."

"Not then. Now. Hu can't be happy that you're here. Why jeopardize a relationship over grinding herbs?"

"Hu expects me to support his decision; so, he should support mine. I'm... doing this for my master."

"Why? He's dead."

"Well, aren't you sensitive?!"

Continue to page 213

Chapter 12 – 4

"Hey, Dui?"

"Yes, love?"

"How old are you?"

"Why? Are you interested? Don't bother, love, I'll only break your heart."

"I was just trying to make conversation!"

The stagnant air resounds with the mortar grinding against the pestle. In time, the awkward moment is broken when his head pokes out from underneath the pile of rugs. Dui runs a hand over his hair, which is beginning to billow into the former fuzzy mat of tangled knots.

"I'm thirty. How about you?"

"Twenty-six."

"Twenty-six-year-old woman not married in this day and age? Once a lost cause always a lost cause, I guess."

"What is that supposed to mean?"

"It means if by the time I'm fifty and you're forty-six and that general of yours is still a bachelor, I'll break form and marry you, love."

"No, thank you!"

Chapter 12 – 5

Our banter is cut short. The little bell on the door jingles happily when a familiar face leisurely enters with another I never expected to see outside of palace walls.

"Minister San An. Qing Hai. Is something the matter?"

"Must something be the matter for us to have this chance meeting, my lady? I must admit, I did not expect to find you in present company." Though his demeanor is covered by a smile, his cold eyes chastise my lack of pleasantries.

"I-I'm sorry, Minister. It's just, most people don't come by our clinic unless there is a problem. I'm happy you're both well."

My attempt to assuage the Minister twists his contempt to condescension. Qing Hai, smiling nervously, steps forth as though to divide me from San An. "S-Same here. I'm glad you're well, Miss Bao Lai. Master Dui."

Qing Hai makes a quick obeisance to Dui, who's prostrated before the Minister. I suppose there are formalities expected in the company of nobility, none of which I was taught. Qing Hai continues smiling nervously. With few words, the young man grabs my hand and then excuses us from the scene.

Chapter 12 – 6

"You saved me again, Qing Hai."

We're strolling around the neighborhood while Dui and the Minister tend to business at the clinic. I hope I haven't left things too difficult for the good doctor.

"Not at all. My uncle's manners could use some work, I admit. Actually, when he heard you were at Master Dui's clinic, he volunteered to escort me. Otherwise, he'd never enter these streets without, at least, a sedan."

Hai grins cheekily. If it weren't for the Minister's previous proposal, I would have been oblivious to Hai's fun. The idea that San An came to find me is a little flattering, embarrassing, and also startling. Mostly, it's an uncomfortable thought.

"So... why did you and the Minister come?"

"I'm not supposed to divulge that."

"I'm Dui's assistant. Anything that affects him will affect me. Besides, he'll tell me anyway."

"Then, it's best that he tells you. Some things shouldn't be discussed in public."

The only secret these men hold that I'm privy to is in regards to He Pi and the assassin. His Highness must still be missing or the assassin hasn't been caught.

Either fact doesn't explain why Dui must be involved. At the moment, another concern is of greater import to me.

"Qing Hai... how is Bai Hu?"

We haven't spoken or seen much of each other since our public quarrel. These days, he purposefully comes home when I start out in the morning and leaves before I return. My notes have gone unanswered and my efforts to force his attention were brushed aside. He's always busy or tired and I am always denied permission into the palace whenever I endeavored to reach him there.

"He's not doing any better than you."

"Huh?"

"He's been moping and taking his frustration out on... *a certain trainee*. My duties in the barracks have tripled. But, something tells me in the days to come, he'll be too preoccupied to notice when I slack off." The young man, sighing in relief, smiles to himself.

Hu's frustrated when we aren't together. I know I shouldn't, but the acknowledgement forces a smile to my face. He must still care about me. That idiot! I can't believe he'd go to such lengths when he misses me too.

"Qing Hai, would you please take me inside the barracks? The guards won't permit my entry into the palace. I have to slap Hu out of it!"

"Don't you mean *snap* him out of it?"

"No."

Hai slightly cringes under my hard response. He's so childlike and innocent that I regret causing him inconvenience. Kind as he may be, Hai ultimately rejects my request, though he reassures that I will have full access to the barracks soon enough.

At the time, I thought to argue. Little did I know, he was absolutely right.

Chapter 13: Promotion to Court

A week after San An's visit, Dui and I arrive at the palace. I'm not entirely certain of the circumstances but we were brought in to replace another physician, who in turn, has taken over our clinic. Dui's griped daily ever since the request was made; however, an offer from Minister San An is not one to be turned down, especially when he personally paid homage, as I've come to learn.

When he comes to us in the courtyard, Hai secretly throws an 'I told you so' grin. I smile back to convey my appreciation. After a short bout of formality, Hai takes the lead inside. I've been so excited for this moment that I haven't been able to sleep for the past three days. Once Dui and I settle into our new post, Hu won't be able to ignore me. I'll come and go from the barracks as much as I'd like. That alone makes this job worthwhile. It was even better when I discovered San An will be paying a hundred times the wage I've come to expect at the old clinic. I'll be able to live like a queen!

Speaking of queens, I don't recall much from my previous stay at the palace. This time, I'm determined to take in the sights. Tall, decorated walls are covered by finely carved redwood motifs. Endless hallways are filled with vintage treasures. Fragranced blooms burst from lacquered vases. The servants in fine silk could be mistaken for lords and ladies. They greet us with such respect that I feel abashed.

The farther we walk inside, the more extravagant the palace becomes. My gracious, is this place beautiful! If I were so lucky in another lifetime, I'd love to be born someone of import and live in the lap of luxury. Hu would be my personal bodyguard and Dui, my court jester. A girl can dream!

"The throne room is that way in case you're ever summoned, and down the hall to my left is the war room. You'll never need to go there, I hope." Hai continues to point out different markers, none of which I'll likely remember after three seconds. "Feel free to explore these grounds as you wish. Just please don't enter the private quarters on the left side of the top floor."

If memory serves, that private quarter belongs to He Pi, which means His Highness must still be missing. As for Hai's warning, it wouldn't have come unless Dui was kept ignorant. Good thing I didn't expose that secret; else, I fear the repercussions should San An finds out.

While I'm mesmerized by luxury, Dui is as excited as can be for another reason. He's been a master practicing in a hovel. At the prospect of having equipments to further work and studies, there comes a twinkle in his eyes I've not seen since his days as an apprentice under Master Tai Hung. His pace matches Qing Hai's and then quickens as though to pull along his young host.

"Is there a room dedicated for surgeries and recovery?"

"Oh, yes! Of course! There's an entire quarter dedicated to that. Master Yu also left his rare herb collection for you in the brewing room. That's adjacent."

"And the herbs are brought in from Mount Chou?"

"Some. Most are grown next to the lily garden past the short bridge out back. I'll show you."

Like two excited schoolboys, the pair seemingly race each other toward the infirmary. Their voices rise and then slowly fade. I'm too busy daydreaming about another life to bother. By the time I glance up, the only one standing in the hallway is me.

"Oh, for Heaven's sake!"

First day in a new job and I'm already lost! How humiliating.

The path in front diverges in two. I run down the hallway to the right, but Dui and Qing Hai are nowhere in sight, so I make haste down a few more corridors. This is ridiculous. There was a hall full of people when we first entered. Why is no one here? Maybe the most logical thing to have done was walked back to the front and asked someone to escort me to the infirmary. As usual, caprice led me astray and I've no idea the way back.

Chapter 13 – 2

"Qing Hai! Dui! Where are you?! Answer me!"

"Is there anyone alive and present who could ignore your shrillness?"

Light chuckles accompanying that melodious voice send my heart to my throat. I stop breathing. Slowly, heavy feet turn a rigid body to meet the owner of that voice. There, a part away, stands the most beautiful person I've ever seen in my life. The red flowing hair, emerald green eyes, white marble skin, and pale rose lips seem ever more charming in contrast to his black silk robe. I can't help but shamelessly stare. For whatever reason, the longer my eyes are glued to him, the wider his grows.

In time, he moves closer, each step quicken my beating heart. I fear I may be in trouble if I weren't madly pining after Bai Hu.

"I-I didn't mean to shout. I'm sorry."

Embarrassed, I try to flee when his long fingers snatch my wrist. His grip feels like iron; his skin feels like silk.

"You are lost. Why run away? Do you not want my help?"

"I didn't want to trouble you... sir."

Chapter 13: Promotion to Court

Emerald eyes narrow though his intention escapes me. They're partially amused and otherwise condescending.

"Trouble me. I implore you."

"Then... could you show me to the infirmary?"

"Are you ill?"

"No. I'm the new physician's assistant. It's my first day. I don't know where to go."

"Already a disgrace on your first day. And you expect soldiers to entrust to you their lives?" Light chuckles turn bright. The stranger reaches out and touches my cheek. It's madness! The moment those piercing eyes cast their spell, my defenses are rendered moot. I can't move.

Cool fingertips trace over my face as though he were drawing a figure from memory. If he keeps this up, my heart won't stand a chance.

"Um... C-Could you please stop that?"

"First, tell me your name. If I am so inclined, I will release you."

"I don't see why I have to suffer your inclinations."

"Oh-ho! Impertinent, aren't we! You have my attention. Tell me your name is Dong Xing and I will grant you my company this instant."

If that is a joke, I haven't the slightest clue why it's funny. Who on Earth is Dong Xing and why is he smiling so tenderly? It's unnerving.

"Look, you have me confused with someone else. My name is—"

"Bao Lai!"

I've been aching to hear that voice, except once more, he has the worst timing! I fly from the stranger's loosened grip; though, in less than two steps, he's embraced me from behind. Bai Hu, fuming, stomps forward with San An following in tow.

"Unhand my wife!"

"*Your* wife?" Pausing, he scans the storming Bai Hu up and down. His arms bind more strongly. "No, this is impossible. I disapprove. You're not fit for her."

"I don't give a damn what you think! She's my wife! Let her go or I'll rip your arms off!"

"That's quite enough, General." San An's steady tone carries daggers, the inherent authority of which draws back Hu's composure. Moving past Hu, the Minister bows graciously to this stranger, who I've finally grasped to be of great import. "Lord Han Bei, Bao Lai is indeed the General's charge. She is due at her new post. General Hu will assure to that. Please, escort me to council. I'm afraid there are dire matters at hand."

Still grimacing, Han Bei's reluctant arms leave me.

"Then let me be frank, Minister. Ning will not dirty her hands in Nan Rong's troubles without reason and the only reason I haven't left is that Bao Lai happened to impede my path. Do not plan to keep her from my company. That would prove to be your greatest mistake and the beginning of the end for Nan Rong."

Immediately after stunning everyone with the audacious declaration, Lord Han Bei parts from our company with a baffled San An. When only Hu and I are left, the air grows stagnant.

"Are you all right?" He finally mutters.

"I'm fine. H-How are you?"

"How should I feel knowing every man happens to be in love with my wife?"

"Every man except you."

"Ah!" Hu, scratching his head huffily, lets out an aggravated grunt. "Why are you here?"

"I work here. Just like you."

"The army doesn't accept women."

"Not as soldiers, they don't."

"Meaning what exactly?"

"Meaning from this day forward, I am the new court physician's assistant. I will be tending to the soldiers. You'll have to endure my meddling whether you like it or not. Now, could you please show me to the infirmary? I'm late for my first day."

"Are you purposefully disobeying my wishes out of spite?"

"I am not doing anything out of spite. I want to treat patients and support you. This is how I can accomplish both."

"Oh yes, I can see your *devotion*." He snaps sarcastically. "Is that why poor Kai is still limping? Dui never refused her treatment before. I wonder what changed his mind."

"What—Dui wouldn't! She's not injured!"

"Kai doesn't have a reason to lie."

"She does if it means you'll fuss over her. She's in love with you, you big idiot!"

My dissonant cries echo down the long hallway. He's staring back in disbelief. While there's more he wishes to say, Hu manages to hold his tongue.

My heart hurts. It hurts when we're close and worse when we're far apart. He's standing right in front of me and I still miss him. Though, I know the sentiment is not mutual. I feel him drifting farther away each passing moment. The novelty of our situation has become mundane. Maybe he's found the woman he loves and I'm keeping him from her. I can't easily let go of what's mine. This much, I've told him before.

How long have we been standing here in silence? It has felt ages. I'm too agitated to acknowledge him and I'm sure he doesn't want much to do with me. Maybe, it's as San An said, I am his charge and nothing more. Once His Highness returns, this charade will end along with the Minister's ruse.

"Sorry about that!" Qing Hai's nervous chuckles abruptly cut through the corridor, retrieving both Hu and me from our silent clash. "I thought you were right behind us!"

They come up, Qing Hai and Dui, the former smiling; the latter, stern. Dui looks from me to Hu and grinds his jaw. "Save apologies for later, Qing Hai. Mother, come with me. It's urgent."

"Bao Lai is your mother?" The young soldier stares blankly. His innocence is something to be desired.

"Might as well be. That, or an overbearing sister. She's a pain in my neck. If it weren't for her skills, I'd hire someone more pleasing to the senses."

For a split moment, he casts a discreet sidelong glance at Bai Hu. Dui's implicitly pushing the idea that the incident at the clinic truly was an accident and there is absolutely nothing romantic between us. I appreciate his efforts at convincing the one man who won't believe me, however futile they may be.

"Come along, Mother. We've draughts to prepare."

Dui waves a hand to call me forward. I bow to a still much-confused Qing Hai and then follow forthwith. Hu says nothing when I walk away. When I look back, he's disappeared down the opposite end of the corridor.

Chapter 14: That Which Cures All

"That looks heavy, Dui. Let me carry it."

"Way to challenge my manhood, Mother. Give me a little credit."

"It's not my fault you're a fragile little thing! Let me help!"

I reach to take the wooden travel case of supplies from Dui, who artfully maneuvers his body to block my attempt, only to then find that his shoulders aren't strong enough to endure the weight. He nearly topples. In turn, I snatch the box and strap it to my own shoulders. His pride having been damaged, Dui looks away, frustrated.

"I carried water daily at the temple so I'm used to this. Don't worry about it. You're more suited to use your brains. Let me be your brawn."

"A regular knight, aren't you, Mother?"

Fretting, Dui takes my canvas satchel across his shoulders. The darn thing is so light, a toddler could carry it. Grinning, I jump up and down with the heavy wooden case on my back just to rub it in his face. Dui tries to steal back his parcel in order to reclaim pieces of his broken masculinity. We run about the courtyard, dodging between the armored horses and grumbling officers, one of whom unexpected catches me in his arms.

"We meet again, my lady. Now that I've caught the rowdy apothecary, what is my prize?"

I know that voice. There's no mistaking it. The tone is smooth and mature; yet, also slightly teasing. Amongst current party, he's the only one in black and silver armors.

Yesterday, after retiring to my new quarters, Qing Hai came to explain that Lord Han Bei is an emissary from Ning, the country to the east of our Nan Rong and a long time adversary, who was brought into the conflict which the assassin instigated. Regrettably, the assassin wasn't caught and now he's attacked Bei Ling's leadership and fled to Mount Chou. Bei Ling is north of Nan Rong. Their generals have entered the South to find the instigator. Nan Rong's council decided to intercept the invasion lest other countries follow suit and take liberties.

Dui was instructed to accompany the troops. As his assistant, naturally, I'm tagging along. Secretly, I've been hoping for this chance. It's been my childhood dream to join the army, as I had promised my friend, but women aren't allowed. This might be the closest I'll ever come. I didn't expect Ning's emissary to take part in this campaign.

"Lord Han Bei? Are you going too?"

"You remembered my name. I'm honored. And yes, I will accompany you, my lady, is that surprising?"

Chapter 14: That Which Cures All

"A little..."

Somehow, my honesty triggered his amusement. The emissary bursts into laughter. His embrace grows noticeably tighter. The weight on my shoulders keeps me from wriggling free.

Dui finally catches up, prepared to tactfully request my release from the overfriendly emissary. However, he doesn't have the chance before another is storming forward to make a scene.

"Didn't you hear me yesterday? Take your filthy hands off my wife!"

Hu's booming, furious voice pierces through the noisy courtyard, sending every man to silence. Even I lost my nerves for a moment. Han Bei remains unyielding. The smile on his face turns to a sneer. His grip refuses to loosen. In moments, opposing hands are tugging at my body, neither of which will yield nor, for my sake, apply too strong a force to claim full custody.

"I've told you, I don't approve of this relationship." Han Bei replies earnestly. "Besides, were she my wife, I would not have her suffer one lonely evening. She was in tears last night. Where were you?"

"Were you eavesdropping?!" Last night, after Qing Hai left, I lost my nerves and succumbed to emotions. Hu's constant disregard wouldn't permit me one moment of peace. I did cry. I just didn't know anyone heard.

"Don't pout," the emissary chuckles melodically. "Your defense is my duty. No unworthy man will have a place by your side."

"Er... Lord Han Bei, you're being overly protective."

"As I should. You are important to me, Bao Lai."

He says my name with such emphatic grace, almost relishing the words, that I can't keep from blushing. His odd obsession is furthering Hu's distrust. The latter makes one hard tug, forcing Han Bei's grip to falter in order to keep me from harm. I collapse against his heavy armors where Hu keeps me shielded from unwanted hands.

"I don't know how it is in your land, barbarian, but in Nan Rong, taking another man's wife will cost you life and limb."

"Life and limb is a small price to pay for a woman's happiness. That is something you selfish Southern dogs wouldn't understand."

"Where do you get off telling me how to treat my wife?"

"I'm the closest thing she has to family and I forbid her union to a fool."

"Family? Don't make me laugh! I don't need your permission. You're not Tai Hung. Find your own damn wife and keep your hands off mine!"

Hu's declaration echoes like a roar of a wild beast, ready to tear his opponent apart. Far from fear or flattery, everything turns numb the moment my master's name is mentioned. The only person I've divulged his identity to was Dui, who already knew him by trade. I look up, lips parted to question the secret he's kept from me. At the same time, Hu sends down a seething scowl.

"And you! You're not coming to Mount Chou!"

"Wh—Yes, I am!"

"Women have no business on a battlefield! I know what you'll say and I don't want to hear it!"

"That's not your call!"

"You're my wife, so it is my call!"

"We're not mar—!"

"Are you two quite finished?" The Minister comes forthwith in full armor, looking as natural in them as he does in the usual long noble robes. A crinkle is spread wide across his brows. He gives a disapproving glare in my direction for nearly breaking form and then a threatening stare at Hu for causing the disquiet. I am Hu's wife. That is the lie everyone must believe, including Han Bei. Denying that will just bring unnecessary suspicion.

"I understand you're worried for you wife, General. However, Master Dui alone cannot tend to every man.

Under short notice, we were unable to secure additional trustworthy assistance. Let's hope both their skills won't be required but should that become necessary, we are best prepared. She won't be forced to face Bei Ling, I guarantee that."

"With all due respect, Prime Minister, were she your wife, you wouldn't let her take one step out of this palace."

"If that is your opinion, then you are more than welcome to stay here and detain Bao Lai. We have a long road ahead. Nan Rong's welfare is at stake and I won't have it jeopardized over a lover's spat."

Despite his usual easy-going attitude, Bai Hu, along with Zhen Yue, are model imperial soldiers. I've seen the admiration the Demon General's induced from others. Now, as I look around, everyone seem to have their noses upturned. In an instant, the respect he's worked so hard to build has crumbled under the eyes of his judging peers. All because of me. San An was right. I was too busy being aggravated by his authoritative tone that I overlooked the reason for it. He's worried for me and thus, doesn't want me to go; just as I worry for him, which is the reason I sought to. Maybe it's too late to save face. At least, I want to try.

"Bai Hu, I'm sorry. You have a point. A woman on the battlefield would be a distraction. I'll stay."

"Is that right? That's disappointing." Han Bei, finding the ordeal amusing, leisurely enters the

232

conversation. "I thought Bao Lai was a woman of convictions—of passion. Your concession came too easy."

"This has nothing to do with you."

"Spoken like a true myopic fool." Han Bei's sharp eyes meet Bai Hu's deadly stare. The force of their opposition is that of two titans ready to draw blood. "I would not waste my time marching under Nan Rong's banner otherwise. My strength and the strength of the East are reserved for Bao Lai alone. If she stays then so will I. If she is displeased, I would not hesitate to whisk her away some place far better."

"You—!"

"Then let us be off. Daylight is limited."

With San An's curt dismissal, conversations come to an end. The caravan prepares for departure. Dui and I assemble behind the generals. The Minister is positioned a short distance in front of us. Han Bei is behind, guarding the rear.

It wasn't until we were on the main road leading to Mount Chou that the ordeal was finally explained to me through Dui's inconspicuous whispers. Nan Rong seeks Ning's alliance and Han Bei is the mean to accomplish that arduous task. For whatever reason, the emissary has taken a liking to me. San An fears Han Bei's departure should I have been left behind. I believe Bai Hu also recognized that challenge, though, Dui is of another romantic opinion which I secretly hope to be true: Hu conceded lest Han Bei steals me away.

Chapter 14 – 2

Bi Xi is a small village near the base of Mount Chou. Unlike the crowded capital full of tall buildings, houses here are spaced far apart and built rather low, each having at least a small, gated yard. Trees are abundant outside the village while inside is rather sparse, with mostly short grasses and small shrubs. Bai Hu is from Bi Xi, which explains why he lives in a house resembling the ones surrounding us, even if that means his commute to work every day takes three times longer.

Hu's not said a word. The Minister strayed toward the back of the lines during our trek to keep Han Bei company and voided the emissary from engaging me in conversation lest that sparked another riot from my grimacing paramour. I never meant to cause more trouble for Hu. I truly would have stayed behind except the decision was no longer mine. Dui secretly mentioned that I am expected to keep up Lord Han Bei's mood. As far as I can tell, there isn't anything I could do to dampen his favor.

"You're staying here."

I turn toward that stiff tone and wrinkled brows, a complete mismatch to the friendly, carefree man he once was only a month ago. Dui and I were reviewing our supplies for the march ahead. At Hu's intrusion, the doctor excuses himself.

235

"Could you please stop frowning?" Both my index fingers reach to push his cheeks upward. We've been at this standoff long enough. I just want to see him smile again. Sadly, the frown doesn't waver under my playful attempt.

"Bai Hu, I... yes, I'll stay if that's what you want. Please, be careful up there. Promise that you'll come back to me safely."

His hard gaze briefly softens and thereupon others' interruptions, turns to stone. Lord Han Bei and San An come hither to confer my orders while Bai Hu retreats to keep from another quarrel. In the end, I was able to satisfy Hu's request to stay in Bi Xi. San An used me as an excuse to convince Lord Han Bei to march under Nan Rong's banner against Bei Ling. An act, which the Minister resolved, will push back the Northern Army without either side having to draw swords.

Chapter 14 – 3

"He'll be fine."

Dui drops a few more herbs into the mortar while I continue to grind with the pestle. Most of the soldiers left earlier with San An and the emissary for Mount Chou. Dui was tasked to Bi Xi by Hu's request. The small village comprises mainly of children and the elderly. Most young adults left for better jobs in the cities. Such as it is, many are in need of treatments but the local physician, aside from lacking proper resources, isn't very knowledgeable. Once they've discovered Dui's talent, the villagers have been coming and going all day from our makeshift clinic. Things have finally settled down but we've still many orders of medicine waiting to be filled.

Light from the setting sun turns the earth on the dirt roads crimson. The weight on my chest grows heavier at the sight; a sore reminder of those days at Tian Mao Yi when I waited for my friend's return by the main road. He left without a single farewell and now, almost twenty years later, I still often think of him. I pray that parting will never repeat, especially not with Bai Hu.

"Mother... Bao Lai! Are you listening?"

I jolt from the irate chiding. He has been carefully rallying my sour mood all day. Despite Dui's kind encouragement, intuition tells me nothing can ever be so easy.

"Is this the last batch, Dui?"

"Yeah. Are you okay?"

"I'm fine. Thank you, by the way, for treating the villagers. I know everyone, Hu included, really appreciate it."

"Eh. Don't make me out to be a saint. I work for the state now. Nan Rong's taxes are funding my services."

"I guess. Still, thank you."

His lips purse. Dui looks away abashedly and then continues to stuff the medicinal mixtures into paper packets. I start for the bucket of dirty bowls that has been soaking since this afternoon. Inexplicably, the moment my hands reach into the bucket, tears surge and I can't keep my shoulders from trembling. I stifle a cry and slosh the water about in the hopes of drowning out my pathetic whimpering. In the next moment, a pair of busy hands is squeezing my bottom.

"What the hell are you doing?!"

I whip about, falling on my behind in the process. Dui's crouched on top of me. The lustful stare is accompanied by a wide grin. His fingers nimbly run up the side of my waist toward my chest and then he leans in close enough for our lips to touch. The ordeal came so shocking that I sit frozen in place, afraid to even breathe.

"Why the long face, dove? My gentle hands can cure what ails you, even your heartache. Come on, let's have a look between those soft, lovely mounds."

Moisten lips lower toward the collar of my shirt. I thought he promised to keep his hands to himself once I accepted employment. Well, I suppose I work for San An now, and not Dui. My hands are fists. This isn't the time for lewd jokes. Fury initiates retaliation. However, right before connecting to his face, my fist freezes. How could I have been so blind? That's truly all this is: a lewd joke.

I fall to the floor, rolling from laughter at the recollection of every woman in An who's reddened their hands from slapping the good doctor.

"What's so funny, love?"

"You've succeeded, Doctor. You've cured my ill mood!"

A pout settles over his mouth. Dui moves away and falls to the floor beside me. Then, proceeds to rub his tired shoulders.

"I meant it, you know. Anything my gentle hands can do for you, I would, love."

"I've formulated that your lechery is actually a method to lift your patients' spirit. There's not one woman who has slapped you and hasn't laughed about it later. Master Peng also said that laughter is the best medicine."

"You're cruel, Mother, making that kind of assumption. I don't ever intend to be the butt of anyone's joke."

"Then, tell me this. While I was out fetching water from the well earlier, why didn't you take advantage of Miss Hong-ji? She's young, pretty, and innocent. Best of all, the pretty miss made no attempt to rebuff your advances. If anything, I saw you withdraw once she took your offer seriously."

"You were supposed to fetch water from the well. How would you have known?"

"I dawdled."

Dui rolls to the side, his back to me, and then curls into a ball.

"It's none of your business."

"I disagree. I'm your mother, at least, an overbearing sister, isn't that what you said? Since we're family, what's the use in keeping secrets? I've reasoned that if your lechery is an act, that would explain the poor hygiene and false detached attitude. And, seeing as how you don't actually want women to accept your advances, would it be crazy to think you aren't really attracted to women?"

My matter-of-fact, partially insinuating rant, expected his retaliation. For a long while, I wait with a grin on my face for him to rebuff. The grin eventually fades during the uncomfortable silence, until he turns back to me with his brows in a knot.

"Dui, what's wrong? I was joking."

"Well... what if... I mean theoretically... what if I... didn't-wasn't...couldn't... is that... strange?"

"Uh... what?"

Pain surfaces behind those usually composed grey eyes. His penetrating stare is begging me, though for what, I don't know. The pleading worsens with the dreadful silence billowing between us and I cease to breathe lest the final thread on his composure comes undone.

"Please... answer me. Is it wrong that I just can't... feel attraction toward women?"

"I... don't think so?"

Our gazes are glued to each other's in an unblinking deadlock. I was only kidding. I've no idea how to approach the subject when it comes back to hit me square between the eyes.

The answer wasn't one he expected. Dui lifts up and then moves to clean our workspace. What's wrong with me? He's helped me so much during my trying relationship with Bai Hu, and when he wants a bit of understanding, I'm stuck in disbelief. No, our current society doesn't find it ordinary but Dui is my friend, first and foremost, and I couldn't care less what his preferences are.

"Dui."

I move to take the mortar from him. He looks up, confused and then offended.

"Just forget it."

"No. I want to know. Really."

"What's there to know? I'm... not natural."

"You're right. You're a genius. All you geniuses are weird."

"Don't mock me."

He snatches back the bowl. I grab onto his hands. The face that arches up is on the verge of tears.

"Dui, there's nothing wrong with you. I've cross-dressed most of my life, who am I to judge? That's not it. You're perfectly wonderful the way you are. Who cares if you prefer men?"

"I never said I preferred men!"

His hands jerk back tersely. Dui's growing more agitated by the stupid things I say. Be that as it may, he's chosen to share this part of him and I want to understand. Thus, I choose to push on.

"Then tell me. I want to know."

"Because you're nosy?"

"Yes, and also because you're important to me. You and Bai Hu are my two most cherished people left in the world. Isn't there anything I can do?"

My endeavor is met with a scoff. Dui withdraws as a mean to distance himself from conversation. For once, he was willing to open up his heart and I was a clumsy fool who fumbled the precious thing to the ground, even trampled on it.

The closer I move in, the farther he retreats.

"Leave me alone."

Dui quits the room, taking his troubles away and tucking them under a mask of complacency where his other secrets hide. While I can't comprehend the reason for his misery, my heart twinges at the idea of his loneliness. I've lectured him this entire time and forced him to conform to a standard in order to find a companion, when in fact, he's tried desperately to be contrary to his nature. Hu and I have each other but we bicker over immature things. For Dui, who has never had the pleasure of experiencing the same bond, it must be painful watching from afar.

In reality, the feeling isn't foreign. How could I have forgotten? Before I became 'Wife,' the idea of being in a relationship was unthinkable for me. I shied away from women because I felt inferior and faltered in society because I didn't understand how to fit in. Whenever I saw couples together, uneasiness settled over my chest. I didn't feel normal. In the end, I lived as a recluse. Despite our differences, a part of me realizes the pain of loneliness he's carrying. Not long ago, they were mine.

Unable to control the rising storm in my chest, I start up and then run after the young master. However, soon as I exit the clinic, the tepid night air brushing against my face is the last things I recall before all else turns to darkness.

Chapter 14 – 4

Three days ago, I woke in this cell and would have picked the lock sooner had my captors been more trusting by leaving me unattended.

From the colors and style of their attire, which are brownish-yellow fabrics fashioned into tribal garments resembling those of the barbarians on the outskirts of Nan Rong, I assume these men must be akin to those slain on the road by the Demon General that night the assassin infiltrated the palace and attempted San An's life. I can't tell if they are in league with the assassin but one thing is certain, their grudge resides with Bai Hu.

"Hey, I need to use the bathroom again."

The young man standing in the corner grimaces when I bang on the cell door. Though rough around the edges, he carries Qing Hai's innocent disposition. Of all the men who come to stand guard, he seems the most likely to be swayed.

"Can't you hold it?"

"Are you kidding me? Hold it until you let me go? My bladder will explode!"

"Then do it in the corner!"

"I'm not a dog! Didn't your mother teach you how to treat a woman?"

"Do I look like I have a mother?"

"Well, someone gave birth to you. Could you at least turn around?"

His eyes narrow. Our staring contest rages on until he can't help but blink; a silent agreement of concession. Leave it up to me to master the mundane arts.

"I weren't planning to look anyway!"

Once his back is turned, I shuffle my clothes to give the impression of undressing while reaching into my hair to retrieve two pins. Then, in the subtlest manner, begin to work the lock on the door. Another mundane skill which my friend from the temple taught to me. I can't believe I still remember how to do this after all these years.

"Are you done yet? I don't hear anything."

"Give me a break! I'm not accustomed to doing this with company. Besides, who said you could listen?"

Growling, his head bangs against the wall from exasperation. Another pin quietly clicks and then the door unlocks. I move back into position near the barred windows. All I need now is for him to leave the room.

"Well, what do you know? False alarm. I'm really thirsty though, can I have some water?"

"I'm not your babysitter!" He swings around, hands balled into fists. "What's a brat like you doing chasing after a grown man like him anyway?"

Chapter 14: That Which Cures All

"Who?"

"The Demon. Talk about mothers, is yours fine with that?"

"Do I look like I have a mother?" I mimic his previous tone. "Speaking of brats, what's a brat like you doing with the likes of these men? Who are you people? What do you want?"

"Can't you tell by our clothes? We're the bandits of Mount Chou!" He answers proudly with a grin and head held up high.

"Yeah... real noble profession."

"I don't have to take any crap from you! We are honorable, unlike the bastards cowering in the capital! They'll get what's coming."

"What does that mean?"

"It means your lover is in for a real surprise."

Rising from behind that boyish smile is lustful vengeance. These men went to all the trouble of capturing only me from the village to use as lure for Bai Hu. While I would deny that the Demon General intentionally slew their comrades without reason, I'm not so sure that was the case. Admitting he had anything to do with the incident will only add fuel to the fire. The unusual circumstance continues to bother me. Why were the bandits from Mount Chou far away from their base, barring the eastern road between Nan Rong and Ning?

"Out of curiosity, how would you mountain dwellers know my lover? He hasn't come up this way until a few days ago. Are you sure your grudge is against the right man?"

"I was there!" The sharp gaze falters to despair. His gritted jaw is fighting hard to withhold tears. "And I know you were there too. I saw you, the other man, and the Demon leave my fallen comrades to rot like animals! Your Minister called our men to the capital, promised us a place in the army, and then massacred everyone! Left me alive to find their mangled bodies just to rub our noses in it. If I weren't positioned so far away, I would have killed him myself!"

"That's not true! I don't know anything about a summon to court, but nothing was staged. Bai Hu was chasing after an assassin who attempted the Minister's life. He couldn't have known your men would be there!"

"So his first instinct was to kill them?!"

"I... I don't know what happened and by your account, neither do you. If their deaths were staged, it wasn't by Minister San An or Bai Hu. Logically, the assassin instigated everything and who's to say he didn't kill your allies?"

"Based on what proof? I never saw anyone else come close to the borders and isn't it convenient an assassin explains everything away!"

"You want proof? Here's your damn proof! Hu chased after that man because he did this to me!"

My heart is thudding so loudly that it's hard to keep steady. It's all my fault. Hu lost control when I was injured by the assassin. The repercussion of which is now apparent. Once more, because of me, he'll willingly walk into danger and this time, intuition doubts that he'll be able to leave unscathed. I am his weakness and he is mine. As long as we are together, this will always be true.

With trembling hands, I pull down a part of my collar to expose the long scar left from my confrontation on the rooftop. I can't keep from violently shaking, fearful for the man who means more to me than anything in the world, while my counterpart is mimicking my anxiety, grieving for his friends. The tears streaming down our cheeks are acknowledged by the other; except, we both know an understanding will not change the outcome of this conflict.

Chapter 14 – 5

'A draught for you daughter,
A brew for your boy.
A philter for your paramour,
An elixir of life.
These I sell and many more,
A wandering apothecary with gifts from the gods.
Knowledge less squandered,
Time well spent.
I have every potion to fill heart's content.
The root of all evil may be greed,
The root of goodness is to be happy.
Nothing's to fret over with all the time in the world.
A concoction touched by Heaven, my signature pearl.'

Such a song is both foreign and familiar to the ear. The so-called medicine men who came down from Hing San often drew in customers back in Pa Xu with similar songs promising perpetual health, love, and immortality. In truth, they were snake oil selling hawkers. I used to listen to their droning, nasally singing when Master Tai Hung and I purchased supplies from the local trade shop. The difference this time is the hawker himself; a true apothecary.

I run to the barred windows just as several bandits shout for his halt. He's approached from a different side of the stronghold. I can't see him. Proceeding with his farce, Dui's convincing sales pitch is mixed with half-truths of herbal healing properties which would confound even the more knowledgeable laymen.

Chapter 14: That Which Cures All

"Is that... possible?"

"Hmm?"

I turn back to the conflicting young man scratching his head. He seems ready to run outside at any moment.

"Love potions. Do they really work?"

Apparently, the chance I've been waiting for has arrived. However, if I sound too eager, he'll become suspicious. I best give him a shove.

"*You* love someone? That's hard to believe. Why don't you just kidnap the poor girl and put her in a cell?"

"Shut up! I... Do you think they're real or a waste of money?"

"That depends. Is she worth the few measly coins it takes to find out?"

He frowns at my frown and then recalls that he can't win against me in a staring contest. Letting out a groan, the young man rushes outside. Once the wooden door to the back slams against the frame, I open the cell door and then sneak out of the detention area.

Chapter 14 – 6

My half-baked plan comes undone the moment I step outside. Dui's distraction helped me escape. Now that I'm free, he's detained. I doubt they'll allow him to leave freely and should they be so kind, Dui's objective wasn't to walk into danger in order to make a few coins. He isn't aware of my plan and I definitely don't know his.

I have to force him to retreat, somehow. The more I look around, two choices come to mind. Which should I take?

The direct approach (Continue to page 253)

Signal to him (Continue to page 256)

Chapter 14 – 7

Signaling to him is too risky. He might not see me and if I'm caught again, we'll both be in a world of trouble. I best take the direct approach.

These men are complete opposites of Bai Hu and akin to Dui. Dirty clothes are piled in a corner out back. A few are hanging from clothesline but they, too, don't smell any better. Maybe the brown coloration on the yellow fabrics weren't intentional. They're just dirty, dirty men. Not much different from many of the monks at temple.

I snatch down a long coat to cover my pink robe, the hem of which is pulled up and wrapped around my waist. Then, with one of the belt cords, tie my hair into a topknot.

"Ah, anything in there to erase memories, Doctor?" I mimic Dui's nonchalant tone when I come up between two men fighting over the last love potion. "My friend won't settle for an apology. I need him to think nothing happened."

Dui looks up, startled from the realization, before rummaging through his box for a suitable draught.

"Don't be a wimp. Real men don't apologize!"

One of the bandits standing nearby slams a heavy palm against my shoulder. On impulse, I slam a fist against his arm, the common reaction when the other students from the temple challenged me. He slightly winces and that is enough for many dubious eyes to lower.

"Shut yer face! I slept with his woman after I bedded his mother. He can't take his wife without thinking what's gone in her and where he's going."

The surrounding men groan from disgust. Dui, on the other hand, is doing his darndest to keep the beet-red face from exploding with laughter.

"H-H-Here you are," the apothecary manages to stifle his humor and mutter at last. He hands over a vial of red liquid in exchange for a few coppers. "Well, gentlemen. Unless anyone is in the market for a hair-growth potion, that's about all for today. I'll come back with a new batch of love potion after I resupply. Have a good day."

Dui shuffles the remaining vials back into the carrier. He throws a quick glance in my direction and then starts down the hill. For some reason, against all my expectations, the bandits don't attempt to rob their coins back from Dui. They're too busy discussing the values in their purchases.

Once he's a short distance away, I call out to Dui as an excuse for my retreat. "Hey wait! You didn't tell me how to use this!"

He turns back just as I come up and then we stand still and pretend to be in conversation over the tonic.

"Shall we make a run for it?" He whispers, his finger pointing at the vial as though explaining the properties.

"No, too many eyes. We won't make it. You go on ahead. I'll walk out back and make my way down the other side before circling around. Please, warn Bai Hu. They're after him."

Continue to page 259

Chapter 14 - 8

I best signal for Dui's retreat. Once he's safe, I'll fly down the mountain on the opposite side then swing around to reconvene in Bi Xi.

These men are complete opposites of Bai Hu and akin to Dui. Dirty clothes are piled in a corner out back. A few are hanging from clothesline but they, too, don't smell any better. Maybe the brown coloration on the yellow fabrics weren't intentional. They're just dirty, dirty men. Not much different from many of the monks at temple.

After snatching a long coat, I climb up the side of the detention area and change into the reeking article. Amongst the dull yellow-brown fabrics, my pink robe can't be missed. I wait patiently until Dui glances up from rummaging through his crate and then wave the lively colored robe.

Shoot! He's not the only one looking this way. A few men who can't wait their turn swarm behind the doctor, distract him from my signal, and nearly expose me. What a terrible plan! At least, no one saw me. I can still try my other idea and approach directly.

A strong tug jerks my body backward once I reach solid ground. A large palm covers my mouth.

"Shh! It's me, Bai Hu. Don't scream."

Chapter 14: That Which Cures All

I shake my head to signal that I won't. His hand moves off. I swing around to embrace him but Hu doesn't waste any time distancing us from the base.

"Hu. Wait. What about Dui? Does he know you're here?"

"He's not my problem. Let's go."

"Hold on!"

"Keep it down. It's him or me and I'm not letting you choose him. Hurry up."

We're pulling in opposing directions. As expected, I'm no match for him. I can't believe he's still stubborn. This isn't about choosing a lover. There's no one I can imagine being with except for Bai Hu. Dui is my friend. He came to save me. I can't just leave him.

"Will you stop? Dui's in danger!"

"So am I for coming alone but apparently, I don't mean as much to you."

"What—That's..."

Resonating thunder suddenly shakes the base. Hu and I nearly fall to our knees. By the time he's recovered, I've slipped from the loose grip and ran back toward the commotion. From the thick smoke, a thin shadow emerges out of the detention area, frantically calling my name. I sprint forward, shouting for him to come this way, when a large group of shadows surround his thin frame.

"Dui!"

My feet fly forward but then I fall back onto Hu, who's latched an impenetrable hold around my wrist. A flurry of blades flail, a deep groan, and then the world around crumple. Dui's lifeless body stains the green grass a sorrowful crimson. He gave up everything for nothing. My friend is gone and so is my composure. I collapse to my knees while Bai Hu draws his blade to meet the advancing bandits. Somewhere in the midst of grief and regret, I fly forward to exact vengeance. That is all I remember before the light of the world fade before my very eyes.

The End.

Chapter 15: The Scuffle at Mount Chou

I'm halfway up the hill between Dui and the compound when a booming thud resonating from the detention area scatters the crowd. The man with the worst timing in the world storms outside. His brown hair waves wildly, the sharp gold eyes tear into his foes, and those fangs are seething from fury. He really is a demon, even without the silver mane.

"Bao Lai!" He screams my name frantically in a tempest rage. *"Bao Lai, where are you?!"*

A clashing of metal against metal, a groan, and then several bandits are knocked to the ground. On impulse, I run up the hill, stopping in my tracks once I've realized that there are too many men standing between us. Distracting him won't be beneficial if I give away my position. Besides, should someone capture me before I can reach him, that won't make things easier.

Instead, I make a mad dash into the crowd, draw a sword from one of the bandits Hu knocked down, and then proceed to feign clumsiness. I *stumble* over one of the men on the ground and slam into another, who in turn, slams into another. A raised foot trips several more. In the heavy crowd, no one's the wiser. The line between Hu and I slowly diminishes.

Strong as Bai Hu may be, his strength is quickly sapped from frantically swinging the heavy blade after having trekked up the mountain. Sweat is beading across his brows and his attacks are growing noticeably slower. My cheap tricks aren't enough. I hasten forward, plunging recklessly through any break between the lines.

We're so close. I leap over the fallen bandit in front of me, prepared to fight by my lover, when another force reels my body backward violently against a hard chest plate. A booming voice projects from above my head, Hu swings to face me and then everything turns numb. Please, tell me this isn't happening.

Terror and shock strike down my voice. My cries are stifled under indescribable despair. The sword lodged in Hu's chest withdraws, leaving a stream of blood to dye the green grass below a dark shade of crimson. I jump forward but the same force pulls back. More bloodstains scatter over the earth. Hu furiously swings the blade, cutting down man after man; his eyes fixated on my tear-stained face. In time, the open wound loses too much blood and he falters to the endless number of advancing bandits. Their swords pierce his torso, his arms and legs, sending him to the ground.

Why is this happening? Why does this always happen when we're together? I always cause trouble and he's always trying to save me. Not just this time or the last. Somewhere inside, I know this is a fate we must repeat. An endless cycle. However, endlessness is not what I fear. He's not moving. I can't lose him. I won't. I won't ever let anyone take him from me!

My heart is ripped in twain. Blood is surging so rapidly, my pulse is in my ears. From afar, a loud explosion shakes the crowd to their knees and inadvertently loosens the strong grip around my wrist. I lunge forward, sword brandished, and swing madly at the men who dare keep me from my dear husband. They strike back without success. Everything is slowed. Time seems to have stood still and no opponent is impossible. The ground is scorched red as anguish cries erupt into the air. Until I am the only one standing beside Hu's slumped body in a thirty feet radius, no man was spared injury.

"Get away from him!" With my echoing voice comes the return of my senses. Time resumes and I collapse next to Bai Hu. The tremors in my knees won't subside. My lungs burn as though I've not breathed since the explosion took place.

"Bao Lai!" Dui moves in between the shaken men, set down his kit beside Bai Hu, and then resolve to treat my beloved.

Tightening the sword in my unsteady hand, I push off the ground. I've lost my advantage; though, I can't recall the method through which it was gained. For the short while it lasted, I've strike enough fear to give a decent bluff. The bandits remain at bay. That is, all but one: the man who distracted Bai Hu which led to his defeat. This dark-haired, bronzed skin, burly man who towers above everyone, slowly moves forward. I can't imagine that without my stroke of luck that I could slay this giant.

"Stay back! Don't make me kill you!"

"We didn't start this war. He did."

The deep, throaty response accompanying the hard stare puts everything to silence. From the corners of my eyes, some the other bandits are cowering. I take it he's their leader and rightfully so. There's a fierce manner in his disposition and I can feel his massive strength just from standing nearby.

"He didn't! I don't know who invited your men to the capital! Hu was chasing after an assassin and your men... I don't know what happened on that road either but I can't imagine he'd attack without a reason!"

"So, you're blaming my friends. Am I to believe a liar? My comrades were supposedly struck down by the Demon General and yet, there he is, bloodied and bruised from a scuttle with a handful of greenhorns. The men I sent were elites. The only person here capable of slaying them is the same one without a mark on her. To add insult to injury, my new recruits are alive. You let them live after destroying their pride. Hell hath no fury like a woman scorned."

Those around lower their heads. Many are holding onto injuries which this man implied I've caused. Did I not kill anyone? More importantly, he believes I am the demon who slew his friends. In a way, they were killed because of me. Hu never would have been on that road had I done as he'd asked.

"It was my fault." The blade slips from my hand. I take one step forward to meet the giant.

"Bao Lai! Don't!"

"Stay back, Doctor! Please, save Bai Hu. I'm begging you, as a friend... as your mother."

He growls at my withered smile, nodding bitterly, before resuming his task.

In front of the giant, I drop to my knees. "I did it. I killed your friends. Deal whichever punishment you see fit but let the Doctor and Bai Hu go. They have nothing to do with this. You'll win back your pride and honor. If not, if you won't honor my dying wish, I'll punish you from beyond and make certain every man here dies a horrible, horrible death!"

Those hard eyes bear down. He momentarily looks away and scoffs. "This is your idea of an apology? Threatening me?"

"It's not a threat if I mean it!"

Silence upon unnerving silence. I've barely closed my eyes to accept my fate when they pop back wide open. He's laughing? Not just the giant but his greenhorns too.

"What's so funny?"

"Hmph. How am I supposed to slay an opponent who pouts like a bratty child? You sound just like my kid sister."

"Meaning... you'll let us go?"

"There is honor amongst thieves. Prove to me the scar you showed Pin wasn't coincidence. Tell me about this assassin."

He's been watching me all along, including my time in the holding cell and the earlier exchange with that boy, Pin. In spite of myself, I'm impressed. For a big man to remain discreet in that small area took quite a bit of skill on his part.

With nothing to lose, I stare directly into his eyes and recount the story, from the assassin's attempt on San An's life to our run-in on the rooftop and Hu's endeavor to punish the man. The bandit chief listens intently, his face remains unreadable, his thoughts impenetrable. Once my story completes, his back is turned.

"Where are you going, Chief?" A bandit to my right suddenly voices the thought I withheld from anxiety.

"To find San An's army. This woman did not lie. The man with two colored eyes delivered the message for us to enter the capital and positioned our men to guard his retreat. The stupid general fell into his trap and so did our men. He expected our remaining troops would take vengeance and clear San An's men from

Mount Chou, making his withdrawal from Bei Ling easier. Two birds with one stone."

"What about Mount Chou?" My curiosity got the better of me and I jumped in without discretion. He turns back, seemingly less stern than he was moments ago.

"The Prime Minister came to subdue Bei Ling's march. Bei Ling wouldn't have advanced without provocation. The man with two colored eyes crossed into our territory but he did not expect to find me. I was supposed to have died in the capital. A miscalculation. I injured him days ago believing he was San An's agent. For that unfinished business, I will join the Minister's rank."

He starts down the hill after those parting words, giving orders for the rest of the bandits to do with us as they'd like. After all, their friends died on that road to Ning and many more were injured here. Even if no one died today, there is still a transgression left unpaid. That doesn't mean I will permit any harm come to Dui and Bai Hu. Once a sword is back in my hand, I stand guard over my friends, praying for the odd affair earlier to repeat should my opponents advance.

A handful of bandits ready their blades.

Chapter 15 – 2

"Bao Lai was too kind. I will not spare the lot of you if one hair on her head is displaced."

That iron voice sends every man to disquiet. Han Bei, in Ning's infamous black and silver heavy armor, walks from the back of the line to the front. A partition forms each step he takes until the emissary is standing beside me.   The crimson blade in his hand is so terrifying sharp, I can almost feel it cut into me from simply gazing upon the relic. Looking over, he smiles.

"You surprised me. Tian Ji Zhong Shi Yan. Now there's a talent I thought was lost to the world. I wouldn't have believed it if I hadn't seen it for myself."

"What's... Tian yi-yi sh...?"

"A gift from the gods to an ancient bloodline. Time stood still, didn't it, from your perspective? From mine, your eyes turned gold; your movements, faster than lightning. Your father would have been proud."

"Are you... my father?"

Han Bei breaks into delirious laughter, nearly tipping over and falling onto his blade. His hand pats my head gently. I don't see why that's so farfetched considering how overly protective he is. Wait, that's not true. He's not protective at all!

"You were here all along? Why didn't you save Bai Hu?!"

"Why should have I? The idiot stormed in on his own accord. Apparently, he also killed their comrades. A man knows when not to interfere. Seeking vengeance for a fallen brother is one of those instances. On the other hand, a gentleman will not permit harm to a woman. I would have intervened on your behalf sooner had you not scared these boys out of their wits. Again, you amaze me."

"I don't need your empty praises! If anything happens to Bai Hu, I'll kill every single last one of you!"

For all my ranting, the most important aspect has been overlooked. Dropping the sword, I run to Bai Hu. He's barely breathing. His face is so pale. With limited supplies and equipment, there's only so much the doctor can do.

"Dui—"

"I'm trying my best but..."

"What can I do?"

"Clean water and an antiseptic. Mount Chou is known for plentiful medicinal herbs. I'm sure if you'll look around—"

"Got it!" I fly forward, almost slamming into the emissary. "Lord Han Bei, please, I'm begging you, watch over Dui and Bai Hu."

Though pretty curved rosy lips retract to a frown, Lord Han Bei shrugs and then steps aside. I run down the hill into the thicket. Surprisingly, the young man who guarded me, Pin, grudgingly comes to assist.

In the end, most of the remaining bandits decided to follow their leader and joined San An's ranks. They aim to avenge their comrades through punishing the man with two colored eyes who instigated the affair.

Chapter 16: The Second Half

Wen Meng's allegiance to San An completed the assassin's provocation and also the mean to his demise. Most of the bandits left to join their chief. The remainder stayed to guard Chou. Yue and Qing Hai came to visit for a few days. Matters in the capital soon called for their attendance, and then only Dui and I are left at the bandits' hideout along with an unconscious Bai Hu, who hasn't woken up since the ordeal. His injuries are too severe. One blade barely missed his heart, the others ripped holes in several internal organs. Multiple wounds were dealt to his arms and legs, severing muscles and tendons. Dui's kept quiet but I know should Hu wake, his days in the military are over. Being a soldier was his life and I've taken that from him.

"It's time to change his bandages again."

The herb mixture has been ready for some time now. I start to undo the rolls of bandages from the basket. Dui gives a weary nod and then begins to remove Hu's dressing. The doctor hasn't had much sleep since the event. Bags under his eyes are growing increasingly heavy; it's a miracle he can still see.

During Hu's scuttle with the bandits, Dui was the one who set off the explosives hidden inside his apothecary's case, the method through which he had originally intended to save me. Through his diversion, my so-called gift, Tian Ji Zhong Shi Yan, was somehow triggered, bringing an end to the melee. He's done so much for Hu and me. Still, he continues to give his all.

"Dui, after this, why don't you sleep for a while? I'll watch over Hu."

"I'm fine, dove."

"You look ready to keel over. That won't do Hu any good. If something appears off, I'll wake you."

"Sleep next to me, dove. Then, I'll consider it."

He gives half a weary smile as a mean to lighten the mood. Guilt seeps into my conscience. No matter how I've offended Dui, I can always count on his support. He's come to defend me again and again, while I've returned his kindness with some very mean and ignorant presumptions.

"I'm sorry."

The words in my head are projected into the air, but it wasn't I who said it. Those woeful grey eyes staring back are heart-wrenchingly apologetic.

"I'm sorry I couldn't protect you... and Bai Hu."

"Dui, it wasn't your fault."

"Being a weak man is a fault. I'm not made for battle. I couldn't raise a sword. Were I stronger, a real man, you wouldn't have had to cry your eyes out."

Chapter 16: The Second Half

"I am mad at you but only for being reckless. You're a healer. You're not meant to raise a sword. Brutes like Hu and me, we're only good for getting into trouble and then we need your gentle hands to mend our wounds. You came to save me—"

"I couldn't!" The bitter words are spit out between gritted teeth. Dui can't force trembling shoulders to steady.

"That's not true. You're brave, Dui. You don't leave a friend in trouble and the things that you're capable of, most men can't handle. If it weren't for you, neither Hu nor I would still be here. You are a person I deeply admire and respect. Please don't sell yourself short."

His cheeks flush from a sharp exhale. With nothing more to say, we silently continue until Hu's bandages are changed. There is more color to his face compared to a few days ago, but he can't heal fully at this rate. Despite Dui's methods to keep his body nourished, he'll eventually wither away unless he wakes.

A warm hand lands on my chin and then a thumb flicks away a speck of water from my cheek. I look up to see Dui on the verge of tears. That's right. He's told me that he's easily influenced.

"Sorry," I pull away and rub my eyes.

"You really love him, don't you?"

"Wh-huh? Love? I... love Hu?"

He gives my wide-eyed stare a once over, smirking at my ignorance. "I'm the last person you should be asking considering my... peculiarity. The way you both chased after each other, I just assumed you were in love."

"I... haven't considered that possibility. He's never said that he loves me and I'm not certain what love is."

"That's odd. Crying over someone constantly, risking life and limb to protect the other, becoming jealous at the drop of a pin, can't imagine being with anyone else. I'm no relationship expert but that sounds an awful lot like love."

My chest is squeezed into a ball. Everything Dui said and more is true of my feelings for Bai Hu. Why haven't I realized it by now? Somewhere along our pretense relationship rose genuine attraction and attachment. More than a boyfriend or a lover, he is my everything. I love him. This must be the feeling I couldn't before now describe; the longing for his touch, the ache I feel when we're apart, the desire to forever remain by his side. I love him, far more than I could ever imagine loving anyone. I've been telling myself our attachment is superficial due to the short amount of time we were together, but now I see that belief is itself, superficial. It doesn't matter how long we've been together. I want to spend the rest of my life with him.

"Please, Bai Hu. Wake up. Please don't leave me!"

Chapter 16: The Second Half

The scent of his cologne is despairingly nostalgic. The first time I buried my face in his chest, he called me a pervert. I would give anything to hear that again. I would trade anything for him to wake.

"Bao Lai, don't press too hard against his injuries."

"Sorry." Lifting off Hu's chest, my fingers trace along the curves of his handsome face, the image of which I never want to forget.

Tears resume shamelessly until a commotion rises outside.

Chapter 16 – 2

Horses neighing wildly, sharp grindings of metal against metal from unsheathing weapons, a call from the bandits for the intruders to halt, and then soon after, a pair of faces I didn't expect to see storm inside the tent. I jump up, unable to contain my shock.

"General Yue. Master Zhuang! What are you doing here?"

Master Zhuang Gu is a famed general from Ji, who served as a self-defense instructor at Tian Mao Yi after retiring from the military. I haven't seen him since Master Tai Hung passed.

"Now, there's a surprise. You've become quite a lady, Little Hung. Tai Hung would have been proud. And this young man must be Dui. I'm sorry about your mother, boy. She was a good woman."

Dui suddenly coughs up a lung, waving a hand to dismiss the master's sympathy; more so, to brush past the subject.

"I assume you came for a reason?" Dui snaps curtly.

The one to first respond is Yue, who holds out the silver mane helmet he's carried at his side since entering the tent. "This will wake Bai Hu."

"You can't be serious," Dui grumbles. "I heard all about his *demonic* form. Split consciousness aside, the idea that a helmet makes any difference is medically impossible!"

"There is much in life which medicine and science can't explain, young master."

"Certainly! But waking someone severely injured from a coma through a mere helmet is downright illogical!"

Master Zhuang shoots back another contention. While the two go about their disagreement between logic and fantastic probabilities, Yue approaches with the relic. The instant the silver hair drapes over Hu's shoulders, the atmosphere in the room changes. That oppressive, frightening air is wholly discernible. His eyelids pop wide open, revealing the golden, taunting glare of a vicious beast.

Dui and I stare at one another in disbelief; our two guests are unfazed. Hu attempts to move but injuries keep him. Instead, a loud, furious growl fills the small room.

"Bai Hu! You're awake! Let me fetch some food and water. Dui, could you please prepare a draught to ease his pain?"

"You *bitch*!" The Demon's bellow is followed by fangs gnashing furiously to subdue the pain paralyzing his body. "This was your fault! Every single time, you do this to me! Once this worthless body can move again, I'll rip out your throat!"

"That's enough!" Master Zhuang moves forward to divide me from the beast. He gives a packet of herbs to Dui and quickly instructs the young master to prepare the draught. "A man never blames another for his failure. I thought you were stronger than this."

"*I* didn't fail! *He* failed because of *her*! I should have killed you when I had the chance!"

The last sentence is directed at his wife. That seething resentment on the face I love so dear is eating me away. He isn't Bai Hu but he is also Bai Hu. Somewhere in his heart, Hu cares about me and in another part, he despises me. The man who calls himself my husband is a gentle soul. This man singlehandedly slew a horde of elite bandits like child's play and without the slightest bit of remorse. Hu didn't kill any of the men who tried to take his head, which was one of the reasons for his defeat. This begs the question why Hu didn't put on the helmet when he came for me. That would have guaranteed success. I look to General Yue whose head is shaking as though he already knows my question.

"Ever since he injured you, Bai Hu gave up his advantage." The stoic general states factually.

"He's an idiot! I really should have killed you when I had the chance."

"She heard you the first time, Bai Hu." Master Zhuang sighs agitatedly but also casually, as though he were speaking to his own son. "Can you pull your other self from the coma?"

"No can do, old man. He's practically dead thanks to that troublesome bitch. Weaklings can't suffer through trauma like I can. If you want him back, better take the gamble."

"What gamble?"

His sharp fangs snap at my encroaching hand.

"I can't stand your stupid face!" Pausing, he lets out a vindictive chuckle. "Ironic. If it weren't for you, I wouldn't exist and now, my one goal in life is to take yours. I'm longing to see the torture on your face when I rip your heart out."

The long tongue wraps around his lips. Bai Hu looks at me almost lustfully as would a starving hunter deprived of joy from taking the life an elusive would-be prey. I love him too much to feel frighten but remorse is overwhelming me to such an extent that I can barely face him.

"What are you talking about? How did I create you?"

"Ask the old man."

"Mind yourselves and ignore the foul-mouthed delinquent, boys. Leave the helmet on or Hu may not wake again. Come, Little Hung. I'll leave the choice to you."

Chapter 16 – 3

We've walked around the bandits' hilly base for the fifth time now and I still can't believe the master's revelation. I've asked the same questions again for the tenth time; the answers haven't changed. Master Zhuang scratches the nubs of his silver beard, shakes his head from time to time, and then continues to humor me.

"Bai Hu was that boy, my best friend from Tian Mao Yi?"

"Yes. The mischievous pair that gave Tai Hung white hair and everyone else, me included, constant headaches. You were both trouble, or maybe trouble followed you. Worse when you're together. Unlike his name suggests, he was hardly a tiger back then. We called him Little Cat, Xiao Mao. In your case, he was referred to as, 'Xiao Meow.'"

Chuckles come both nostalgic and painful. I remember how much he loathed the nickname. He was always mean to me and I often retaliated with my fist. We hated one another and that's why we were best friends. No wonder from the moment we met on that road and thereafter, our time together felt natural. I didn't hide my nature from him, because he already knew. My friend, whom I love with all my heart, is buried somewhere under another part of himself that despises me. I should have taken his advice and made the most of our precious time together.

"You're the one who removed Hu from temple."

"That's right. When it became apparent he wouldn't be able to overcome the trauma, I took him to Bi Xi and left him with my wife's relatives in hope that a quiet country life would make him forget the awful event."

"And he killed that man... because of me?"

"Yes. I never discovered why you were that assassin's target. Tai Hung covered up the incident and kept everyone hushed on the ordeal. As for Hu, I can't imagine an adult capable of his strength, and only at ten years old. Love is a curious thing."

"What do you mean? Hu didn't love me."

"Everyone realized it but you two." Master Zhuang smiles sadly. "We secretly called you *the old married couple*, because while you both bickered constantly, there weren't anything you wouldn't have done for the other. Tai Hung and I even made a bet. I said given time, you would grow out of your boyish nature and return Hu's worship. He didn't share my confidence. It seems I've won and the old codger isn't around to keep his end of the deal."

Master Zhuang glances over and sighs. He pats my back gently, the way Master Tai Hung used to when I was upset. I clamp down my lips to keep from bawling but it's becoming more difficult by the second. Through a stifled cry, I push another question. "Then what happened?"

"If you want to cry, then cry, my child. There's no shame in being human."

Once I nod emphatically, the master, with hands cupped behind his back, resumes.

"Any soldier will tell you that every life stolen is another burden on the soul, not another notch on a belt. There is never an age when taking a life becomes mundane. Hu broke down and I thought Bi Xi could restore his spirits, but by the age of seventeen, his nightmares returned and then he couldn't stand to carry the sin. I... did what I thought was best. I buried the violent, severe, vicious part of him created from self-degradation, fear, and hatred into that totem. In the process, it took another part of him. His true strength was robbed by the other half to guard and protect his weaker self. Hu will abstain from killing. The Demon has no reservation. I have tried to subdue him. It is not possible."

Hu mentioned a falling out from his lover, Feng You, at the age of seventeen because she found him too serious. I thought he was joking. The Demon was right. I did this to him. Each time we are together, another groove is carved into his soul because of me and the troubles I bring. He's been hiding the truth to protect me from guilt this entire time. I've been too proud to force down the wall between us and love him unconditionally as he had done for me. I've never admitted to Hu that I love him, the part of him which loves romance and sweet words, loves to tease his wife, and loves to take late naps in the afternoon on days off. To admit these affections now to the Demon would be an insult to the kind man who has always placed me first. I can't shake the overwhelming fear.

"Little Hung—Bao Lai. Have you made your decision?"

Master Zhuang snaps back my wandering mind. There remains an important judgment I have to make. The Demon didn't lie. The Bai Hu I've come to worship can't wake from his injuries. He gave up his stronger half to keep from harming me, and in the process, gave up the part of himself which could bear the pain. The only way to possibly recall him to this plane is to unite the two parts of Hu. He has to become whole again. The gamble, which the Demon mentioned, is for me to decide. Anything could happen once both sides merge; assuming, he could survive the ordeal. Bai Hu may be lost forever while the Demon reigns. The reverse could also be true. Or, neither is true and he will become another person altogether.

While I may lose my husband, the bigger price will still be paid by Hu. He doesn't wish to become the Demon and he doesn't wish to carry the burden from that original sin. He's sacrificed too much to keep that half from dominating. I could wait for him to wake on his own or I could force him to wake and let Hu suffer losing himself in the process. I know which he would want and I know which is best for me. Either method has a price and benefit—a gamble. The question then becomes whose wants do I put first?

Wait for Hu to wake (Continue to page 283)

Force him to wake by merging his two halves (Continue to page 285)

Chapter 16 – 4

"Hu has always put me first and I will return that favor. I can't permit him to suffer regret through the Demon's influences again."

"Are you certain, my child? It is your choice but do consider the consequences. The chance of Hu waking from his injuries isn't any better than Hu succeeding the Demon in this trial."

"Yes. I trust Hu will come back to me."

Master Zhuang compresses his lips to keep another opinion from luring me to distress. I know his judgment. I admit that he's right but the right answer for him and for me isn't the right answer for Bai Hu. He doesn't wish to lose himself. I'm helpless but that much I can still do for my beloved.

Once we return to the main party, Master Zhuang leaves a few instructions to Dui and then he and General Yue leave Mount Chou. The Demon howls a deathly cry when I remove the silver mane, signaling the end of his reign.

Days and weeks have gone by. Dui and I are constantly by Hu's side. Dui is on the verge of collapse from fatigue and I've nothing left but hope. The doctor won't leave despite my barrage of persuasion. Two lives depend on Bai Hu. He'd never consciously leave those in need, I know that. I desperately pray that he'll wake, cry for him to wake, and so far silence has been my only reward.

While his body has begun to heal, his soul is still somewhere distant. I will wait for him no matter how long it takes. And if by chance he has no choice but to leave me alone, I await the day we are reunited in the next plane.

The End.

Chapter 16 – 5

"Hu has always put me first and this time isn't any different. I am doing this for me but I also know he would want this for me, being the selfless man that he is. Hu has to come to terms with himself and I can't accept losing him."

"You're not selfish, Bao Lai. Hu would want to remain close and protect you in any way possible. Just remember, the Demon is also Hu. If his consciousness wins over the man you love, he isn't any less Bai Hu."

"I pray that won't happen but in case it does, will my Hu ever come back?"

"Difficult to say. I imagine he'll always be somewhere inside, same as the Demon. Even now, Hu isn't always aware of his counterpart's actions but the Demon is often aware of Hu's desires. According to General Yue, that's why he couldn't kill you. With Hu fully asleep, nothing is holding him back."

"Then why does he wish to merge?"

"Because his existence is based on that totem. The moment it comes off, especially now with Hu's critical condition, there's a great chance he'll fade away. He's made for war and therefore, cannot live a normal man's life. He's that helpless child Hu used to be who doesn't know what to do with himself after the bloodshed was over. However, no different from everything else, he fears death. This is a last resort and he's betting on victory."

"I... understand. No matter what happens, he is Bai Hu and I will learn to love every side of him."

"Well said. Have faith. As I've mentioned, love is a curious thing."

Master Zhuang's words are taken to heart. I have faith in Hu. This belligerent side of him was created from having protected me. If anything, he is the embodiment of that love and sacrifice. I won't cower before the Demon. For as long as it takes, I will ensure his happiness as he had for me.

Chapter 17: The Trouble with Dui

"It'll be okay." Dui squeezes my hand again. Tremulously, I squeeze back.

The draught that the doctor prepared for Master Zhuang was taken into the shabby shack and then we, including General Yue, were ordered away. It has been hours. The skies are dark and stars have come out in droves, lacing the heavens in a glowing net extended as far as the eyes can see. While the beauty above serves to tempt away anxieties, I feel no relief.

Night on Mount Chou is chilly. Dui and I are gathered in another quarter for shelter while General Yue, as unaffected as ever, stands out in the cold despite our urging. Dui fights to keep awake though fatigue and stress are lulling him to slumber. His shoulders are cramped, he's pale as a ghost, and worst of all, what I had thought were solely my tremors were also his. I fear without sleep, he won't be in any better condition than Hu.

"I'll wake you when Master Zhuang comes, I promise."

"That's my line, Dui. You haven't slept in days. Please, get some rest."

"I won't let you wait alone. Believe me, I know what you're going through. Having no one to hold your hand in a time like this is the worst thing in the world."

"Does the experience... have something to do... with... your mother?"

Broadened eyes look away, followed by a scoff. "Boy, for having been raised by monks, you sure lack manners."

"I'm sorry! I didn't mean to pry but either sleep or I'll continue to dredge up the past."

"That's some threat, *Mother*."

His purposeful sulking drives away my angst, forcing half a smile to my face. Maybe he's right. Having someone to hold my hand during troubled times is inexplicably comforting. I give up the notion of forcing him and instead, hope that silence and boredom will eventually drive him to sleep over my nagging.

For a long while, the crackling flame in the brazier is the only residual sound between us. I continue to silently pray for Bai Hu until the words inside my head become a chant. Through the darkness bearing down, Dui's sudden snickering forces me from desolation.

"You do that a lot, you know, mouth your thoughts."

"I-I do?"

"Yup. I didn't say anything before because I thought it was funny. Anyway, don't worry so much. After witnessing a medical impossibility today, I don't know what to believe. I was taught the human body. Apparently, human nature escapes me." He chuckles shortly. Dui stares out the window for a time in quiet contemplation, and then as though having formed a resolve, turns back. "I think she always knew my defect. That's why she made me promised to marry a nice girl by the time I turned thirty. As you can see, I've failed."

"She, as in your mother?"

"Yes, Mother. You badgered me then to find a nice girl, and fifteen years later, you still badger me now."

"Heh. I'm sorry."

"What? That's all? Don't you have a million more questions, curious one?"

"I know you're trying to distract me so I won't bawl like an infant but don't torture yourself. There are some things not meant to be shared. Thank you for being here with me. I can't ask for more."

"Secrets? Me? Nonsense, dove! I always willingly share every part of me to a pretty girl, as long as she'll bare all her parts to me." Dui nudges my arm teasingly, forcing another smile to my face. "It's the least I can do since you've graciously left my fingers unbroken after their... exploration."

The memory of his busy hands makes me quiver. I try to pull my away when his grip tightens.

"About that. Are you certain you don't like women?"

"Who said I don't like women? I like you just fine." Pausing, his eyes roll to the thatched roof. A flood of colors flows to his face. Despite my urging to stop tormenting himself through these revelations, Dui remains adamant. He resumes, much slower this time. "I've tried to feel... something, anything... for the fairer gender. As a physician, I've seen every part of a woman and simply the attraction isn't there. And before you say anything, no, I am not attracted to men. Women's bodies may not invoke anything in me but I find touching a man's body repellent, and unless it's medically necessary, I'd rather not even look."

"Then why grope your female patients? Is that to drive them away?"

"Ah, not really. Truth be told, I couldn't continue my first relationship due to lack of affections on my part. We weren't able to... *advance* our attachment. Since then, I've practiced getting used to women. What I mean is—"

"Your inappropriate touching is a method to force yourself to feel attraction for women and not a result of feeling attracted."

"Right."

"Well, Dui, patients aren't test subjects. I don't blame those girls one bit for slapping you silly."

"I know. Neither can I. It was supposed to be a onetime thing but I've done it so much that it's become compulsory. I can't help myself. Unlike a pervert, there isn't any satisfaction to be had. I'm not a real man. I don't know what I am."

"You're Dui—"

"Oh god, please not a useless pep talk! Let me guess, I should just accept myself as I am because it's *fine* to be different! Is that what you intend to say? Well, don't bother!"

"Hey! You're the one who kept talking after I've told you to shut it! Don't sass me, mister! I was surrounded by many handsome men at Tian Mao Yi but I didn't fall head over heels. Bai Hu was my best friend. Until recently, I hadn't realized that I was dependent on his companionship and our previous love-hate relationship was childish preconceived notions of love and attraction. Meaning, I've always loved Bai Hu, even when I didn't know it, and I didn't know it because I forced myself to believe I was one of the boys. So maybe I know a thing or two about being unnatural. First of all, stop living your life to please your mother. You're a successful, talented doctor who's genuinely kind-hearted. A rare breed! There's nothing to be ashamed of. Second of all, maybe you don't feel attraction for women because you haven't met the right one. Maybe you're still waiting for the female version of my Hu."

"That would be one very large woman."

"You know what I mean! Just because most men lose their minds at the sight of big breasts and wide hips, doesn't mean that is expected of every man. Most women would prefer a man who only has eyes for her."

"Yeah, well, let's say you're right. What if I never meet her, this woman who could make me lose my mind? Or, what if she's taken?"

"I'll help you find another."

"Oh, please! I've traveled the five lands, from villages in the mountains to those by the sea. I've crossed the ocean for a time to study from foreign masters and even their exotic women couldn't provoke anything in me. If there is one such woman made for me and she's been claimed, it would take a million years to find another."

"Then... why do you need anyone at all?"

"Come again?" The hard glare is accompanied by a frown. This time, he tries to pull away but I hold on steadfast.

"Why do you need anyone? You're worrying over marriage because of your mother. If you can start living for yourself instead and if you are content with remaining alone, then why bother with marriage at all?"

"Easy for you to say. You already have someone. You just wouldn't understand."

"Then make me understand."

Our standoff from many nights ago resumes. Dui is important to me. I don't want him to shoulder his pains alone; the same way he's never let me shouldered anything alone.

"I... I can't be selfish. My life is not only mine to live."

"How's that?"

"You are really nosy, dove."

"And that actually surprises you?"

He looks away and lets out a conceding sigh. "Fine. I've already embarrassed myself. What's the harm?"

The physician shuffles, smoothing his wrinkled shirt little by little as though to buy time or gather his thoughts. After a long while, Dui settles into position.

"My family was poor—poorest in the poorest neighborhood. My mother alone couldn't feed both my brother and me. He was older and stronger. Yu Qi was sent away to an uncle somewhere east to work his land and earn daily meals. He even managed to save a few coins to send back to Mother whereas most boys who came from nothing would have spent it on themselves. That's the kind of son he was. Anyway, a great flood came soon after and decimated the area. We never heard from my uncle, his family, or Yu Qi again. They were presumed dead. I am the only child left in our bloodline. It was my duty to care for my mother after the sacrifice she'd made to keep me, a sacrifice she never forgave herself for making. I studied medicine because she told me to, because my brother wanted to become an apothecary. He was a good son. He would have made her proud. I'm supposed to continue our line but how am I to do that unless I marry a woman I don't care to come home to?"

"But, don't you think it's time to start living for yourself? I've never had a mother. I can't imagine things from your point of view. Master Tai Hung had plans for me too, of which I'd strived to accomplish the opposite. Despite my insolence, the master cared about my happiness first and foremost. I'm sure your mother felt the same."

"Shows what you know. My mother wasn't exactly the coddling type like your master. She couldn't have been with the life she had. It was her way or a switch to the backside. I hardly ever saw her smiled. After Yu Qi left, half of her was gone. I just... wanted to make her happy, the way my brother did when he was alive."

"Where is she now?"

"With Yu Qi. Her heart was weak. She had bouts of fatigue after which she became bedridden for weeks. Master Tai Hung pushed me to leave Pa Xu to find a cure with the promise that he'd watched over her in my stead. Earlier, when Master Zhuang offered his condolences, well... I managed to find a method to subdue her illness. Years of hardship took its toll, which couldn't be undone, but I could have eased her pain and let her lived to a ripe old age. As with everything else, I'm a failure. My revelation came too late. In the end, I couldn't do anything but watched her die. That was her last wish, for me to find a wife."

Chapter 17: The Trouble with Dui

Under glistening eyes, Dui clamps down his jaw. The memories are too much to bear and they haven't become easier with time. When Master Tai Hung was bedridden, I was convinced somewhere in his notes was a potion for immortality. To me, he could do anything. He was my idol. I often sat in his library screaming to myself that he kept secrets from me, that if I could find the instructions, I would make him live forever so I could torment him. In those days, I should have just remained by his side as long as I could. Maybe my regret is also Dui's.

"Ah, well, enough of my stupid problems!"

"They're not stupid, Dui. You are a good son. I bet your mother wanted a wife for you so that someone could continue to care for her beloved son when she couldn't."

"If you say so. In that justification, I don't need a wife. I have you. You've been nagging in my ears since the day we've met."

"I also combed your hair and made you bathed at least thrice a week. I am your mother."

He frowns at my grin and then leans back against the wall.

"That you are."

Fatigue, stress, and now suppressed anguish have finally dominated his will. With our hands still joined, Dui concedes to slumber. I continue to pray, especially to Master Tai Hung for Hu's recovery, for Dui to find his path, and for me to find the ability to support both my friend and my beloved.

Somewhere in my somnambular mumbling, I fall asleep until light peaks in through the window to reveal a new day.

Chapter 18: Blood to Blood

Master Zhuang's effort to reunite both parts of Bai Hu was a success; that is to say, he survived. I'd never felt so relieved in my life only to soon after, suffered a terrible blow to the heart. My Hu, the goofy carefree man who called me, 'Wife,' is buried somewhere underneath the Demon who seeks my death. Even now, the vicious smile of victory on his twisted face won't leave my mind. He remembers me and our time together; the novelty of which won't amend his hated opinion of a woman who has put his life in danger countless times and caused him endless sorrow since two decades ago.

Regardless of Master Zhuang's confidence that the Hu I've come to love will eventually emerge from behind the Demon, I knew his words were only for encouragement and nothing more. Perhaps, that was the reason Master Zhuang decided to stay on Mount Chou to continue Hu's medical treatments while Dui and I were forced to return with General Yue to the capital. My presence served to hinder his recuperation. The best thing I could do for Hu at the time was to stay away. Besides, Dui and I are the new court medics. With conflict on the horizon, it becomes evident that war waits for no one.

Through Wen Meng's support and Han Bei's authority, Minister San An was able to negotiate an interim retreat with Bei Ling's generals. However, soon after the caravan returned to Nan Rong's capital, an attempt on Lord Han Bei's life was made, resulting in current predicaments.

"I can assure you, we've taken measures to increase security and the assassin has been promptly dealt with."

"The timing was certainly perfect. An assassin's ploy brought me to Nan Rong, another assassin directed my attention to Bei Ling, and upon my return, yet another assassin waits to take my life. Tell me, Minister, how many more assassins with impeccable timing should I expect until your intent is made?"

San An's usual perfect composure nearly falters from the accusation. Somehow, he manages to find another leeway to move conversations forward. Dui and I tarry a ways behind. I'm not sure why we were invited on this stroll. Dui thinks Han Bei is kinder when I'm near. I fear to think the man he is without that *kindness.*

"This is all your fault, Mother." Dui leans over and whispers in his usual annoyed manner. "I could be watching herbs dry instead of listening to this pathetic conversation."

"How is it pathetic?"

"Seriously? The Minister is clearly begging for Ning's alliance and the emissary is toying with him."

"San An would never kowtow to anyone. Is Ning's alliance that crucial?"

"Apparently so. I bet Lord Han Bei will agree as long as he gets something from you."

Upon Dui's facetious remark, Han Bei abruptly swings about with one of his own. "The Doctor is more observant than I thought."

He and the Minister are far enough away that the features on their faces are obscured. Yet, the emissary managed to hear Dui's low whisper which I barely caught. Han Bei's attention then directs toward me as a mean to beckon for my company. I advance with Dui following suit.

"Minister, I couldn't care less if your assassin thought to take my life or pushed me to ally with Nan Rong. One fact remains. I have not left because of Bao Lai."

"The assassin was an agent from Bei Ling, Lord Han Bei." San An reasserts politely. "I'm afraid the man who could send Bao Lai to be your handmaiden is currently recovering at Mount Chou—"

"If I were inclined, I would seize her by force." Han Bei replies curtly. "There is a lie you've been insisting, Minister, and a truth I've hidden. If Bao Lai can tell me your lie, I will tell her a truth."

His brash challenge forces all eyes on me and I... am drawing a blank. By the creases on San An's brows, I have to assume his secret must be one I also currently hold; one he would never divulge under any circumstance.

"Um... Lord Han Bei, I don't—"

"Before lying to me, Bao Lai, consider this consequence: for your sake, I may aid Nan Rong given the truth and through your lie, Ning will never ally with the South."

He's not giving me a choice. I turn to the Minister who's looked away in concession. With nothing else to do, I admit His Highness's disappearance.

Shortly after, Dui and San An are sent away, while I continue the stroll with Han Bei in order to receive a truth. However, that too came with another price. I've spent the past hour explaining the circumstances that led me to the capital. I never realized how boring my life was before An. For whatever reason, the emissary finds my stories interesting.

"Do you like it here, Bao Lai, working under that shrewd physician and conniving minister? Haven't you ever wanted more?"

"Dui is a good man and the Minister has been nothing but kind to me. Please don't speak ill of them. I'm not entirely sure what you mean by wanting more, Lord Han Bei. I have Bai Hu. That is enough to make me happy."

"Except, you're not happy. As I've said before, I do not approve of your relationship."

Chapter 18: Blood to Blood

"With all due respect, I don't need your permission. Why does it bother you that I love Bai Hu?"

"Bothered is a strong word. Concerned is more fitting. I've come to see you as perhaps... a younger sister. In another lifetime, that might have been true."

"Do I remind you of someone?"

"More than you can ever imagine." He glances down shortly, a little troubled, before a soft smile curls over the perfectly curved lips. "That truth I still owe you: Tian Ji Zhong Shi Yan. It's a rare gift from an old bloodline which originated from Bei Ling, usually passed down to the son. You've proven it's possible for a daughter to inherit that trait too; except, you don't seem to have knowledge of the skill or how to control it."

"Does that mean I'm from Bei Ling?"

Han Bei glances down again. The troubles in his eyes deepen. His lips purse and a quiet sigh escapes. "Are you certain this is the life you want, Bao Lai?"

"Would you answer differently if I say no?"

"Yes, I will tell you a different truth if you say no. However, once I do, your life in Nan Rong cannot continue. You must return to Ning with me."

"Aren't you being a little dramatic?"

Soft chuckles become a laugh. Han Bei suddenly sweeps me into an embrace and then just as quickly, releases his hold. He shuffles back as though it were a mistake.

"I... am losing myself to those eyes," the emissary mutters. "Tell me you're happy here, Bao Lai, and I won't ask again."

This man is becoming more confusing by the minute. I want his secrets, but if that means leaving Nan Rong and never seeing Hu again, the answer is clear. I confide my happiness to Han Bei, which brings to him both pain and comfort.

"Then, it reasons that your bloodline ties to Bei Ling." He resumes the path with both hands cupped behind his back. "As the story goes, Tian Ji Zhong Shi Yan was a gift from the gods bestowed upon the great warrior, Fa Zhen, who established the first kingdom of Song after slaying the demons who terrorized the area. Song, of course, is current day Bei Ling."

"Demons are real?"

"That would depend on your perception of real. More or less, the stories served to exaggerate Fa Zhen's accomplishments and instill his authority over Song. The demons mentioned are thought to have been a group of barbarians who lived and died through war and chaos. Their skills paralleled the God of War; unmatched by other mortals. That is, until most of their lines were slain. I imagine a handful might have escaped Fa Zhen's massacre and merged with other societies. For a long time, the demons' strength was thought to have vanished. Like you, his existence mitigates that belief."

"His existence... Bai Hu?"

"Yes. I've heard tales of a silver-haired demon who could best a thousand men at once. His presence on the battlefield signaled the end. Whether that is true or not, Bai Hu has certainly earned a reputation for being a brute. I wonder, perhaps his docile nature comes naturally in your company. A demon and a demon slayer; possibly in your case, a demon tamer."

"What are you saying? My ancestors... slew Hu's ancestors?"

"Annihilated is a closer term. As I've said, I do not approve of your relationship. The blood in your veins is not compatible with Bai Hu's. What I had thought were mere fairy tales and political propaganda turned out far from baseless. Your gift is a mean to destroy him."

"But that's just coincidence and assumption! Gods and demons aside, I love Hu! Our blood has nothing to do with it!"

"Convincing me won't change anything. I simply wished to share this truth with you, to spare you further pain. The man who was injured by those bandits was Bai Hu. The Demon was nowhere in sight. Would he have spared you had his real self surfaced, or would you have had to rely on Tian Ji Zhong Shi Yan to subdue the beast, as had Fa Zhen?"

Lord Han Bei leaves me with those confusing words before retreating inside the palace. I can hardly breathe let alone move from the spot.

My blood seeks to snuff out Hu's bloodline. That thought alone is too frightening to consider. I may not have raised a weapon against Bai Hu but that doesn't change how he's suffered because of me. He nearly died saving me. And maybe, he did. Bai Hu is no more. The Demon has taken over and will seek vengeance against me while I seek to stop him. What if both Lord Han Bei and Kai were right? I have to stop being selfish and give up Bai Hu. At least, let him keep living after I've already stolen his life.

Around, the skies have turned dark. By the time I notice my own shadow, I'm standing in twilight. The cycle is repeating. Nearly twenty years ago, after Master Zhuang took Bai Hu to Bi Xi, I was left waiting for him on that road near Pa Xu, from dawn until dusk. Blood doesn't matter. What's in my heart does. I can't imagine being without him another twenty years nor will I ever leave him to shoulder another burden alone.

Chapter 19: the Demon Slayer

By some grace, Lord Han Bei left to prepare a sum of reinforcements from Ning. For that which has benefited Nan Rong, San An coined me a *dangerous woman.* The Minister began distancing himself more than usual. I don't mind since we have had very little to say to one another. Sometimes, I do wonder if the path not taken would have been best, for Hu and for me. I could have accepted San An's proposal, but in the end, I can't imagine loving anyone but Hu. I pray that this conflict will be resolved soon, so that I can leave everything behind and return to Mount Chou.

In the mean time, Dui and I have spent our busy days in the barracks examining soldiers, their living conditions, and the measures needed to mitigate future injuries. Several men were unaware of personal fractures and broken bones. With repetitive blows to the same area during training, the small injuries will become something worse. Others were ill and spreading their contagions. Dui set apart a quarantine and recovery area in the barracks to nurse the weary, sick, and broken soldiers back to health, earning their reverence along the way.

Sometimes, I hear the soldiers' whispered conversations and learn the extent of Dui's impact on their lives. Many who joined the military didn't have better options. Many more don't have family. For the first time in their lives, the men feel that someone is looking out for their welfare. That alone brought a few teary eyes. Dui is more than a healer of the body. Unbeknownst to him, his gentle hands can also heal the spirit and the heart. Someday, I hope the right pair of gentle hands will heal Dui and provide the felicity which he's been searching.

"Can you bring in a new crate of bandages?"

I was gathering the dirty bowls of medicine when Dui called over his shoulder. He's come to acknowledge my superior brute strength and has been requesting heavy labor jobs which he would have before tried to do himself. It might hurt his pride but it certainly brings a smile to my face.

"You got it, Boss!"

I rush from the quarantine area toward the supply storage on the west end of the barracks. The instant I step outside with the large crate, a looming shadow encroaches, and then a silver flicker swings down from above. With my hands preoccupied and not enough time to move away, I close my eyes and prepare for the impact, though none comes.

"Hmm."

His doubting sigh makes one eye prop open. I fully upturn my head to see Wen Meng with a hand on his chin. He's so tall; his shrouding shadow is blocking sunlight from casting over me. Even so, he's seems less intimidating than I remember from our first encounter.

Chapter 19: the Demon Slayer

Actually, there's a hint of unassuming kindness on the rough face. That doesn't mean I care to speak to this brute who stopped me from saving Bai Hu. His men injured my beloved. No matter the reason, I won't ever let the transgression pass.

"Excuse me," I spit out a soft grumble and start to traverse around the giant. A large palm brusquely ceases my right arm. I nearly topple. "Take your hand off me or I'll drop this crate on your foot!"

"Are you strong or weak? You injured my men without beading a sweat and then just now, couldn't dodge a simple sword swing." The withdrawn hand proceeds to stroke his chin. "I could have killed you."

"Well *thank you so much* for not killing me in cold blood! Do you expect my gratitude?"

He returns my curtness with a dubious stare. "Are you really a woman? Your attitude lacks femininity."

"*My* attitude?! You swung a sword at my head and put your dirty hand on me! Should I be complacent?"

"My hands aren't dirty."

"Yes, that makes it *fine* then!"

"Wait."

Once more, he tugs back my arm, the force of which loosens my footing. I fall against his broad body, dropping the heavy crate on his foot by mistake. Common courtesy calls for an apology, and I almost did, before realizing that this may be the only opportunity to exact whatever little vengeance I can for Bai Hu. Disappointedly, he lifts the heavy crate off with one hand as though it were a pebble.

"What did I say about touching me?!"

"Again, my hands are clean. Demon Slayer, I want to test your skills. Let me reclaim my men's honor. At worst, take what is left of mine so that I may face the others and tell them we've faltered to a true warrior."

"I don't want anything to do with you."

"After you've flung yourself at me? That is hard to believe."

"You're the idiot who pulled me!"

"And yet, you've not made any effort to separate. Desire conveyed through inaction resounds louder than false belligerence. If you can best me in battle, I will concede and take you as my wife. Our strong bloodlines will accomplish much for the world."

Of all the revolting things to say with a straight face! I can't find the words to express disgust. Instead, my foot rams against his shinbone. The giant falls back. Quickly, I snatch up the crate and run to the quarantine tent.

Chapter 19 – 2

Sometime after dinner, while reviewing the list of Dui's inventory, a gentle knock lands against the door. Believing it's Dui, I open without question, turning pallid at the sight of the giant whose head is touching the arch of the doorway. By the time I thought to slam the door close, his large hand is forcing the wooden panel wider.

"You have the wrong room."

"Not at all. I came as you expected."

The candor conveyed through forthcoming, earnest eyes makes me uneasy. I fall back from confusion while he advances in suit. His stoic posture reminds me of General Yue, and for that, I suddenly find him intimidating.

"I-I'm sorry, when did I ask you to come?"

"Earlier today when you accepted my challenge and bested me; a deed no other has accomplished. Hence, I have come to fulfill my promise. I am a man of my word."

Wen Meng's large palm extends toward my face. I jump aside, nearly falling on my behind. "Are you insane?! I didn't accept anything!"

"Then why did you kick me?"

"Because you didn't keep your filthy hands to yourself!"

"I can assure you they were clean."

What is wrong with this man? I would say that was pure sarcasm except his tone lacks any notion of deception. Stranger still, that plain, simple disposition belongs to this tall, burly, fierce figure. He seems a very large child, a faint reminder of the old Bai Hu. For that, I'm not able to hold onto my vindictive grudge and all the more reason my chest is burning.

"L-Look, I am sorry I kicked you out of spite. I never intended to fight you. What happened on Mount Chou was a fluke. It won't happen again. I can't best you in battle. I forfeit. Please excuse me. I have records to review."

"You didn't intend to fight me? Are you saying that you defeated me without a single thought?"

"What?"

"Action without thought. A pure reaction. This is your secret, Demon Slayer? You must be even stronger than I imagined. Yes, I understand now. Your ability to move flawlessly in battle, the recent advances you've made to gain my attention, and the method you've used to bring me to your bedchamber; all without thought, as time and destiny certainly wields mankind without pause. There is no denying fate. I have fallen to your whim. Greater than domination of the body, you have subjugated my will. Our union must be."

"Have you listened to a word I've said?! Our *union* will never happen!"

"You are a woman past your prime and without a husband. Doesn't it reason that you should accept the only offer you'll ever have?"

"Excuse me?! *Who the hell taught you*—?!"

"There you are, love."

Dui's voice floats coolly past the threshold. I cease my shaking fists just as Wen Meng turns to the wily physician who strolls into the room and then leisurely extends an arm across my shoulders.

"Would you mind leaving, sir?" He addresses the bandit chief casually. "I've been so busy that my lover's felt a bit lonely. I intend to satisfy her needs this night. Unless you wish to observe *our* union, kindly be on your way."

"I thought the weak-willed general was your lover."

Wen Meng directs the remark to me and it's becoming more difficult to keep my hands steady. No one is permitted to insult Bai Hu except me!

"Hu is not—!"

"Her lover anymore," Dui cuts off my defense with a quick lie. "I am. No brute is a match for a man with gentle hands. I have the brains and she has the brawns. Strength without intelligence serves no purpose. For the sake of this world, *our union* is fated."

"Were your claims true, she wouldn't look so uncomfortable in your arms."

"She's fidgeting. Such is the reaction of a shy woman wanting. Do you mind?"

Wen Meng, still adamant, refuses to budge. Dui shrugs. Without hesitation, and to my horror, both arms strap around my waist and pull our bodies tightly together. His lips cover mine while those *gentle* hands make their ways up and down my back before descending downward, cupping my lower cheeks in their fondling grasps. I can't push him off without encouraging Wen Meng's insane proposed conquest. As a result, I follow Dui's example and lace both arms around his neck.

For a long while, all is silent except for Dui's soft sighs escaping from his venturing lips. I hold my breath until air is in short supply. My hands move off Dui. However, immediately upon pushing against his shoulders, thin arms pull us back together and then a warm tongue pushes at my lips begging for entry. My next instinct is to step on his toes.

"Ow! What was that for?" Dui flies off, clutching at his foot.

Chapter 19: the Demon Slayer

I thought we were alone but once our bodies part, Wen Meng is still leering from the stoic pose. On impulse, I grab Dui's waist and lean my head against his chest.

"I'm sorry, honey! It's just so embarrassing having someone watch! Could you make him leave?"

"What can I really do about perverts, dove?"

Traveling fingers cup my backside again. My body turns rigid from the continuous stroking. Dui wears a contented smile. Wen Meng doesn't appear affected by our lewd display.

"I'm not a pervert." The giant stares purposefully into my eyes. "Our business isn't over. I will not leave until there is agreement."

"I refuse to take part in your breeding program!"

"That doesn't concern me anymore. If I can best your lover, then I shall have you, but your lover is a healer and I won't raise my hand against a man who saves lives. I want to challenge *you*, Demon Slayer. Let's see whose blood is superior."

"Eh... Are you saying you're a descendant from the Demon bloodline?"

"A very diluted bloodline, but yes. My people claimed Fa Zhen was a coward who kidnapped their women and children and forced the men to surrender. Massacred almost everyone as a result. A few escaped

313

through help from sympathizers while others without family ran south. I saw your capabilities. A person of that talent could conquer through the sword alone. Let me know the truth."

"Why? Whether Fa Zhen was brave or cowardly, what rights did he have to exterminate your tribes? Knowing where it came from, I'm not particularly proud of my blood."

"Not even when the counter stories have my people killing every other group around the Northern Territories, including Fa Zhen's?"

"I... don't understand what a battle between us will prove. Who will ever really know the truth? Besides, I can't use Tian Ji Zhong Shi Yan on a whim. At Mount Chou was the first time that ever happened."

"I see. Because your lover was in danger, the dormant skill surfaced."

His sharp eyes immediately pierce Dui. I jump in front of the physician lest Wen Meng follows through with the dangerous idea. When his heavy arm extends, my eyes close, prepared for the impact, until a large palm lands on my head and gently musses my hair, the way Hu used to do. A smile appears on the gentle giant.

"You're very strange, defending a comrade when your head barely reaches his shoulders. You should learn your place. Haven't anyone taught you that a woman should be protected by a man, not the other way around?"

"What the f—!"

One of Dui's hands wraps around my mouth, the other wraps around my waist, before pulling hard against his chest to stop my outburst. With muffled cursed words resounding in the room, my arms flail violently. Same as before, Wen Meng remains unaffected.

"Calm down!" Dui whispers discreetly. "He's not purposefully insulting you!"

Dui's right. Wen Meng is a very simple-minded man but acknowledging that doesn't dampen my irritation. My pointless tantrum ceases and then Dui lets me go.

"I won't fight you! Leave me alone!"

"I won't leave you alone until we fight," the bandit throws right back.

"I can't summon Tian Ji Zhong Shi Yan!"

"I know. But I can."

What a confident thing to say! He smiles at my wide-eyed dubious stare.

"You're not laying one finger on Dui."

"That is a fact. I won't. Tomorrow at dawn break; in the barracks. Come to me then or I shall go to you."

He treads back toward the door, ducking his head under the archway upon exiting. For someone so large, his footsteps are as light as a cat's and his movements, as swift as a dancer's.

"That was... confusing. Thanks for saving me, Dui, even if you did go a little overboard."

"I wanted to test something out!" He chuckles in a stupid manner, running a hand behind his head, while his face bursts into flames. Unlike Wen Meng, he's far from sincerity.

"I still think you're a perv."

"Whatever. *How do* you manage to win every man's favor?"

"By being belligerent."

Smirking, Dui moves to the bed and leisurely settles atop. "I didn't come to thwart your proposed midnight tryst, by the way. San An wanted me to relay a message. In two weeks, Ning's reinforcements are slated to arrive. At that time, you and I should be ready to march."

"I thought Bei Ling retreated."

"Scouts on Mount Chou sent notice. There are movements to the north. It figures. The entire ordeal seemed too easy. I knew this would escalate to full warfare."

"Sounds as though you're speaking from experience."

"In a way. I've traveled far during my studies. War is a common theme everywhere and peace is the result of battered nations unable to wage war. The rest is poetic idolatry."

"Well, aren't you an optimist!"

"I try my best." He lazes onto the bed, stretching his long arms in the air. "So, what are you going to do?"

"What do you mean?"

Dui scoots over to make room for me to sit on the bed. Troubled eyes cast upward toward the canopy. "San An summoned me to replace Master Yu. I have an obligation. You don't."

"Dui, I'm not leaving."

"You joined because of Hu—"

"And I'm staying because of you. You'd never let me face danger alone and I want to be here for you."

"People with someone to live for shouldn't be reckless."

"Same to you. Everyone in this palace depends on you, Dui."

"That makes me *so* happy."

Following the lethargic sarcasm, Dui turns his back to me. The awkward events of the day have stiffened my shoulders. I lie down with my back to him. Dui shuffles.

"You're awfully friendly. I may not be attracted to women but my traveling hands won't discriminate."

"Not even when the woman is your mother?"

The air grows tepid from his seething displeasure. "Hey Dui, do you plan to stay here forever?"

"Assuming I survive this conflict? Maybe until I'm forty. At some point, I'd like to return to Pa Xu and find a few apprentices. No matter how many cures are found, more diseases and illnesses will surface. Someone needs to keep up with the times."

"You'd make a great teacher. Tian Mao Yi would definitely take you in and there's plenty of room for students."

"No, thank you. The last time I was there, Tai Hung's pup tormented me. That place is nothing but bad memories."

"She's really sorry! What can the pup do to make things up to you?"

Yawning, he reaches up a hand to scratch his messy hair and mumbles sleepily. "Ask me again when this conflict is over and if there's still a Nan Rong."

Chapter 19: the Demon Slayer

The impact of those words suddenly bears down. With multitudes of strong men in our midst, coupled with Bei Ling's previous retreat, I never imagined the outcome of this conflict would be against Nan Rong. The truth about war is unpredictability. Despite my unwillingness to take part in Wen Meng's test, I hope his bold claims will have merit. To preserve the Southland, Fa Zhen's gift may yet redeem its previous destroyer role and come to play savior.

Chapter 20: Dui, the Defender

A few weeks later, Bei Ling sent a small group to Mount Chou in order to distract Nan Rong from their larger force, which was sent to Feng Jia and then to Lan Yue Pass. Wen Meng and his bandits easily routed the diversion and the first regiment, led by Zhen Yue, was sent to push back Bei Ling's larger force. Accompanying the first regiment is Qing Hai, Dui, and me.

For the past week, both sides have been at stalemate. General Yue is a force to be reckoned with but Bei Ling has the advantage in terrain. We're fighting an uphill battle; worse, our number is half of Bei Ling's. Reinforcements won't arrive for another week. By then, I fear the victor at Lan Yue will have already been decided.

Dui's had little sleep since the march started. With the count of those injured and dying increasing daily, the physician hasn't had a moment to breathe. I do my best to help, though all efforts seem futile at this rate. There is only one method to keep our men from harm and that is to rid of the threat.

"Don't even think about it."

Dui shoots a hard glare over when he sees my hand clenched tightly around the charm Wen Meng presented during the course of our duel. An old relic his people managed to pry off one of Fa Zhen's descendants who was also gifted with Tian Ji Zhong Shi Yan. Similar to Hu's silver mane, it can induce my gift to surface.

Nothing grand comes without a price. Those of the Demon bloodline often lost themselves during battle, slaying friends and foes alike, and thus killed themselves from grief in the aftermath. Those like me who carry the Demon Slayer blood trade a short momentary advantage with our lives. That is, each time the skill surfaces, the impact to our heart is unpredictable. I felt my heart on the verge of exploding the last time. Who can say what may happen when I next use my talent? Still, my one life compared to the hundreds suffering around me is inconsequential. Despite his objection, I know the physician would do no less in my shoes.

"I thought you don't believe in this whole bloodline nonsense, Dui."

"I don't. I attribute your skill to an extreme adrenaline rush. There have been various recorded cases of hysterical strength. Infants lifting horse carts to save their parents, and parents lifting boulders to save their children. The cost is usually extensive damages to nerves, tissues, organs—everything. Doesn't that sound familiar?"

"I've used the skill before and I haven't suffered any drawbacks."

"Yes, dove, it's called luck. The thing about luck is best not to chance it."

"What about this relic?"

"Psychological suggestions, I assume. Whatever you may believe, I don't want to see you injured or worse. Understand?"

"You're not the boss of me."

"Actually, I am your boss. And recently, your teacher and caretaker."

"Now who sounds like whose mother?"

"How would you know, Pup? You've never had one."

Frowning, my fist slams against his slender arm. Dui moves away, hissing from pain, while rubbing the point of contact.

"Sssss! Ow! Why are you so mean, Mother?"

"What was it you said? It was your mother's way or a switch to the backside? Did you forget?"

"That wasn't my backside!"

"Then turn around!"

"Ah-hem." Yue enters the tent, as agitated as his stoned face would allow. Dui and I freeze in place, embarrassed for our cheery banter in the midst of trouble. The General approaches me, giving Dui no regards.

"I need your help," he begins succinctly.

Chapter 20: Dui, the Defender

"Sure, what is it?"

"Qing Hai's scouting unit was sent out four days ago. We've lost contact. I need you to find him."

"Qing Hai's missing?"

"Wait just a minute!" Dui's immediately on his feet with both hands clamped around my left arm. "Isn't that a task for your recon team? I need her here!"

"Dui, please. I'm worried about Qing Hai too."

"So... what? Use your skill to run past Bei Ling, have your heart explode by the time you reach the end of their lines, and then keel over?"

"But—"

"Enough." His usual flat voice, when slightly raised, thunders like a raging storm. Yue's patience is dwindling. In one swift movement, a sheathed dagger lifts off his side and lands in my hand. "You're the least conspicuous person we have. Take this and make your way north of Feng Jia's capital, to Bu Xin. If Qing Hai is still alive, he'll be there. Retrieve his report and then return immediately."

"Where in Bu Xin?"

Yue shrugs, leaving the room posthaste after passing these vague instructions. I start after him just as Dui, believing I would leave for Bu Xin, tugs back my arm.

"Bao Lai. You're not going!"

323

"What about Qing Hai?"

"There are other *inconspicuous* people the General could send."

"And you could have sent Lord Han Bei to save me at Mount Chou, so why did you go alone? Dui, he's my friend too. I want to find him."

"Uh-huh. That sounds great, Mother. Which way is Feng Jia's capital?" His arms folded, Dui's sulking stare carries pure condescension. Damn him for knowing me so well!

"Um..." I look around and ultimately decide to point right because it's better to chance an answer than to admit being wrong.

"He's in Ye?"

"I... Shut up and draw me a map!"

"I'd give you a map but it still won't do you any good. Either we go together or you're staying."

"What about your patients?"

"That's on your conscience, love."

Another standoff. Is this how we must conduct the entire course of our friendship? He doesn't play fair and I can never win against him. I, on the other hand, don't know when to quit. Once I return a false concession, our row ends.

Chapter 20: Dui, the Defender

We had little to say to one another for the rest of the night and come sunrise, with General Yue's directions, I'm well on my way to Bu Xin.

Chapter 20 – 2

Nan Rong is bordered east by Ning, north by Bei Ling, west by Ye and northwest by Feng Jia. Of the five countries, Feng Jia is the smallest with little resources to fuel a decent army. For that reason, the nation is subservient to more powerful neighbors, leaving the territory in disarray and its people poor.

From Lan Yue Pass to the capital of Quan Ming is nearly a day's trek. I was told to take the Mei Hua Road, which travelers and merchants often used, in order to avoid detection. As my face is that of a teenage girl and not an adult woman, I was able to pass through border gates with the excuse of going to visit my mother.

The instant I step into the capital is the same moment I understand why Feng Jia wasted no time in kowtowing to Bei Ling. There must be slums in Nan Rong better off than this city. Every other person is a beggar. The ones who aren't, hardly have enough to share. Men in Bei Ling armors march around town to exert their authority; pushing feeble citizens aside, taking whatever they please, and after filling their fat bellies, throw away scraps to find amusement in the beggars' scramble. It makes me sick to my stomach but interfering won't solve anything. I have to find Qing Hai so that Nan Rong may end Bei Ling's influence.

With conscience writhing, I move hastily away from the distasteful scene, and then soon after, find myself in front of a large, dilapidated palace, dulled by time and lack of upkeep. The amount of Bei Ling guards stationed on the perimeters outnumbers Feng Jia's men. At this rate, Feng Jia might as well become part of Bei Ling.

"*Boo!*"

"Ahh!" A hand slams over my mouth as the small scream escapes. I nearly keel over from all my nerves firing at once.

"What a cute reaction. You *can* be feminine!"

"D-Dui?! What the hell are you doing here?!"

"So much for femininity." He scoffs. "Lower your voice, dove. Screaming in public is hardly inconspicuous. Anyway, I've been following you the entire day. How did you not notice?"

"You were asleep when I left!"

"Yes, I knew you were perverted. Sneaking into my tent in the middle of the night. Did you see anything good?"

"Just a dirty look on your face from a dirty dream. Are you sure you're not attracted to women?"

"Maybe just to a certain woman."

"What?"

His mumble was quick and nearly inaudible. If I hadn't seen his mouth moved, would have never caught the supposed confession. Even then, I couldn't have heard what I thought I heard, but when I attempt to prod, his fingers pinch my nose.

"As if I would ever believe you'd give up that easily, dove. I took an early nap during dinner and then put on a good show for the *voyeur*."

"What about your patients?"

"Lucky you. I knew we'd be short-handed so I asked San An to send another physician long before the march. Master Yu arrived yesterday morning to take over most of my duties."

"And you didn't tell me?"

"You're not the boss of me," he replies sarcastically, quoting my previous tone. Dui moves away from the shabby palace, pulling my wrist along. "You're going the wrong way. The northern gate is in this direction."

"Wait, you're not coming Dui."

"A little late for protests, don't you think?"

"Hey! This is hardly a joke. There are people depending on you."

"Others are always dependent on me, dove. That won't change. For once, I want to be useful to those important to me."

"What makes you think you haven't been useful? You've helped me more times than I can count!"

"Conceited much? I meant Qing Hai. He's my friend too."

"Oh—well, yeah—but—"

"You'll need a better argument than that, dove."

"Are you... in love with Qing Hai?"

His messy hair shoots up on ends. Dui whips around. The sunken frown is accompanied by deadly predatory eyes. I never knew he could look so scary.

"I'm kidding!" My hands fly up defensively.

"Say that again, love, and there will be a healthy dose of senna in your dinner."

"You wouldn't!"

"Try me. I'm a doctor. Everything I do is medically necessary."

"That's a bunch of—"

"Would be ironic if you said 'crap.' It's almost dinnertime and I do have senna in my emergency pack."

"Do I even want to ask why you'd carry senna of all things?"

"Protection. You have your method to subdue others, I have mine. So, dinner?"

"I'm not sure I want to say, yes."

All this toilet talk is making me queasy. Not to mention, who needs senna when this entire city is a dump? I can't imagine anything here free of food-borne pathogens and maybe Dui's grasped the same. The doctor reaches inside his pocket and produces a packet of dried nuts.

"It's safe, I promise."

"I'm not hungry. Dui, I'm not stopping until I reach Bu Xin."

"So? I can manage. Bu Xin's not that far."

"That's not the point. General Yue tasked this to me. He's probably expecting you. You should go back."

"No can do, love. I was in the tent when he said my friend is missing. The implication was clear. Besides, when did he say I couldn't assist?"

"But... You can't go! You're needed elsewhere!"

"Uh-huh. You think I'm that stupid, I don't know what you really mean?" Drawing back the packet of nuts, he stares pathetically at the ground. The bushy hair may serve to conceal wavering eyes but his tone betrays him. "The feeble doctor isn't strong. He'll only get in the way. You keep saying others need me because you don't."

"That's not true."

"Isn't it? I doubt you'd reject help from the generals, Lord Han Bei, or even Wen Meng. They are the type of men more fitting to walk beside you, right?"

"That's... not... true..." I find myself repeating the same poor defense because I don't have a valid response. For what feels an eternity, we stand frozen in twilight where long shadows spread across the ground, shrouding everything in a miserable grey tone. I do respect Dui but a part of me can't deny his charges. He is physically weaker than the other men I've come to know but that has never stopped him from coming for me whenever I needed help. An unarmed man without great strength is far more courageous for his heroics than others who boast with their swords. I've been telling Dui his deficiencies are nonexistent, while I've been subconsciously treating him otherwise.

Still, that doesn't dull the truth. Dui is weak and I am worried for him. I'm not strong without my latent talent and I don't know if I can protect him if needed.

"You're mouthing your thoughts again."

"I—"

"Fine. I'm sorry for being *such a burden*. Not everyone can be as special as your boyfriend."

"Wait!"

A sharp slap brushes my reaching hand off his sleeve. Dui moves quickly into the crowded streets. In the poorly lit district under dark clouded skies, I lose sight of his slender form. I was fine traveling alone but having him with me for a time brought about a sense of ease I didn't know he instilled until now. A chill spreads across my chest. I suddenly feel lost and afraid.

"Dui! Dui! Wait for me, Dui! I'm sorry! Come back!"

What started as mere shouts became delirious panicked cries. My heart won't stop beating out of my chest and I can barely breathe. At the same time, my feet won't cease. Wherever they're taking me, he's nowhere in sight. My friend seemingly disappeared off the face of the earth. Tears blur my already limited vision, heightening my fear and quickening my steps. Without recourse, I unthinkingly tread on until slamming into something solid.

"I-I'm sorry!" The words fly out my mouth as I fall on my behind.

"You!"

His familiar tone resounds in the chilly night air. I happily rub the tears off my eyes believing I'd assail the man I was searching for. Instead, the bone-chilling chuckle that follows makes my hairs stand on ends. Why is everything I do a mistake?

"I remember you, little girl. Do you remember me?"

The scoundrel I would never forget peers down with a bloodlust grimace, not far from another lustful expression he once conveyed during my misstep down a dark alley. Beneath the scarred cheeks and deformed jaw line remains light colored eyes surrounded by dark curly lashes. Whatever beauty he once had is long gone; the resentment of which casts an uglier shadow over his brows than wretchedness. My breathing stalls and then on impulse, I scramble in the opposite direction.

Chapter 20 – 3

The event from that night comes back to me; the fear now tenfold. However that man managed to escape Nan Rong's dungeon, of all places to have met him again, why here? One word from him that my lover is a Southern general and all the soldiers around will descend. No matter how fast my legs fly, the pursuing thumping footsteps on the dirt road become increasingly louder. Worse, I hear three sets of distinct steps, meaning he has friends. The memory of the other two perverts who accompanied him that night makes me cringe.

If only I'd accepted Dui's help, I wouldn't be in this mess. Why did I insult him after everything he's done? The doctor thinks himself less than a real man. As his friend, I shouldn't have emasculated him through my superiority complex. Without my gift, I am weak and so I keep trying to prove myself strong, as I've done all my life to fit in with the monks. Dui is stronger than any man I know. He always tries to do what others can't and for my sake, has always done what I thought he couldn't do.

At this rate, I won't be able to find Dui and I'm not anywhere closer to Qing Hai. This has to stop.

Making a hard turn, I run down another section of streets toward a crowded area, squeezing between pedestrians after pedestrians. Once I manage to slip out the other side of the throng, someone's hard boot

Chapter 24 – 2

"Hello! Master Lo Han! Master Lo Han, are you home?"

I'm fairly certain this is the right house. Years ago, Master Tai Hung and I visited here once or twice. Aside from Master Zhuang who taught me self-defense, Master Lo Han was another I looked up to, mainly for advice which a younger person's perspective was needed. He was sort of an elder brother though secretly I had a crush on him for years. It wasn't love by all means. Well, I say that but my heart is racing from anticipation. How long has it been since I've last seen him?

A subtle click and then the door draws open. At the sight of fluttering smooth brown hair, I turn on my heels.

"I'm sorry! I thought this was Master Lo Han's house!"

"Wait. Little Hung?"

That deep silky voice turns by entire body rigid. Memories of childish adulation well in my chest, making it difficult to breathe. I turn around to catch glimpse of that handsome face, kind eyes, and strong jaw line. Age may have left its mark but that's him all right.

"Master Lo Han? You have hair!"

"It's rude to point, Little Hung. What are you doing here and wearing pink for that matter? I thought you hated pink."

"I... do. Sorry for the intrusion. I was hoping you would be here unmarried—I mean single—I mean alone! Ahaha! C-Can I come in?"

"Of course."

He moves aside and signals for me to enter. My heart is on the verge of exploding. I thought he was gorgeous bald. He's so tantalizing now that it's a shame he's a monk. What a terrible, terrible thing to think!

"You still think I'm handsome, huh?"

"Wh-What?"

"Mouthing your thoughts again, Little Hung."

Master Lo Han's smooth chuckles are just as I remember except they now carry a teasing implication. And what does he mean by *still* think he's handsome? Did he know?

"You've grown into a fine young woman, Little H— Bao Lai. How time flies. I miss the days when you were at my heels at Tian Mao Yi."

"You make me sound like a stalker."

"Not at all." Master Lo Han, signaling for us to sit at the table in the center of the room, smiles impishly to himself. His house is small but quaint, clean and smells of incense. The clay bird figurine I made for his twentieth birthday remains by the windowsill where he'd placed it over a decade ago. Nostalgia of days gone by is unbearable.

"I missed my adorable cross-dressed little sister, is all I meant. What brings you to Liang Bi?"

"Well, it is a rude thing, showing up out of the blue and asking for your help but I didn't know where else to turn."

"Not rude at all. Families live far apart and look to each other in times of need. That's natural. I'm honored you consider me your family, Bao Lai. As always, I'm here to listen."

"What a way with words! You're still as gallant as a prince, Master Lo Han."

"Hmm, that would be ironic considering you're the princess."

"Come again?"

For my confused wide-eyed stare, his insinuating smile widens. I can't bear to look any longer at that endearing smile or else my swooning will worsen. Just as my nervous gaze trails away, the master lets out a laugh.

"I should have known from his audacious flirting that he was an imposter."

"Huh?"

"I heard Master Tai Hung passed. I'm sorry. I sent my condolences too late. My letter to you was returned by Master Zhu. Had I known he and the others planned to eject you from Tian Mao Yi, I would have raced back. By then, you were gone. So when we met again in the capital, I offered to take you back to Tian Mao Yi."

"Um... You're confusing the life out of me, Master Lo Han. I haven't seen you in almost ten years."

"Precisely. The person I met wasn't you. I shouldn't have let my eyes fool what my heart knew to be untrue. The high priests faltered to his temptation and when the truth was revealed, lost whatever pride they had and exposed their indecency. Through his own strange methods, I feel he must have accomplished that for you. Your gender never severed their ties to religion; his gender couldn't keep them bound."

"He? Wait a minute, don't tell me you met—"

I clamp down my lips, unable to continue. No one is permitted to know He Pi is missing. That was the reason I became entangled in this political mess. To displace the awkward silence, Master Lo Han smiles reassuringly.

"Yes. I met His Highness, He Pi."

"He *is* alive. That's great news! Where is he?"

"He left for somewhere north was all I gathered. His Highness didn't say much about himself but he was more than interested in you. I'm afraid I might have divulged too much about you."

"I don't mind. There's not much to me."

"Always selling yourself short, Bao Lai. Maybe this will change your mind."

The master produces a letter from his breast pocket and urges me to look inside. There are two names mentioned, one of which makes me nearly fall out of the chair.

"Master Tai Hung sent for you and Bai Hu? Why?"

"Yes. This was his second letter after his first didn't receive a response. I was away at a northern temple to provide aid after a landslide. I'd only meant to stay six months and instead, stayed the year after an earthquake hit the neighboring town. So he sent another notice, this one included Bai Hu; whichever of us could fetch you first. You'd left by the time he arrived. Bai Hu said he would try the villages near Pa Xu. I apologize for not joining in his efforts extensively. Other obligations kept me but I'd hope to run into you during my excursions."

Though the confession was made through sarcasm, Hu once said our meeting was fate. It was never chance. He was supposedly near Kou with Yue and Hai searching for His Highness that day we met; maybe, he was actually there looking for me. His conduct was rough and he never told me the truth about our past but at heart, he knew who I was and took me into his care as

Master Tai Hung requested. Not only did Bai Hu take me in, he loved me, looked out for me, and provided everything I needed. Why couldn't he have told me the truth? If only I'd known. I love this pink robe. I love it more than anything! It is proof that I am his wife.

"Bao Lai. Are you all right?"

"I... um... yes, I'm fine."

"Don't lie through your sobs."

Master Lo Han's sleeve suddenly brushes against my cheek. I hadn't noticed he's moved to my side. In a loving, familial manner, one arm is around my shoulder, the other continues to take the tears away.

"Is this about Xiao Mao? You both were close. I'll send him a letter to call off his search."

"It's not that. Bai Hu found me. He's... incapacitated at the moment. I came to ask your advice. Bei Ling is advancing through Lan Yue and I'm not sure how much longer Nan Rong can hold that front. If Ye falls into this mess, I don't see this conflict ending well for anyone."

"Why are you involved?"

"I'm the court physician's—Dui's—assistant. Dui, you remember him, right?"

"How could I forget poor Dui? Are you still tormenting him?"

"I guess you could say that."

Chuckling, Master Lo Han pats my head. "Master Tai Hung's efforts were for naught. He sought to keep you from political troubles and yet here you are."

"You're confusing me again, Master Lo Han."

"Just Lo Han. You've left temple and so have I."

"You've what? Why?"

"Story for another day. As I mentioned, I might have told His Highness too much. He managed to find the edict Master Tai Hung kept in his study. You'll think I'm crazy but at least hear everything I have to say first. You are Ning's missing princess, the rightful heir to the Eastern throne. For that reason, an attempt was made on your life shortly before Xiao Mao left. He managed to thwart the assassin. Master Tai Hung didn't go into details, but that much he did tell me, in the hopes that I would come to look after you once he passed. If he ever intended to tell you the truth, the assassination attempt made him held his tongue permanently."

"Then why are you telling me?"

Lo Han stares back hesitantly and then slowly withdraws his arms. "You don't sound at all surprised."

"Oh. I am. Maybe the shock hasn't set in. It's just that your incredible claims validate Lord Han Bei's strange behaviors. He makes sense to me now."

"The Grand General of Ning, Lord Han Bei? So much for severing ties. The Master utterly failed. He must be rolling in his grave."

"Don't say that! He did what was best for me."

"And so am I. Isn't this the answer you sought? Your connections to the East can play a vital role in this conflict."

"Lord Han Bei is our ally but what about Ye and Feng Jia? Bei Ling's men are teeming in both countries. Nan Rong is struggling at Lan Yue. What chance will the South have once Bei Ling coerces the two border countries to join in their siege? Nan Rong needs more soldiers."

Lo Han leans back against the sofa and stares at the ceiling. He usually sits in this pose during tedious contemplations, all the while stroking his jaw. During these moments, he often loses track of time and his surroundings. Knowing this to be his custom, I follow suit and also lean back, prepared for the wait. After twenty minutes of twiddling my thumbs, Lo Han shifts into proper posture and slowly resumes. "Strength in number is a fine option. However, victory isn't gain through force alone. The best weapon strikes at the heart."

"Meaning what?"

"Strong men are just as fallible to beauty as any man less talented. Here. Take this to Mei Gui Guan in the Zui

District and ask for Ma Tai Tou. The clever woman should be able to provide further instructions."

Walking to the cabinet, Lo Han fetches a faded woven box underneath a pile of prayer books. From the simple patterned box is produced a lacquered comb covered in red blossoms. He hands it to me; though, I hesitate to reach.

"Um, Master—I mean Lo Han, if I remember correctly, Zui District is between the lower Red Light District and the upper nobles' quarters, right? Mei Gui Guan, Rose Pavilion... that sounds an awful lot like a brothel."

"Yes, that's right."

"Oh! R-Really?!"

"Not officially but everyone knows the private *services* offered along with the usual affairs. Foot soldiers often spend time in the Red Light District and their commanding officers frequent Mei Gui Guan. The ones with more authority usually have more to share."

"I see." Liquor loosens tongue and around pretty girls and flowing wine, most men tend to lose all inhibitions. This upper echelon brothel might provide useful information; though, it's strange that Lo Han would know the name of the madam. Curiosity gets the better of me and, in clearing my throat, thrusts up a dubious stare. "So... h-how do you know Ma Tai Tou?"

"Let's just say she made a man out of me."

401

My whole head in scorched from the unrelenting images that suddenly flash. I stare at Lo Han, unable to form half a word. He can't be serious! A man of his quality would frequent a brothel? Are they the types of women he prefers? Is that why he quit the priesthood? I can't believe I'm more jealous than appalled! What is wrong with me?!

"What a strange face you're making!" Smiling innocently, he presses the comb onto my palm. "Ma Tai Tou took me from the streets, provided a roof over my head, three square meals a day, and an education. She sent me to Tian Mao Yi to further my studies. I owe my life to that woman and I certainly wouldn't be the man I am today without her guidance."

"Oh, that's what you meant."

"Of course. Why? What were you thinking?"

It's painfully obvious that he's teasing me. As usual, his prince-like smile shakes me to the very core. I look away, embarrassed, and then soon after, annoyed.

"Growing up surrounded by pretty women must have taught you much. No wonder you're so charmingly smooth, Lo Han."

"Ha! Just to you, Bao Lai. I'm not this sweet to anyone else but my adorable sister."

"I said smooth, not sweet."

"We both know what you really meant."

Chapter 24: Lo Han

There he goes inducing another heart attack with that smile. Worse, he refuses to leave out the note that I am a sister to him, rendering my swooning to utter turmoil. I had hoped this childish crush would have subsided by now, but the more we are together, the more nervous I grow.

"I-I should be going. Thank you, Lo Han. You always provide a path for me when things are obscured. I knew I could count on you. Someday, hopefully I can return the favor."

"Nonsense! We're family. Just be sure to visit more often. Next time, we'll camp out under the stars the way we used to do and then spend the night together in my tent, hmm?"

What happened to my sweet-natured Master Lo Han? Or, has he always been this way and I hadn't noticed? My whole body bursts into flames through his casual assertion, fueling that princely smile to broaden. The mask on his perfect face is stretching thin and underneath is revealed a mean, teasing man. There's only one method to fight back.

"I think His Highness might have rubbed off on you, Lo Han."

"He's taught me a thing or two."

"I take that to mean of all the holy men he seduced, you weren't spared."

"Are you implying that I'm seducing you, Bao Lai?"

"Of course not. You're like a brother to me."

The broad smile slightly contracts. Lo Han's smooth hand reaches down to cup my jaw. "Yes, that's right. At one point, I too thought you were a brother to me, especially those carefree days when you ran topless in the training fields."

"Give me a break! I was five years old and flat-chested!"

"And now my sister is a swan."

Lo Han's thumb runs over my cheek, sending uninvited heat to my face. He's won and I'm a sore loser. Frowning, I draw back and bow low. A quiet sigh escapes from my host, signaling his disappointment that the games are over before they began.

"One more thing before you go, Bao Lai. Mei Gui Guan has recently been entertaining a large number of Bei Ling's men. You'll draw much attention as a woman and even more attention as a man. Be careful."

"I will. They won't notice a thing. Should I give Ma Tai Tou your regards?"

"Don't bother. She's a woman of fine taste. Regards are too cheap for her palette."

I hope he's joking. I've nothing to offer a woman of fine taste. And maybe, that's why Lo Han presented this comb for my benefit. The quality is beyond anything sold in common trade shops. Even those in expensive boutiques pale in comparison. I glance up to question how he came to possess such an impressive item but my host merely shrugs.

"It's getting late. If you'd rather spend the night here, sweet little sister, I won't mind having you climb into bed with me. It'll be like old times."

This is both his nice and mean way of telling me to leave. I bow to my old friend once more and then head west toward Zui District.

Chapter 25: Night in a Brothel

Mei Gui Guan, true to its name, spares no expenses to line every walkway with roses of every color and fashion. Large fragranced blooms burst from expensive vases which are tastefully placed on tables, mantels, and walls. The same luscious blooms decorate every maiden's hair. What beautiful women! After witnessing the prostitutes calling from the windows in Nan Rong's Red Light District during my faulty excursion, I'd expected the same gaudy, tired, dolled-up display. This place is more of a grand palace, crowded by celestial maidens, and overflowing with wine. No wonder men of wealth and significance spend all their free time here. Even I feel a bit entranced by the scenic view.

"Where are you going, handsome?"

I'd clenched the gauntlets to steel my nerves before walking past prying eyes into the backroom when she suddenly tugs on my arm as a mean to distract my mission, smiling sweetly through perfectly painted petal lips. Soon after, a soft giggle bursts. "My, that armor is a little big for you, isn't it? Wouldn't you feel more comfortable if I help you out of it?"

"Erm... No, thanks. Excuse me, Miss, is Ma Tai Tou around?"

The pretty face suddenly turns to disdain. Her head cocks to one side. The lady frowns. "We only serve *men.* Little boys should return to the Red Light District."

"Well, that's rude. I need to speak to Ma Tai Tou. What's the problem?"

"She's not here."

"When is she coming back?"

"Not anytime soon."

Her foot taps the glossy floor. Her hands are on her hips. I see. I was hoping not to bring him into this but I'm also curious as to how close he is to this brothel.

"That's too bad. Lo Han, my very good friend— we're like brothers actually—assured me she was here. And I'd brought such a fine gift for Ma Tai Tou."

Abrupt sparkles break across wishful eyes. She went deaf after hearing his name and couldn't care less for anything I said after. The brimming smile returns.

"How is Lo Han? I didn't know he was back! That man! He promised to visit! When you see the Master, tell him Ai Qi is very mad! No, wait, tell him Ai Qi is saddened by his abandonment."

Behind the heartbreaking pout, a melodramatic tone surfaces, and behind that, is a determined glare. Gracious. I'm glad I didn't fall for Lo Han else every woman here would scratch my eyes out.

"Um... okay. I'll tell him whatever you want if I can speak to Ma Tai Tou."

"Tsk! That's all you wanted? Why didn't you say so in the first place? She's this way."

I did say so but contending won't do any good. I clamp down my lips and follow the happy Miss who skips merrily down the corridor on the right.

Chapter 25 – 2

"If that isn't the worst disguise I have ever seen, I don't know what is."

She waited for Miss Ai Qi to leave before lifting off the large carved mahogany chair resembling an empress's throne. On the wide table are ledgers and client lists, next to which is a lockbox which requires an unordinary key.

Ma Tai Tou comes closer; her loose silk robe waves elegantly. Though a madam, she is just as painted as her girls and if she were twenty years younger, would put them all to shame. I wonder what Lo Han thought of her during those prime years.

"Stand up straight and stop mouthing your thoughts! How do you expect to be taken seriously when you're slouched over like a drunk?"

"Y-Yes, ma'am!"

For whatever reason, she scares the life out of me. I'm not the obedient type, Master Tai Hung could attest to that, so I've no idea why I feel the need to obey. This is how it must feel to have a mother; at least, Dui's mother. It was her way or a switch to the backside. I wouldn't be surprised if this woman had one hidden under her sleeves.

"There are few things I will tolerate, young lady, and deception is not one of them. My customers pay good money to enjoy everything Mei Gui Guan has to offer. I don't need riffraff coming into my establishment causing trouble. If you want a job, wait for recruitment season like everyone else."

"Er... I-I'm not. M-My name is Bao Lai. I-I came t-to—"

"Don't stutter! Either speak with convictions or stop moving your mouth so your brain can catch up."

"I-I'm not doing this purposefully!"

"No one likes a whiner!"

What is with this woman? We've just met and she has a problem with everything I am. I didn't come for charm lessons. Apparently, opening my mouth makes things worse. Instead, I retrieve Lo Han's lacquered comb from my breastplate and hold it out to the irate madam. It sparks her interest and then just as quickly, earns her wrath.

"I don't take bribes."

"It's a gift."

"Then present it as a gift. Walk back out that door. Knock and ask for entry. Greet me properly and then kindly offer this gift. Once we have settled into conversation, bring up the subject which you wish to discuss. That is the civilized way to behave. You have the look of a country bumpkin but you weren't raised in a barn, I hope."

Chapter 25: Night in a Brothel

"Are you... serious?"

"Dead serious. Pausing midsentence is just as bad as stuttering. Learn to be a lady first before pretending to be a man. Now go."

I have many choice words for this *lady*. Considering Mei Gui Guan is just another brothel, she sure has some nerve looking down on me.

"Don't wear your thoughts on your sleeve, girl. Obstinacy will take you far but tactfulness will take you farther. The moment you stepped through that door I saw pride in those eyes. Despite your opinion of me and my girls, we did not request your presence. You came for our help. So, tell me, who's better than whom?"

Hard eyes bear into mine, rendering me speechless. I hate to admit it but she's right. Regardless of my prejudice, this woman saved Lo Han. He respects her more than anyone and for that, so must I. I came for her help and had the gall to waltz in without proper introduction and civility. The men I grew up with preferred the direct method, straight to the point, but I'm not a man and this isn't Tian Mao Yi. Courtesy comes before consideration. The real world is both difficult and frightening.

Bowing low, I march back out the door to catch my breath. In time, a slight knock rumbles when my fist beats softly against the hardwood. I ask for entry and my host complies. She starts from the chair as before, only this time, I make the effort to grace my host with proper greeting, introduction, and the expensive gift before we sit down for tea.

She asks the most mundane questions and I play along until a slight nod signals that she's ready for my request. And so, casually inserting Lo Han's name, I explain the situation to Ma Tai Tou.

"Was that all? Indeed, I will look into it. Bei Ling's men are running my girls ragged. I don't care if they have more money than our usual customers; they certainly don't have any class."

"Thank you! Is there anything I can do in the meantime?"

"Appealing to me was a good start but I can't provide the support you'll need against these soldiers. There is another woman your time would be well spent in persuasion. For that, you'll need to brush up your disguise. Whose armor did you steal?"

"It was a loan."

"I can hardly believe that! They aren't the common suits loitering in the Red Light District. No, these are lightweight but sturdy. High quality smithwork specially made for a very important man. Two ways to disarm any man are through sheer brute force and temptation. Which did you use?"

"I—! It really was a loan! Technically, a spare!"

"Now, now, don't get upset." Ma Tai Tou chuckles amusedly in an oddly familiar fashion, resembling Lo Han. "When your honesty is challenged, a smile is the best defense and composure is the best offense. Snapping back shows two things, you're either too eager to argue because you're lying or you're excessively juvenile rendering anything you have to say to disregard. Sit up straight and try again."

She's a busy woman. I can't imagine these impromptu lessons are for her own amusement. Whoever this other woman is whom I need to persuade must require the proper approach. And so, I straighten my hunched back and take another deep breath before a smile forms. "Yes ma'am. The suit was a spare. My acquaintance was kind enough to loan it for a time."

"In exchange for what favor?"

"In exchange for protecting his brother and Nan Rong."

"Better, but now you've given too much information. I could use them against your acquaintance. Next lesson, to answer honestly without any honesty."

"Isn't that just lying?"

"Limiting and redirecting information. A lost art which requires conveying a high level of sincerity. Try again and don't place your acquaintance's family in danger. Armor this rare is easily identifiable. I could

413

find your acquaintance and this brother of his by morning."

"Then, what is the proper response?"

"Think for yourself and I'll correct you as necessary. When the time comes, I won't be present to hold your hand. Let's not form that crutch now."

"Right. Thank you."

I wrack my brains for an answer and after several more mistakes, manage to find the right one. We continue until sunset, going over speech, presentation, and body language. The more I learn, the more I realize how little I knew.

At the end, Ma Tai Tou took Yu Qi's armor for modifications to my size and with stilt inserts so I could match his height. Her plans are still unclear, though, I'm not worried. She's bossy, strict, and outright mean but behind the cantankerous front is a kind and highly capable woman who looks after her own. I feel safer in her hands than in the company of armed bodyguards. The latter may raise a sword but Ma Tai Tou can raise an army.

Chapter 26: A Lesson in Persuasion

"We've given Bei Ling access to our territory in exchange for staying out of this conflict. This is unreasonable!"

Neng Cao's wavering voice is followed by a glance begging for support from her primary council, a man of great personal beauty who goes by the name Zhang Mang. Since I've stormed into Ye's palace donned in Yao Ying's disguise, which was prepared by the ladies from Mei Gui Guan, everyone I've crossed have either rescinded from fear or kept their heads down. Everyone, that is, except this Zhang Mang. He's staring at me with a certain amusement. Those snickering emerald eyes reminisce of another powerful man who exudes the same level of condescension to his opponents: Lord Han Bei.

In the throne room are my hosts Zhang Mang, a handful of Ye's military leaders, and Emperor Neng Cao, secretly a cross-dressed, frail woman with little authority. From all those at council, only Zhang Mang gives the lady any regards. For that, he sits by her side as an equal.

A week ago, after my visit with Ma Tai Tou, her best skilled girls worked to coax information from their Bei Ling customers. The North doesn't intend to spare the western countries claiming neutrality. Feng Jia will be forced to march upon Nan Rong while Bei Ling's men continue to lay siege on Mount Chou. Ultimately, Ye will

415

be coerced to join the fray for the single purpose of distraction. The two smaller countries will be annexed, specifically Feng Jia after their suspected failed invasion. That is, Bei Ling expects that Feng Jia will be decimated, but in the process, serve a major blow to Nan Rong. Without an army, the North will waltz in and insert their new government. By then, Ye will not have much choice. Neng Cao must abdicate or Ye will be brought to its knees.

Given the dire news, Lo Han donned his former kasaya and traveled south to deliver correspondence to San An. Everyone's done their part to give me this chance. It's my turn.

Flattening out the middle of my tongue and taking a proper breath from my diaphragm, a lowered, deeper, controlled voice resembling Yu Qi's continues to pour out. "From the beginning, our discord has been with Nan Rong. Ye submitted to our use of *her* territory however we deemed fit. This is merely another step in that agreement."

My purposeful hint at her gender makes the lady turn pallid. No matter how desperately she tries to conceal the secret, it's one that's widely known amongst nobles, according to Ma Tai Tou. Neng Cao fidgets, and in her place, Commander Ru squares his proud shoulders; though, his eyes are still casted at the ground.

"Ye's courtesy shouldn't be mistaken for submission. Bei Ling was permitted to use our roads and only our roads into Nan Rong. Our soldiers are off limits."

"Ye's courtesy pales in contrast to Bei Ling's courtesy to have used your roads and only your roads until now. Roads are easily destroyed and rebuilt; same as any country."

The hardened tone in my voice forces back Commander Ru's pride. I may lack Yu Qi's natural imposing authority but not one man has had the nerve to retaliate against my insolence. The evidence of Yao Ying's intimidation is palpable. However, just as relief begin to wash over me, Zhang Mang cocks up his head.

"So, what do we get in return for helping you?"

"A trade would imply Bei Ling was open to negotiation. I'm not here for negotiations."

The young man's smirk slowly becomes an amused smile. In the next beat, an invisible force shifts the atmosphere, as though he were letting parts of his hidden self escape to quash my arrogance. He's powerful, as powerful as he is beautiful, and full of murderous intent. I know this air. There's no doubt about it. This man is an assassin.

"You have soldiers and we have soldiers," he begins flippantly with a shrug. "A pawn is pawn; all civilians are pawns. For everyone one of ours who dies in the process of killing one of yours, at the end, we'd still have plenty left to dig graves for everyone else. So, let's try this again. What do we get in return for marching to Feng Jia?"

"The... half of your army that would otherwise be slain. A-And the other half Bei Ling would undoubtedly put down for insubordination!"

Darn him! The cheeky smile on that infuriatingly charming face is not helping my nerves. Who would take me seriously now? I paused, stuttered, and lost composure. Worse than that, gave a stupid answer befitting a child. If the real Yao Ying were here, swords would have clashed before excuses. Without my special skill, I doubt that I can best this man in combat.

"*Scare-ry!*" Rolling his eyes, Zhang Mang snorts. "Your discord is with Nan Rong, said so yourself, so why target Feng Jia? Those poor bastards have nothing to take and Ye has nothing to gain."

There he goes again, throwing that confident, condescending glare in my direction. His lips curl upward smugly and then soon after, frowns. I frantically search for a quip, the pressure of which makes my thoughts grow more erratic, filling the room with more silence and hence, increasing the pressure I already feel. I'm on the verge of losing whatever advantage Yao Ying's reputation provides. Those green eyes refuse to yield. Unable to find recourse, I stare back. In an instant, his head quickly tilts to what I think is a nod.

Chapter 26: A Lesson in Persuasion

So, that's how it is.

Taking another deep breath, Yu Qi's voice continues to project. "Feng Jia has nothing and therefore, has nothing to lose. Bei Ling has the advantage in strength; Nan Rong in, distance. That leaves Ye."

"What are you saying? Feng Jia plans to invade Ye?!"

His strident assertion moves the detached military leaders to the edge of their seats. Their attention lifts off the ground, hands balled into fists with determination burning furiously. In mere seconds, they're prepared for war. This Zhang Mang is really something! His voice can stir that which mine would never reach.

Momentum is right in front of me. A flurry of words claw at my throat, ready to push the eager warlords forward; that is, until Zhang Mang looks quickly from the men on his right to those on his left, as though shaking his head, before a direct stare comes back to me. Ying is a man of few words. The less I speak, the better they are convinced. Instead, I give an emphatic nod, sending the room to uproar.

Neng Cao leans to her council for advice. By her expression, I can tell the woman is in love. She'll do whatever this man says. I just hope we're on the same side.

Time eventually subdues excitement. Amongst the leaders, Commander Ru stands up and taps a fan against the long polished mahogany wood table, calling all to order. Zhang Mang's unfazed attitude toward Yao Ying has given the Commander more confidence.

"Let's say Feng Jia is plotting to overtake Ye. How did you come by this information? Furthermore, Zhang Mang has a point. What does Bei Ling gain by helping us and why should we give you command of our military?"

Commander Ru's brave challenge rescinds to an awkward aversion the instant my eyes slide over in his direction, glowering in the manner Yu Qi imparted when I'd asked to borrow his armor. However, the questions placed cannot be ignored. They want answers. This one, at least, I have ready.

"Nan Rong's aggression forced our vigilance. Feng Jia cannot hide their intentions from my watchers. I will lead your army to Feng Jia in Nan Rong's colors and change their target to the southern country."

"Clever!" Zhang Mang, clasping his hands together, chirrups. "Make our enemy destroy your enemy. I shouldn't have expected any less from you. The Yao Ying Sun is truly a creature to be feared. Feng Jia should have tried harder to keep you, traitor. Vengeance is a deadly poison."

I thought we were working toward the same goal and then he goes and provokes me again. Despite Ying's past irreparable actions, Diao believes he defected to Bei Ling in order to save Feng Jia. I hate that his honor is tarnished but I also know what Yu Qi would do. Starting up, I make a short obeisance to Neng Cao and then part from the throne room.

Chapter 26 – 2

Loud banter ejects from the other side of the door. I wouldn't have interrupted if she hadn't called for me. Three knocks against the hardwood, the lively conversation comes to a standstill, and then Ma Tai Tou gives her blessing. I walk in and promptly greet the lady and her guest.

"Darling!" The overfriendly, gorgeous woman in light green robe starts up and runs to my side. Her lithe body and my strong armor collide. I jump back from panic but can't escape the kiss promptly planted on my cheek. For that, her teasing smile widens. Wait a minute. I know that smile.

"Zh—"

"Mu Dan!" She chimes quickly while pressing a hand hard against my mouth. "Your lover, remember? No? One night and then I'm nothing to you, Master Ying? You're a cruel, cruel man!"

He giggles at my bulging eyes. Tremors are crawling over my skin. Was Zhang Mang a woman all along or does Ying prefer the company of men? This person is absolutely a man... I think.

The confounding situation throws back old habits. I mouth empty sounds, and as a last resort to unravel tangled thoughts, reach over and run my hands across Mu Dan's chest.

"Pervert!" He screams. An open palm immediately flies across my cheek. "Keep your hands to yourself!"

"Same to you! You started it! They're not real, are they?"

"How rude! Didn't your mother teach you any manners? Don't go around groping people. How would you like it if I do it to you?"

Both his grubby hands land squarely on my chest. Though Ying's armor wouldn't have permitted Zhang Mang to feel the bounded rises, instinctively, I draw back from embarrassment and swing a gauntlet at his face. He dodges, cackling noisily.

"Enough! Some of us have to work for a living! Quit wasting my time!" Ma Tai Tou's irate shout makes my hair stands on end. Conversely, Zhang Mang casually shrugs as though he were used to her wrath.

"Oh, well. Fine. Ruin my fun, why don't you? Guess I have to get back before the little empress goes looking for me." He flips the long brown hair, smiling impishly through cherry lips. "I'll see you later, Tai-Tai."

Zhang Mang bows graciously to Ma Tai Tou. When he walks past, keeps a meaningful, teasing pair of green eyes to my face. What an irksome man. Furthermore, he's provoked my jealousy for that natural gliding gait. Zhang Mang must have practiced this craft many times before. I just wonder the reason.

"W-Wait!"

The revelation then hits me. I can't believe I'd forgotten.

Zhang Mang turns back, annoyed by my low bow. "Hmm? The damage has been done. I won't spend the night with you no matter how long you beg."

"Zh—Mu Dan. Whoever you are. Thank you for all your help."

"I don't know what you're talking about." He replies airily. With another casual shrug, Zhang Mang disappears down the hall.

Yesterday, I was aggravated by his behavior in the throne room. However, if he hadn't been my opponent, the others would have been suspicious by his later support. I played the part for less than an hour and nearly failed. He plays many roles without ever taking off the mask. What an extraordinary person he must be. Under different circumstances, I'd like to believe we could have been friends.

"And here I thought you had common sense. He's not the type to fall for anyone."

"That's too bad. Neng Cao might be under different impressions."

She smiles at my lack of usual defensiveness. Ma Tai Tou pushes a scroll across the table. To the right of the inscriptions inside is a familiar red seal. It's a decree.

"He's done it!"

"Take credit where it's due. He couldn't have done it alone. Give him another week. Kang Lang will have Feng Jia's men ready to march."

"Who's Kang Lang?"

"The boy who goes by many names. Now—for Bei Ling—it's almost time for the first show to begin. Find Ai Qi and Mei Qi in the Hong Ying Tea Room, they'll help with preparations."

"Thank you, Ma Tai Tou. I couldn't have done anything without you." Bowing to the lady, I hope my earnest gratitude reaches her.

"No need for flattery. I help those who help themselves." She moves off the chair and comes closer. Ma Tai Tou lifts me up and then presses the lacquered comb into my hand. "You've grown since that tactless girl walked in here a week ago. Take this. It's for you."

"The present was from Lo Han."

"It belonged to me. An heirloom from my mother. I gave my most prized possession to Lo Han as a present for the girl he meant to wed; whenever that day would come. That was before he insisted on joining the priesthood. Imagine my surprise to see you waltz in sporting this very thing. A mother is often hard on the woman her son loves. I admit I was a little hard on you."

"Not at all. I wasn't as respectful as I should have been. My master taught me better. I'm sorry. Lo Han intended for me to earn your support through this comb. Besides, he quit the priesthood so he may yet find a wife. If you wish, I will deliver it back to him."

"He didn't give away this comb with the intention of having it back. Either that means he chooses to never marry or you are the woman he loves. Take it. Give it to your own child. I don't want my heirloom in a display case in some boutique or worse, a decoration on some rich girl's head."

I started to contend that I can't be the caretaker of this precious item but the offended stare on her face calls for retraction. I reach for the expensive comb, worth more money than I'll ever have combined, and carefully hide it in my breast pocket. At this point, I don't know if I'll ever have children. Marriage and family seem to be far off notions. Still, I guess only time will tell. Should life take me down that road, I will pass on this comb and the stories of the great Ma Tai Tou, a woman as valiant and talented as any commander.

"Thank you. I'll treasure it."

"Good. Now go on. Don't make those antsy girls wait."

I bow to her once more and then retreat to the Hong Ying Tea Room. My disguise requires touchups and I need guidance from the ladies for my performance. The nobles at Ye's palace, I could fool through the right armor and basic disguise techniques, but Bei Ling's commanding officers know Yao Ying's face well. Even with the false mask, they would be able to tell I'm not the real thing. And so, Ma Tai Tou suggested enlisting the aid of liquor and exploiting skewed perceptions.

Tonight's show has the necessary pawns present. Once they're inebriated, lost in good company, Ying will appear to end their fun. He'll order the lot back to assist Bei Ling by way of Feng Jia. They'll retreat believing Bei Ling is suffering major losses against Nan Rong, following which, Ye's men in Nan Rong's colors will proceed under the belief of invading Feng Jia while giving the appearance that the South has advanced far. This is the next step in repelling Bei Ling's forces and freeing Feng Jia.

Chapter 27: Actions and Consequences

General Zhen Yue and Nan Rong's reinforcements were able to route Bei Ling's men at Lan Yue. Following the short victory, several more assault units continued to scatter along the borders, leaving Nan Rong's forces preoccupied. At the same time, Ning crossed into the northeastern Ying Ling borders to keep an eye on that front though the East doesn't appear to be invested in this conflict.

In the West, Bei Ling soldiers retreating from Ye prompted their allies stationed at Feng Jia to fall into disarray. Despite doubts since many claimed that Yao Ying never left Feng Jia, watchers substantiated the large group marching north to be wearing Nan Rong's colors. In believing that the South is advancing after having captured Ye, Bei Ling's men fled from Feng Jia, taking with them a deadly infliction worse than destruction: fear. Stories in the North boast Nan Rong's massive strength, having captured two countries and is aiming for Bei Ling.

Feng Jia, now freed from Bei Ling, faces an encroaching enemy. In the days after the North's retreat, Ying gathered Feng Jia's small army and prepared to meet Ye. Then, once the two sides come face-to-face at Yuo Muo, Zhang Mang seizes the opportunity he's been waiting for.

Drums reverberate from both lines. I stand beside Grand Commander Zhang Mang in Ying's spare armor.

The truth is, I did borrow his armor, but it wasn't he who agreed. Diao fetched the spare after he turned me down sorely. It is she who now stands aside the Yao Ying Sun. Her eyes smile each time she glances at the irate Ying.

"Long time no see, traitor." Zhang Mang rides out with sword readied. No wonder he realized I was an imposter. He and Ying are far from strangers.

Ying moves forward on the black armored steed to meet his challenger. I'm becoming unnerved. We agreed this wouldn't be an actual melee between Feng Jia and Ye. Zhang Mang seems to be of another opinion and his actions are beginning to cause dissension in Ye's ranks. For that same reason, Commander Ru steps forward.

"What is going on here? Which is the real Bei Ling commander? Why is that one leading Feng Jia? We came here by his orders—"

"You marched through my orders!" Zhang Mang shouts back. "Pull your head out of your ass. I've been leading this army! I am the Grand Commander! You got a problem with that? Come up here and say it to my face!"

With one hard glare over his shoulder, the wrath Zhang Mang usually hides exudes into the chilly air. The magnitude of his strength is almost oppressive. He is a reaper.

The line behind falls silent. Commander Ru, though thoroughly intimidated, can't banish the embarrassment he'd suffered in front of the men formerly under his authority. He looks at me and then at the real Ying. Upon discerning that he's been fooled, even cowered before a fake, the proud commander's resentment billows. His hands clench. Commander Ru steps forth to reclaim his honor.

"I accept your challenge, Grand Commander." Ru's mahogany mare gallops out to meet Zhang Mang, his halberd raised into the air. "To reclaim my position as the one and only commander. Ye's army belongs to me!"

Zhang Mang, shrugging, twists the orange steed to face Commander Ru. He's happy, too happy, at this chance to prove his leadership to the confused soldiers. Somehow, I think he planned this. Zhang Mang didn't intend to battle Ying, he aimed to take Ye's army under his full control. However, that leadership comes with a price: Commander Ru's head.

"Commander, back down!" This time, I enter the fray. I'd never learned to ride. Hence, I'd marched with the soldiers. As I run into the space dividing the two armies, Commander Ru sends down a disgusted glare.

"You! I don't know who you are but I'll take your head after I run him through! Ye will not be mocked by outsiders! I shall reclaim our honor!"

"Commander, Ye's honor is not lost. Ye expelled Bei Ling from Feng Jia. Is that not reason for satisfaction?"

"We marched to stop Feng Jia from invasion. That was through *your* persuasion!" Turning to Ying, Ru brandishes his halberd. "And you, Bei Ling's commander. Have you betrayed them as well? Is there not one man here capable of honesty and loyalty? In whose name do you lay down your life?!"

"I serve only Princess Diao!"

Ying's shout is nearly muffled by the echoing roars from Feng Jia's rank. Diao's cheeks flush red from his unexpected valiance. She looks at me so happily that my heart lightens. Youth was not a hindrance after all. Somehow she managed to give back her broken people their spirits and have Ying see her as an equal.

Regretfully, that same sentiment is not shared by Ye. The men look at one another, unable to grasp who is truly in charge; Zhang Mang, Ru, or me. Soft grumbles become loud mumbles. Contention threatens to tear them apart. They can't trust their leaders and from that, begin to distrust the men standing by their side.

Zhang Mang's low growl and piercing eyes immediately direct at the instigator: me. His method, however cruel, served to mitigate this very thing. I stopped him from killing one man and in turn, many more lives are in danger. My cries to subdue the men fall on deaf ears. Weapons are raised. In moments, factions are formed. Then, someone from the back of the lines cries out that Feng Jia's the real enemy, forcing tension and resentment to rise from both sides. All hell is on the verge of breaking loose.

"*Enough!*" Zhang Mang lets out an unearthly bellow, spreading soul-rending chills through his bloodlust eyes. None of the soldiers at the front dare even breathe for fear of becoming his first victim. When he continues, the magnitude of his aura is indescribably terrifying, so that even Feng Jia's men are frozen from sheer terror. "You cowards should learn your place! I am in command and I'll send anyone who says otherwise straight to hell! Get on your knees and beg for my forgiveness, Ru. Do it and I'll let you run home with your tail between your legs!"

A devilish grin bears down, clearly conveying his threat is hardly just that. What a sadistic man! Ru's pride would never permit him to beg. Zhang Mang's *forgiving* gesture drove him into a corner. While Ru knows he can't win, he also can't accept to live without honor.

Under different circumstances, my resolve would be clear. However, others around are also watching carefully. If they fall into disarray again, Zhang Mang's wrath won't be able to subdue the chaos a second time. Ru's finally grasped his folly. It's him or them.

Ru closes his eyes to steel himself and make peace with his maker. A grim expression overtakes his countenance and then the halberd is raised once more. Zhang Mang, smirking, brandishes his sword. For the short duration that follows, both sides of the field are deafly silent. My conflicting heart is beating out of my chest. Ru's horse neighs, signaling its charge. I...

Stop Commander Ru (Continue to page 434)

Stop Zhang Mang (Continue to page 436)

Chapter 27 – 2

"Stop, Commander!"

I dash out in front of his horse just as it takes off. The startled creature abruptly kicks both forelegs high into the air, sending Ru to the ground. The Commander is out cold and the confrontation is over before it began.

With no one left to challenge his authority, Ye definitively rallies under Zhang Mang's leadership.

"Listen up! We're taking this fight to Bei Ling! Those brazen bastards will regret ever stepping foot into the Western Territories. What say you, Feng Jia? Let us through or we'll cut our way through!"

Ying's brows rise from Zhang Mang's half question, half threat. Diao giggles, drawing the men's attention. She rides forward next to Ying.

"Grand Commander Zhang Mang, was it?" She begins. "Feng Jia too has endured subjugation by Bei Ling. We've let them trampled on our pride in exchange for false promises. Honor is pointless without life and yet life without honor is not worth living. Our people have united and we ask the same from you. Join us for the duration of this conflict and let our two countries build a beneficial union."

He studies the young girl for a time, glowering quietly from her brash proposal. Then, out of the blue, his usual moods come about. Zhang Mang shrugs.

"Who has ever said no to a cute girl? Fine, you can tag along but don't get in our way. As for you, old man, our differences will be settled another day."

The last part he said to Ying, who makes no acknowledgment either way.

Continue to page 445

Chapter 27 – 3

"Stop, Zhang Mang! This infighting is pointless! Emperor Neng Cao conferred your role as Grand Commander. You are in charge!"

"Damn right, I am!"

"Then, as the leader, give those under your command the benefit of the doubt. Everyone is baffled by our plan. We aimed to expel Bei Ling from Ye and Feng Jia. That was accomplished. Let's continue with our goal to end Bei Ling's conquest once and for all."

"Stand down." Ru's hard, though controlled voice, cuts in from behind. "Don't muddle the situation. I couldn't care less what your reasons are. We, Ye's servants, were pawns on a chessboard, trapped in a friendly match between Nan Rong and Bei Ling. I take it you're both from Nan Rong."

"Commander Ru, we share a common foe."

"That doesn't make us allies. Bei Ling used us and so has Nan Rong. Trading masters does not equate to freedom; neither is following a fool. Emperor Zhou failed our people when he left the throne to Neng Cao."

Without another word, the determined commander dashes forward. I'd barely jumped aside to avoid being trampled when the heavy echoes of metal clashing against metal resound across the battlefield. Ru's halberd strikes swiftly, and given the advantage in reach, should have sent Zhang Mang to the ground. The Grand Commander easily dodges, closing the distance before Ru has the chance to recover. The green blade flicker and then the duel is over. Zhang Mang emerges victorious, untouched and seemingly bored. He flicks blood off the thin blade. Then, turning to Ye's terrified soldiers, paces a hard stare steadily across the ranks.

"Anyone else who wishes to challenge me, step forward now!" The acrid cry is met with absolute silence. No man dare breathe a sound. Thus, he continues in a tone as hard as ever. "No? Then listen up! Freedom comes with a price and Nan Rong has bore half of the burden. Bei Ling's claws were removed from Ye and authority was returned to His Highness Neng Cao. Men of honor do not leave debts unpaid. What say you? Who here will join me and take this fight to Bei Ling?"

A flurry of cheers billows to deafening heights. Zhang Mang continues to rally the men, turning former dissension toward a unified goal.

"Those brazen bastards will regret ever stepping foot into the Western Territories!"

Another round of wild cheers breaks across Ye's ranks. That is, everyone except me. Shock numbs my senses. I can't believe how easily he turned the men, whose eyes were lusting to take his head, to now seemingly ready to die for his cause. He's frightening. Aside from his lack of consideration for human life, his words alone can slay thousands and yet, he's also strong enough to single-handedly slay thousands more. If he were gifted with Fa Zhen's ability, I would fear for the world.

Somewhere in my trance, his eyes suddenly catch hold of me. My breathing stalls and then tremors move down my spine. He smiles, amused by my terror, until our fixed gazes awkwardly diverge.

"So, what now? Let us through or we'll cut our way through!"

The Grand Commander cocks his head in Feng Jia's direction. Ying's brows rise from Zhang Mang's half question, half threat. Immediately, Diao rides forward and takes a position next to Ying.

"Grand Commander Zhang Mang," she begins. "Feng Jia too has endured subjugation by Bei Ling. We've let them trampled on our pride in exchange for false promises. Honor is pointless without life and yet life without honor is not worth living. Our people have united and we ask the same from you. Join us for the duration of this conflict and let our two countries build a beneficial union."

He studies the young girl for a time, glowering quietly from her brash proposal. Then, out of the blue, his usual moods come about. Zhang Mang shrugs.

"Who has ever said no to a cute girl? Fine, you can tag along but don't get in our way. As for you, old man, our differences will be settled another day."

Chapter 27: Actions and Consequences

The last part he said to Ying, who makes no acknowledgment either way.

Chapter 27 – 4

"Hey! What is your problem?"

Ye's soldiers are currently settling in Feng Jia's guard quarters. The events of the day are still fresh in my mind and so, given a spare moment when he was alone, I approach Zhang Mang to express my resentment.

"Sounds to me like you're the one with the problem."

He turns around, grinning like a mischievous young boy. If one didn't know better, would have thought he were still capable of innocence. The more irate my scowl grows, the wider his smile becomes.

"Commander Ru didn't do anything wrong! He didn't deserve to die!"

"Half of that is right."

"And?"

"And, what are you going to do about it?" With arms folded, he leans against one side of the wall under the arched tunnel leading to the back of the courtyard.

"You—! How can you take people's lives so lightly?!"

"That's my line. Had his life meant that much to you, then you should have challenged me earlier in front of everyone. Don't act all high and mighty now. It's not my fault you're a coward."

"He wasn't a threat to Nan Rong. Did you plan this from the start? Pressed him into a corner to usurp control over Ye's army? No, you know what? I don't give a damn what your reasons were! You had no right!"

"Stop berating me. Is an apology going to bring him back? *I'm so sorry*! Happy?"

"You're a real bastard, you know that? How can anyone trust you to lead when clemency is a foreign concept?"

"Tsk," Zhang Mang clicks his tongue. Then, lifting off the wall, closes the distance between us. The emerald eyes are carrying the same daggers from the battlefield. He's annoyed again. Without thinking, I step back while he continues to move in until I hit the wall. By the time I realize my mistake, his arms have already reached out to confine me in between. He looks down; the smile is anything but amused.

"Don't be an imbecile. No one life is above consequence to one nation. Why would I have wasted my time killing that idiot unless he posed a threat? It just so happened that a stupid girl thought cross-dressing was fun and of all the men to dress as, the very one she would undoubtedly meet in Feng Jia. If Ru had kept his mouth shut, another keen observer would have stepped forward and things would have still ended the same. I did what I had to do in order to fix *your* mistake! Think things through before you act! Every great feat has great penalty. You screwed up and someone had to die. It's that simple. Just be glad I didn't have to slay a hundred more to keep things calm after you butted in."

"But—! I didn't think he would... I butted in because... You're always one step ahead! You knew my blunder. Why didn't you say anything?!"

"Not my problem. Don't point fingers at others. It won't change the fact that you screwed up. Besides, I didn't ask for your help. My plans to expel Bei Ling were already set in motion. Your interference merely sped things up."

Pausing, the grimace across his petal lips is now a derisive smile. "Hmm, depressed already? Yes, it was your fault Ru died. You might as well have shoved the blade through his chest."

I stop breathing from the sudden accusation. Once the thought looming in the back of my mind is projected, guilt becomes a sin. I walked into Ye without the least notion of how my actions would influence others. All that mattered to me was Dui and Hu's safety. For that, one faultless man was killed right before my eyes. How many others have suffered the same fate behind my back? As he said, great feat comes with great penalty. I can't begin to grasp the consequences Bei Ling's men will face for their failure.

Chapter 27: Actions and Consequences

"*Interesting!*" Zhang Mang's sarcastic smirk is followed by an index finger against my forehead. "Look at you! So *serious*! Well, don't strain yourself. Keep rationalizing your mistakes, it won't change anything. The way to make up for any mistake is to continue after learning from it or make so many more mistakes that there's nothing left to fix. Either way, getting worked up over nothing is a waste of time. Bei Ling still needs to be taught a lesson so there's no time to waste."

Everything he said is true, however heartless his ideas are. My self-absorbed scheme to protect Nan Rong ignored the welfare of the other countries and their people. I'm not in any authority to correct those mistakes but maybe as he'd said, continuing on is the answer. The least I can do is continue to work toward ending Bei Ling's aggression, even if that too, has consequences.

"What? No backtalk? I thought you were full of opinions."

"I have an opinion of you, Zhang Mang. You're definitely full of something else."

"Oh! Sassy!" He cackles incessantly. "I can *feel* your rage through those burning eyes. It warms my heart. Here, let me feel them a little closer."

The irritating person leans in. My mind turns blank and I inadvertently swing a gauntlet at his face. He easily tilts back out of arm's reach, smiling a most devious smile. For a moment, what I thought was a severe look of lust enters his expression, turning my body to ice. Zhang Mang, realizing the same, suddenly shakes his head and moves back.

"You're purposefully turning me on, violent woman. Too bad your costume is also a complete turnoff. Oh well, another time. I'll bring the outfits and then we can role-play. There's a much cuter man whom you could pretend."

Shrugging, Zhang Mang stretches both arms in the air and takes to the path leading to the back of the courtyard.

"Wait! Just who the hell are you? Who sent you?"

"Me? I'm just a passerby. Pretend I'm not even here."

The flippant answer sends me to run after him. He throws back a word of advice to not keep my guest waiting. Diao suddenly calls out from behind. Once I turn back, Zhang Mang's disappeared.

Continue to page 448

Chapter 27 – 5

Ye's soldiers are currently settling in Feng Jia's guard quarters. Commander Ru lived but every ounce of respect he's earned throughout his entire career was destroyed in one swoop. None of Ye's men will pay the pitiful commander any regards. I, in turn, don't know the right thing to say that could fix his unwarranted punishment. For the duration of late afternoon, Ru remained withdrawn and distant, like a man who's lost his soul. By sunset, the humiliated soldier had already left camp.

The events of the day are still fresh in my mind and so, given a spare moment when he was alone, I approach Zhang Mang to express my resentment.

"Hey! What is your problem?"

"Sounds to me like you're the one with the problem."

He turns around, grinning like a mischievous young boy. If one didn't know better, would have thought he were still capable of innocence. The more irate my scowl grows, the wider his smile becomes.

"Had I not frightened his horse, you really would have ended Commander Ru, a brother-in-arms and ally, without a thought, wouldn't have you?"

"And?" With arms folded, he leans against one side of the wall under the arched tunnel leading to the back of the courtyard.

"You—! How can you take people's lives so lightly?!"

"That's my line. Had his life meant that much to you, then you should have challenged me earlier in front of everyone. Don't act all high and mighty now. It's not my fault you're a coward."

"He wasn't a threat to Nan Rong. Did you plan this from the start? Pressed him into a corner to usurp control over Ye's army? He may have lived but you've taken his life. You had no right!"

"Tsk," Zhang Mang clicks his tongue. Then, lifting off the wall, closes the distance between us. The emerald eyes are carrying the same daggers from the battlefield. He's annoyed again. Without thinking, I step back while he continues to move in until I hit the wall. By the time I realize my mistake, his arms have already reached out to confine me in between. He looks down; the smile is anything but amused.

"Don't be an imbecile. No one life is above consequence to one nation. Why would I have wasted my time unless he posed a threat? It just so happened that a stupid girl thought cross-dressing was fun and of all the men to dress as, the very one she would undoubtedly meet in Feng Jia. If Ru had kept his mouth shut, another keen observer would have stepped forward and things would have still ended the same. I did what I had to do in order to fix *your* mistake! Think things through before you act! Every great feat has great penalty. You screwed up and someone had to pay.

It's that simple. Just be glad the men didn't fall to hysteria and slit their own throats after you butted in!"

"But—! I didn't think he would... I butted in because... You're always one step ahead! You knew my blunder. Why didn't you say anything?!"

"Not my problem. Don't point fingers at others. It won't change the fact that you screwed up. Besides, I didn't ask for your help. My plans to expel Bei Ling were already set in motion. Your interference merely sped things up."

Pausing, the grimace across his petal lips is now a derisive smile. "Hmm, depressed already? Yes, it was your fault and it's not over. I was planning to finish what I started tonight but the coward ran away. People who lose pride often become petty and Ru's not above pettiness. By having stopped me, any future lives lost to that vengeful coward will be on your shoulders."

Zhang Mang moves away and continues to the courtyard. His words, which bring a pang of guilt to my chest, sounds like an ominous foreboding of things to come.

Continue to page 461

Chapter 28: The Western Alliance

"Your Highness, did something happen?"

"Highness? Please don't stand on ceremony. Friends and formalities are contradictory." She pouts shortly before a grin spreads across the flower face. Diao glances up and down my disguise, giggling. "Master Ying was right. You do look very dashing!"

"He said that?"

"Yes, but he was also very sarcastic. Master Ying would have come with me but he's too proud to admit that he's shy. Bao Lai, you have our gratitude."

"That's really not necessary!" I reach to raise up the bowing princess. "I didn't do much of anything!"

"I wouldn't say that. If nothing else, you gave me quite a fright, leading Ye's army here. Because of your actions, Bei Ling retreated. Did you plan this from the start?"

"More like made things up as I went. I had help from extraordinary people. That's why I don't feel like I've accomplished anything. I'm just... sorry Ru had to die."

"That was a sad turn of event. Unexpected. Despite his opposition, I think him an honorable man. Only a strong person would stand his ground knowing defeat is certain. That's why I really don't know what to make of this Zhang Mang. Master Ying thought he was rational but I, well, I'm not sure. What do you think?"

"Zhang Mang is... necessary. He played no small part in persuading Neng Cao and we'll need his strength in the fight against Bei Ling. That said, he is still a manipulative conman without any remorse. Something in my gut tells me he cares about Nan Rong the way Ying cares for you and Feng Jia. I know that isn't what you wished to hear."

"It is. I will keep an open mind since you and Master Ying share an opinion. I'll do my part and remain vigilant. Besides, no matter how he tries to keep me sheltered, I know the troubles Master Ying's caused. He's not an innocent man and his hands have been drenched in blood. Redemption for his sins, redemption for me who has stood idle for too long and let him carry Feng Jia's plight alone, will begin by ending this conflict. And, though it isn't much, I will ensure for Commander Ru an honorable burial."

"He was a loyal servant of Ye. I'd like to send him home."

Diao nods sadly. Many lives have been claimed since this conflict began and undoubtedly, many more will be claimed before it's over. It reasons then to end this conflict as soon as possible.

"I'm very proud of you, Diao. When I first came to Quan Ming, it was a ghost town. You've managed to bring back life and give the people hope."

"You give me too much credit," her eyes avert shyly. "I couldn't do much on my own either. I, too, had help. Master Ying is always ready to support me and Mr. Dui was very inspiring."

Dui. Just hearing his name makes my heart swells with conflicting emotions. I haven't sought for him since entering Feng Jia because I felt guilty and I haven't asked about him because I'm afraid of the consequence. Zhang Mang wasn't wrong. I really am a coward.

"What's wrong, Bao Lai? Are you crying?"

"N-No." My denial is hardly believable when more tears are flowing than my sleeve can soak up. "H-How is Dui?"

"Is that why? Silly, he's fine! I knew you'd come back. I encouraged him to stay but he's as stubborn as the woman he loves. "

"What do you mean? Did he leave? Where did he go?!"

Giggling, Diao tugs on my arm and starts for the gardens. She refuses to give into my frantic badgering until we're past the gates. "A week ago, Mr. Dui returned to Nan Rong. He said there were people waiting for his services."

"Are you sure? You can't trust that man to keep from mischief."

"Really? He said the same about you. In fact, he talked about you so much that I couldn't sit idle. I understand why he idolizes you. From our conversations, I came to idolize you too. I thought bowing to Bei Ling was the answer but that merely served as bandages on a festering wound. I wanted to be like you, strong and proactive; someone Master Ying would feel proud to stand by."

"And has he reciprocated your affection?"

"Not yet but I won't give up!" Sparking eyes and nervous giggles brighten the scene. Diao looks around before leaning in closer, smiling happily. "Can I tell you a secret? Don't be mad. I think that when I spent endless days with Mr. Dui, Master Ying became very annoyed. Jealous, even! So, I might have spent more time with Mr. Dui than I should have. Nothing happened though, of course. I mean, once you love someone with all your heart, no one else can dominate any part of it. Don't you agree?"

"Um..." More awkward silence. She's waiting for my approval and though I should agree, though I want to agree, my mouth is moving and nothing will project. The answer should be simple. Love is finite. The heart doesn't change. That is the epitome of loyalty.

"Bao Lai? Don't you agree?"

"I don't know," is my embarrassed response.

"Oh? Oh! I-I'm sorry! That was very rude. General Hu, right? I'd forgotten. Wait, so if you don't know does that mean Mr. Dui still has a chance?"

"Eh, what? Just how much did he tell you?"

"Enough to know that he's *madly* in love with you!"

"Please don't say that." The thought is killing me, only because I feel happy.

"What's wrong with Mr. Dui?"

"Nothing's wrong with Dui. He's important to me and so is Bai Hu."

"Does Bai Hu love you as much as Mr. Dui?"

"He... did. It's complicated."

"Hmm, I bet! Must be difficult having two great men in love with you!"

"Until everything is settled with Bei Ling, I don't think having ten men in love with me will make a difference. Besides, I would be surprised if Dui's forgiven me. Before I left, I pushed him to fall for you."

"No! Bao Lai, that is too cruel! Mr. Dui is not fickle!"

"Then wouldn't I be fickle too if my affections for Hu shifted to Dui?"

Having perceived my troubles, she looks contemplatively at the sky during the drawn moment. Sometime after, a thought forms and then she resumes the path. "Well, fickle only for convenience's sake. Not if you really love him. I couldn't love Mr. Dui no matter how sweet he is because Master Ying is my one true love. It would never work. Your situation is different."

"Convenience's sake, huh? I think you are giving convenient answers, Diao. Thank you for trying to cheer me up but I insulted Dui, aggravated Bai Hu, and caused trouble for both. I acted without considering the consequences. I was egotistical to say the least."

"I wouldn't stop being an egotistical troublemaker if I were you. Mr. Dui seems to like all your vices."

An elbow nudges my arm. Diao giggles jokingly. I throw back a weak smile for lack of a comeback. Our stroll then winds down a wider path. For a long while after, we enjoy each other's company without exchanging many words until the thumping of boots in the distance from the evening patrol brings conversations back to the task at hand. The two western territories have now been united. There's only one path to go from here.

Chapter 28 – 2

As it turns out, Zhang Mang and Ying are very well acquainted and also very adamant to end the association through the sword. The last time we were all gathered in the throne room, a brawl nearly broke out. The only reason it didn't was that Diao interceded with breaking for lunch. Since then, Her Highness and I have been mouthpieces, exchanging information which are then relayed to our charges kept in opposing ends of the palace. In short, Diao and I have become babysitters.

Zhang Mang wants to lead the joined armies to Bei Ling while Ying is against the idea. His argument is that Feng Jia's men have sat idle for too long, are untrained, and should not become pawns to Zhang Mang's authority. I see validity in his concerns. Should Feng Jia lead the charge, their inexperience will result in defeat and create a terrible blow to morale. Should Ye lead the charge, victory will go to Zhang Mang, the albeit belligerent but charismatic leader, who has been increasingly popular amongst Feng Jia's men. Ying has Diao's interest to secure. She can't lead Feng Jia in the aftermath with everyone idolizing Zhang Mang. He could easily step in and rally both western territories for Nan Rong; an idea that is hardly farfetched considering his unwavering loyalty to the South. What this equates to is lack of solution unless another leads in her authority. That is, Ying wants me to lead the charge in Diao's authority.

Chapter 28: The Western Alliance

A few days later, another familiar face arrives at court. Lo Han comes bearing gifts from San An. For this occasion, the rivals are invited to the throne room. In the large trunk the runners brought in, He Pi's crimson armors and sword are laid.

"Prime Minister San An wishes for you, Bao Lai, to take the charge from Feng Jia as His Highness, He Pi. This will reinforce the rumors of Nan Rong's domination in the West. Bei Ling's morale will be crushed."

Lo Han's plan is met favorably by Zhang Mang and as expected, disdain from Ying.

"Nan Rong was recognized for freeing the Western Territories. Since the continuing charge will be led from Feng Jia, Nan Rong's role should end here. He Pi will not twice accept feats he neither accomplished."

"Don't be petty!" Zhang Mang also stands up and moves to the center. "Is this really the time to discuss credits? Wang Liang must be dispatched. That should be our primary goal. After that, if you wish to carve up Bei Ling four ways, I won't argue."

"False promises from a man who's been working to divide Feng Jia. You've been furtively recruiting our soldiers. That is not a secret to anyone."

"Huh, so I'm the bad person here for being affable? Well, excuse me for questioning your loyalty. Wasn't it you who instigated this nonsense in the first place for Wang Liang?"

"Wait, Zhang Mang, this conflict was started by Wang Liang?" I now join the fray. The belt buckle I'd tasked Qing Hai to deliver to San An had Nan Rong's royal insignia. Wang Liang is Bei Ling's prime minister. That makes no sense at all.

"That's right," Zhang Mang frowns with hands on his hips. "You didn't know? That's brash! Here you are on the verge of bringing Bei Ling to its knees and you don't even know who is behind this mess? Stupid is too kind a word for an ignoramus."

"Then enlighten me. Why is Bei Ling doing this?"

"Men of power don't need reasons to accumulate more power, darling. To them, it's a right. Had I known our *friend* here turned traitor to Wang Liang, this ordeal could have been taken care of much sooner. So, what's your excuse for not running a sword through that bastard's heart when you had the chance?"

Ying doesn't answer. He's not a man who naturally feels compelled to defend his honor, especially against an agitator. Nevertheless, the hardened assassin I first met not too long ago has somehow softened since his return to Yu Qi. He cares for Dui and perceptively, has also come to openly show his fondness for Diao. With her urging, Ying lets out a quiet sigh.

"Wang Liang rarely ever leaves his stronghold. His runner, Su Jian, sends instructions to me. Except, my research concluded her real name is Yan Lei. Further sleuthing produced that Wang Liang is Su Jian."

Ying's eyes fall on me to convey expectation of a revelation that should be obvious. I stare back, dumbfounded. That still doesn't explain why Wang Liang targeted Nan Rong.

"God! It's *painful*! That lost puppy look is agitatedly adorable!" Zhang Mang's index finger digs into my right cheek. I slap away his hand and then he moves back, laughing. "Su Jian is from Nan Rong, my dear oblivious pet. A prince no less. Well, *was* a prince. Everyone thought he died. Funny how that works."

"Wang Liang is He Pi's brother? Why attack his own home? Why now?"

"What is it with you and reasons? Who cares why? I just want to send him back to hell where he belongs." Pausing, his tongue clicks. "Makes sense why the illustrious minister wished for He Pi to charge at Bei Ling. With Nan Rong's colors surrounding them from two sides, the former prince won't know which direction to retaliate."

"Those were his exact thoughts." Lo Han finally reenters conversations. "His Highness is currently inside Bei Ling working with another group to overthrow Wang Liang. Bao Lai, confusion is a potent tool. Wang Liang's worst fear is His Highness.

Coincidentally, you both share a face. We should use that to our advantage."

"Well said, old man."

"Not so fast." Ying overthrows Zhang Mang's enthusiasm. The latter is already fetching armor from the trunk. "Nan Rong will not use Feng Jia to claim another victory."

"This again? I'm not interested in this piss-poor country and neither is the South. Look at the big picture. You have your freedom. So Feng Jia won't have a stake in Bei Ling's wealth and the little miss won't have the people eating out of her palms as you wish. Oh, well. That's your damn problem. Should have thought about that before siding with a criminal."

"Zhang Mang!"

"Yes, darling?" He turns and smiles boyishly. "Stop getting so worked up. You're turning me on."

"Must you keep insulting our allies? Ying has a point."

"No, he doesn't. Anyone who thinks so is an idiot and deserves to be taken out back and shot. From the beginning, he's known Wang Liang has strong-armed Bei Ling's council. Their emperor, Cai Pai, is a puppet and will continue to be a puppet until the day he dies. Ying was drawn to a traitor because he too is a traitor. A traitor to Ning, Feng Jia, and now Bei Ling. The list of people after his head would fill this entire room. So, as a last redemption because his enemies will never permit him to part from this conflict unscathed, he's trying to secure wealth and authority for the little princess. Love is a foolish thing, isn't it?"

Diao and I stare at one another and then at Ying. He won't acknowledge Zhang Mang's claims, especially the last part. I keep overlooking his crimes because he is Dui's brother. A life with Diao in any society would be near impossible after everything he's done. Despite his fate, Ying only thinks of her, the way Dui always puts me first.

Tears swell and then threaten to fall. I clamp down my jaw to keep from wavering. In succession, another trembling voice calls for everyone's attention.

"Master Ying, is that true?"

Diao's pleading is met with a quiet sigh. She moves to take his arm but Ying gently withdraws. She loves him without a doubt, without question, in the absolute. I have never witnessed anything so pure and perfect. My conflicting heart pales in comparison to their devotion and yet, I still have a choice.

The sight of their unfilled happiness rips at my heart. I started to speak on her behalf when Diao, overflowing with sorrow, pushes back the surging tears. Her once rosy cheeks take on the maturity of pallid lilies. She comes to a greater revelation during the ensuing silence which neither I nor others in the room could grasp. With a hardened countenance, Diao gives her attention to Zhang Mang.

"I will ride with you and Bao Lai. No one territory will claim victory. We do this together."

"It's too dangerous," Ying softly contends.

"Then protect me as you have promised my father. This is my choice and I will see it through. It won't be easy to break their defenses but I'm counting on you, Master Ying. And also on you both."

"Nothing of worth ever comes easy," Zhang Mang snorts. "Try not to get in the way."

I look to Lo Han for advice and through his meaningful smile, concede. Although I'm against Diao on the front line, arguing is pointless. Her determination won't waver. She's riding out to protect Feng Jia and earn her people's reverence and trust. Another part aims to keep Ying close. She would never let him go without a fight. And I, if possible, will help her keep him forever.

Continue to page 468

Chapter 28 – 3

As it turns out, Zhang Mang and Ying are very well acquainted and also very adamant to end the association through the sword. The last time we were all gathered in the throne room, a brawl nearly broke out. The only reason it didn't was that Diao interceded with breaking for lunch. Since then, Her Highness and I have been mouthpieces, exchanging information which are then relayed to our charges kept in opposing ends of the palace. In short, Diao and I have become babysitters.

Zhang Mang wants to lead the joined armies to Bei Ling while Ying is against the idea. His argument is that Feng Jia's men have sat idle for too long, are untrained, and should not become pawns to Zhang Mang's authority. I see validity in his concerns. Should Feng Jia lead the charge, their inexperience will result in defeat and create a terrible blow to morale. Should Ye lead the charge, victory will go to Zhang Mang, the albeit belligerent but charismatic leader, who has been increasingly popular amongst Feng Jia's men. Ying has Diao's interest to secure. She can't lead Feng Jia in the aftermath with everyone idolizing Zhang Mang. He could easily step in and rally both western territories for Nan Rong; an idea that is hardly farfetched considering his unwavering loyalty to the South. What this equates to is lack of solution unless another leads in her authority. That is, Ying wants me to lead the charge in Diao's authority.

A few days later, another familiar face arrives at court. Lo Han comes bearing gifts from San An. For this occasion, the rivals are invited to the throne room. In the large trunk the runners brought in, He Pi's crimson armors and sword are laid.

"Prime Minister San An wishes for you, Bao Lai, to take the charge from Feng Jia as His Highness, He Pi. This will reinforce the rumors of Nan Rong's domination in the West. Bei Ling's morale will be crushed."

Lo Han's plan is met favorably by Zhang Mang and as expected, disdain from Ying.

"Nan Rong was recognized for freeing the Western Territories. Since the continuing charge will be led from Feng Jia, Nan Rong's role should end here. He Pi will not twice accept feats he neither accomplished."

"Don't be petty!" Zhang Mang also stands up and moves to the center. "Is this really the time to discuss credits? Wang Liang must be dispatched. That should be our primary goal. After that, if you wish to carve up Bei Ling four ways, I won't argue."

"False promises from a man who's been working to divide Feng Jia. You've been furtively recruiting our soldiers. That is not a secret to anyone."

"Huh, so I'm the bad person here for being affable? Well, excuse me for questioning your loyalty. Wasn't it you who instigated this nonsense in the first place for Wang Liang?"

"Wait, Zhang Mang, this conflict was started by Wang Liang?" I now join the fray. The belt buckle I'd tasked Qing Hai to deliver to San An had Nan Rong's royal insignia. Wang Liang is Bei Ling's prime minister. That makes no sense at all.

"That's right," Zhang Mang frowns with hands on his hips. "You didn't know? That's brash! Here you are on the verge of bringing Bei Ling to its knees and you don't even know who is behind this mess? Stupid is too kind a word for an ignoramus."

"Then enlighten me. Why is Bei Ling doing this?"

"Men of power don't need reasons to accumulate more power, darling. To them, it's a right. Had I known our *friend* here turned traitor to Wang Liang, this ordeal could have been taken care of much sooner. So, what's your excuse for not running a sword through that bastard's heart when you had the chance?"

Ying doesn't answer. He's not a man who naturally feels compelled to defend his honor, especially against an agitator. Nevertheless, the hardened assassin I first met not too long ago has somehow softened since his return to Yu Qi. He cares for Dui and perceptively, has also come to openly show his fondness for Diao. With her urging, Ying lets out a quiet sigh.

"Wang Liang rarely ever leaves his stronghold. His runner, Su Jian, sends instructions to me. Except, my research concluded her real name is Yan Lei. Further sleuthing produced that Wang Liang is Su Jian."

Ying's eyes fall on me to convey expectation of a revelation that should be obvious. I stare back, dumbfounded. That still doesn't explain why Wang Liang targeted Nan Rong.

"God! It's *painful*! That lost puppy look is agitatedly adorable!" Zhang Mang's index finger digs into my right cheek. I slap away his hand and then he moves back, laughing. "Su Jian is from Nan Rong, my dear oblivious pet. A prince no less. Well, *was* a prince. Everyone thought he died. Funny how that works."

"Wang Liang is He Pi's brother? Why attack his own home? Why now?"

"What is it with you and reasons? Who cares why? I just want to send him back to hell where he belongs." Pausing, his tongue clicks. "Makes sense why the illustrious minister wished for He Pi to charge at Bei Ling. With Nan Rong's colors surrounding them from two sides, the former prince won't know which direction to retaliate."

"Those were his exact thoughts." Lo Han finally reenters conversations. "His Highness is currently inside Bei Ling working with another group to overthrow Wang Liang. Bao Lai, confusion is a potent tool. Wang Liang's worst fear is His Highness.

Coincidentally, you both share a face. We should use that to our advantage."

"Well said, old man."

"Not so fast." Ying overthrows Zhang Mang's enthusiasm. The latter is already fetching armor from the trunk. "Nan Rong will not use Feng Jia to claim another victory."

"This again? I'm not interested in this piss-poor country and neither is the South. Look at the big picture. You have your freedom. So Feng Jia won't have a stake in Bei Ling's wealth and the little miss won't have the people eating out of her palms as you wish. Oh, well. That's your damn problem. Should have thought about that before siding with a criminal."

"Zhang Mang!"

"Yes, darling?" He turns and smiles boyishly. "Stop getting so worked up. You're turning me on."

"Must you keep insulting our allies? Ying has a point."

"No, he doesn't. Anyone who thinks so is an idiot and deserves to be taken out back and shot. From the beginning, he's known Wang Liang has strong-armed Bei Ling's council. Their emperor, Cai Pai, is a puppet and will continue to be a puppet until the day he dies. Ying was drawn to a traitor because he too is a traitor. A traitor to Ning, Feng Jia, and now Bei Ling. The list of people after his head would fill this entire room. So, as

465

a last redemption because his enemies will never permit him to part from this conflict unscathed, he's trying to secure wealth and authority for the little princess. Love is a foolish thing, isn't it?"

Diao and I stare at one another and then at Ying. He won't acknowledge Zhang Mang's claims, especially the last part. I keep overlooking his crimes because he is Dui's brother. A life with Diao in any society would be near impossible after everything he's done. Despite his fate, Ying only thinks of her, the way Dui always puts me first.

Tears swell and then threaten to fall. I clamp down my jaw to keep from wavering. In succession, another trembling voice calls for everyone's attention.

"Master Ying, is that true?"

Diao's pleading is met with a quiet sigh. She moves to take his arm but Ying gently withdraws. She loves him without a doubt, without question, in the absolute. I have never witnessed anything so pure and perfect. My conflicting heart pales in comparison to their devotion and yet, I still have a choice.

The sight of their unfilled happiness rips at my heart. I started to speak on her behalf when Diao, overflowing with sorrow, pushes back the surging tears. Her once rosy cheeks take on the maturity of pallid lilies. She comes to a greater revelation during the ensuing silence which neither I nor others in the room could grasp. With a hardened countenance, Diao gives her attention to Zhang Mang.

"I will ride with you and Bao Lai. No one territory will claim victory. We do this together."

"It's too dangerous," Ying softly contends.

"Then protect me as you have promised my father. This is my choice and I will see it through. It won't be easy to break their defenses but I'm counting on you, Master Ying. And also on you both."

"Nothing of worth ever comes easy," Zhang Mang snorts. "Try not to get in the way."

I look to Lo Han for advice and through his meaningful smile, concede. Although I'm against Diao on the front line, arguing is pointless. Her determination won't waver. She's riding out to protect Feng Jia and earn her people's reverence and trust. Another part aims to keep Ying close. She would never let him go without a fight. And I, if possible, will help her keep him forever.

Continue to page 490

Chapter 29: The Demon's Revenge

Three flags signaling the alliance give the impression our combined army is three times larger than actual size. Our march is met with little opposition and rare skirmishes end quickly. We pass through gate after gate unhindered. Soon, their walls will appear in the horizon, giving end to this discord.

Around the campfire on this cold night, Diao and I huddle together for warmth. Ying and Zhang Mang have gone off to scout our surroundings and Lo Han has retreated to his tent. I'm unsure why he chose to come; though, I would be lying to say that I mind his company. He's my mentor and at times like these, I still need guidance.

"Would you like more to eat, Diao?"

"No, I'm fine." The gloom hasn't left her since the incident from the throne room. Diao throws a few more sticks into the fire and then rests her head on her knees, sighing.

"It will be okay, Diao. Give him some time to consider."

Shaking her head, another weary sigh escapes. "You're so naïve Bao Lai."

"What do you mean?"

Chapter 29: The Demon's Revenge

"Time can't change what the heart refuses to acknowledge. After all these years, I'm still just a sister to him. I'm fine, really. I knew. And I... don't want to discuss love anymore."

"Sorry. I didn't mean to be nosy."

"You could have said concerned. I would have been none the wiser." She smiles. "Since you're openly nosy, could I tell you a story?"

"Of course."

"Thank you. It's nice to have a sister." Diao taps her knees a few times to collect her thoughts. "My father, a very courageous and talented man, wanted a worthy son to lead Feng Jia. He wasn't blessed. My mother died when I was born and though his advisors encouraged the idea, he refused to remarry. He loved my mother too much. Honesty and devotion were the bases of his character. All my life, I'd admire that in him and strived to mirror him, so that he may one day feel proud. When he brought Master Ying home, I knew I'd been replaced. I couldn't compete. Instead, I threw tantrums and tried to make him leave.

Except, Master Ying never once thought himself better. He protected me, guided me, and swore his loyalty. He thinks I am the most capable person to lead Feng Jia. To honor my father and for my benefit, he's done unspeakable things, most of which were behind my back. That doesn't justify his actions and whether on Earth or in the afterlife, he will have to answer for his crimes. Despite that, Bao Lai, please protect him. I'm not strong enough to save Master Ying. Before he ever faces trial by peers, I fear a trial by swords awaits."

"Diao, you're not exactly asking the right person. For a time, I was one of those people who wished him trial by swords. Because of him, my beloved will never be the same. Even now, there are still resentful parts of me. For you and for Dui, I've attempted to give Ying the benefit of the doubt and overlook his offenses. I can't make false promises. I'm not as strong as Zhang Mang or Ying."

"You are with Tian Ji Zhong Shi Yan."

"Wh—! How? Dui! That blabbermouth!"

"Not at all," she giggles. "Your eyes turned faint gold during the standoff at Yuo Muo. Most wouldn't have noticed but I couldn't miss it, because my father was the same. He had the Demon Slayer blood, too; a descendant of Fa Zhen. See? We *are* like sisters."

"We... are. I still can't make false promises."

"Because using the skill might cost your life."

"No, because I can't put all my faith in my blood. I can't promise that I will keep him safe but if you will permit, I can promise to try."

Diao looks up at the star-laced sky wistfully, smiling an ambiguous smile. In time, hopeful, nearly pleading, eyes fall on me. "Bao Lai, if you could strive to protect

Master Ying and keep him on this Earth even a second longer than fate has decided, I will forever be grateful."

"That is a promise I can make. I will do everything in my capabilities."

Chapter 29 – 2

Seconds after I call for him, Lo Han, smiling seductively, draws back the entrance flap to his tent. I can't believe he's adamant about teasing me at a time like this.

"Coming into a man's tent in the middle of the night, Bao Lai, is too forward, even for you."

"Your sister has already been to your house many times, Lo Han."

"To my house as a sister; to the bedroom that is my tent as a woman."

"All the while cross-dressed as He Pi."

Lo Han, seemingly enjoying himself, smiles genuinely at my inappropriate blushing. "The comfort of warmth which only the flesh can impose is much more important than any cold armored shell. Wouldn't you agree?"

"Don't poke fun at me, Lo Han. It's not fair for you to know my secret."

"What secret would that be?"

"That... your sister admires you greatly."

"More than admire, I hope."

Chapter 29: The Demon's Revenge

Meaningful, sultry eyes take my breath away. I'm feeling faint again, in spite of myself. "Someday, Lo Han, the right woman will torture you in my stead."

"That torturous woman is closer to me now than any other. Is something causing your anxiety, Bao Lai?"

He brushes past the ambiguous declaration, smiling kindly as though he hadn't said anything at all. I know that smug look. He wouldn't tell me even if I try to beat it out of him. Whoever she is, I am certain he doesn't mean me. Acknowledging that eases my rioting heart.

"There is. I heard the soldiers whispering, mostly idle gossips, but something caught my attention earlier. They said Wang Liang is as powerful and crafty as he is ruthless. We've been marching for a week now. I am surprised by his lack of retaliation."

"You're afraid we're marching too fast?"

"Yes. Morale has been high and momentum is building but what if we're getting ahead of ourselves? I trust Ying and even Zhang Mang but I don't know anything about Wang Liang. Are we heading for a trap?"

"Worrywart. How would we know until we get there?"

"Very funny."

The smile on his lips flattens. Lo Han paces slowly around the tent, lost in thought with hands cupped behind his back. Once paused, he moves to draw back the tent flap and drifts a steady glance at the dark sky.

"It's close to midnight, isn't it, Bao Lai?"

"Yes, I think so."

"Then, it is already too late."

"Oh. Sorry. I saw your light on. Didn't think you'd mind. I can come back in the morning."

Following an alluring chuckle, he turns back, smiling so sweetly that it's almost devilish. The unholy sight makes me lose my breath.

"Such an innocent answer. You are too naïve. It's a pity, dear little sister. I am too fond of you to watch you die. If only you'd come to me sooner, I could have spared you the pain."

"What... are you saying?"

"The deadliest trap requires the least effort. The well-placed trap under your noses has already taken hold. Death is moments away from claiming his first victim. The new day marks the end of the Western Alliance. Find solace within this sentiment: you won't die alone."

"Stop joking. You're saying dangerous things, Lo Han."

The inconceivable notion that my mentor has deceived me is slowly sowing into my doubts.

Chapter 29: The Demon's Revenge

Simultaneously, I know that without his help, Bei Ling would still dominate the West. In exchange for my blank stare, his smile deepens to fondness. He comes close and envelops his warm body around mine. This moment, which I'd dreamt those many years ago at Tian Mao Yi, comes too late. I attempt to shirk off the inappropriate embrace, though unsuccessfully.

"You're acting strange, Lo Han, more than usual."

"That's where you're wrong. Usually, I am out of my real character. Usually, I wouldn't dare put my hands on you. If you had come to me in Liang Bi and asked for my love and devotion, I would have given without hesitation. I promised Tai Hung to look after you and I promised myself to give whatever you'd ask. You asked for the wrong favor."

His arms constrict. A soft sigh laces into my hair. I can't grasp anything he's saying but the idea is more than frightening. He's one of the few people left in the world I'd entrust everything. I don't want to lose him.

The only thing I can think to do is shake my head and grab onto his shirt, silently pleading for him to retract from whatever it is he's planning.

"Don't cry, little one."

"I am not little! Don't talk to me like a child! What are you doing, Lo Han?"

"Two birds with one stone. Justice for myself and for my family."

"Your family? When we first met, you said you didn't have any."

"I didn't. I don't have anyone because of people like you."

"What is that supposed to mean? And don't circle the truth! Be honest!"

"You don't have long to live and this is how you choose to spend your last moments? Fine. Allow me to sate your curiosity. Centuries after the purge of the northern barbarians, they still hunted us like animals. Thirty years ago, food was scarce in Bei Ling and jobs were plentiful in the West. My family and hundreds of other migrants headed for Feng Jia along the old Han Shan Road. It didn't take long for highwaymen to exploit the opportunity. Every other family put their own first and left useless prayers for the unfortunates targeted by the riffraff. Half a day's trek away from Feng Jia and then we came upon a one-horse cart in dire. My father couldn't live with himself if he permitted their young daughters defiled and their men slaughtered. For his good deed was in exchange, his life. His Demon blood was exposed and the very people he saved turned him in to the guards. My father was executed, as was my mother for being his *whore*. I did as Mother instructed and ran like a coward until Ma Tai Tou brought me into her protection. I thought I could let the past go and then I met you."

Chapter 29: The Demon's Revenge

Lord Han Bei's warnings shoot across my conscience like a paralyzing bolt of lightning. My blood seeks to destroy theirs. It's not superstition. It is fact. Fa Zhen's descendants won't stop until they've obliterated every Demon.

"You knew... about me... all this time? Why? Why didn't you tell me? Why were you kind to me? Why have you been letting me torture you?!"

"Have I been kind, Bao Lai?" He shoots back languidly. "By happenstance, I discovered your identity through an assassin operating for a discreet Ning faction. I didn't care why their faction sought your death. I just wanted vengeance for my people. I told him where to find you and how to evade the temple's security."

"You were the one who sold me out to the assassin that Bai Hu killed?"

"Yes. Bai Hu. For a temperamental boy, he amazed me. You were always bullying him, treating him unkindly for being small and inferior, the way your people have treated mine. But he saved you, nearly died for you, without any benefit to himself. In effect, he lost himself, the same as my father. I couldn't raise my hand against you after that; otherwise, I would have dishonored my father's sacrifice. You want to know the heinous truth after all? Your childish infatuation was agonizingly insufferable! I hated you. And then ironically, I hated myself for finding pleasure in your company. I started to fall under your spell and the path to my destruction. So, I left Tian Mao Yi; lost the place to call home."

"I... am so sorry, Lo Han. What can I possibly do—"

"There isn't anything you can do. You haven't sinned against me even if everything inside you inherently seeks to destroy my existence. It is nature, as water is to fire and light to darkness. And naturally, I seek to preserve my pointless life and take vengeance against the unjust. Diao. That girl is also Fa Zhen's descendant. Her father put mine to death. I couldn't find justice for him. I will for myself."

"You can't be serious. Diao is just a child!"

"She's no more of a child than you are."

"But, Lo Han, you can't. You're a man of the cloth."

"Not anymore."

"You are at heart! You've helped countless people and performed innumerable good deeds."

"And what have I to show for it? No family. No justice. I must pretend to be like everyone else. Content. At the first notion of my bloodline, there's a place at the gallows marked for me. Now that you know what I am, what will you do, Bao Lai?"

Surging waves of pain and confusion stagnate inside my chest. Those eyes on the face so dear to me bear both distraught and anger. My lips part and yet nothing comes to ease his pain. The helpless feeling destroys my composure. As a last resort, I shake my head and bury my face against his chest, grasping his shirt ever tighter.

"Don't feel sorry for me, Bao Lai, because I haven't for you. The antidote is written on a note I swallowed the moment you came inside. You'll have to slice my belly open to find it or watch every man and woman here die."

The ghastly proposition sends me off his chest, stumbling back clumsily.

"Antidote? Lo Han, what have you done?"

"I have not done anything nor will I. The stars foretold Wang Liang's ambition and I have chosen to not intervene. The water you've all been drinking is laced with a new poison, the likes of which no healers can cure."

"Except you?"

"I am not a healer. By having stood idle, I am as guilty as Wang Liang. I am not innocent. Do the right thing. Save everyone."

"Are you insane? Why are you doing this?"

"Vengeance is the easy answer. Vengeance through the only method I know how. I can't raise my hands against you, Bao Lai."

"And I won't raise my hands against you! Lo Han, I'm asking you. Please, stop this!"

"It's too late for favors. You should have petitioned for my love."

In another time, those words would have rendered me deliriously happy. I wish that I could return then to undo all the pain and suffering my blood has brought to those I care most. The unbearable guilt makes my mind go blank and it's not until some time has passed do I realize that the world hasn't stood still. Lo Han's arms have encircled my body. His lips kiss me with passion more fantastic than I ever imagined him capable, passion more intense than anything I've ever felt, and while my heart is pounding furiously, I know this isn't romantic love. I do love him but my heart is taken and likewise, his is filled solely by vengeance. This kiss is merely another act of retribution.

"Lo Han! Don't! The poison!"

I push him off and move back, cupping a hand over my mouth. My mentor smiles. At last, he is satisfied.

"I've taken your poison, Bao Lai. Whether you kill me or not, I will die through you. There is only one choice left to make."

"You—! What happened to preserving your *pointless* life? You're not making any sense at all!"

"You're crying. Having someone shed tears over me in the short time remaining is a sign my existence had meaning. What a sensational feeling."

Chapter 29: The Demon's Revenge

He's gone mad. His despondent view on life has robbed Lo Han of all sense and sensibility. Saddest of all, this view isn't newfound. He's carried this anger inside for decades. I didn't notice because I always came to him with my problems, never worrying too much over his troubles.

"Stop over thinking. You don't have much time. Most if not all will die within three days. The weakest will be taken in mere hours. It will be on your conscience unless you do the right thing."

He moves to the mat set on the dirt floor and takes a prayer pose, signaling that he won't retaliate. Outside, murmurs ignite to vociferous clamors. I rush to find a handful of men sprawled on every side of camp, groaning from pain while others falter to panic.

Chapter 29 – 3

The uproar brought back Zhang Mang and Ying. They're both so perceptive, I fear for Lo Han's life. He doesn't deserve to die; after all, it wasn't he who poisoned our water. I knew he had a talent for star reading but it was never this accurate, to pinpoint the exact moment in time or find the antidote to an exact poison. In other words, he guessed, and killing Lo Han would prove futile. He doesn't know the antidote either. The lies were meant to expedite his death. That is an ambition I refuse to fulfill. If I have it my way, he'll have to keep his misery and live to a ripe old age.

The initial symptoms of tremors, stomach pains, paresthesia, and cold sweat make me think a neurotoxin may be the root. However, a few men are also exhibiting blisters; none are displaying necrosis. I have no idea what this is and with each minute, more symptoms arise. Ying's background in medicine and poison acquired from his trade put him in the lead position to find an antidote. While we work through a list of possibilities, Zhang Mang stands guard. The camp is vulnerable without defense. Men continue keeling over; half of which are due to hysteria. Diao, who claims to feel fine, tends to the soldiers.

Despite his indifference, the nagging thoughts keep returning. I can't help but glance toward Lo Han's tent out of concern. After a while, Ying catches me in the act.

"Does he have something to do with this?"

"Who?"

"The flippant monk!"

"No. He's been in his tent since we made camp."

I manage to employ that confident tone practiced during my time with Ma Tai Tou. His dubious nature would otherwise chance a glimpse of the truth but with more soldiers falling to panic, Ying lets go of the idea.

"Yu Qi. You and Zhang Mang were away for most of the day. Your canteens contained water from the River Huan, right?"

"Either address me as Ying or don't," he grumbles. "Someone could have contaminated the rations for all I know. But, yes, I have been drinking water from Huan."

"And you feel fine?"

"So do you. Stop asking pointless questions."

Ying continues paging through the worn booklet, notes kept from decades of experience. With my limited knowledge in toxins, there's nothing I can accomplish by standing here aside from distracting him. I start for Diao in the newly designated quarantine area at the southwestern part of camp.

Chapter 29 – 4

Lo Han's warnings are slowly fulfilling. It's been over an hour since symptoms broke out. Several men have died and many more will soon follow.

"Is Master Ying close?" Diao runs toward me, wiping the stains from her cheeks with one sleeve. Hope laces her teary eyes and then burn to despair when I shake my head.

"No. I'm sorry. This is all I have. It's not much but it's all I have."

Diao grasps the trembling hand that's produced a handful of willow leaves from my pocket. No matter how detached I've told myself to become, to keep from faltering to irrationality, anger and sadness surge when faced with good people pointlessly losing their lives. This was another mistake, a consequence to an action, as Zhang Mang pointed out. I pushed them to end Bei Ling and in the end, Bei Ling will be the death of us all.

"Stop it, Bao Lai!"

I look up, wide-eyed, to Diao's controlled chiding. She's taken the leaves from my hand and crumpled them in hers.

"Pointing fingers won't help anyone! Now, as I recall, willow leaves can relieve slight pains. It's better than nothing. Although, what a peculiar thing to carry in your pocket!"

Chapter 29: The Demon's Revenge

She smiles to lift my moods, as she had been doing for the soldiers. A smile as bright as the sun, the kind eyes, and gentle demeanor. No wonder the men in this area, facing inevitability, appear more tamed than I expected. Diao played no small part in that miracle.

"I couldn't help myself on the way out from Feng Jia. Dui said to always carry willow leaves in case I can't tell if a patient still lives."

"Why's that?"

"Because willow is so disgustingly bitter, no person alive can remain still."

His ridiculousness brings a smile to my face. The fact that I believed him makes Diao smiles too. That silly doctor. If he were here, this crisis wouldn't be as daunting.

"Any new symptoms?"

"No, none that I see." Diao scans the morbid scene behind, fighting off impending tears as best she can manage. "He didn't discriminate between soldiers and civilians. Who knows how far his poison has spread down river? The men, they..." She pauses to choke back a few tears, steeling her nerves before continuing.

"They're more worried for their families than themselves. Several volunteered to deliver messages to Feng Jia, Ye, and Nan Rong. At this rate, they might not make it. Our carrier pigeons won't arrive for several days. I threw multiple letters into jars and sent them downstream. Hopefully someone will fetch the note in time. This cruelty... I won't let it go unpunished! I pray that I may live long enough to bring Wang Liang to justice!"

I don't have a response. Words have little meaning without actions. Diao's done all she could. I can't say the same.

While Diao busies mashing the willow leaves for the suffering soldiers, a runner comes to fetch us back to Ying's tent. Zhang Mang is showing signs of the symptoms. The thought that Ying won't be far behind is causing panic to escalate. He's our only hope. If he falters, we're doomed.

"You make a cute He Pi," Zhang Mang pokes my cheek the instant I settle beside him on the thatched straw mat.

"Thank you? How are feeling, Zhang Mang?"

"I'm dying. What do you think?" Frowning, he lets out a barely strained sigh. Zhang Mang isn't the type to show his weaknesses. He's suffering more than he lets on. In fact, if he were suffering from the symptoms earlier, the stubborn man wouldn't have admitted to it openly.

"When was the last time you drank from your canteen?"

"This afternoon, after I refilled my container."

"When did your symptoms *really* started?"

"What's with the accusing tone?" He winces, in spite of himself, and then hurriedly covers it with a grin. "Don't make that face. Let me see. Maybe... a few hours before sunset."

"And you were up river."

"Yeah, so?"

"The rest of us have been drinking water throughout the day and we've just now felt the effects. That must mean the toxin was recently released."

"Assuming tolerance doesn't play a factor, then sure. You seem swell. You and that traitorous bastard over there giving me the eye. He was upstream too."

Ying ignores Zhang Mang's grimace. A scholarly pose overtakes his expression in the same manner I've often witnessed on Dui's. "Yesterday afternoon was the last time I filled my canteen."

"Oh right. And three days ago was your last drink I bet. I'd forgotten you're a camel. Lucky you!"

"Calm down, Zhang Mang. Getting worked up might worsen your symptoms."

"Don't censor a dying man!" Pausing, he lets out a sardonic chuckle. "Well now, let's see how you fair when it's your turn. Feeling faint?"

Soon as the words leave his mouth, my vision begins reeling. Light tremors shake my body. I feel cold, nauseated, and weakened all at once.

Zhang Mang manages to pull my crumpling body onto his before I hit my head against the ground. He smiles happily in the embrace as though his thoughts are far and away; undoubtedly, with He Pi. My stomach is cramped into a knot. I can't fight through the pain well enough to answer any of Diao's cries. At this rate, I doubt I can last the hour.

"I'm sorry, Bao Lai!"

She shoves the entire wad of gnashed willow leaves into my mouth. The disgustingly bitter paste, no less than poison itself, shocks me from my pain-induced delirium. I spit out the grotesque thing, tempted to lick dirt off the ground to rid the horrid taste. However, the shock was short-lived. Immense pain is slowly creeping over.

"Diao, are you... all right?"

"Yes, I feel fine! Master Ying, isn't there anything you can do? Bao Lai, is there anything I can do?"

Faced with my own mortality, the list of what ifs frantically runs through my mind. I should have stayed with Dui and then gone back to Nan Rong. That would have been best. Instead, I dragged everyone else into my ambition, including Lo Han. I never knew how much he hated me and how much he also cared for me. At least I can say that I will die in the company of good friends. He's all alone. Lo Han's always alone. I don't want him to be lonely anymore.

"Diao... could you... help me to... Lo Han's tent?"

Through choked back sobs, she pulls me to my feet. Zhang Mang grudgingly releases me while Ying returns to his trial antidote.

Continue to page 499

Chapter 29 – 5

Three flags signaling the alliance give the impression our combined army is three times larger than actual size. Our march is met with little opposition and rare skirmishes end quickly. We pass through gate after gate unhindered. Soon, their walls will appear in the horizon, giving end to this discord.

Around the campfire on this cold night, Diao and I huddle together for warmth. Ying and Zhang Mang have gone off to scout our surroundings and Lo Han has retreated to his tent. I'm unsure why he chose to come; though, I would be lying to say that I mind his company. He's my mentor and at times like these, I still need guidance.

"Would you like more to eat, Diao?"

"No, I'm fine." The gloom hasn't left her since the incident from the throne room. Diao throws a few more sticks into the fire and then rests her head on her knees, sighing.

"It will be okay, Diao. Give him some time to consider."

Shaking her head, another weary sigh escapes. "You're so naïve Bao Lai."

"What do you mean?"

Chapter 29: The Demon's Revenge

"Time can't change what the heart refuses to acknowledge. After all these years, I'm still just a sister to him. I'm fine, really. I knew. And I... don't want to discuss love anymore."

"Sorry. I didn't mean to be nosy."

"You could have said concerned. I would have been none the wiser." She smiles. "Since you're openly nosy, could I tell you a story?"

"Of course."

"Thank you. It's nice to have a sister." Diao taps her knees a few times to collect her thoughts. "My father, a very courageous and talented man, wanted a worthy son to lead Feng Jia. He wasn't blessed. My mother died when I was born and though his advisors encouraged the idea, he refused to remarry. He loved my mother too much. Honesty and devotion were the bases of his character. All my life, I'd admire that in him and strived to mirror him, so that he may one day feel proud. When he brought Master Ying home, I knew I'd been replaced. I couldn't compete. Instead, I threw tantrums and tried to make him leave.

Except, Master Ying never once thought himself better. He protected me, guided me, and swore his loyalty. He thinks I am the most capable person to lead Feng Jia. To honor my father and for my benefit, he's done unspeakable things, most of which were behind my back. That doesn't justify his actions and whether on Earth or in the afterlife, he will have to answer for his crimes. Despite that, Bao Lai, please protect him. I'm not strong enough to save Master Ying. Before he ever faces trial by peers, I fear a trial by swords awaits."

"Diao, you're not exactly asking the right person. For a time, I was one of those people who wished him trial by swords. Because of him, my beloved will never be the same. Even now, there are still resentful parts of me. For you and for Dui, I've attempted to give Ying the benefit of the doubt and overlook his offenses. I can't make false promises. I'm not as strong as Zhang Mang or Ying."

"You are with Tian Ji Zhong Shi Yan."

"Wh—! How? Dui! That blabbermouth!"

"Not at all," she giggles. "Your eyes turned faint gold during the standoff at Yuo Muo. Most wouldn't have noticed but I couldn't miss it, because my father was the same. He had the Demon Slayer blood, too; a descendant of Fa Zhen. See? We *are* like sisters."

"We... are. I still can't make false promises."

"Because using the skill might cost your life."

"No, because I can't put all my faith in my blood. I can't promise that I will keep him safe but if you will permit, I can promise to try."

Diao looks up at the star-laced sky wistfully, smiling an ambiguous smile. In time, hopeful, nearly pleading, eyes fall on me. "Bao Lai, if you could strive to protect

Master Ying and keep him on this Earth even a second longer than fate has decided, I will forever be grateful."

"That is a promise I can make. I will do everything in my capabilities."

Chapter 29 – 6

As I near Lo Han's tent, the owner storms from around the back in a panic. He's as pale as a ghost and jittery to boot. Barely have I called out his name, strong arms pull me into a protective embrace.

"I'm sorry. It's too late. This isn't how things should have ended! I don't want to see you die!"

"What are you saying?"

"Tian Ji Zhong Shi Yan can't save you. Don't use it. The poison will spread faster. Vengeance never seemed as meaningless until now. For the remainder of our time on Earth, spend each moment by my side."

"Lo Han, you're not making sense! What poison?"

"The one circulating in your system; same for everyone else here. Time was wasted reading the wrong stars. Instead of hers, I should have read yours."

Lo Han always had a knack for star reading. I know better than to refute his warnings. They're usually accurate. Wang Liang's lack of retaliation thus far has been in the back of my mind and I was coming to find Lo Han for that very reason. This isn't even close to what I'd expected. My talent can't provide relief for his unpredicted method. However, I know someone else who can.

494

Chapter 29: The Demon's Revenge

Ying's trade naturally permits him to be well versed in poisons. He's the best candidate to find an antidote. Regrettably, both he and Zhang Mang have left camp to scout our positions from upstream.

My endeavor to leave Lo Han's side fails. The tight grip takes my entire body into his arms. The dizzying force is followed by another confusing, startling intensity which renders my knees weak. I collapse against his chest while the light touch of his lips against my own grows deeper into a conflicting passion from which I can make neither heads nor tails. Each time my weary arms push away, his strong ones pull forward, adamant to keep our bodies entwined and inseparable.

Had this moment occurred a year ago, I would gratefully remain lost in this unimaginable heaven and yet, little could I surmise that in mere seconds, hell would break loose.

A whistling of arrows light the skies blood red. Sharp cries and inferno rise over the camp. The men scramble into position against the storming raiders. Hard gallops against the dirt ground are drowned under screams and maddened shouts. Metal grinds against metal and flesh. The harrowing sound of death fills the former quiet air. Above it all, the voice of a dead man who has come back a reaper.

Lo Han swings our bodies out of harm's way just as an arrow whiz by, torching the small patch of dry grass below our feet into a puff of heat which then extinguishes. I manage to pull away from him during the tumble and start for Ye's former proud Commander Ru now leading the raid from our rear. Compared to Ying and Zhang Mang, Ru never had a chance. Against common soldiers, his talent is undisputable. Men fall at his feet left and right. The steeled look of a killer on his face is not one that will permit clemency. I'd stopped his execution by Zhang Mang and in turn, Ru will become our executioner. This was my doing.

"Bao Lai, don't!"

I'm trapped in his arms again. While I don't wish to hurt Lo Han, he's not making the alternative easy.

"I can't just let everyone die!"

"They will die regardless of your interference! Ying won't return in time. Look, it is already too late."

Our allies are dropping like flies, not from injuries inflicted by Ru and his cohorts, but sudden crippling phantom pains, making them easy targets for the ruthless raiders. Fear takes over judgment, sending a handful into hysteria, and many more into panic. At this rate, we're done for.

"Stay with me until the gates of hell open. We won't ever walk apart again. Let me keep you safe until eternal darkness comes."

Trembling. Faced with my own mortality, my body is trembling uncontrollably in Lo Han's arms. The breathy whisper of eternity lulling in my ear and the sweet kisses pressing against my cheek is so utterly tempting, I want to succumb to his whims, whatever they may be. And yet, in this moment before absolution, there is one thought that dominates me: love. I love Bai Hu and I also love Dui. I owe the former an explanation and the latter an apology.

When she suddenly appears from one of the burning tents with an unconscious man in her arms, I finally recall another love at stake.

"Diao!"

The line of soldiers keeping the raiders at bay are dwindling while the surrounding fire continues to scorch, consuming the camp and filling the air with smoke. It's difficult to breathe.

She casts over a quick glance and then goes back to retrieve more unconscious soldiers. A pointless task when there's no escape. There's courage in stupidity and in stupidity, hope. Ying and Zhang Mang will return. They cannot save the men dying by the hands of these raiders but whoever is left may yet be saved by Ying, including Lo Han. I can afford them that advantage. I can save at least one love.

"Lo Han, should we pass into the next world tonight, I'll never let you walk alone. Should your path continue, I'll wait for you but please, don't remain unaccompanied until that day comes."

"Don't! It is futile! You can't change fate! Let me love you in the time that's left!"

497

"I'll leave that up to the stars."

The throbbing in my chest grows louder until everything is drowned out in hollow echoes. In mere seconds, even the flames have stood still. The burden on my shoulders for having let Ru lived becomes heavier with his death and the deaths of the men under his order. After a few burning tents are cast away, an explicable pain paralyzes my body. The poison has finally overcome my advantage. While I lie still waiting for cold hands to pull consciousness under, Lo Han's handsome face evokes nostalgic memories of days gone by. They were wonderful days. When the time comes, I'll be near to take his hand and then, together, we'll return to those days and live in them once again.

The End.

Chapter 30: This is Where We Part

Hobbling through the tent flap, I fall over, taking Diao with me. She couldn't continue holding up both He Pi's heavy armor in addition to my weight. That short walk was more than I could muster. I lie on the ground, gasping for air while Lo Han dashes over.

The man I once considered, still consider, my mentor is a good and benevolent person. Resentment clouded his mind which only destruction can absolve. In my final hour, I'd like to believe that he's forgiven me.

"Why did you come? I don't want to watch you die!"

His callous attitude is nowhere to be found. He calls out my name in the kind manner just as I remember. My Master Lo Han is himself again.

"I like... being a pain." My stupid grin can't clear unshed tears glistening in his eyes. Lo Han recoils before giving away reservations and snatches me into his arms. "How are... you feeling?"

"Worry about yourself! You!" He directs the last remark at a trembling Diao. "Has your assassin found an antidote? He must have. How else are you not afflicted? A frail little thing like you can't naturally outlast Bao Lai!"

"Lo Han... don't."

499

"No, he's right." Diao fumbles her fingers together nervously, glancing every which way as a mean to suppress the culminating expression of guilt that suddenly surfaces. "I-I've been thinking that too."

"And? Out with it! Redeem your wicked bloodline. Think of someone else for once!"

"Lo Han!"

"*He's right, Bao Lai!*" On the verge of tears, she rocks back and forth on the dirt ground. Whatever shame she's hiding, Lo Han's threatening tone pushes her nerves farther over the edge. However, it's not until I plea in his stead that Diao finally succumbs. "He's right. I think it's my blood."

"What are... you... talking... about?" The pains in my abdomen are worsening. Breathing is now a chore. Lo Han plops a finger on my lips to keep me from continuing and in my place, recommence interrogations.

"You're Fa Zhen's descendant. So is Bao Lai. What's your advantage?"

"Not Fa Zhen's blood. T-The Demon's blood. I-I'm not supposed to tell anyone."

From the unthinkable admission, Lo Han's grip on certainty is beginning to loosen. The arms holding me are trembling uncontrollably. His fists clench to steady composure but in the end, loses to three decades of pent-up fury.

"I should cut out your lying tongue! Your father indiscriminately killed *everyone*—men, women, children—with one *speck* of the barbarian blood in their veins! If you were a mutt, he would have suffocated you at birth!"

"M-My father was a kind man! He would never do anything so horrible!"

"You're delusional! The man was a monster! After nearly a thousand years of persecuting my people, his laws continued to call for our execution!"

"He didn't! Those laws came before his time. The people felt safe with them in place so he couldn't... he did eventually!"

"Yes, on this deathbed. After how many died?!"

"One!"

I grip Lo Han's sleeve but he either pretends not to notice or is completely lost to everything else in the world aside fury. There isn't any sign of him yielding and the same can be said of his counterpart. She respects her father too much to suffer his dishonor, even though his guilt is slowly unveiling, and thus unraveling her own. It was only a theory but one she's kept silent. The possible bloodline advantage could have expedited the antidote's discovery. Through her silence, many never had a chance. On her face is clearly remorse; on Lo Han's is another expression altogether.

"At least *two*," Lo Han spits bitterly through his teeth. "Indisputably, at least two!"

"One!" She fends off his attack through thick sobs, croaking back a hoarse reply. "Just one. He didn't know his soldiers would... no one sane ever openly admits to carrying that bloodline and absolutely no one had been charged for several centuries! When he heard the shocking news, my father ran to the gallows and stopped that woman's execution!"

"Which woman?"

"Murong Sang Diep. Empress Cong Hou. My mother."

Chapter 30 – 2

How embarrassing. I lost consciousness from shock the moment that incredible revelation, in actuality insinuation, was made. Could it really be? Diao is my mentor's half sister. Since I'm a sister to him, that makes her my sister. And since she is a sister to Ying who is Dui's brother, does that make Dui a brother to me? I can't wait to tell him only because I know he'll frown.

"You're in a good mood for someone who nearly crossed over."

My stiff neck was turned toward the exit. I didn't notice him sitting on my other side. Painstakingly, I squirm until the former gloomy monk comes into view. A smile beams down. Sadness and resentment, which plagued his demeanor, have faded to certain contentment.

"Are you sure I'm not dead, Lo Han?"

"I'm as sure as you are. Never trust a figment of your imagination."

"Then I shouldn't trust that advice either. Is everyone well?"

"The men who survived long enough to have been administered the antidote, yes." Lo Han's smile softens, hinting slightly at melancholy. "I really thought you were done for. Don't do that to me again."

"How *did* that happen? Did you give me your blood?"

"Nothing as unhygienic as that! Ying is a man to be envied. A brute and a genius. By the time you lost consciousness, he was making his way over with the practiced antidote. Thankfully your condition made you a perfect test subject. No objections whatsoever."

"I guess so. What was the poison?"

"We're not sure. He realized Diao's tolerance was the key and apparently, whatever special vector in our barbarian blood has been long decoded by the genius. Mimic that vector to naturally resist the poison and find a safe method to pass it from the body. That was his vague explanation. Still, much of the damages prior to application of the antidote can't be undone. Are you all right?"

"My muscles feel stiff and weak. Besides that, just really thirsty. What will we do without water?"

"Ah, well. The star reader has been dabbling in geomancy the past few years. He managed to find few water sources outside from River Huan."

Lo Han brings the canteen to my lips. I drink to my heart's content until my stomach begins to cramp. Then, exhaling sharply, I fall back on the mat and thank the heavens for being surrounded by such talented, resourceful people.

Chapter 30: This is Where We Part

Not long ago, the impending shadow of doom slowly crept over the camp. Every man I met had an icy cold hand latched onto his collar, prepared to draw him through the other realm. I, too, had a glimpse across the veil, and there's no doubt in my mind that if one fraction of a second, one sparse moment in time went awry, I would have awoken in that other world. I don't know why I lived when others died. Once more, those left behind are given a chance to stop Bei Ling and ensure that the lives lost weren't in vain. I don't want things to return to the way they were because then nothing would have changed. I want every country to aim higher, for peace and prosperity. It's a farfetched idea but so was the idea of seeing sunrise last night. I don't want to be held back by uncertainty anymore.

"Wait a minute, Lo Han. Did you say '*our* barbarian blood?' Diao is your sister, isn't she?"

His eyes broaden. He looks away and then gives a sidelong glance. "Yes."

"I know it's not my place to say this but you should give her a chance."

"That is a given." He mutters softly. "I realized my disdain for Diao was stemmed from her resemblance to my mother. I saw... Empress Cong Hou... once when her caravan passed through the markets. I thought... I couldn't accept that my mother would marry the man who had my father killed and also forgotten me. At the time, it was easier to hate Fa Zhen's successors than to admit my mother betrayed our family and her people."

"That can't be. At temple, you said that you didn't have any family, but in the few instances when you mentioned a woman named Sang who cared for you, the wonderful pictures of a kind mother you painted were genuinely formed from respect and love. She meant the world to you and you to her. Something must have happened."

"You would give a woman you've never met the benefit of the doubt when her own son finds it difficult to swallow Diao's claims?"

"Which are?"

"The convenient excuse that my mother's memories were lost from the shock of losing my father. The second baseless claim, somewhere in the back of her mind, she sought for her son. Diao thinks Ying was mistaken for me and was taken in after Mother passed."

"That isn't farfetched. Ying lost his memory too. He would have been inclined to agree."

"Again, convenient."

"Conveniences aren't lies. We live in a very small world."

"The world is small and everyone is suffering from amnesia. Conveniences are as good as lies."

"I'm... sorry."

Chapter 30: This is Where We Part

"For what? I was a stubborn fool who sent an assassin to have you killed. Have you forgotten what I've done?"

"No. I understand why you were angry. You needed someone to endure that frustration. Regrettably, Bai Hu suffered, not me. Recent events were not your fault. Wang Liang will be punished."

Aside from the clamors outside and a few heavy breezes lashing against the canvas, silence suddenly owns the atmosphere. Naturally, I can't keep from shuffling. Lo Han closes his eyes. In time, reopen them with newfound humor sprouted across his lips.

"How gallant! I can always rely on you for constancy, *General* Bao Lai."

"Don't make fun of me."

Another of my secrets he knows well. At Tian Mao Yi, I'd dreamt of becoming a great general after spending countless hours in the training halls listening to war stories from former military men. Everyone laughed at my ambition; that is, everyone except Lo Han and Bai Hu. I didn't know the master was laughing at me on the inside.

"Not at all. I'm amazed. You've surpassed your dream. You're practically commander."

The unexpected compliment sets my cheeks on fire. I glance away awkwardly, fueling his satisfied laughter.

It's really unfair for him to exploit the chinks in my armor. For once, I'd like to cleave through his shield.

"Say, Lo Han. You drank water from the river yesterday too, right?"

"Yes."

"So you were poisoned long before I barged into your tent last night."

"What's your point?"

"My point is I couldn't have poisoned you through that kiss since you were already poisoned. Why did you kiss me?"

"Are you obsessing over something so trivial? If I said I'd wanted you to die wracked with guilt, would you believe it?"

"Not if you put it that way."

"Then what if I said I simply wanted to because I love you?"

The airy response makes my heart leaps into my throat and then his pretentious smile delivers a finishing blow to my ego. Why is it so difficult to overcome my former girlish crush for this cruel man? I don't love him that way and yet, I can't stop my heart from beating wildly in the midst of his company.

He purposefully torments me for his own amusement. In a sordid way, I might have been doing the same to Dui. Ever since we parted, I keep wondering what I could have done to earn his love and if I were ever truly that ignorant. It's possible that I knew his worship long before the admittance. The greater question then, is why did I stay by his side? I'm either a terrible person or a very conceited ass. There isn't much difference between the two.

"Don't think about other men when you're with me."

Soft lips press against my cheek, causing my whole body to quiver. He chuckles amusedly in my ear, resting his chin on my shoulder before repeating the token.

"I don't have a choice when you taunt me this way, Lo Han. Here. Ma Tai Tou said I should keep this but it doesn't feel right. This belongs to your betrothed."

The lacquered comb was too precious to leave lying around. I've carried it in my breast pocket, wrapped inside a few layers of fabric. My counterpart stares at the object dejectedly. Shortly after, he closes my fingers around the comb.

"It's yours. I gave it to you and I meant it."

Honesty is clearly conveyed through his adoring gaze; the same look I've seen on Dui's face many times before. The implication forces involuntarily blushes to my cheeks; though, admitting his consideration is too frightening. Instead, I yield, relieving the duty of guarding the comb from him back to me and replace it inside my breast pocket.

"Thank you. I'll keep it safe. Now that things are settled, when do we resume marching?"

"A few more days for the men to recover and then we'll continue. However, this is where we part. It's time you return to Nan Rong."

"Why? I'll recover by then. I promise to carry my weight."

"That's not why. The soldiers are divided. Half admires Zhang Mang, the rest look to you and Ying. I couldn't care less about Ye but Feng Jia should look to Diao. Once the conflict is over, she won't be able keep the country together if she keeps standing behind both your shadows. She needs to take the reins now, before it's too late."

"What about Ying?"

"His fate is obscured. Your star is clear. The paths you've taken—the stars tell me your destiny isn't in the West."

"But Diao can't do this alone, especially not with Zhang Mang lurking about. He's clever and dangerously manipulative. Someone has to... Will *you* stay with her?"

"Yes. That is my intention. I've spent my life in anger over the loss of family. Like it or not, she's family. I don't want to lose what I've missed all these years over anger."

Chapter 30: This is Where We Part

That mature attitude was one of the reasons I came to admire Lo Han. Back then, his maturity was a farce, a result of restrained resentment. He's opened up to me these past two days more than he had the two decades prior. I can finally see a genuine smile on his face, so contagious, that I feel my own mouth curl upward.

"She'll be happy and I hope you will too."

"I'll settle for contentment." Smirking, he raises off the floor to stretch his back. "When you see Bai Hu, tell him I apologize."

"Tell him yourself. That's your punishment."

"As cruel as ever, little sister."

"I'm not your sister. She is."

On cue, the silhouette lurking outside the tent flap nervously scrambles inside. She gives me a nervous smile and Lo Han an uneasy stare. Somewhere in the midst of her silent panic, Diao manages to request an audience with her brother. The latter lazily complies in an almost annoyed manner, purposefully giving his sister a hard time, though she apparently requires more exposure to adjust to his superficial bullying. She leaves and Lo Han, smiling humorously, shortly follows.

"Wait, Lo Han. In case I won't have another chance, thank you, for everything."

"Don't put it in such harrowing terms. We'll meet again, Bao Lai. The stars told me so."

"I mean it. Whatever happens, please know that I'll always be grateful our paths crossed."

"As am I. Although, in another universe, another timeline, not just crossed; we would have walked side-by-side." He leaves the confounding message to my anxiety, smiling complicatedly to himself during the retreat.

Another universe. Another timeline. Sometimes, I can't tell if he intends to be factual or metaphorical. Both are beyond my comprehension. Lo Han is an enigma. Perhaps, some riddles are best left unsolved. Such are revelations. To pass the threshold means to give up everything that came before. I'm not willing to forfeit his significance as my friend, my mentor, and as the man I've idolized all my life. Someday, I know he will be unraveled. The person to accomplish that feat cannot be me. There are others waiting for me in this time and in this universe. My place, as is my heart, is in Nan Rong.

Chapter 31: Fa Zhen's Redemption

Several days later, the alliance convoy resumes marching. At the helm are Zhang Mang, Lo Han, and Diao. The former is back to his old crudeness. The latter is heartbroken by Ying's departure. At the same time, another part of her is visibly mending from having the support of an overly protective brother. I would be lying to say that I'm not jealous for having lost Lo Han's attention but I am also excruciatingly happy for him beyond a doubt. He's found a place to call home and a person to call family.

Messengers were dispatched days ago with the antidote instructions. On one horse, Ying and I set out for Zhong Ren, Nan Rong's northern base, to provide relief. Well, that was our stated intention. My ulterior motive is to find Dui. I'm worried about him. I really hope he returned to camp; otherwise, I don't know what I'll do.

"Stop fidgeting or you'll fall off!" Ying snaps over his shoulder. The feral tone startles me from daydream. Inadvertently, I cling to him tighter.

"I'm sorry!"

He doesn't respond. This always happen when we're alone together, uncomfortable silence and random barking. They're such complete opposites, Dui and Ying, that I can't imagine they're brothers. Dui mentioned their strict mother loved the eldest best. If

Ying took after her then I understand why Dui was so obedient, is still obedient, to her wishes.

"Hey, Ying." I call to my counterpart who's already glowering. "After this is over, will you return to Nan Rong with Dui or to Feng Jia with Diao?"

"Don't meddle in others' affairs."

"We're not strangers. You're important to people who are important to me."

"You're not important to me," he replies coldly. "I'm not obligated to humor nosy women."

"Oh, don't be like that! It's a long ride to Zhong Ren."

"Keep up the interrogation and I'll shorten the ride."

"How's th—"

The horse neighs wildly, coming to an abrupt halt and kicking both forelegs into the air. Suddenly, I'm paralleled to the ground. My mind turns blank. I cling to Ying for dear life, squeezing his body so tightly that the light scent from his shirt escapes through the chainmail. He smells just like Dui.

Two hoofs slam against the dirt road, kicking dust into the air. Still fearful of the consequence, my trembling arms constrict. Ying leisurely exclaims, "There's a large rock on the road."

I peek around his body to the path in front. The large rock he mentioned is barely a pebble. An infant could have stepped over it.

"That was a mean thing to do!"

"What was?"

"Don't give me that! What if I'd fallen off and broken my neck?"

"Then your boredom would have ended sooner." His shoulders shrug in an odd manner as though he were shaking.

"Are you... laughing?! You—You're a real jerk, *Yu Qi*!"

I touched a nerve. He's gone rigid. In the next instant, the steed dashes forward at lightning speed and I nearly lose my grip.

"Keep at it! You can't intimidate me, *Yu Qi*!"

"I'd merely hoped to shut you up."

"What do you have against me?"

"Your arrogance."

"What arrogance? Have I slighted you?"

"Stealing my armor, tarnishing my honor, and making a mockery of my reputation weren't enough? To top off insults, you're awfully friendly toward every man who happens to cross your path. Look how you're clinging to me. Dui deserves better than a harlot with wandering eyes."

"Excuse me?! I have to *cling* because you're trying to kill me! The first parts might be true but Dui and I are not a couple, you judgmental jerk!"

"Do you expect me to believe he nearly died for a mere *acquaintance*?"

"He is a selfless man! A true physician who always puts others first!"

"What does that make you? A fickle woman whose only quality is to lead on others? Your lover would be appalled to see how you've dragged him along. I don't know why you bothered to take my armor. The pretentious mask on your face makes a better disguise."

"I'm—! Don't turn this on me! I asked first! Are you in love with Diao?"

"Hmph! What an unbelievable question. The answer is obvious."

"No, it's not. That's a lousy answer!"

"You asked a lousy question."

The steed's pace increasingly quickens. This man despises me. Yet, he's doing everything to keep my arms latched around his body to prove a point. From then on, no matter how obnoxious or clever I strive to become, he neglects all my attempts at prodding.

516

Chapter 31: Fa Zhen's Redemption

Day turns to night but I dare not sleep lest he leaves me stranded. The next morning, the ornery man rides even faster to test endurance in my arms, weakened from lack of sleep.

Diao asked me to save her beloved but I'm beginning to think I am the one in need of saving from this sadistic man.

"Get off."

Those commanding words come too soon. We're on the outskirts of the northern base, if I'm not mistaken. Closing the remaining distance on foot isn't a chore but parting here wasn't my intention.

"Aren't you coming to Zhong Ren? They need our help."

"Nan Rong is not my priority."

"Is that really the reason? I'll ask San An for your pardon. After everything, he has to—your antidote—"

"Enough. I never would have taken you this far if it weren't for Diao."

"Oh, yeah? I promised Diao to look after you."

"Never make promises you can't keep."

A hard elbow knocks against my breastplate, loosening my grip, followed by a sweep of his gauntlet. The world above was still spinning when the sound of hoofs recede into the distance. He Pi's crimson armor is covered in dirt.

"Yu Qi! Wait!"

He's as stubborn as his brother and rude to boot. My first impulse is to run after him. The second impulse reins back the ridiculous thought. He can outrun me but I won't let him escape.

Chapter 31 – 3

Qing Hai swings nervously from me to San An, who's not taking my disobedience in good stride. Once I arrived at Zhong Ren, learned that Dui and the generals have resumed marching. Yu Qi was also heading toward Bei Ling. That is where I must go. However, the Minister has other plans in mind.

"Lord Han Bei discovered your absence from Nan Rong. He is refusing to budge until you are recovered." The Minister explains for the third time. He would rather believe that I'm dense than defiant.

"Why didn't you ever send for me?"

"I wanted to end this as soon as possible. Your position in Feng Jia was better served. I see now that Wang Liang won't easily submit. Without Ning's reinforcements, we couldn't have held our position against Bei Ling until their expulsion from the West. Unless backed into a corner, they will continue. Go to Ning. Convince Lord Han Bei. We can't leave that front exposed."

"But... I don't want to."

His finely trimmed eyebrows rise in arches. The look of disgust is ruining his handsome face. "I hope that isn't your best argument."

"B-Bao Lai's intuition has been on point, Uncle. M-Maybe we should give her a chance!"

Chapter 31: Fa Zhen's Redemption

Qing Hai inches next to my side, rubbing the back of his head nervously. He's afraid to challenge San An as though the Minister were his strict father. The scowl sent back suggests that might be the case.

"I will not argue with two children who don't know their place. In His Highness's absence, my word is law."

"O-Oh yeah? Well, His Highness isn't absent. I'm standing right here."

Arms folded and shoulders squared, I stare at San An's widened eyes. He made the mistake of sending He Pi's armor and I intend to exploit that mistake.

"I'm going to Bei Ling, Minister. This is a family affair. Besides, you wanted me to scare the life out of Wang Liang. I'm here, let me scare him from this front."

San An isn't amused by my flippant attitude but apparently, someone else is. His sardonic chuckles float into the tent. A young man with hazel eyes and dark hair emerges, donned in Ning's black and silver armor. Momentarily, those distant yet judging eyes burrow into my face and then just as quickly, lose interest.

"Captain Xian. I wasn't expecting you. Is anything amiss?"

"What do you take me for, Minister, a harbinger? So much for Southern hospitality. I waited at the gates and no one came to receive me. I had to escort myself in."

"The watchers' drums didn't sound."

"What does that tell you about the poor defenses protecting this base?"

"I... suppose we can't be too careful. Just as well, perfect timing on your part, Captain Xian. Bao Lai is here."

"Is she invisible? I don't see a woman. Or, is one of you naturally keeping secrets? I should have known the Minister was too pretty."

"*A-ha, it's me, Captain!*" I raise my hand to bar San An's quivering lips from exploding expletives. Well, he probably wouldn't, but he's aching to. "I didn't want the men to feel uncomfortable. Nice disguise right? What do you think?"

"You didn't want the men to feel uncomfortable so, you're dressed as He Pi? Nothing like having the boss looking over your shoulder to feel at ease."

"Be that as it may," San An bears an empty smile to cut off the frivolity. "She is here. You wouldn't mind escorting her to Ning, I'm sure."

"Of course, I mind. That would be a waste of time. I reported her disappearance to Lord Han Bei. I can simply send notice to my lord that she's returned."

"So, this was your doing."

"I can't take all the credit, Minister. Nan Rong's cowardice extends to its citizens. My lord joined the pointless alliance for this woman. I saw no reason to continue once she ran away."

"I didn't run away!"

At my outburst, Xian smirks, thoroughly satisfied for making Nan Rong seem inept. Behind the indifference, Xian also suggested that he can send notice to Han Bei, never promising that he would. Ma Tai Tou's teachings haven't left me. I see through his amusement; the joke's on him.

"You know what, Minister. I think you're right. I should go to Lord Han Bei. Just to be safe. Plus, he told me I could never stay in Nan Rong given the truth and I happened across the truth. My place is in Ning, wouldn't you agree, Captain? If you're busy, Qing Hai will take me."

In an instant, he's gone pale. The Captain involuntarily stammers, ending frustration with a low growl. Our irate stares are at stalemate. I have to ensure he'll report to Lord Han Bei and he needs assurance that I'll stay away from the Grand General. Xian knows my ties to the Eastern throne, and should I claim that which is rightfully mine, he will be forced under my authority, the authority of a Nan Rong citizen; a fate, to him, worse than death.

"Lord Han Bei doesn't have time to indulge bothersome women. I will deliver the message." Xian turns away, waving a hand in the air to dismiss any further notions of my proposed venture, and also to signal a compromise. "Ning will do her part. Make yourself useful. Lead a unit to Yue Na."

"Why Yue Na? Isn't that on Bei Ling's eastern front?"

"Hmph." Xian snorts, smiling to himself. "Bei Ling lost their advantage in the West. Their last resort with Huan also failed miserably. They are staging another gamble. Soon as soldiers close in Yue Na, their markers will detonate, killing everyone within the area. Our men have already withdrawn from Ying Ling. After the explosion, let those cocky fools march east. Ning will destroy them once and for all. This conflict will be over."

"Erm... Maybe I misunderstood, did you just... volunteered to sacrifice Nan Rong soldiers?"

"Why else would I have come to Zhong Ren? Set off the explosives and Ning will bring about the end. Quid pro quo."

"Are you *insane*?! Who told you about the trap in the first place?"

"People." Xian shrugs half-heartedly. "If you have a better idea, let's hear it."

"I don't have a better idea but having our soldiers blown to bits is out of the question!"

Ignoring my unhelpful criticisms, San An calmly intercedes a logical alternative. "Must Ning traverse through Yue Na? What of Ming Na and Er Na?"

"Packed with even more explosives. Yue Na is the least populace city; hence, the least casualties. Unlike you, Minister, I do have a heart."

San An sighs softly. His eyes pace across the large map spread on the table. Without Ning forces repressing Wang Liang from the East, there's no telling what he might do.

Following the drawn silence, Qing Hai nervously steps forward. I could be imagining things but he's seemingly eyeing San An quietly, as though seeking approval. "I don't mean to interrupt, um... don't the people in Yue Na know about the trap?"

"Of course they do. They're the ones tasked with detonation."

"What's keeping them from leaving?"

"*Really*? I thought by now one of you would have had the sense to request all the facts instead of resorting to this pointless back and forth."

The Captain settles on a chair near the table and begins fumbling with the marker on the map denoting Ning forces. "Look. Here is Wang Liang's kind nature at work. Explosives were placed in Yue Na, Er Na, and Ming Na after all women and children were seized. If Ning or other foreign armies break through any of those

525

cities, all hostages will be killed. However, if a city successfully fends off intruders, and in the process, kills all their current inhabitants, the *reward* is freedom for hostages from that city. The men have considered evacuating the areas before detonation, hoping their families are released, but that plan was quickly brushed off. Wang Liang won't tolerate being cheated—and he will find out—all hostages will be killed. In conclusion, Yue Na will result in the least casualties and Nan Rong should lead by example and march first."

"You can't be serious. Couldn't we free their families?"

He turns to me, smiling unnervingly wide. "Okay. Sure! Where are they?"

"Er... s-somewhere around."

Those snickering eyes are familiar attributes on another Ning soldier I remember well. Lord Han Bei doesn't strike me as the type to permit harm to women and children. This man is the same. Thanks to Ma Tai Tou's short lessons, I've learned to see partly through superficial derision. Captain Xian isn't honestly suggesting we sacrifice Yue Na; he's just very bad at asking for help. That doesn't change the fact that I don't have an answer.

"Everybody is 'somewhere around,' *Your Highness*. We thought to send agents but the men won't let anyone inside their cities. Can't blame their caution.

One mishap and everything worth living for will disappear in an instant."

Shaking his head, the Minister begins pacing beside the table. "If Wang Liang has become a sadistic madman, then the same trap could await Nan Rong and the Western Alliance. You did not mention it. Are we spared, Captain?"

"Unfortunately, yes. Your vantage points are spared our fun."

"What is he planning? Nan Rong has been at the helm of this conflict. Basic tactics call for removal of the head."

"I didn't think you of all people would feel disappointed, Minister. Ning's military is a monolith. Bei Ling's focus on the Eastern front is meant to drive back everyone else."

"That can't be the entire basis for this ruthless plot. The Western Alliance is closest to Bei Ling; second is Nan Rong. Ning has retreated from Ying Ling. He's focused on the wrong side. No. There has to be another reason he's looking east."

"Hmph." The Captain tips over the Northern Army's marker on the wide map, and then using an index finger, meticulously push the icon toward the three outskirt cities, as though he were carefully measuring the distance. "That is odd. These cities are isolated from the rest of Bei Ling. I'm guessing it takes over

527

three days from Yue Na to the closest post. Maybe you do have a point, Minister. They're not far from the old To Ba Ridge."

San An's pacing ceases. His face lights up from having come to revelation. "The E Mo tribes."

"Those are also my thoughts," Xian nods.

For once, the two men are in agreement and all I can do is stare blankly from one to the next. Qing Hai casually shrugs the moment our eyes meet. He doesn't know either.

"Um, what about the E Mo? Who are they?"

"Nuisances to Wang Liang." The Captain stands up and stretches. In contrast to the leisure attitude, his eyes are burning. "The E Mo, like most tribal people scattered across the Northern Regions, are descendants from old, powerful barbarians. The majority isn't anything special but once in a while, someone like your Demon General comes along. Then the tribes might become greedy and demand the same rights as the civilized. Wang Liang and his cohorts can't have that but killing a Demon isn't very easy. Plus, eradicating the E Mo might bring unpredicted backlash. He's baiting Ning to handle their extermination and at the same time, deal a devastating blow to our army."

"He's kidnapped their families! How is that keeping his hands clean?"

"What is innocence but perception? If Wang Liang said he's safekeeping their families from Ning's aggression and justifies slaughtering their women and children when the men fail by claiming the E Mo sided with the invaders, then who in the capital will challenge that view? There are many ways to wash the hands clean, usually in the blood of others."

The cruel tactics Wang Liang implemented against the E Mo is the same story Wen Meng recounted about Fa Zhen. This is personal. Before Lord Han Bei's revelations, I never knew this divide existed in the world. People were just people and animals had their place. When people are exploited like animals, my ignorance is challenged, and then I don't know where to turn.

"Why are you crying?"

Xian's harsh tone snaps back my wandering mind. He's looking at me accusingly. I can't rebuff. I am a Demon Slayer. My ancestors had no small part in the destruction of the Northern tribes, whether right or wrong.

"It's frightening. I can read your mind just from your expressions."

"Excuse me?"

"You're one of Fa Zhen's prized descendants, if memory serves. I didn't know you lot were this arrogant, believing you're responsible for the persecution of an entire group of people long before your great grandparents were even a thought. Spare me the self-deprecating woeful eyes."

"I'm not feeling sorry for myself! The E Mo needs help. There must be something I can do."

"Maybe. There's always a price. If cost isn't an issue, it can be done."

"The Minister pays really well but... how much do you need?"

Xian's rolling across the table. I turn to San An for an explanation but he's looked away.

"I don't know why you're laughing, Captain."

"Obviously! That's why it's funny. I think I'm starting to like you. Having a dumb person around to make me feel smart is not so bad!"

"You shouldn't talk about a woman that way! Bao Lai is just trying to help which is more than you deserve!"

Qing Hai, who's been idly standing away from conversation, suddenly puts everyone to silence through his fuming shouts. I didn't know his voice could raise that high. None is more surprised than his uncle. The Minister, scowling from embarrassment, slowly clears his throat to disband the tension.

"Yes, that is... correct. Let us never speak ill of a lady. Thank you, Qing Hai. And forgive me, Bao Lai."

The young man nearly keels over from surprise. San An's embarrassment was against himself. The gentleman in him didn't come to my defense; though, that's understandable since I'm not dressed as a lady. Xian's amused stare rounds the table and while he has more to say, manages to hold his tongue.

"What is this cost you're expecting, Captain?"

Shrugging, Xian plops down on the chair. "Not one you can pay, Minister. Tian Ji Zhong Shi Yan requires a trade only Bao Lai can make."

"Is that all? Why didn't you say so in the first place? I know all about that. Tell me what I must do."

"Don't haphazardly volunteer. You might regret it. Fact is, we don't have to march through the outskirt cities. Lord Han Bei has considered using Nan Rong's roads to reach Bei Ling but that leaves the East exposed. If the capital of the largest and grandest nation falls, the other countries won't be far behind."

"So, you're saying if Wang Liang thinks you're advancing from the center, their forces will extend east? Couldn't Ning *pretend* to march from the center and then quash Bei Ling forces once they reach Ying Ling?"

"What do you know? Not so dumb after all. I hate people who feign stupidity. Hmm? Don't give me that sour look, Minister. I was saying Bao Lai isn't as stupid as I thought. It's not an insult."

"Neither was it a compliment, Captain. Go on. What role must Bao Lai's special skill play?"

"Saving the hostages, of course. Rumors have Wang Liang seizing children for his training camps. He makes the act sound universal as though everyone in Bei Ling must ban together for a greater good. So far, the only people actually seized were the folks from the outskirt cities. When it comes down to it, I wondered whose children he would sacrifice. Now that I know the E Mo are involved, I bet he's thinking the little barbaric ones would make a good shield for the other two fronts. I wouldn't want to raise my hands against the little tykes anyway."

"How could he? That's heartless!"

"That is war," Xian coldly rebuffs my frantic cry. "Wang Liang can't win through strength alone. Confusion, misdirection, and intimidation are his tactics. Last resort, attack the conscience. Too bad he never accounted for the meddling cross-dresser who's already too confused to fall for his confusion."

"Please stop insulting Bao Lai."

"Which part of that was an insult, Minister? She's exactly what we need. If Wang Liang uses the hostages, armies will pause and infighting will ensue. There will be those who seek victory and those who seek to avoid vengeance from the Divine. We don't need to fall for his divide and conquer strategy. Now that I've thoroughly bored you with the why, let's get to the how."

Xian positions three markers over the three cities and a fourth one on the closest post, Xia Pa. Then, picking up a donkey, looks to me.

"This is you. Now, since the three cities are on guard at all times and their people are on edge, ready to die at any moment for their families, we can't come close. I need your special skill to carry me and Qing Hai across Yue Na undetected."

"Why me?"

"Are you complaining, boy? I hear you're the best tracker Nan Rong has to offer. Help me find the hostages, starting in Xia Pa."

"Couldn't we infiltrate from the middle? Going through Yue Na is a big risk, for us and the E Mo."

"We'd still have to waste two weeks making our way to Xia Pa and then trace backward to find the hostages. That is, if we aren't stopped by the heavily guarded garrisons blockading that front. They have hundreds of them stationed for miles. They're not just going to let us walk through without making a fuss. Bao Lai's heart might give out after two gates. Plus, once we find their holdings, Bao Lai will need to infiltrate and kill everyone who becomes an obstacle."

"Excuse me. You want me to do what?"

"Kill everyone who gets in our way. You can't expect Qing Hai and me to take on an entire city alone, can

533

you? We're just two average men. You're a freak of nature."

"There's nothing average about you! Ugh. Fine. I'll... do something if needed. Qing Hai, are you okay with the Captain's asinine plan?"

"I don't think I have a choice," the youth replies while rubbing the back of his head nervously.

"Wait, what happens after we have the hostages? Will Ning still advance from this direction to draw out Bei Ling?"

"Why wait? Ning has the armors; Nan Rong should find men to wear them. Corporal Niu will take my place and lead the march from the center. Should Bei Ling move past Ying Ling, Lord Han Bei will make them regret it."

"Doesn't that defeat the purpose of our task? You're baiting Bei Ling to march east where Lord Han Bei will quash their forces. The North will fall and the E Mo will be free."

"Why are you so naïve? The fact that we push them into a corner will equate to Wang Liang stopping at nothing to win. As callous as you think he is now, the man is currently relying on rationality and inhibition. Threatening to harm children for their mothers to run into our camps strapped with explosives is not above him. I'd rather not have any more innocent people die!"

For a moment, the detached mask was lost, at which time, hazel eyes turned stormy grey. Diao said my eyes turned gold when I lost composure, just like her father. I wonder, did he know all along that the E Mo were in trouble and this façade was to recruit our help without exposing his secret? Maybe we aren't much different. He could be a Demon or a Demon Slayer.

"I didn't mean anything by it. I'll gladly help. Fa Zhen's blood owes them this much."

"Fa Zhen means nothing to me. Let's trade the hostages for all of Wang Liang's explosives stowed in the outskirt cities. I'll gladly return them to his doorsteps."

Xian's sudden, excited cackling is borderline malevolent. Eyes are alighted as though he were a boy witnessing a fireworks display. I'm glad he thought to save the E Mo women and children but this is a little overboard.

"Captain Xian, we're only going to save the hostages. Putting Bei Ling civilians in harm's way is not right."

"Can't I at least set them off on Bei Ling's army?"

"No!"

Pouting, his fingers tap the table rhythmically in annoyance. "You Southerners are an unimaginative, boring lot. I'm leaving before you bore me to death."

In the end, the Minister urged Qing Hai and me to follow the Captain.

I had believed after leaving Feng Jia that this conflict was coming to an end. Dui and Bai Hu were so close and now I wonder if we'll ever meet again.

Chapter 32: The E Mo

"Are you all right?" Qing Hai pulls our bodies closer as we make our way through the road to Xia Pa. He's practically dragging me along.

"*I'm dying!*"

"Stop being dramatic." Xian, who's ten steps ahead, snaps over his shoulder. "If you were to die from that, you would have already. Hurry up. The temperature is only going to drop from here."

An hour ago, we were outside of Yue Na. I used Wen Meng's charm to induce Tian Ji Zhong Shi Yan and carried the Captain and Qing Hai across the small city, which really was more of a village. Not only was he heavy, Captain Xian packed several large parcels which required multiple transports, one of which contained a set of armors. That alone would have made me fall over from fatigue without the impact of my latent skill.

My heart is beating profusely and my body is shaking violently. I can't catch my breath. I was confident my will could handle the cost. After the fact, I realize how reckless that was. Dui risked his life in Feng Jia to keep me from this very expense and then I chanced everything just to carry Xian's luggage. I think the Captain is trying to kill me.

"Captain, she's really not doing well."

"Then leave her. Weaklings without use should be left behind."

"Captain!"

"*All right.* There's no need to yell." Xian whips around and drops his luggage on the spot. "You should be thanking me. At least, I didn't make her carry my horse. We'll rest here. In a couple hours, this desert will be one endless block of ice. I hope you've packed the essentials. No? Figures."

My desperate grip around Qing Hai is slipping. I'm not joking about my mortality anymore. A black shadow is seemingly lurking beside me. Its icy cold hand is ready to reach out and pull consciousness under. No matter how I try to stave off the darkness, it is futile. The speck of light in the center of my field of vision is diming and then all around, darkness encroaches until there is nothing left.

Chapter 32 – 2

I can't believe we're in trouble again. Master Lo Han is leaving for Ye Li Temple tomorrow. I fashioned a good luck charm a few days ago. Xiao Meow hid it, I know he did. 'Stop kissing up to Lo Han,' he said. 'How can you expect to find a man when you keep dressing like one?'

I gave Xiao Meow a good beating during our spar on the training fields. He cut my hair when I wasn't looking. Another fight followed and then we fell down the steps in front of the Lotus Pavilion. Master Tai Hung smacked my head. Master Zhuang smacked Xiao Meow's. And now, as punishment, we have to wash every piece of clothing and bed sheets in the entire temple, including the ones from the guest quarters.

There goes Master Tai Hung's new apprentice, the scrawny twig, walking so proudly behind my master. That kiss up. If Xiao Meow weren't always pulling me into mischief, I could outdo my master's new prized protégé in a heartbeat!

"Eww! Gross! Don't put that loincloth on my head! Ack! Get back here! Xiao Meow! I'll give you a beating you'll never forget!"

"Miss Bao Lai! You're choking me!"

"Huh?"

The single speck of light within the shrouded darkness fades and then from darkness, reveals a new light. I'm clinging to Qing Hai's collar with one hand. In the other is a fist.

"Wh-What's going on? What happened? Where are we? Why are you dressed like that? Why am I—?"

"Calm down. Your voice is raspy. Have a drink."

Until he mentioned it, I didn't realize the thirst overtaking me. My lips are dry and cracked. My throat feels like sandpaper. He takes up the jug and I steal it from him, drowning myself in water until my stomach cramps.

"Don't overdo it! Leave room for food. You've been unconscious for nearly a week."

"I-I have? Where are we?"

"Hui Fu, a little west of Xia Pa. Look, if anyone asks, I'm your brother and we're E Mo, okay? I'm Qiang and you're Tui Tui. Please don't make that face, it wasn't my idea. Also, Captain Xian is Fei. The little old lady who owns the inn is taking care of us until the Captain delivers us stragglers over to the guards for a reward in Man Wan. We'll see where they take us from there. Do you understand?"

"I think so. Wait. You carried me all the way from Yue Na? I'm so sorry."

Chapter 32: The E Mo

"I didn't. Cap—Fei did. He was worried you'd freeze to death, so he—"

"Come, children! Lunch is ready."

The door opens with such force that the shabby wood nearly cracked from slamming against the wall. Xian, frowning, walks in with a tray of food and tea. He's dressed in Bei Ling colors. Those are the armors he made me carried across Yue Na.

"Finally awake, Tui Tui? Good. No one needs dead weight."

After placing the tray on the low table next to the window, Xian moves to take my wrist and then closes his eyes to check my pulse. He's nodding but I doubt he even knows what he's doing.

"Uh. I see. I knew it. You were pretending all along. Well, get up. I'm tired of carrying you around."

"You say that, but you wouldn't let me help, Captain."

"Fei! Get it through your tiny E Mo brain, boy! My name is Fei!"

"Eh... Which one of you changed my clothes?" I'm in tribal garb, same as Qing Hai. The unsettling thought suddenly dawn on me. Qing Hai's head tilts left toward Xian. A cheeky smile breaks across his face.

"Don't flatter yourself, girl. I don't have any affinity for wild women. I couldn't have your brother changing

541

your clothes. That's borderline incestuous. Besides, my perfect wife is a celestial maiden descended to Earth."

"Pff! *You* have a wife? That poor woman!"

"At least I'm married. The Demon isn't really your husband, is he? No one wants you."

"Great accomplishment! Just how *did* you manage? I bet you bullied her into marriage through one of your asinine schemes."

"Take my scheming as a lesson. You'll need it with your lack of charms. Try baiting the Demon with a fake pregnancy and see how that turns out."

"You—!"

"Leave her alone! Miss Bao Lai may not be perfect but at least she's genuine! What makes you so sure your perfect angel is not in bed with another man right now?!"

The unexpected outburst captures our wide-eyed stares. Xian and I exchange glances. Qing Hai's flushed cheeks and furrowed brows carry more than embarrassment. He's on the verge of falling apart.

"Qing Hai. Wait. Qing Hai, wait!"

He's out the door the moment my quaking voice disrupts the awkward silence. I start up but can't fully support my body. The room is spinning. Darkness is threatening to retrieve consciousness back into its grasp.

542

Chapter 32: The E Mo

"Tsk! What is he thinking, running outside dressed like that? The guards will have his head! Stay here and eat your lunch! I don't need you fainting again!"

Xian's gone from the room by the time I look up. If only I could run after Qing Hai and calm his frustration. I should have known better than to start a petty argument with the Captain. Qing Hai is always defending me. This time he overreacted. I never knew under his usual sweet, innocent mannerisms, was such repressed temperament. Hopefully, the Captain finds him soon. I need to apologize to them both.

A bitter gastric taste is surging from my empty stomach into the back of my throat. I feel like vomiting and all my muscles are suffering from tremors. One hand in front of the other, I crawl toward the food tray on the low table near the window and scarf down whatever I can.

How strange. A few pieces of bread dipped in curry and everything suddenly feels calm. The tremors have subsided but I also can't lift my arm. Neither can I move my legs. The last to fall limp are my droopy eyelids and then darkness again consumes all senses.

Chapter 32 – 3

This is starting to become a habit though I guess I can't complain. Each time I faint, I wake up closer to my goal. This time, I'm in a holding cell with the E Mo hostages taken from the three outskirt cities. I'm not sure what happened but my guess is the food at the inn was drugged and the old lady who owns the place made a nice sum from handing over a wanted barbarian to the guards. I hope the Captain and Qing Hai escaped her opportunistic grubby hands.

The E Mo immediately knew I was an outsider and even after everything they've been through, kept silent and nursed me back to health. It's been almost three days since I woke. My temperamental body has settled and I can freely move again. However, once bitten, twice shy. I'm scared to invoke Tian Ji Zhong Shi Yan. Besides that, there are too many civilians involved that I can't be my usual reckless self. In this cell alone are twenty people—twelve females and eight males, ages from five to seventy-five. There are ten cells like this as far as I can see. Many more reside beyond the doors leading to the next blocks. The areas are tiny, drafty, and worst of all, stinky. Half of the time, we all breathe through our shirts.

"Are you all right? You're jittery." Mo Bi pats my back kindly. He's one of two E Mo in the cell who can speak my language. The others usually converse in a different dialect I've never heard before.

Chapter 32: The E Mo

"I'm fine. Thanks. Just a little claustrophobic."

"You and me both. I'm not used to anywhere that doesn't have wide-open skies. Wait a month, though. You'll get over your fear."

"How long have you been in here?"

"Three months ago when I came back to Ming Na. There's a man in Sai Mi named Zhang Tang who teaches the E Mo your language and gives us a decent education. He said our people can't be accepted and find better lives if we keep ourselves locked up in the desert. I don't know if he's right but I'm willing to try. Anyway, that's when I was taken in with the last group. Others have been here longer."

"This is inhumane."

"To most people outside of our tribes, we're not humans. Barbarians should be chained. I'm worried about my father and big brother though. I hope they won't do anything crazy to protect us."

"Me too. Things will be okay. Just give it some time. I'm sure help will come."

"I like your optimism but help never comes for our people. Several have already died from illness and malnourishment. The poor babies can't handle the cold and some women are having a hard time with the guards."

"You mean..."

Mo Bi nods sadly. He's only fourteen and yet, he sounds much older. There's a sense of innocence about the E Mo and also a maturity earned from hardship. This is particularly true about Mo Bi.

"You're shaking again, Miss Bao Lai. Are you scared?"

"No. I'm not."

Taking these people away from their homes and keeping them hostage is bad enough, but to violate the weak and defenseless too is unforgivable!

Memories from the Red Light District and again in Feng Jia surge through my trembling fists. During those times, I was terrified though I managed to escape the disgusting fate, a fate no one deserves to suffer. To think these women are treated like toys, used and then tossed aside, is enough to provoke the destroyer in my blood. If Xian and Qing Hai don't come soon, I might just do as the Captain suggested.

Chapter 32 – 4

Stale bread and dirty water. These are the rations the guards distribute during their second round. Same as yesterday, this marks the short time before the sun descends. With its eventual retreat, damp coldness soaks into the bones. The wailings of infants echo in waves. Little children bury their heads inside their mothers' coat to keep from the horror. Mo Bi leans a little closer to me for warmth and with my urging, leans his head on my shoulder.

A few hours later, the sounds of keys jingling, muffled chatters, and thumping boots signal the new set of guards come to relieve their counterparts. They usually stay away from this block. I couldn't grasp the reason before now. Most of the population here are elderly women and young children. The night guards must have their hands full harassing the young women located in the next blocks.

"Hey, Mo Bi. Do you know how to pick a lock?"

"No. Li Li can."

Li Li is the other E Mo in our cell who can speak my language. She doesn't talk unless spoken to and as usual, being addressed makes her uncomfortable. She gives a shy nod and hides her face in her knees.

"Here." Taking two small pins from my hair, I present them to her. She looks at me and then at Mo Bi, who takes the pins to remove pressure from Li Li.

"Miss Bao Lai, are you planning something?"

"Not yet, but when the rescue team comes, I need someone to help me pick all the locks."

"I grow envious of your optimism."

"Ha! I'm just a troublemaker. The notion of causing trouble excites me. I've been holding back for everyone else's sake."

"Well... what kind of trouble would you consider making?" Mo Bi stares at the ceiling, his voice quaking nervously, the innocence of which makes me think of Qing Hai.

"Don't provoke me. Once I formulate a crazy idea, I tend to see where it goes. Not this time though. Everyone's safety is at stake."

"I knew you weren't brought here by mistake! If you can do it.... anything at all! We'll die in here, Miss Bao Lai, and if we don't, they'll send us to die out there for a war we didn't start. I heard all the stories in Sai Mi. Anything would be better than this."

"Didn't you say you were worried for your father and brother? They wouldn't want you to do anything reckless either."

Chapter 32: The E Mo

"Everyone outside is stuck. They could run away if it weren't for us. Why should everyone have to suffer? Please Miss Bao L—!"

Two sets of heavy boots thumping hard against the ground send everyone to silence, even the children who were fussing for attention. Most facing the pair put their heads down to avoid drawing attention. The two slowly walk into the center of the block and scan the area. The looks on their faces resemble those of window shoppers.

They pass cell-by-cell, bringing tension and fear to each group within their sight and those adjacent. Once they move past our holdings, I thought maybe they'd grow bored and leave everyone alone. Instead, Lord Han Bei's warnings hold true. My blood is meant to bring troubles to Demons and such as it is, the guard on the right suddenly moves back in front of our cell. His bushy brows plant on Li Li.

"Hey, girl. Come here."

The soldier puts a hand through the bars and calls her over. She's shaking terribly. Li Li is thirteen years old and she certainly looks her age considering the tiny stature, braided pigtails, rounded cheeks, and big jade-colored eyes. This man has to be in his late thirties; not that age even matters in this sickening event.

"Are you deaf or stupid? Don't you understand, barbarian? I said *come here!*" He bellows the command as though being loud and obnoxious would induce her to speak his tongue if she hadn't already.

Li Li looks around for support. Panic keeps her and she doesn't notice my lightly shaking head. When she thought no one would provide relief, slowly stands up. Mo Bi stumbles forward to keep her back but the poor girl's already decided and refuses him. She doesn't want to bring the soldier's wrath upon the others. Li Li's obeying like the good girl that she is and so, she's forced my hand.

"Hey! What's the big idea? You're calling on a girl when there's a perfectly good woman standing right in front of you? Talk about insulting!" Pouting, I stand up and fully turn to face the guard, signaling for Li Li to sit down. This sassy persona is one I picked up from Miss Ai Qi at Mei Gui Guan.

"Who are you, girl? Didn't think any of you rats could sound human."

"Uh! Girl? I'm twenty-six!"

"You look fifteen."

"Flatterer! She and I might look the same age but I'm more developed in mind and body. See? Not all of us are made equal. Some are naturally better."

"Apparently. That one's more my type. Call her over here and tell her to come quietly."

Chapter 32: The E Mo

"And you continue to insult me? What does she have that I don't?"

"Innocence and timidity."

"Huh! You mean mousy and inexperienced. She's a stick! What? Still chasing after little girls because your equipment hasn't matured enough to handle a real woman?"

The other guard standing three cells down stifles a burst of laughter. The one before me suddenly tenses.

Attack a man where he hurts most and always in front of his peers, if possible, because he'll never hear the end of it. That idea came from Ma Tai Tou. There isn't a more painful strike to a man's pride than aiming below the belt.

"You agree with me, don't you, sir?" I call down to the other guard. "Only scared little boys harass scared little girls. Has he ever picked on anyone his own size?"

"Shut your damn mouth!"

His gauntlet flies against the metal bars, sending a resounding shock throughout the cellblock. Everyone instantaneously shrink back, me included. I was worried about opening my big mouth. As Zhang Mang said, every action has consequences. Same as the challenge with Commander Ru, sacrificing one for many would have been better than sacrificing all for one. However, I just couldn't do it.

"Geez, calm down, Jai." His counterpart moves adjacent. Patting the irate man's shoulder, he laughs. "Why are you even pissed? The lady's practically throwing herself at you. Of course she will get offended when you overstep her for a younger woman. It must get lonely in there, doesn't it, sweetheart?"

"That's an embarrassing thing to ask a woman." Turning away bashfully, my head nods a quiet confirmation. Thereupon the cell door opens and a hand extends from Jai.

"Be careful what you ask for."

"Same to you. And what about you, sir? What do I call you?"

"I'm Yang. You certainly have a lot of nerve acting this greedy. Sorry, I already have a lover."

"What's wrong with wanting everything? People without ambitions get nowhere in life. Oh well, that's too bad. You're quite a catch. Would any of your friends here be interested? How many are there during the night shift? Ten? Twenty?"

For experienced men, they're actually shocked by the suggestion. I'm disgusted for insinuating the idea but since confrontation can't be helped, I might as well have all the guards together when my skill is triggered. The worst scenario would be permitting any to leave and alerting reinforcements. That won't end well for the E Mo.

Chapter 32: The E Mo

While Jai continues to blush profusely, Yang's brows furrow into a dubious stare. He was standing too far away prior that I didn't fully grasp the indisputable sharpness about him that isn't common in soldiers patrolling these blocks; the same quickness Captain Xian exhibited. I tried to end this too quickly and as a result, my eagerness might have been overplayed.

"I thought you were just protecting that girl." Yang's lips thin into a line. His eyes glide from me to Li Li and then back again. "What did you say your name was?"

"I didn't. My name is Tui Tui."

"Where are you from?"

"Yue Na."

"You don't look like it to me."

"Then, let me out. Who wants to be in here anyway?"

"Hmph." Further thinning his lips, Yang falls silent.

"So what? Who cares how she looks? It stinks in here. Let's go already."

Jai, antsy for the fun night to begin, reaches out again. Yang knocks him back. Then, placing a gauntlet on the hilt of his sword, begins to rattle off a series of sentences he finally recalled. The intonation is familiar and a few of the words I can recognize from having listened to conversations in my cell. He knows a fraction of the E Mo's language, which is still considerably more than I do. I can't bluff a reply and the truth won't solve anything. In this case, pushing the lie is my best option.

"Don't speak to me in that revolting tongue! I hate being lumped with these savages! It's not my fault! I never chose to be E Mo!"

"Self-degradation and proffering pleasure to curry favors with your enslavers. You're either a sad excuse for a human being or a liar with tricks up her sleeves."

"Since when do people like you think we E Mo are human beings? Do you lock away half of your own in cages like animals when they aren't criminals? I'd do anything to escape this life! Until you've walked a mile in my shoes, where do you get off judging me?!"

"So, you're just a terrible person then." Yang, smirking, removes his gauntlet from the hilt. "Terrible people don't know when to quit lying. All it would take is a change of clothes to leave the E Mo life. Your face isn't E Mo. Your voice doesn't even hint at their dialect. If you were really this *eager*, there are plenty of brothels and teahouses to find a fool who will take you home."

"With no money, how would I come to acquire these things, fancy clothes and travel? The moment an E Mo walks into town, either the guards hold their throat by the sword or everyone else busies with formulating the price they'll fetch from the highest bidder."

Chapter 32: The E Mo

"And now you're playing a victim? Someone with your imagination could run into a city stark naked and claim bandits attacked to win sympathy from the guards. There are very few soldiers who would deny a defenseless, unclothed woman a warm meal and a warmer bed. You're out of excuses and out of chances for redemption. I don't know who you are or why you're pretending to be E Mo but this nonsense ends now."

The blade quickly draws from the scabbard, echoing the sharp grinding of metal against metal. The tip juts forward. A force knocks my body back a few steps and then Li Li's screams send the block to uproar. He moved so quickly that neither Yang nor I noticed in time. Blood drips down his left arm, soaking the light brown fur coat a bright shade of red. He cups a hand over the wound and falls to the floor.

"Mo Bi! Are you out of your mind?!"

Blood won't stop pouring from his wound no matter how hard I press. Li Li crawls over, tears streaming down her cheeks, and buries her face into his right shoulder. She desperately clings at his coat, nuzzling their cheeks together.

He always makes certain she has enough to eat and often sit shivering in the cold from giving his coat to keep her small body warm. I hadn't realized until now that he has been sitting next to me these past few days, opposite of Li Li, to have a better look. No wonder he'd sometimes blush without provocation. And, he knew the E Mo were seized by Wang Liang but still returned to Ming Na. Mo Bi volunteered for this imprisonment to watch over Li Li. Their predicament suddenly brings back bad memories from Feng Jia. The endless tears on her face were ones I shed then for Dui.

"Miss... Bao Lai." The hoarse, feeble whisper sounds just like Dui's. He holds out my hairpins and smiles. "You're here... for a reason. Nothing worthwhile comes... without a price."

"You dumb kid! Keep quiet! Why would you do that?! She loves you, idiot! Can't you understand how important you are to Li Li? She needs you and you're always reckless. Always doing stupid things to protect others. Stop trying to save me! What am I supposed to do without you? I need you, Dui!"

The weight settling over my chest causes an ache to erupt inside that was absent the last time I'd confessed. But, Dui's not here and neither is Bai Hu. Qing Hai and Captain Xian can't help me. Only worn, sad, hopeless faces peer from reclusive shadows. I never should have waited until now, after forced into this quandary, to help the E Mo. Actions may have consequences but sometimes inaction is worse.

"Send for someone. Have this trash taken outside. We don't need his bloody corpse stinking up the place. It stinks enough."

Chapter 32: The E Mo

Yang barks the cruel orders. Li Li clasps Mo Bi tighter, screaming in that language foreign to me. I can't think to do anything else until he stops bleeding.

"Who told you to draw your sword? You caused this mess, you clean it up!" Jai barks back. In an instant, Li Li's tiny figure is jerked off the floor and then the brute drags her down the opposite end of the block.

"Leave her alone! Wait. What...?" Air pinches out of my lungs. The hand reaching beneath my collar for the relic returns empty. It's gone. My advantage was stolen along with my freedom by the greedy innkeeper. The situation keeps growing direr. I can't move past the cell door. Yang's blade is lifted again, only this time, the tip is pointed at Mo Bi.

"Take your pick, *Champion of the Savages*. Save the girl and I'll kill this boy. Stay with him and hear her scream. Maybe she'll kill herself like that other one a few blocks over."

"How can you be so heartless? She's just a little girl!"

"I haven't done anything against her. You're the heartless one. This is your fault. This is what happens when you undermine Bei Ling's authority and make a mockery of our soldiers. Last chance to clear your conscience and maybe I'll spare the boy. Who sent you?"

"Miss Bao Lai, just go!"

Jai slams open the northern door leading to the next block, Li Li's crying her eyes out, and Mo Bi's pushing against my leg. I should

Save Li Li (Continue to page 559)

Save Mo Bi (Continue to page 561)

Chapter 32 – 5

"Please just go! Help her, Miss Bao Lai!"

Li Li's screams send a chill down my spine. The sheer terror on her face induces me to move without consideration. My feet fly forward, bursting through the wooden door to the northern block. Once Jai grasps that he's been followed, keeps one hand on Li Li's collar and draws the blade latched to his hip. All around, horrified chatters and jeers drown out my furiously beating heart. The E Mo knows the consequences they'll face for my failure and as it is, unarmed and without my advantage, I'm on the verge of failure.

"Let her go!"

"Or what? This little savage is mine. I'd slit her throat before I give her back."

The heart-wrenching scream nearly makes my knees buckle. I thought Li Li was terrified by Jai's threat but her gaze is directed at me; more so, someone from behind. All in the boisterous room falls to silence except for Li Li.

Mo Bi's lifeless body is thrown at my feet and in Yang's hand is a blood-laced blade. He killed a helpless boy who couldn't fight back and dragged his body to boast the disgusting victory. The kid never had a chance.

"Heartless bastard!"

An indescribable heaviness storms the air, overlapping my shout. A flood of wind rushes past at the same moment I lunge for Yang. I know this feeling of madness and rage. A reaper has appeared whose aura mimics the Demon General's. Her jade colored eyes, which are burrowing into my face, stain blood red. The instant I notice them, the blade she's taken from Jai have penetrated through Yang and me.

The End.

Chapter 32 – 6

"Please just go! Help her, Miss Bao Lai!"

I can't look away from Mo Bi's wound or the unnatural creeping paleness over his cheeks from loss of blood. Charging after Jai won't do any good unless I can match his sword. I need a weapon and there's one pointing at Mo Bi's nose.

The woeful stare on my face that's quietly peering down signals to Mo Bi my hesitation and apology. The terror overwhelming his countenance grows tenfold. His lips tremble. The corners of his eyes wet with tears.

"Miss Bao Lai, please! Save Li Li!"

In tandem with Mo Bi's frantic cry, I run past the cell door. True to his threat, Yang's blade raises and then lowers in a swift arc, flying to the ground in a loud clang along with his body. He fell for misdirection and in turn, I've tackled him to the floor. The soldier scrambles but heavy armors keep him from recovering before a fist slams against his nose, knocking the flustered man unconscious. It's a cheap trick, not the easiest to accomplish unless at close range, but effective against opponents when unarmed. That was from the first week of Master Zhuang's training at Tian Mao Yi. He told us not to, but the students tested that theory on each other. We all had bloody noses that week.

"Hold on, Mo Bi! I'll be right back!"

561

Swooping up Yang's blade, I scramble through the doors leading to the north block. All around, horrified chatters and jeers drown out my furiously beating heart. I can't understand anything they're saying but half must be frightened for Li Li, the rest are frightened for their families. The offense I've committed against the guards won't go unpunished and retribution will not be isolated to the offender.

"Where is she? Where's Li Li?! *Li Li*! Where did he take her?"

Two doors are ahead, each leading north and west respectively. I can't hear her cries anymore from the increasing madness. Half of the prisoners are pointing west, the others point north. I pick a random door and fly through only to find another puzzle with three doors and the same incomprehensible shrillness abound creating an impasse for any progress. Each step forward feels another step back. I could be running in circles and not even know.

"The girls! That way!"

Among the throng of unfamiliar shouts, my ears naturally pick up recognizable words. A young woman in tears is flailing her arms through cell bars. Once she captures my attention, points furiously to the left door. Her eyes roll upward, seemingly searching for the right words in my language. I imagine she's another student studying under Zhang Tang, the man from Sai Mi who promoted education to the E Mo. What a difference a few words of mutual understanding can accomplish. My futile course may finally progress.

"That way! Up!"

"Straight ahead through that door?"

"Yes! Careful!"

"Thank you."

With advancement comes rising anxiety. Time is limited and I don't have the luxury of a well-thought plan. I've not seen one guard since running after Li Li. If they're congregated ahead, I'm not certain what this one sword can accomplish without my advantage.

Past another door and then distinct chatters and distraught cries burst from the area obscured yet by another barrier, built larger than its predecessors and made from heavier wood. My heart stops the moment the storage room door opens.

The fate which I was twice spared is forced upon those before my very eyes. Some are my age, others much younger. Li Li is in a corner with her chest half-exposed and tears streaming down flushed cheeks. She stifles a cry upon the disturbance, as do the other women and children, while the guards pause the atrocity to draw their swords.

"Who the hell are you?"

The guard who poses the question has the most distinguished armor amongst the group. Compared to

Bai Hu and Zhen Yue, this man makes a mockery of soldiers and sullies the honor of leadership. He isn't the only one guilty but having led through example and permitted these heinous transgressions under his command makes him the most deserved of retribution.

"Let them go!"

"What's this? Not one of the savages, are you? Good. These animals were starting to bore me."

His sword brandishes and then the others under his command follow suit. However, the leader waves for his men to withdraw. "Don't bother. Continue your fun. She came to save these animals. Let her die witnessing failure."

"W-Wait just a minute! This is between us, let them go!"

Against my outrage, the soldiers move back into position to continue their abuse. Resounding screams from the E Mo douse composure in ice water. Rising panic inside tears my attention from the melee against the guard captain. Li Li is struggling to keep Jai's filthy hands from her innocent body. Every time I make a mad dash, a sword comes for my head. His swings are heavy, sapping the strength from my shaking arms each time our weapons collide. To make matters worse, he's fast and skilled, as expected from a well-trained soldier.

"Li Li!"

Chapter 32: The E Mo

Little hands frantically cover her fully exposed chest. Jai sends a gauntlet across her face. She falls back, whimpering from the assault that left a cut across her cheek. Blood flowing down her face is suddenly matched by blood flowing down my arm. In the fraction of time I looked away, the opposing blade sliced through the fur coat and into my flesh. The sword that was in my hand is lying a ways away.

Giving no quarters, the smug look on his face blurs upon the next wave of assault. I manage to evade the first few strikes before fatigue wins over will. The next few strikes rip at the fur coat leaving tear marks and trickling pools of blood.

"You're the best those fools could send? *Pathetic.*"

There's undeniable truth in that mocking tone raining down amusedly. I came with a sword but didn't intend to kill. As a result, everyone around is suffering and I'm going to die. I wanted to be strong, to protect those important to me, and yet once presented with the advantage, I've been innately ashamed of the blood flowing through my veins despite my continuous dependency.

"Stop it!" Li Li's sharp cry in familiar tongue startles her assaulter along with the guard captain whose sword is raised above my head. She's looking at me, begging for my life to be spared while hers isn't in better predicament.

"Well, how about that? You can sound human. This will be more fun than I thought." Chuckling to himself, Jai pins her trembling wrists to the wall. The filth buries his face into her neck.

"Get away from Li Li!"

Master Tai Hung said it's wrong to take a life. I've lived by his creed but in this moment, witnessing beasts attack those innocent, I finally understand Fa Zhen. His gift was meant to stop Demons, in whichever form they may take. And yes, it has been a gift, a blessing all along; one I finally accept with pride as a true part of me.

The surging feeling inside my chest is filling to the brim. I yield to the slayer blood flowing through my veins and let my nature dictates the sin it will carry.

The E Mo victims' stagnant faces are warped by grief and pain. The guard captain's raised weapon aimed to end my interference is frozen in midair. Li Li's tears have ceased flowing. Through Tian Ji Zhong Shi Yan, time is standing still. Each step forward is mechanical. This body of mine is moving without any control. In an instant, the chaos ended.

Chapter 33: Yu Qi's Solution

"Bastard!" Another fist flies against Captain Xian's face. He could easily dodge the assault; instead, lets me take out my aggravation, which aggravates me even more.

"Bao Lai, don't you think that's enough?"

"No!"

I shake off Qing Hai's restraint and slam another fist into Xian's cheek. His once handsome face is black and blue, none of which was a result of last night's event. Last night, once time resumed, most of the guards fell over unconscious from my assault and the rest ran off from witnessing the instantaneous event. They called me a demon, which was close to the truth, and brought the remainder of the guards on duty to subdue 'the beast.' With their security preoccupied, Captain Xian and Qing Hai easily snuck inside and took care of the rest. What that means is the Captain was outside all along.

"I-It was my fault too. I shouldn't have acted so childish in Hui Fu. You can blame me."

"Stay out of this, Qing Hai. This was his plan! And a lousy one at that! Why didn't you storm in?"

"I didn't think *you* of all people needed saving or would even want to be saved for that matter. Besides, I've told you, your job was infiltration and killing

567

everyone who gets in the way. Qing Hai tracked our way here and I... made sure that anyone who left the prison to alert Wang Liang would be punished."

"So for the past three days, you've been waiting outside for me to cause trouble in there?"

"One, actually. Your friend's the slow tracker, not me. Anyway, Lord Han Bei said you were a troublemaker by trade. I abided my time by watching the base. You can thank me. Wang Liang won't hear about this until one of *you* blab."

"You—! I'm not thanking you for anything!"

"Just calm down. Everything's fine now. It was my idea to wait until nightfall. The Captain was really worried, he almost ran in before sunset—"

"*Ahem!*" Xian smacks Qing Hai's shoulder sharply. "You'll be the first one to blab to Wang Liang, won't you? Look, I don't need anyone dying under my command. Makes my record look bad, then who'd want to follow me? They'll take away my cushy job. Now, are we done here? These people should return home before the men in those three cities blow themselves up and this boy still needs medical care."

"Right. Sorry. Are you feeling all right, kid?"

"Yeah... I'll... be fine." Mo Bi replies through strained breaths. He looks much better than yesterday but it will be a long while before that wound heals.

Chapter 33: Yu Qi's Solution

"Good. Then I guess this is goodbye. Mo Bi, take care of Li Li."

"Where are you... going, Miss... Bao Lai?"

"To Sai Mi. I have a promise to keep. Mo Bi. Li Li. Qing Hai. Captain. Good luck."

Squaring my shoulders, I march off in the opposite direction, facing the rising sun. Just as my pretentious heroic retreat begin, a burst of laughter springs from behind. That's the last person I expected to hear.

"You're going the wrong way." Li Li smiles brightly. "It's that way."

"I-I knew that!"

"Adults shouldn't lie." Li Li giggles timidly. The previous somberness over her demeanor seems to never have existed. She's acting more her age. The suffering she'd endured last night couldn't faze her spirit. "Should I go with you?"

"Er, I'll be fine. You should go home. Your families are waiting."

Throwing a withered smile, my feet whip toward the road Li Li pointed. Once more, my forced composure unravels and progress comes to a halt in the midst of the gallant march, only this time, through a rock slamming against my right shoulder and then several more against my head and back.

"Hey! What the hell?!"

Shouts and jeers drown out my defenders' attempt to calm the sudden rising mob. The other E Mo have kept to themselves this entire time, whispering to one another as they had in the prison. I thought nothing of it. However, the hatred burning in their gazes, the unrelenting resentment and anger, I can't understand a word they're saying but those eyes aiming to tear me apart fully convey whom they see: Fa Zhen.

Those women from the storage room last night must have told the others about my gift. Fa Zhen's gift made their people outcasts and his gift also gave back their freedom. Li Li desperately tries to calm the mob from advancing but it won't do any good. The wound that has marred their spirits runs too deep. I can't undo the past or heal the offense in one night. They have a right to be angry just as I have a right to feel offended.

Despite their hatred, to see this many Demon descendants still alive after having meddled in their affairs, makes me indescribably happy. Lord Han Bei wasn't entirely right. My blood is meant to destroy demons, but only when I decide it. At this harrowing moment, I can choose to invoke Tian Ji Zhong Shi Yan and stop the abuse or I can simply walk away.

And so, I'm running to escape the hail of flinging rocks and to keep my friends from trouble. My friends include Captain Xian. While I'm still chary about his character, I can't help but be thankful for what he's done. His actions may have redeemed Fa Zhen more than I have. Besides that, at least now I know for certain. Hu and I are always in trouble when we're together because the both of us have been troublemakers from the day we were born. Our nature is so much alike that we were effortlessly drawn to each other. He protected me the only way he knew how and I will find a way to make amends to Bai Hu. The happier days we've lived together will resume.

A burden is lifted off my shoulders. With lighted heart, I skip to Sai Mi.

Chapter 33 – 2

"That's really pricey for wormwood."

"Quality often comes with a high price."

"Uh-huh, and is that tongkat?"

"Yes, ma'am. They're imported from far southern countries."

"How long ago?"

"Just came in last week."

"Hmm. Fine. Take twenty percent off the tongkat and I'll buy two packets of the pricey wormwood too."

"I'm sorry, I can't do that. That's our entire margin. These came from very prestigious herbalists you know."

"I can clearly see the stamp on the side of the crate. This was purchased from Wang Di Medicinal Herb Farms. I used to visit there once every three months. Wholesale, that wormwood is a quarter of the price you have listed. Twenty percent off the tongkat would still bring you to fair market value for the wormwood at sixty percent list price."

Ugh. I sounded like Dui just now and the shopkeeper is giving me the same look he usually receives from trade shops. I came to search for Yu Qi and instead, wandered aimlessly after realizing finding one person in this massive city is impossible. Somehow,

I stumbled into this medicinal herb shop and have probably spent a good two hours browsing. I'm really surprised to find tongkat. Wormwood is just good to have on hand.

"How long do you plan to hold up the line? Some of us actually have places to go."

"As long as it takes to pay market value for wormwood," is the snappy reply I send over my shoulder to the irate customer standing behind me.

"Let me guess, trying to bribe the doctor with that tongkat so he'd take your unfaithful self back?"

"Eh...?"

Sharp eyes of a hawk on a narrow face; spiked tufts of hair. Aside from not wearing armor, there's something different about him.

"What's with the eye patch?"

Yu Qi leans down and, taking a deep breath, whispers inconspicuously. "It's my disguise. I'm a pirate."

"*Pfff*... haha! And you said that with a straight face! You're kidding, right?"

"Only simpletons laugh without reason. Now move out of the way, country bumpkin. No one haggles in these high-end shops. If you have to then you can't afford the merchandise. Get out."

"Rude much? I was here first. Besides, they're ripping people off at these prices."

"Taxes, wages, and rent are different here. You're only looking at inventory cost. Don't forget overhead."

"Oh, I see. That makes sense. Are these normal prices for Sai Mi?"

"For above average to top quality, sure. I guess you can check the markets on the other end and haggle a better deal but then you never know how old those herbs are. You see, those merchants buy from places like this, when the stores have to throw out inventory, and from random dealers who sell small batches. You never know if there's consistency which can be bad if the potency is too high or low. So, unless you harvest and dry your own, I'd pay more to not have to worry about that headache."

"Oh, uh-huh. I get it. Wow, you sure know a lot about business!"

"I've picked up a few things here and there. Often times, I've thought about opening my own apothecary shop."

"That would be great! Do you usually dry your own herbs?"

"Usually, but sometimes it can't be helped."

"Are you two going to buy anything?"

Whoops.

Chapter 33 – 3

That was awkward. For a moment, I'd forgotten I was speaking to Yu Qi, probably because he didn't insult me for once. It was nice.

"What's in the bag?"

We're walking abreast down the road leading to the poorer side of the market. The pricey wormwood was forgone and I settled for tongkat. Yu Qi won't let me look in his satchel.

"None of your business. Quit following me."

"I have to. I promised Diao. What are you planning anyway, Yu Qi?"

"My name is not Yu Qi. Go away."

"You know, that cranky old man attitude is the reason I like annoying you."

"There isn't a man alive you won't *annoy*. I'm not falling for you."

"O... kay. Thank you?"

I should have known better than to attempt civility. He's such a curmudgeon.

"Who are you calling a curmudgeon?"

"Whoops. I was mouthing my thoughts again, huh?"

"When do you ever quit? Speaking of bad habits. I know you stole my belt buckle, kleptomaniac. I want it back."

"Um. You purposefully dropped that for me... right?"

"Me? Give *you* anything? That's preposterous."

His voice is hard and serious, though he often sounds that way even when I'm more than certain he's joking. That is, when a normal person would be joking.

"But... it had the Nan Rong royal family seal. Weren't you trying to tell me that Su Jian is behind this?"

"Why would I? What could a simpleton like you possibly do? Here you are in Sai Mi and instead of using your special gift to put down Su Jian, I caught you haggling for mediocre wormwood. What a waste of talent."

"Me? What about you? I thought you were in a hurry after throwing me off your horse and then I find you in the same shop. Seriously, what's in the bag?"

"Herbal oil for my hair."

"Very funny."

"What's funny about it? Hair this smooth and fine don't grow naturally."

Yu Qi flips his head, making the spike tufts shimmer like feathers in sunlight. I started to laugh believing he's joking but his stone face blocks the attempt.

576

Chapter 33: Yu Qi's Solution

"So... you're a narcissistic curmudgeon?"

"Ugly people wouldn't understand."

"Oh, wow. That's a nice thing to say. No wonder you're single. Diao must be out of her mind to be so fond of you. Don't let her get away."

"Dui suffered from severe head trauma, that's why he's so fond of you. I told him to run away."

"*Hmm.* Fair enough."

I must be suffering from severe head trauma because for a moment, I thought a corner of his mouth curled slightly upward.

"Yu Qi, are you coming back to Nan Rong? Dui—"

"No."

"But—"

"Be quiet. I have work to finish. Don't bother me."

In front of an old house the size of a closet, Yu Qi produces a key and unlocks the sturdy door. Believing he aims to keep me out, I push his slim body through the threshold and squeeze inside. Aside from a table, chair, brazier, and trunk, there isn't much furniture available. Also, it smells weird.

"Is this how you seduce all your victims, attack when their backs are turned? I won't let you have your way with me, succubus."

"Er... I wasn't. I thought you wouldn't let me in."

"Correct. This is trespassing. Get out."

"I'm already trespassing so, I'll stay. Hey, Yu Qi, what's in here?"

Frowning, the curmudgeon locks the door and lights a candle on the table. Then, slipping the key hung around his neck from underneath the tall-collared shirt, unlocks the trunk. Inside are a brewing kit, another large satchel filled to the brim with materials, his armor and sword, and a substance I know well.

"Is that... senna? You two really are brothers."

"I don't know what that means." Yu Qi prepares the table and lights a fire in the brazier. Most of the raw ingredients laid out are familiar. Several large jars are filled with potent tonics and tinctures. Others even have dead snakes and scorpions inside.

"Eww. I hate snakes."

"Stop touching my things! Quit poking that jar!"

"Okay! What are you making? Let me help. Like I said, Diao sent me look over you so, that's what I'll do."

Letting out an exaggerated sigh, Yu Qi slaps my hand to keep it from poking the jar with snakes again. It's so gross. I feel compelled to poke it.

"A poison. You don't know anything about poisons."

Chapter 33: Yu Qi's Solution

"Poison? Don't tell me you're returning Su Jian's favor. Actually, it's been a while since we left Diao and Zhang Mang. Shouldn't their forces have reached Bei Ling's gates by now?"

"Difficulties delayed their march. Wang Liang is hiding in the palace. Defenses are too sturdy."

"So, you're flushing him out with senna?"

"Was that a joke? You're not funny."

"Aww." Dui would have appreciated that one.

"I'm not Dui. Get it through your head. I'm a killer. Because of me, your lover and Dui barely escaped death. Did you forget? I couldn't care less the things you promised Diao. The moment you keep me from accomplishing my ambition, I'll end you without a thought."

He's right. We aren't friends. In fact, for what he's done, we are rightfully enemies. I hated him until his real name was discovered. Then I knew him as Dui's brother, Diao's secret love, and the man who saved me through his genius. Those mixed feelings have battled inside my mind and I know, also in his. He can't return to Yu Qi but he also can't remain Ying. I wonder, given more time, will Bai Hu become this way?

"Stop staring. Take vengeance for the Demon as you wish; otherwise, get out."

"No. I'm mad at Ying. He's not here. And you're right, neither is Yu Qi. Whoever you are, just let me help. I can't make poison but I can deliver it straight to Wang Liang."

I hold my breath in the ensuing silence, keeping my eyes directly to his sidelong glance until he grows contented, or maybe exasperated, and finally turns away.

"You're as stubborn as that doctor," he replies almost mockingly. "Want to dirty your hands? Fine with me. The poison isn't for Wang Liang. His death won't be peaceful. This is for everyone else blocking my way."

"W-Wait. You can't be serious. I can use my advantage and take us both inside."

"Yes, I know you wish to lay hands on me. Were I that desperate, your proposition doesn't outweigh the benefit. Behind the thick crowds of guards stationed at the front are two tall walls, a massive door which requires the strength of two to open, long corridors, and an antechamber which leads to another maze. I could be optimistic and believe your heart won't give out after passing the exterior defenses but you won't have the strength to move. I don't need dead weight and I certainly don't need Wang Liang's guard to heighten when his men find your limp body."

"But those people are just doing their jobs. That's not right!"

Chapter 33: Yu Qi's Solution

"Then don't volunteer to help a killer. The longer conflict goes on, the more people die. Just standing here wasting my time with your self-righteous lecture, another man on the battlefield just *doing his job* fell dead."

"Y-Yeah, but... there has to be an easier way to get inside. An old escape route. Don't all these palaces have one?"

"Go find it and come back when you do. If I haven't finished my poison by then, we'll do it your way. Oh, and when the thousands of guards come to stop us, be sure to tell them you're just *doing your job* and maybe they won't jam their swords through your chest."

I have nothing to say to that. Chances are Bei Ling's guards won't give us a fraction of sympathy. At the first notion of danger, they'll be inclined to take our heads. Furthermore, I'm still sore over the E Mo's mistreatment by Bei Ling's men in Ji You. If I didn't have a choice but to kill all the guards who were in my way, even the ones who only performed their duties, in order to free the hostages, I would have. It's the same thinking, taking lives, differing marginally by rationalizations. In short, I'm a hypocrite, just as Dui said.

In the quiet room, Yu Qi continues to prepare the concoction, paying no regards to my silent shuffling. His techniques are precise and practiced. The serious expression of focus is a mirror image to Dui. At first glance, they're complete opposites and at heart, they are

581

one and the same. I bet Yu Qi would have been a kind doctor, just as his brother is, had he not suffered the unfortunate incident at such a young age. Despite everything, I feel sad for Yu Qi.

Sometime after, he reaches for the satchel from the herb shop, dumping onto the table several ingredients including a bottle of oil which was mentioned earlier for smoothing his hair. One of the ingredients is rather unusual.

"Isn't that wisteria?"

"Are you still here?" He replies curtly without looking up.

"Your poison isn't meant to kill, is it? Temporary sickness to cause hysteria. I knew you were nice!"

"Yes, nice people tend to poison water supplies and kill hundreds without hesitation. I dread to know the type of people you consider evil. This sympathy for the devil act has gone on long enough. I don't have time to humor you."

"Yes, yes. You're a grumpy old man. Someone still needs to dump that into the palace's water supply. Why not let a young person help? I can run in and out with my skill before anyone notices."

"Assuming you won't fall over dead halfway inside."

Chapter 33: Yu Qi's Solution

"True, but ever since my skill last surfaced, I realize I can induce it at will. It's also not as taxing on my heart as when I used that relic."

"No idea what you're talking about."

"Look, I can do it. There might be soldiers at the site and like you said, we can't afford for Wang Liang to be on greater guard. Plus, your pirate disguise can't fool anyone."

His face turns sour. Yu Qi mutters inaudibly under his breath. Expletives, I imagine. No wonder Diao is fond of this strange man. He's really fun to aggravate.

"Keep laughing at me and I'll cut out your vocal cords."

"Uh-huh. That means you expect me to stay, which means I can help, right?"

He doesn't say more and silence is as good as concession.

Chapter 34: Sai Mi Under Siege

He won't admit it but he's glad I tagged along. The private well, which provides water to the main palace, was kept discreetly under lock and key behind a tall gate in an abandoned area on the west side of town. In front of the entrance were at least twenty soldiers and three sentinels. Wang Liang is really paranoid; though, I suppose for good reason.

Infiltration took longer than expected, tiring my heart substantially. I've slept a good portion of the day in a rented room on the top floor of the Long Hu Tavern. It's now dark outside. From the windows, there appears to be commotion at the palace.

"Hey, Yu Qi, come see this."

No answer. The lump on the bed adjacent to mine is still. I knew it. He must have left the moment I fell asleep. The least he could have done was not insult me by stuffing pillows under the sheets. I gave him the more comfortable bed too! What a waste!

Oh, well. Until things at the palace escalate into hysteria, I might as well rest in the big fluffy bed Yu Qi didn't bother to use. My chest is still tight. There isn't much I can do for now.

"*Ahhh*! Y-Yu Qi?! I-I'm so sorry!"

"Now you're attacking me in bed? What's the excuse this time? Do you want me that badly?"

Chapter 34: Sai Mi Under Siege

"I thought you'd left!"

"Right. Sure. That must be why my figure was protruding from beneath the blanket. *Your* bed is over there. What's the reason for jumping into mine? "

"Because—! You won't listen either way, will you? Fine. I was trying to seduce you, Yu Qi. *You're so handsome, strong, and smart*! I've never been more attracted to anyone in my life! Happy? Geez. Get over yourself, Narcissist."

"So, you finally admit it. Hmph. Don't bother. Shameless women aren't my type, especially ones who have been used."

"Excuse me?!"

"Be quiet."

He jumps off the bed and runs to the windows. Same as before, there is commotion at the palace but hawk eyes are directed elsewhere. Distinct shadows flicker, as swiftly as mere twinkles of a star, before disappearing completely. I would never have noticed these seeming figments of imaginations hadn't Yu Qi's gaze relentlessly pierce the hazy apparitions lurking near the perimeters of the massive structure, moving as though to surround the place.

"Who are they, Yu Qi?"

"How should I know?"

"What should we—"

From the southern gates, drums and whistles tear through the calm night air. There's franticness in the loud, muddled signals, which then abruptly ends in an eerie silence. Below, shadows moving to surround the palace momentarily backtrack from the unexpected interruption. In that short fraction of time, light from one of the buildings nearby breaks across a familiar face: mine.

"Is that His Highness?"

"Where?"

"Right... He was right there, I think. Gosh, he moves fast!"

"You're easily impressed for someone who can stop time."

"Well, I can't *really* stop time. It's more like—"

"Shut up. I didn't ask for your life story."

"Rude much?"

He walks to the wrapped parcel by the bed and takes out the suit of armor. "I'm changing. Get out."

I couldn't utter half a word before the door behind slams shut and then I'm left standing alone in the empty hallway.

Chapter 34 – 2

Only perverts would purposefully intrude on another person dressing. I wonder if it makes me less of a pervert for merely eavesdropping. For the past fifteen minutes, Yu Qi has been preparing for the big performance. I've listened once or twice for signs of clothes rustling or armors clanking. He's as quiet as a mouse. Also, he won't return my calls. I fear making brash assumptions lest I suffer another round of his accusations. I don't know why I care what he thinks.

"Yu Qi! What's taking so long? I'm dying of old age out here! *Bah!*"

A force the like of earthquakes, and as loud as roaring thunder, knocks me to the floor along with just about everyone else inside the tavern. Hectic shouts and screams immediately echo from below. Long Hu Tavern's entire foundation shook so violently that large cracks scatter about the former polished hardwood walls. The northern side of the inn is raised, leaving all furniture slanted or sliding to the southern end.

"Yu Qi, are you all right?" I scramble inside the room, shaking from shock and fear, to then tremble from silent rage. Though his armor and a short blade remain on the bed, he's disappeared with the long sword.

A million frightful thoughts are surging, followed by a million expletives. I can't believe him!

Another loud, deafening crash; this one farther away on the other side of the city. In succession are several more scattered explosions giving reminder to the E Mo's near-fatal fate.

That awkward event at the gates moments ago is starting to make sense. As jumbled as it was, those drums meant to send an intruder alert. Has the Alliance advanced this far? I hope Wang Liang isn't planning to raze Sai Mi to the ground!

Chapter 34 – 3

The acrid scent of smoke, deafening cries resounding from all around, which are then drowned beneath several loud explosions, send Sai Mi into utter chaos. People are shoving and trampling over each other just to run in circles. There isn't safe shelter anywhere to be found.

After having climbed down the railings on the side of the tavern, I break into a run toward the massive edifice. From Long Hu Tavern to Sai Mi's palace is a short walk but due to disarray, the short distance become a long trek. I'm still not any closer to palace gates and the more I push forward, the more civilians and soldiers alike are pushing back.

This doesn't make sense. Guards should be rushing from all over Sai Mi to defend the palace. Why are more and more running from that side toward the southern end?

"Demons! Demons are at the gate! Run for your life!"

A guard scrambles past me toward the opposing group of Bei Ling soldiers coming forthwith. He's screaming nonsense. Each time the hysterical man mentions 'demons,' the others fall into silent terror.

Strange. None of the E Mo women or children kept in Ji You could invoke the old bloodline advantage. This could be their men's doing but that doesn't seem right either. The E Mo aren't particularly interested in outside affairs. Once their families were returned, I would have thought they'd find new and safer homes, away from Wang Liang's grasp.

In spite of his warnings, the soldiers leave the mumbling man behind and run to the southern gates. Since I can't move forward in this crowd, my other option is to follow them.

Once we're halfway to the gate, a horde of soldiers, many covered in blood, are running in the opposing direction. Their cries mirror the prior hysterical man, leaving the advancing group in front of me to conflict. Some are adamant to move forward, a handful prefer to stay put until the threat comes and launch an ambush from above, while a few others drop their weapons and retreat.

In the midst of their argument, sheer oppressive terror takes over the atmosphere. The feeling of a reaper, a thousand times deadlier than Zhang Mang's killer aura, forebodes of the abyss opening, intending to swallow everything whole. It's the dreadful sensation of oblivion. It's a feeling I know well. Once the force makes itself known, it's clearly the man I love. Fear can't overcome happiness rising in my chest to see him well.

Bai Hu, in red Nan Rong armor and without the influences of the silver mane, boldly marches up the streets. Those wishing to keep their lives part to both sides and fall to their knees in concession. His sword is covered in blood. His eyes lust for carnage. The soldiers standing to my front, unable to fully grasp the approaching danger, draw their weapons.

"Retreat! You can't defeat him!"

Against my warning, the foolish half charges for the Demon General. In an instant, the remainders are frozen to the spot when their allies fall with hardly any effort from Bai Hu. He cleaved through their weapons and armors as though the hard metal were merely paper. No wonder those men thought there were demons. He can accomplish alone that which a thousand men would struggle to imitate.

"Run away, idiots!"

The trembling men won't budge. The encroaching look of satisfaction on that face so dear to me has rendered his opponents helpless. They're whimpering as though that is their only option. Regardless of my tugs and pulls, their feet are lead.

"Damn it! Move already!"

On impulse, my right shoulder slams against one of the men, who in turn topples onto another, and then another. The shock was enough to bring back their senses. The soldiers run for dear life toward the palace, screaming the same madness that brought them here.

That hard frown clearly conveys his opinion of my intrusion. His eyes, void of emotions, bury into my face as though to claw out my inner turmoil.

I'm not afraid of him. I have to keep reminding myself that this is Bai Hu. Somewhere inside is a man who loves me, who would never hurt me, who sacrificed himself time and time again to keep me safe. However he has become doesn't change who he is.

"Hu—"

"Heh. Found you at last."

His sword swings upward from where he stands, which is a substantial distance away from me. The twisted smile that springs to his face slowly morphs into a mean grin. "I'll send the next one to your heart."

"Send what?"

A heavy frown settles over his mouth. I look to my left arm where his eyes are directed to find a pool of blood slowly dripping down my sleeves. That's impossible!

"How did you—? Hu, I—"

"Get down!"

Someone sends me to the ground just as Hu delivers another invisible wave meant to tear through my heart. The scent rising from the intruder's shirt has become instinctual for me. I don't know why he came back but I'm glad.

"Use your skill! Use it now!"

Yu Qi suddenly falls silent, stiff as a stone statue. Hu's stuck in a rigid pose. Even the flames around have stopped flickering. That was a close one. The wave sent from Hu's sword to slice Yu Qi and I in twain has become visible. Faint, but still visible. I've heard Tai Chi masters boast about their abilities to emit energy into attacks but have never witnessed a single person proved the phenomenon. It's unearthly!

As impressed as I am, now isn't the time to be effusive. Once Yu Qi is out of harm's way, I rush to disarm Bai Hu. However, the moment I reach out, his eyes dart downward and then, like a statue come to life, the Demon General shakes off whatever restraint has kept him. I thought Tian Ji Zhong Shi Yan wore off but Yu Qi is still immobile and so are surrounding flames.

"B-Bai Hu? What—How?"

"Demon Slayer, huh?" His left gauntlet flexes as to adjust to this new state. "Not all that impressive. I see through your cheap tricks. You won't kill this demon easily."

"I don't want to kill you! Bai Hu, stop it!"

"Shut your mouth!"

The upward strike of his sword misses by a hair's breadth. I tumble back and draw the short blade Yu Qi left for me at Long Hu. The fact that he missed is surprising and also proof that Tian Ji Zhong Shi Yan is still in effect. He's broken through my spell, but not entirely. We're now matched solely based on skill. Even his wave attacks are frozen soon as they form.

"Bai Hu, I'm sorry! I never meant for you to get hurt!"

Heavy strikes come in succession. His attacks may have slowed compared to their former alacrity but he's still the stronger opponent. Each time our blades connect, a ripple spreads over my chest. The cost of keeping my advantage in effect is wearing down my strained heart. To remove my advantage would mean slaughter. It's simply a waiting game to see which will kill me first.

"Talk to me! Stop behaving like a child! Tell me how I can make amends! I know you love me. You don't want this!"

"Shut up! Don't act like you give a damn about me! That assassin tried to have me killed. No wonder you're both chummy!"

Feral eyes fall on the frozen Yu Qi. In the next instant, Hu charges at the defenseless man.

"Stop!" Our blades collide as I scramble to intercept. Flames on a nearby wall momentarily flicker. Time is wavering around us, mounting my fear for Yu Qi. "This man has joined the alliance against Bei Ling! He is Dui's elder brother!"

"He's related to Dui so it doesn't matter that he set me up to die?"

"That's not what I meant! He made a mistake!"

"So did I! I should have killed you when I had the chance!"

His target changes back to me. Every time my short sword deflects his heavy blows, lights on the wall flicker; each time more drawn out than the last. I've never invoked the skill for a duration this lengthy. Chances are the moment flames on that wall fully resume, I'll be dead.

"Is that what you want? Will that make you happy, Bai Hu?"

"Nothing would make me happier!"

He doesn't mean that. He couldn't! I don't want to believe it even when the proof is right in front of me! I want to believe this insanity is overreaction and at heart, he would never cause any real harm. Bai Hu loves me just as I love him. There is a reckless method to prove that. What do I have to lose except for my life which is guaranteed to be lost at this rate? On the other hand, he listens best through the sword. I should

Go on the offense (Continue to page 596)

Take a reckless gamble and drop my sword (Continue to page 601)

Hu's blade sweeps at my side. My blade parries and then counters with an upswing. Until now, I've only used defensive maneuvers. The sudden unexpected retaliation causes him to draw back a step. Several blows follow in the rush of momentum. If nothing else, I have his undivided attention.

"Not that long ago, you risked life and limb to save me. Am I to believe that you came here for the sole reason of ending my life? How does that make any sense?"

"*Shut up*! Had I known you and Dui ran away together, I wouldn't have bothered!"

"I was kidnapped! He tried to save me when you recklessly interfered with swords blazing!"

"Oh! *I interfered*! So, it finally comes out!" The Demon's fangs grind furiously. His vicious eyes send a trembling shock over me and I can't move. "Bai Hu nearly died for an unfaithful woman! *I* nearly died for *you*! Where were you when he was alone? Where were you when I lied dying on Mount Chou?! Miserable woman! Take away your troubles! I wish I never met you!"

A heavy strike slams the blade from my hand to the ground. The tip of his weapon is immediately at my throat.

He's still referring to himself as two different persons. The conflict of that struggle is clearly displayed on his twisted face. I've misread him this whole time. He isn't angry for the reason I thought.

"Xiao Meow! Stop it! You big dummy! I love you!"

The angry stare in those feral eyes quiver, same as the sword in his hand. Master Zhuang was right. The Demon General is that little boy from Tian Mao Yi who didn't know what to do after the horrible event which robbed his innocence. For having saved me, he was hidden away, left alone, and I wasn't there for him. I didn't do anything different on Mount Chou. I left while he suffered. Any excuse I have would be just that.

Through our linked eyes, I pray my affections for the man I love so dearly will reach his hardened heart. Maybe, we haven't truly seen one another until now.

"I love you, Xiao Meow—Bai Hu. I'm sorry for leaving, for not having put you first. I've missed you."

I reach out, believing the lowered gaze signals that he's come to his senses. Hope is dashed aside the moment his hand bats away the encroaching touch. Those former angry eyes are filled by another temper more frightful: apathy. Bai Hu moves past me. His complete disinterest and disregard rip at my shaking heart. Everything feels cold and there's a knot in my stomach tightening by the second. I can't breathe. Every step I take after him sends another sharp pang to my chest. The world around suddenly collapse from stagnation. Tian Ji Zhong Shi Yan has shattered. The toll on my vigorously beating heart is turning everything to darkness.

"Stay awake!"

Faint scent floats into the night air. A wad of grassy material is crammed into my mouth, shocking away the icy grip reaching to cease my vividly beating heart. There it is again, my desire to lick dirt to rid of this taste. They really do think alike!

"Swallow it!"

A rough hand prohibits the bitter paste from expulsion. I can't do else except swallow the disgusting thing, shuddering from revulsion before collapsing onto his arms. Yu Qi taps several channels around my heart, slowing the alarming rate to nearly normal beats. I can finally breathe. After a time, echoing tremors and pain subside.

He leans back and sighs. Try as he might to hide it, there's relief on those brows. "You're a real pain in the ass."

"I... know. Thanks. Yu Qi. I thought... you were at... the palace. "

"What's the point? That opportunist, He Pi, exploited our diversion for his insurgency. Two forces against one is hardly a fight. The Demon seemed more interesting. Leave it up to you to steal my prey."

"Is Hu... all right?"

"You're worried over a man who left you to die?"

"Hu wouldn't. He's... complicated."

"If you say so. Hmph. Isn't this wonderful? The world around is burning and I'm left babysitting an invalid."

"Sorry."

"Your apology is worthless. The conflict is not over and Nan Rong has already laid claim to victory. Make yourself useful. Ensure Feng Jia receives the recognition it deserves."

He looks toward the burning red sky, swallowed by rage and terror. Each time Yu Qi mentions Feng Jia, I believe he means Diao. He and Dui are truly brothers, naturally sweet and caring toward those closest to their hearts. The sight of Yu Qi brings up memories of the kind doctor. I miss him. I've missed him since leaving Quan Ming.

"Can you focus on anything for more than two seconds?"

"O-Oh! Sorry! Yes, I'll make sure Diao receives recognition."

Those narrowed eyes thought to correct my implication but ultimately rescind. Yu Qi stands up and dusts off his clothes.

"Your breathing is steady now. I'm going back."

"I thought you won't bother with Wang Liang."

"He's not my problem."

"Then why?"

"Self-centered woman. You're not the only person injured."

Yu Qi continues to move forward without looking back. Each moment after his awakening, he's become more of a knight than an assassin.

Distant cries move in waves and troughs. The genius Yu Qi disappears into far shadows on the path he's chosen, a path which follows the Demon. Where one leaves a trail of blood, the other is resolved to bring salvation.

Continue to page 603

Chapter 34 – 5

"I want you to be happy, Bai Hu."

The sword drops onto the ground in a muffled thud. With my arms opened wide, I close my eyes in anticipation of Hu coming to his senses. As long as that important part of him still exists, the man who called me, 'Wife,' would never hurt me.

Seconds pass by without any sensation. If he hasn't taken the opportunity by now then he won't.

"Bao Lai."

His sweet, tempting voice calls out my name and melts my heart. Once my eyes spring open and the world comes back into view, the sadistic smile on the Demon's face precedes the quick thrust of the sharp blade into my abdomen.

"Die with your eyes open!"

"Xiao... Meow."

He's far from that boy who risked his life to save me, far from the man who loathed himself for having mistakenly caused my injuries. One thing hasn't changed. When we're together, there is always dissonance. Moments from now, I'll be free from this life and every painful memory crossing my heart. Pain for him has just begun. Why did I call out his name? Those dazed eyes are looking back as though lost in a trance. Light tears are streaming from the corners but he's not able to grasp the reason.

Trembling legs crumple as a rising surge of blood boils to my throat. Time has resumed and so has the last broken pieces of his memories.

"N-No. Bao Lai, don't go! Don't go! Bao Lai!"

Our bodies are rocking back and forth. Those big arms are wrapped around my body. He continues to call to me through thick sobs. I want to stay, to tell him everything will be all right, but the icy hand that has reached for me many times since this conflict began finally has a full grip. The more I fight, the more I realize this is a losing battle against the reaper.

My only solace is to know that he will live on. Until that day comes when we can once again walk side-by-side, I will wait for my friend and beloved at Tian Mao Yi.

The End.

Chapter 35: The Last Score to Settle

Once golden sunlight sweeps across Sai Mi, obscurity and terror fade. The impacts from last night's raid become clear. Several buildings toppled, many more were damaged, and while the palace suffered multitude of barrages, the majority remained sturdy, giving new appreciation to the ingenuity of its architect who built the masterpiece nearly a thousand years ago.

After I woke in the makeshift infirmary, the man called Shu Jin, whom I'd met at Nan Rong's palace, came to watch over me. He explained that the insurgency staged by the White Crane Order, an underground faction which he and He Pi had joined, used the opportunity provided by Yu Qi to further draw out Wang Liang's defenses. They staged random explosions around the city. Bai Hu's unexpected charge at Sai Mi's gates further thinned Bei Ling's palace defenses, which permitted the Order to easily retrieve His Highness, Cai Pai, the child emperor. Jin also mentioned that due to my resemblance to He Pi, the Order was able to weed out a traitor who could have caused them the plot, though I don't know what he meant by that.

From time to time, Yu Qi and His Highness, He Pi, come to my side. The former made me suffered his usual mean barking. I hugged him anyway for saving me. The latter, I had a hard time prying his perverted fingers from around my waist. He seems to think that since we look alike, I somehow belong to him. I know I shouldn't hit the emperor of Nan Rong, but I did.

In the end, miraculously, there weren't any civilian casualty. The majority of the injured was treated by Yu Qi and returned home. Sadly, the same couldn't be said for the Order and their adversaries. Although Wang Liang managed to escape, his army was decimated, releasing his hold over Bei Ling. The men under his command either surrendered or were put to death. Emperor Cai Pai was placed in the White Crane's protection, personally under the care of Zhang Tang, the man whom Mo Bi had mentioned as his mentor. He consistently looks somber but I do think he is a good man at heart.

As for Bai Hu, popular stories of an invincible demon in red armor are spreading like wildfires amongst the children, as had the stories of Feng Jia Yao Ying Sun in my time. I heard he single-handedly pushed back Sai Mi's entire army until the lot surrendered to the White Cranes for protection. Exaggerations would have been my opinion had I not been his opponent.

Hu broke through Tian Ji Zhong Shi Yan and walked away unscathed. I'm happy he's well but our strained relationship is still obscured. I don't know if he's forgiven me. Hu parted shortly before I woke, leaving He Pi only the message that he was going home.

Chapter 35 – 2

"Your sordid tactics won't work on me. I won't be swayed by lustful women."

"Uh-huh. Well, I'm not letting go until Diao arrives."

My arms have been latched around Yu Qi's since this afternoon. The Western Alliance is due tomorrow and Nan Rong's forces should arrive near sundown. I won't let him run off again. As such, he's been walking around town at a severely quick pace hoping to loosen my grip.

"If you wish to keep your arms attached to your shoulders, remove them from mine."

"That's some threat, Yu Qi. I noticed your face turning red earlier when those women were staring. They must have thought we were a couple. That really bothers you, doesn't it? A-ha! So bashful! Just the opposite of Dui!"

"Who wouldn't feel flustered by having your association? You're an embarrassment."

"That's mean! Fine. I'll let go if you promise to stay."

"I don't negotiate with brutes."

"Don't you want to see Diao and Dui? They'll arrive soon."

"And what would I say to them?" He pauses shortly under the shade of a tall fig tree whose large extended branches scatter rays of sunlight down over the shadows of his expression. There's sadness in those once gentle eyes, clearly relaying silent remorse.

"Yu Qi, I'll ask for your pardon. I know why you helped Su Jian."

"You don't." He swallows a hard lump and then lets out a sigh. "Neither you nor Diao knows anything about me. I've killed more people than I can remember and through my actions, countless more have died. You cannot absolve my sins."

"Then why did you do it? I just can't imagine you'd wake up one day and decided to kill. Someone sent you down this path."

"It's a path I've freely walked for a long time now. Don't feel sorry for me. Your sympathy is better reserved for the thousands of lives I've destroyed through this conflict alone, yours included."

"That's not true! Wang Liang wouldn't have been any less dangerous without you, and because of your help, his reign was toppled."

"A simple-minded rationalization. Your allies won't think the same. Should none personally seek retribution, I'll be chained and dragged in front of their court. Maybe punishment is the only path to forgiveness and maybe... repentance is the path to salvation."

Yu Qi's distant gaze trails upward to the thick leaves covering the fig tree. Far beyond the canopy, his eyes pierce the sky, toward heaven.

I've kept hoping for a happy ending; for Yu Qi to have Diao and Dui by his side. I foolishly believed that an apology would equate to forgiveness when, had Wang Liang been caught alive, he would never again have seen the light of day, regardless of his regrets. To me, Yu Qi has been an exception. His heroic deeds call for lightened punishment. However, that doesn't mean his freedom is guaranteed. There are too many after his head who will overlook the change in his heart.

I want to keep my promise to Diao but despite keeping him alive, holding a man captive is the same as taking away his life. He wants to repent, I wholeheartedly believe that, and maybe Yu Qi should be allowed to repent in his own way. On the other hand, how is running away repentance? There is no freedom in hiding. He has to face his crimes and accept punishment. I will do everything to find leniency. If he stays, maybe Yu Qi can live a normal life.

Make him stay (Continue to page 608)

Let him go (Continue to page 611)

Chapter 35 – 3

Despite chaos, life goes on. By late afternoon, most of the vendors in Sai Mi have reopened shop. Patrons are swarming restaurants and teahouses to discuss last night's events. Those who've worked since morning to clear the wreckage have retired for the day. The quiet atmosphere of Bei Ling's capital is turning livelier.

Yu Qi wasn't permitted to escape but the smell of tempting food is causing resolve to dwindle. I haven't eaten since yesterday morning and he hadn't since the night before.

"Yu Qi, I'm hungry."

"Do me a favor and chew off your own arm."

"I would but it doesn't taste very good. I don't have the strength to drag you to the markets. Please, stop your stubbornness."

"Who's more stubborn than whom?"

Yu Qi wriggles the arm seized by my death grip. In truth, he could easily separate us but then he couldn't use the excuse to wait for Diao and Dui. He's so transparent.

"Oh, hey! The drums are sounding. Dui's here! Come on, Yu Qi!"

"Stop acting like a child. It's unappealing."

Chapter 35: The Last Score to Settle

After enough encouragement—by that, I mean pestering—the cranky old man finally moves away from the large trunk of the fig tree. He seems nervous to greet Dui as Yu Qi.

"Everything will be fine."

A doubting sigh escapes in exchange for my premature optimism. He halfheartedly nods and then permits me to drag him forward.

In mere moments, sunlight is obscured under a giant shadow. A loud clang shatters the calm atmosphere followed by a low hum. I'm trying to recover from the shock of slamming against the ground but the world around is hazy. Yu Qi pushed me out of harm's way; else, the indiscriminate giant would have taken my head to reach his opponent.

"Wen Meng, don't!"

Barely have I started to Yu Qi's defense, the two titans have leapt a distance away. They fly forward at lightning pace. Quick flickers of swords reflecting sunlight, the grinding of metal against metal, and even a few sparks ignite from contact. Loud echoes reverberate into the air. Yu Qi's sword parries Wen Meng's but the latter launches several more powerful strikes, riling the wind around their heated battle.

"This is not your fight!"

Yu Qi's bellow stops my brash resolve. After I woke in the infirmary, he warned against using Tian Ji Zhong

Shi Yan. His chi control technique subdued my heart from exploding last night but if I invoke the skill again before the month is over, the barrier he's placed will likely break. I'll keel over before having the chance to stop Wen Meng.

Through one heavy blow, Yu Qi's sword flies out of his hand, nearly hitting my foot. Yu Qi has speed and agility but Wen Meng, with his stature, skill, endurance, and bloodline advantage was bound to be victor.

He makes a mad dash when I reach for the fallen blade. Our distance was considerable. Somehow in the short speck of time it took for me to lean down, our fingers slightly graze. Yu Qi manages to retrieve the weapon. Those hawk eyes momentarily link to mine and then a sharp pain slams against my shoulder.

Continue to page 617

Chapter 35 – 4

Yu Qi stares curiously. With a nod, I release his arm and encourage his departure.

"I understand. From this day forward, you won't take another life, Yu Qi."

"Is that an order?"

"Yes, I guess you can say that. Dui tried to live your life and I've tried to make you live his life. You're alive. Hopefully, he'll live for himself now. And, since you've regained that lost part of you, I'll pray that you'll find whatever you're looking for. I won't ask where you'll go because I'll be tempted to follow. So... let's make this quick, I'm not good at farewells."

There I go, crying again. I can't help it. I'll really miss annoying the curmudgeon.

"Stop calling me a curmudgeon. I don't call you a harlot half as much. Tsk! Why did that make you cry even more?"

The sour old man, still grumbling, presses a sleeve against the corners of my eyes. He can be gentle; he just chooses not to be most of the time.

"Sorry. I'll miss you, Yu Qi. Maybe because you're Dui's brother, I feel like you're mine too."

"Meaning what? Dui is like your brother or Dui is your fiancé and I'm the brother-in-law?"

"Erm... neither."

"Hmph. Idiot."

The silence that follows isn't uncomfortable. He stares off into the distance, lost in thought as though recalling the past, and then after some time, sighs deeply, as though finally seeing a future.

"I guess it wouldn't be the end of the world for me to call you, 'Sister.'"

"What?"

"I don't care about your love life but... if you choose Dui, you have my blessing."

He moves away, out of the shade of the fig tree, and into the overflowing sunlight. My imaginations could be running wild from this emotional event but Yu Qi somehow seems calmed and renewed; a truly changed man. Soft hawk eyes glance quickly in my direction. For the first time, a real smile appears over his mouth.

"Bye, Yu Qi! Thank you for saving me! Good luck!"

I call out to his turned back. Though he does exactly as expected and makes no acknowledgement during the retreat, still in my heart, I hope we'll meet again.

Chapter 35 – 5

Late afternoon, Nan Rong's flags wave jovially a distance away from the gates of Sai Mi. The White Crane Order, Shu Jin, and Emperors He Pi and Cai Pai are waiting at the forefront to greet our allies. I'm standing behind Shu Jin, away from He Pi's groping hands. His Highness keeps looking over his shoulder and winking in my direction. I can't tell if he's actually a pervert or if he's only making fun of me since we share a face. I never knew how unnerving it was to be toyed with by me.

From an occasion that should have been rather uneventful, dust suddenly kicks into the air from the back of Nan Rong's lines. Flurries of charging steeds led by the giant Wen Meng, who's spinning an enormous blade above his head, come upon our party. The guards on our end ready their weapons. In mere moments, the giant leaps off the horse and takes a direct path.

"Woman. Where is he? I know he was with you."

A few months ago, I shared Wen Meng's ambition to end Yao Ying. I know how he feels. That rage will never relinquish until the assassin perishes.

"He's dead. The assassin we were looking for, Ying, is dead. Wang Liang killed him. His body burned in the fire set off by the explosions."

It's not a complete lie. Ying is no more. There is only Yu Qi burdened with Ying's memories. These thoughts are repeated in my mind to help convey honesty, as learned through Ma Tai Tou's lessons. However, I know it's difficult for Wen Meng to accept never having his vengeance. He studies every inch of my face while burrowing dark eyes deeply into mine. I hold my breath to keep steady, that is, until He Pi's right hand lands on my behind.

"She's right. Ying's gone now. Wang Liang was too strong. No one could subdue him. I'm lucky to have escaped." He Pi accompanies his reinforcement with a few squeezes of my bottom. I'd swing at him if I didn't need his help.

Disappointment spreads across the giant's face, followed by regret for having arrived late. I made the right choice and allowed Yu Qi's departure earlier. This confrontation couldn't have ended well for either side.

A sigh of relief nearly escaped my lips just before Wen Meng whips around with narrowed eyes. He glances at He Pi's impish grin and my twitching fists. The giant is confused. "Woman. Have you changed lover again? Without a strong man, you are fated to repeat fickleness. Come with me to Mount Chou. I will teach you to loyally submit."

"You kiss your mother with that mouth?!"

"Now, now. Don't take offense, lover. Unlike me, Wen Meng can't appreciate your *wild promiscuity*."

Chapter 35: The Last Score to Settle

"Argh! Take your hand off me, you little imp! And you! Whoever taught you how to speak to women should be slapped! I don't want either one of you! I love Bai Hu, damn it! My Xiao Meow! Bai Hu!"

"Aww. You're hurting my feelings!"

He Pi's groping hand draws back when I raise my right fist. I can't believe this man is the emperor of our great country. Why would anyone even bother searching for this pervert? I can't imagine he does anything at the palace aside from harassing servant girls.

Laughing, He Pi hides behind Shu Jin. I turn back to continue giving Wen Meng a piece of my mind, forgetting to breathe when instead, I see his face. Dui, standing amongst Nan Rong's ranks, as somber as when we last spoke, uneasily looks away. He must have heard everything.

Come the end of this conflict and my mind may yet change. Those were his thoughts. My perception of Dui has changed drastically and so has Hu's perception of me. However, my love for Bai Hu will never fade and neither will my attachment to Dui. I never meant to hurt him. It seems old habits die hard. Hu and I are always trouble together and I never stop tormenting Dui. Useless apologetic words won't erase his loneliness.

"Hey, brother dear!" He Pi's chirrupy voice suddenly breaks the awkward silence. He waves to another somber man quietly making his way forward.

"Your Highness." San An bows to the younger man, sighing an annoyed sigh. "Shall we proceed?"

"Always business! You're no fun, San An!"

"If I am too serious, it is to compensate for your lack of focus and poise, Your Highness."

"Was that an insult?"

San An bows to Cai Pai and ignores the sulking He Pi. Nan Rong's caravan prepares to enter Sai Mi. I move aside to wait for Dui but do not have a chance before His Highness links our arms together and forcefully escorts me inside.

Continue to page 625

Chapter 36: Until We Meet Again

I should have just let him leave.

By the time I roused, Yu Qi and Wen Meng have disappeared without a trace. Trackers were sent to find the missing pair but to no avail. Even Qing Hai's tactical searches returned empty-handed. I wanted a happy ending for my friends. Instead of returning Dui's brother, my choices have robbed his freedom.

After a week without progress, Dui, unable to cope with not knowing whether his brother lived or died, resolved to personally conduct the hunt for Yu Qi. The doctor suffered that torment for most of his life, and through my poor choices to keep Yu Qi, has fallen into despair. I didn't know else to say except for apologies. He spent the majority of our short reunion in silence.

I would have followed him to make amends had Dui not given reminder of my obligations. There are patients in need of treatment until a new court physician is hired. In spite of his loathing, Bai Hu is my priority.

"Besides, Yu Qi could have left at any time. He chose to stay. It wasn't your fault. Forget everything. Go home and be happy." These were the parting words said to me. The doctor's demeanor was stiff from grief but still, he tried to cheer my somberness by relieving apparent guilt.

Days after my dearest friend left, another caravan from the west arrived. Again, I was faced with disappointing another person dear to me. Unexpectedly, Diao did not shed a tear; at least, not in front of the court. She kept poise, spoke with articulate passion, and impressed Cai Pai who promised to build ties with Feng Jia through Zhang Tang's assistance.

To keep my promise to Yu Qi, I urged He Pi to do the same. San An wasn't keen on the idea but His Highness agreed without hesitation because as he'd said, he would not deny pretty girls anything.

Not long after, the Southern caravan started for Nan Rong. The conflict is finally over but returning without Dui feels lifeless and joyless. I keep wondering if I should have followed him but every time that thought comes, memories of Bai Hu conquer all rationalizations. Hu needs me and I need him. Dui didn't want me to interfere and neither did Yu Qi. I've inserted my will over their lives and made everything worse. Maybe the best thing I can do for Dui and Yu Qi is to leave them be.

Chapter 36 – 2

Two weeks ago, I ran home to find the house empty. Terror overtook all my senses and I flew all over An to find Bai Hu. He was with Kai the entire time. Not at the restaurant but at her house. The new Bai Hu doesn't see the lovely creature with silky hair and perfect flower face as merely his friend anymore. He likes her. More than like, he needs her. He laughs when they're together and smiles at her in the manner I'd only ever thought was reserved for me.

When he comes home, the somber hard eyes refuse to acknowledge my calls. No matter how I've pushed for his attention, intruded upon his privacy, and chased after him, the results have been the same. I thought giving him what I've failed to provide would bring the old Hu back; instead, the new one has withdrawn. We haven't slept in the same bed since I came home. He leaves the house whenever I enter his room and spends the night at Kai's. To keep him, I've slept in the living room. Even then, he finds other reasons to abscond. The final blow came two days ago when he told me to leave permanently. Maybe for that reason, I've been afraid to go home, to hear those words again and realize they weren't part of a horrid dream.

Try as I might to hide in this luxurious palace, a new physician is slated to arrive and take over my duties tomorrow. Master Yu, who usurped Dui's old clinic, has agreed to hire me, but I can't sleep in the backroom because he needs space for a massive book collection. That just means I can't keep hiding. It's time to go home.

Chapter 36 – 3

That's odd. The door's open. We live in a safe neighborhood but Bai Hu always locks the door. I suppose there are many things about the Demon I should grow accustomed to from now on. His changing moods, for one.

"Bai Hu, are you home? It's me... *Wife*. Hello? I brought your favorite steamed buns from Bao Bao. Hey, are you—"

He's looking at me as though nothing out of the ordinary is happening, as though I should feel ashamed for being shocked! The disgusting sight has robbed from me the ability to move, speak, and breathe. Apparently, the same can be said for Kai, who's lying in *our* bed beneath Bai Hu's naked torso. The rest of their parts are covered under *our* blankets. I don't even want to consider that sight! Words are surging to the back of my throat; the wrong ones may end things between us. I best choose them carefully.

"*What the hell are you doing, Bai Hu?!*"

"Why are you in my house?" He shoots back my tactlessness in the most carefree tone I've ever heard.

"Excuse me? This is my house too."

"I'm not your babysitter anymore. You don't have a reason to bother me."

"The hell I don't! Who dragged me to the capital against my will in the first place? Better yet, who went to find me in Kou? I know you love me, Bai Hu. Why are you doing this?"

"Aren't you arrogant? Why should he love a cheater? Did you come crawling back because the lanky perverted doctor rejected you too? That's so sad!"

She's clinging to his bare shoulders and pressing her cheek against his chest as if to mark her territory. Every fiber of my being wants to rip her off his body and throw her from the house so the neighbors can see her *virtues* exposed.

"Stay out of this, Kai. One more insult against Dui and every man in this neighborhood will have a good look at your behind!"

She clings to him tighter as if playing the victim, pouting and gasping from the supposed insult. I couldn't care less for her dramatics. My gaze is directed at my everything.

"Bai Hu—Xiao Meow, for the last time, there is nothing between Dui and me. He's my good friend but I only love *you*. You know that! I left Mount Chou because I didn't want to aggravate you further. You were injured! Master Zhuang said... it didn't matter though, did it? I shouldn't have left. I'm sorry. However I can make things up for abandoning you, I will! Just say the word! Please... I love you."

Chapter 36: Until We Meet Again

My nerves are on fire. I'm shaking uncontrollably from terror of his rejection and simultaneously fearing the involuntary reaction is coming off as insincerity. That unfeeling stare of his makes me want to burst into tears. It's difficult enough to keep from faltering to foolishness; I don't need *her* scoffing at my pain too.

Hu's eyes close and then he turns away. "Unless you want to watch, get out. I'm busy."

"Bai Hu! You can't be serious! I l—"

He can't hear a word I say with his head buried in her hair. The erotic moaning, the insipid giggles, and the incessant groping make me want to vomit.

I don't want to run away anymore and yet before I know it, surrounding me are bright lights of the night markets. Everything is as I remember and still, nothing is the same. Unlike last time, no one's going to give chase and take me home. I don't have a place to call home anymore.

Chapter 36 – 4

Dawn spreads new light to a new day. I've walked around the markets all night replaying the horrid scene along with everything I've done wrong until now. There is no solution. The past can't be changed. I can't live in then and I don't want to accept now. Maybe I should take Zhang Mang's advice and continue on. Things will work out or I'll make more mistakes, so many in fact, that I couldn't do any worse. One thing is certain, walking around feeling sorry for myself solves nothing.

Dui was my crutch. I ran to him whenever I needed help and with him, there was always a place to call home. Those days are gone. I can't keep living in the past. It's time to move forward. After everything we've all been through together these many years, only Dui has become an adult. Bai Hu and I are still bratty children throwing tantrums and running from each other. I can't do it anymore. I won't.

Continue to page 642

Chapter 37: A Test of Faith

Days after, another caravan from the west arrived. Zhang Mang and He Pi were too happy to meet again; the former clearly happier. I've never seen two men that close. It makes the mind wander. Lo Han didn't accompany the party; Dui and I couldn't have our planned Tian Mao Yi reunion. Diao was saddened over Yu Qi's departure but understood the reason and kept silent as not to rile Wen Meng's insatiable lust for vengeance. In front of court, she kept poise, spoke with articulate passion, and impressed Cai Pai who promised to build ties with Feng Jia through Zhang Tang's assistance.

To keep my promise to Yu Qi, I urged He Pi to do the same. San An wasn't keen on the idea but His Highness agreed without hesitation because as he'd said, he would not deny pretty girls anything.

Other leaders eventually trickled into Bei Ling, including Captain Xian in lieu of Lord Han Bei, who accompanied a handful of E Mo elders, and Ye's Empress Neng Cao to discuss maintaining peace between nations. The North was represented by Zhang Tang, Bei Ling's soon-to-be prime minister.

After a week or so, the summit finally ended.

Chapter 37 - 2

"When are you going back to Pa Xu?"

"Tomorrow morning, probably, or whenever I finish packing. At the latest, noon tomorrow."

Two weeks ago, I ran home to find the house empty. Terror overtook all my senses and I flew all over An to find Bai Hu. He was with Kai the entire time. Not at the restaurant but at her house. The new Bai Hu doesn't see the lovely creature with silky hair and perfect flower face as merely his friend anymore. He likes her. More than like, he needs her. He laughs when they're together and smiles at her in the manner I'd only ever thought was reserved for me.

When he comes home, the somber hard eyes refuse to acknowledge my calls. No matter how I've pushed for his attention, intruded upon his privacy, and chased after him, the results have been the same. I thought giving him what I've failed to provide would bring the old Hu back; instead, the new one has withdrawn. We haven't slept in the same bed since I came home. He leaves the house whenever I enter his room and spends the night at Kai's. To keep him, I've slept in the living room. Even then, he finds other reasons to abscond. The final blow came two days ago when he told me to leave permanently. Maybe for that reason, I've been afraid to go home, to hear those words again and realize they weren't part of a horrid dream.

Chapter 37: A Test of Faith

I've followed old pattern and dawdled beside Dui when I feel alone. But, Dui is leaving soon. I'll miss him dearly. He's been a good friend. Just the thought of not seeing him makes me feel as though I'll lose a piece of me. Chances are, once our paths diverge from here, we won't likely meet again. I can't keep clinging to him when I'm also his misery.

For Dui's services to Nan Rong, San An granted his request to leave court. He's tired of war and politics. The doctor just wants to treat wounds and cure diseases, as he's always done. He aims to start early on that plan of opening a clinic in Pa Xu and someday soon, train apprentices to take over. In truth, a part of me wants to walk that path with him.

"I see. Seems like yesterday when I first pulled a prank on you at Tian Mao Yi during your apprenticeship under Master Tai Hung. You'll soon become a master with pups of your own. How time flies. Master Tai Hung would have been proud of you, Dui. I am."

"Hmm." He shuffles in place, stacking a few notes together and then putting them back onto the table, repeating again as though he doesn't know how to proceed. "I... I might not have another chance to say this, so... thanks and I'm sorry."

"Why?"

Dui inhales deeply, though his hands still tremble. The doctor turns and smiles shortly. "Well, you know, thanks for helping my brother escape and sorry for saying stupid things. I can't win against Bai Hu. I see that now. Not after you shouted your love for him to everyone in Sai Mi. Can't say I'm not disappointed but, hm... as long as you're happy."

"Dui, I'm sorry."

"No big deal. I'll find another, maybe. Or just not bother at all with that madness. Probably shouldn't. Lots of things to do. Don't have time. By the way, take care of yourself, love. Maybe, I'll see you around."

He grabs a stack of papers from the table and dart from the room. When he spoke, his voice shook as if he wanted to cry, which makes me want to cry. That tightened pain in my chest is back. I don't want him to leave but I can't ask him to stay.

After battling with myself, I realize that I can't keep hiding here. Dui's going home and so should I.

Chapter 37 – 3

That's odd. The door's open. We live in a safe neighborhood but Bai Hu always locks the door. I suppose there are many things about the Demon I should grow accustomed to from now on. His changing moods, for one.

"Bai Hu, are you home? It's me... *Wife*. Hello? I brought your favorite steamed buns from Bao Bao. Hey, are you—"

He's looking at me as though nothing out of the ordinary is happening, as though I should feel ashamed for being shocked! The disgusting sight has robbed from me the ability to move, speak, and breathe. Apparently, the same can be said for Kai, who's lying in *our* bed beneath Bai Hu's naked torso. The rest of their parts are covered under *our* blankets. I don't even want to consider that sight! Words are surging to the back of my throat; the wrong ones may end things between us. I best choose them carefully.

"What the hell are you doing, Bai Hu?!"

"Why are you in my house?" He shoots back my tactlessness in the most carefree tone I've ever heard.

"Excuse me? This is my house too."

"I'm not your babysitter anymore. You don't have a reason to bother me."

"The hell I don't! Who dragged me to the capital against my will in the first place? Better yet, who went to find me in Kou? I know you love me, Bai Hu. Why are you doing this?"

"Aren't you arrogant? Why should he love a cheater? Did you come crawling back because the lanky perverted doctor rejected you too? That's so sad!"

She's clinging to his bare shoulders and pressing her cheek against his chest as if to mark her territory. Every fiber of my being wants to rip her off his body and throw her from the house so the neighbors can see her *virtues* exposed.

"Stay out of this, Kai. One more insult against Dui and every man in this neighborhood will have a good look at your behind!"

She clings to him tighter as if playing the victim, pouting and gasping from the supposed insult. I couldn't care less for her dramatics. My gaze is directed at my everything.

"Bai Hu—Xiao Meow, for the last time, there is nothing between Dui and me. He's my good friend but I only love *you*. You know that! I left Mount Chou because I didn't want to aggravate you further. You were injured! Master Zhuang said... it didn't matter though, did it? I shouldn't have left. I'm sorry. However I can make things up for abandoning you, I will! Just say the word! Please... I love you."

Chapter 37: A Test of Faith

My nerves are on fire. I'm shaking uncontrollably from terror of his rejection and simultaneously fearing the involuntary reaction is coming off as insincerity. That unfeeling stare of his makes me want to burst into tears. It's difficult enough to keep from faltering to foolishness; I don't need her scoffing at my pain too.

Hu's eyes close and then he turns away. "Unless you want to watch, get out. I'm busy."

"Bai Hu! You can't be serious! I l—"

He can't hear a word I say with his head buried in her hair. The erotic moaning, the insipid giggles, and the incessant groping make me want to vomit.

I don't want to run away anymore and yet before I know it, surrounding me are bright lights of the night markets. Everything is as I remember and still, nothing is the same. Unlike last time, no one's going to give chase and take me home. I don't have a place to call home anymore.

Chapter 37 – 4

Dawn spreads new light to a new day. I've walked around the markets all night replaying the horrid scene and everything I've done wrong up until now. There is no solution. The past can't be changed. I can't live in then and I don't want to accept now. Maybe I should take Zhang Mang's advice and continue on. Things will work out or I'll make more mistakes, so many in fact, that I won't do any worse. One thing is certain, walking around feeling sorry for myself solves nothing. There's still one task left undone.

"Hey, Dui."

Exiting the courtyard, he jostles the apothecary case at the sound of my voice. The look on his face is bittersweet; I imagine that's also the look on mine.

"Come to see me off, dove?" The doctor throws a crooked smile.

"Yeah. I couldn't let you go without saying good-bye. And thank you, for everything."

"That's awfully kind of you. By the way, if you're still interested in medicine, Master Yu is looking for an assistant at the old clinic. The new physician San An brought in, Ren Zhong, doesn't like women much, so I hear. You're welcome to stay but he might give you a hard time."

"*Really*? I'm tempted to annoy him but, maybe not. Unlike another physician I know who only doles out threats, this Ren Zhong might actually dose my food with senna."

"Oh, come on! I'm more dangerous than mere threats!"

"Yeah, I know."

During the silent nostalgic pause, the stubborn pain in my chest resumes. We've parted ways before but this time is real. Dui means a lot to me, more than I imagined. He's always on my side, always helping me, and I always feel accepted no matter the stupid things I do and say. I'm going to miss that. I'm going to miss him. I miss him already.

"I better get going. It's a long walk to the next rest stop. Good-bye, Bao Lai. I hope we'll meet again."

This is my final chance. My crutch is gone. I can't keep living in the past. It's time to move forward. After everything we've all been through together these many years, only Dui has become an adult. Bai Hu and I are still bratty children throwing tantrums and running from each other. I can't do it anymore. I won't.

Stay with Bai Hu (Continue to page 634)

Go with Dui (Continue to page 635)

Chapter 37 – 5

"Good luck in Pa Xu, Dui!"

"Thanks. Same to you." Dui calls over his shoulder one last time before disappearing down the road leading to the south gate.

I watch him leave while pushing back thick sobs knowing that this is really good-bye. He's going to build a future for himself, moving forward to another chapter of his life after leaving a painful one behind. Dui's taught me many things. This is another lesson I must apply for myself.

Continue to page 642

Chapter 38: Master Tai Hung's Pups

"Wait, Dui. Let me go with you. I mean, may I?"

He swings around, giving an incredulous stare. Dui furiously chews his lips for a while as if stalling for time to build courage. "Are you asking to come... because of his rejection?"

"You're important to me, that much is obvious. I care about you. I couldn't break my commitment to Bai Hu. I wanted to know he'll be taken care of, that he'll be happy. Kai may not have been fair to me but as long as she will love Hu and give him the happiness he deserves... I won't stand in the way of his happiness.

"His affections may yet return."

"My affections have already changed. I now see what is best for Bai Hu and for me. He needs someone to love and support him in the manner I can't. I need to continue following this path I've set out for myself; the path Master Tai Hung wanted for me. I respect you, Dui, and your intellect. Treating wounds and saving lives, that's what I want too. Wherever you're going is where I want to go. Let me become your first apprentice. Please, take me with you."

Come what may, I can't look back. Bai Hu is clearly happier without me and I would be happy to have a life with purpose. I'm not asking for love or devotion. At the moment, I'm simply looking for a place to belong. I feel that place is by Dui's side. I respect him more than anyone else. I need him.

"Dui."

I call to him when he's seemingly spaced out. The absent-minded stare is rather adorable. Grey eyes dart back and forth as though woken from a dream.

"Are you sure?"

"Yes. I'm sure. Here. Maybe this will help. I meant to give this to you earlier."

Stormy eyes light up at the sight of expensive tongkat, more so for its use than its worth. He's so easy to please.

"Is this a good enough bribe?"

"That depends. Is this the missing ingredient to Tai Hung's potion?"

"You still haven't figured it out? The first recipe in your test journal was correct. Master Tai Hung lied to make you leave Pa Xu. Don't frown at me. You prepared every other possibility except that one for me to judge."

"Why couldn't you just tell me?"

"Because... I thought it was funny to see you scramble."

The frown line of his mouth sags deeper against my nervous chuckles. Picking on Dui is almost a bad habit, formed from two decades ago. I might have gone overboard this time.

"*Please*, Dui! Let me be your apprentice. I promise I'll make it up to you!"

"Hmm. I see. Swooning for the doctor with gentle hands is a bad idea." He replies in that familiar lecherous tone I've not heard for some time now. "Coming with me is a twenty-year commitment, love."

"That's fine. I wasn't planning to do anything much for the next twenty years."

"And I thought I was lazy. No, this won't do."

"Why not? I'll work hard. I won't let you down!"

"That's not why I'm worried. You're not getting any younger, love. Young women should marry and raise families while they can."

"We're practically family, Master Dui. I don't need more than that."

"Got an answer for everything, don't you? Fine. I didn't intend to take such drastic measures but since you've forced my hand, in twenty years, if we're not married to other people, let's go crazy and tie the knot."

"Heh. You got it, Doctor!"

The physician frowns when I mess his slicked back hair. He's had it kept that way since our reunion in Sai Mi. This new Dui, serious and mature, doesn't suit him.

"I like your hair messy. It's more natural that way, the way you usually are."

"Did you just insult me?"

"Not at all."

We start down the road toward the south gate, side-by-side. Having him near makes me happy. This homely feeling of comfort is why I want to walk with him always.

"Hey, Dui. I'm glad we're still friends."

"Crueler words have never been spoken. Here. Take this. It's your punishment."

"Wh—? Why do I have to carry it?"

He's taken off the apothecary case and handed it to me. On impulse, I swing the heavy thing around my shoulders.

"Because you're a brute. My intellect can't be bogged down by manual labor."

"You just don't want to admit that you're a fragile little thing, Doctor."

"Way to undermine my manhood. You're lucky I don't make you carry *me* to Pa Xu."

"Well, I could, you know, since you're a fragile little thing!"

"Hmph. I'm glad I packed senna."

"You wouldn't!"

"Think so? Let's see if you eat dinner tonight."

"Ah! You're just like Yu Qi!"

"Whatever that means. Speaking of my brother, maybe I should have taken his advice. Tormenting me is a sort of hobby for you. I should have run away when I had the chance."

"He told me that too. I thought he was joking. Still wouldn't do you any good. I can outrun you any day, Doctor."

"Is everything a competition with you? Hey, what's that?"

"What's what?"

"Ha! Can't catch me, Pup!"

"That is completely childish, Dui!"

Darn him! As if carrying this case weren't heavy enough, I have to run after the speedy doctor too. He really does run fast. I might have let it go if he hadn't pinched my cheek before taking off. This calls for vengeance and it will be mine!

And so it seems as one chapter of my life closes, another one opens. I'll never forget my time in An, the people I've met, and the experiences I was given. I'm grateful to have known love, however fleeting was the encounter. The special place in my heart forever reserved for Bai Hu will never fade. I'll carry him with me and find new happiness to fill the spaces left empty. For him, I hope the same. I wish that he's happy, now and forever.

At the moment, the elation welling in my chest is a feeling I've not experienced for a long time. His smile makes me smile. I want to see him smile always. We're walking into the unknown, Dui and I, but it is a path I'll gladly follow if it's with him. For the next twenty years and long after, I hope we'll continue on this path, a future we'll carve for ourselves learned from the past that has brought us together.

Copyright 2017. Lenne Penry.

The End.

Chapter 39: Odd Happenings

I have a commitment to Bai Hu, not just to the man who called me, '*Wife*,' or to the boy at Tian Mao Yi, but all of Bai Hu; every version of him. The adult thing to do isn't to throw tantrums or run away. I want a future with him. I have to relinquish the past.

"Welcome home. Go wash up. Dinner will be ready in a few minutes." Thanks to Dui, my cooking is now edible for normal people with taste buds and not just monks who couldn't care less the gruel placed before them.

Bai Hu throws his helmet onto the table by the door. I can understand why he's staring dubiously. While contentions from my unwilling lover are expected, I will absolutely keep from another senseless argument.

"Why are you still here? Didn't I make myself clear?"

"Yes. Perfectly. I don't have a right to stay but I'm asking you to let me."

"Don't need another mouth to feed."

"I'll pull my own weight. I'm working at Master Yu's clinic now. The salary San An paid was also hefty. I won't be a burden. And... I know this will be awkward for Kai so, I'll be sure to stay out of the way when she comes by. I'm here for you, Bai Hu, and only you."

Chapter 39: Odd Happenings

Chiseled lips pucker, prepared to snap his agitation, but something inside holds back the accustomed belligerence. Hu moves inside, lets down the long hair, and sighs wearily. "He's not coming back, the one you're waiting for. I'm him and he's me; one consciousness. This is it. This is me. I remember my fondness for you, our time together at Tian Mao Yi, and our recent intimacy. I just don't care. I can't force feelings I don't have just because you want me to."

"Understood. I won't stand by the road near Tian Mao Yi waiting for Xiao Meow anymore. I want to support you, Bai Hu, this you, here now. When I can no longer fill that role, then I'll do the right thing for us both. So, is it all right? May I stay?"

Maybe there are miracles. I'd hoped but never expected for him to agree. Well, he really just shrugged and retreated inside his room. That's good enough for me!

Chapter 39 – 2

Time sure flies. Before I know it, leaves are turning red and orange. Their lovely hues are mesmerizing but a pain to rake when they're scattered all over. The neighbor's rogue maple trees with branches extended into our yard are making it difficult to keep things tidy. At least, the weather is cool and the sunset makes the neighborhood picturesque. On days like these, I take my time and wait for Bai Hu to walk through the gates. Sometimes, he doesn't completely ignore me and returns my greetings with a nod. The old me would have thought this existence pathetic; the new me understands the meaning of love and devotion.

Today is Tuesday, which means he'll leave for Kai's and I shouldn't bother with dinner. It'll just be me again. Master Yu's ledgers need updating. That will occupy most of my evening. Speaking of Master Yu, he eerily reminds me of Master Tai Hung, especially his tone of voice when I make a mess, which I usually do. I miss being coddled by Dui. He usually jokes when I mess up and then show the correct method. Master Yu makes me suffer thirty-minute lectures. I really do miss Dui. I hope he's found what he's looking for.

"Hey! You're home early. Welcome home, Bai Hu! Um. What's wrong? Are you okay?"

Oh no. I know that look on his face. With weather changes lately, the clinic has been filled daily by patients suffering from cold and flu. Hu's ready to topple from exhaustion. His face is completely red.

Normally, he wouldn't behave this obediently. Once I force him to lean on me, we make our way inside. His fever is rapidly climbing. Hu can barely open his eyes. His lips are cracked from dehydration. His hands and feet feel like ice. It's a miracle he was able to make the long walk home in that heavy armor. That must have taken everything out of him. He's not responding to my call.

"Bai Hu. Stay awake a little longer. I'll have a draught to lower your fever and ease the pain. It's almost done. Hold on."

Last time Hu was bedridden, a friend was there to hold my hand. That luxury is gone. From now on, it's just Hu and me, a scary and also amazing thought. I finally feel that I am here for Bai Hu and I can stand on my own two feet.

Chapter 39 – 3

Well into the night, his fever finally dropped. He's resting quietly. I wish I could have made him swallow a few more spoonfuls of the porridge. Hu should be fine until the next dose. I should start on those ledgers to pass the time.

"Stay, Wife."

The nearly inaudible words came so naturally, I thought I must have imagined them. While still fast asleep, his left hand has taken hold of my mine. I'd forgotten how large his hands are. The roughness covering them can't overshadow their gentleness.

"I'm here, Bai Hu."

In returning his grasp, hope sends my heart soaring and then reality crushes my foolish elation. He repeats those same words in delirium and I realize he'd called for Kai and not Wife.

Inexplicably, the woman of his dreams comes waltzing into the house and straight into the bedroom. Her pretty face twists into a sour glare the moment she notices our quaint predicament. I wonder if Hu gave her a key or if I'd forgotten to lock the door.

"I would have come sooner but some of us have real jobs. Should have known, I turn my back for a moment and you're advancing on my sick lover. The rumors around town were right about you."

"Yes, I've heard all the rumors people with *real jobs* had time to spread. Look, he just fell asleep. Could you not start another spat? I don't want him to wake."

"Fine." Kai shrugs. Throwing her shawl onto the nearby chair, she moves to take my position.

I feel terrible for prying his hand off mine but I know whose hand he thinks he's holding.

"When is he supposed to wake for the next dose?"

Kai settles onto the chair adjacent to the bed and then, taking up the medicine bowl, sniffs Master Tai Hung's secret brew. Her tongue sticks out from disgust.

"Are you going to tell him that you brew the medicine too?"

"Oh, don't be petty, Bao Lai! Hu's health is important to us both. Does it matter who he thinks cared for him as long as he recovers?"

I know what she's doing but she's also right. As long as Hu is well, that's what matters. Besides, if she's here tomorrow then I can work at the clinic. Master Yu is getting along in years. He's not able to keep up with the numerous patients coming and going all day long; more sick people are coming each day. Fliers were posted for another assistant but he hasn't had the time to interview candidates. Until the first wave of patients decreases, this might be the best arrangement.

"In four hours.   Make him finish the rest of the porridge if you can and plenty of that tonic in the green cup to wash it down. It'll help with dehydration."

"See? Was that so hard?" Flipping her long hair over the back of the chair, Kai takes his hand and leans over to press a kiss on his forehead.

The bedroom door closes, preserving the loving scene hidden on the other side.   I hate to admit it but they are picture-perfect together; a general and his princess.

Chapter 39 – 4

Ever since Bai Hu fell ill, odd things have happened. I came home from work the day after and Kai wasn't there. While I have my reasons for despising the lady, I thought her worship for Bai Hu was genuine. She'd left him untended, didn't fetch new porridge from the pot, or refilled his tonic as I instructed. Hu wouldn't respond to my griping and Kai never came back. Stranger still, while I sat by his bedside one night working on the clinic's ledgers, he started conversation which barely lasted half a minute. I don't recall what was said but I'm still overjoyed by the breakthrough.

The event from this morning topped all oddity. Unbeknownst to me how it happened, I fell asleep on the sofa in the living room, as usual, and woke in Hu's bed. My heart nearly gave out when he caught me trying to escape from beneath his heavy arms. An entire minute was spent incoherently stammering plausible reasons for why I might have accidentally climbed into bed and attacked him in his sleep, followed by another minute of awkwardly staring at one another in silence. I finally found an excuse and ran from the house as fast as I could. Master Yu gave another earful lecture for coming to work late and in my pajamas no less.

The day has been amusing to say the least. It wasn't until noon that I realized Hu didn't make a fuss this morning which means I could very well try slipping into bed with him purposefully tonight and every night thereafter. I'm not a saint. Kai has her dirty tactics and I'll have mine. I'm not against winning Hu back in any manner possible, as long as he's in agreement. Tonight, we're having his favorite meal and I've asked for a few hours off tomorrow so that Hu and I can watch the sunset together. I've lost many battles but I won't surrender this war just yet.

"Good-bye, Master Yu. I get pay tomorrow so don't spend all your money at the Red Light District!"

The old man waves a hand to dismiss my insolence. Earlier this morning, a patient mistook him for another who caused a ruckus at the Red Light District last night, illegal gambling and fistfights to boot! Master Yu is a quiet bookworm whose only pleasures outside of the clinic are having tea and watching checkers matches. It's inconceivable he'd ever set foot in the Red Light District, but the patient was so insistent that everyone made various stories of the master's secret life. We had fun at his expense and in turn, he made me stay late to clean all the dirty bowls, which was triple the usual volume.

A strong breeze rushes by, tossing the loose robe wrapped over my pajamas playfully; a quaint reminder of an old friend. The grey robe belonged to Dui. He'd left many articles behind at the clinic. This one still carries his scent. I hope it'll never fade.

"How romantic. Publicly sniffing the perverted doctor's shirt and yet won't leave to find him. I do believe you are standing in my way out of spite."

Chapter 39: Odd Happenings

Her casual voice sends a chill down my spine and shortly after, fire to my chest. I've had enough of this meddlesome woman intruding on my life. I could stand to forgive her for many things but leaving Bai Hu unconscious from high fever an entire day, no food or water, and without sending for me was a heartless act I won't soon forget. He would have been well days ago if she'd hadn't deserted the post usurped from me.

"What a scary face you're making, Bao Lai! Since you're already mad at nothing, let me give a valid reason for your wrath. You'll see who should rightfully take offense."

Whether or not I'll willingly suffer her nonsense, she'll talk anyway. Thus, I give the lady peace to express her plight. Never did I think the more she rambled on about her troubles, the more troubling things would become.

Chapter 39 – 5

Another oddity. I ran home to confirm Kai's unbelievable claims and, upon stepping into the yard, hear fire crackling from behind the house. The smell of grilled fish over open flames is intoxicating. I haven't had the chance to cook outside since those days of living alone.

He's sitting on a wooden stool flipping the skewered fish as though it were only natural. I've never seen him cook. Every meal that wasn't prepared by Kai or me has come from vendors down the streets or the markets. I'm not sure what to make of this.

"You're cooking, Bai Hu? Isn't that what restaurants are for?"

He glances up, seemingly embarrassed, and then resumes turning the fish as a mean to avoid engagement.

"Oh, I see. My cooking hasn't improved much, huh? Sorry. What was it Dui said? Always too much onion, not enough salt. But when I add a bit more salt, it comes out *really* salty for some reason!"

"That's not why."

"Hmm?"

Chapter 39: Odd Happenings

Hu heaves a sigh, presses his lips together, and then looks up. "I can't retire if I continue spending every coin I make."

"You're thinking about retirement?"

He nods and looks down again.

Another oddity; too many in one day. I wonder if I'm still asleep somewhere. The old Bai Hu wouldn't quit the military for anything. It is his life, has been his life, since he was seventeen. Then again, the old Bai Hu never considered marriage either. I thought Kai's claim was baseless, an attempt to drive Hu and me apart. This turn of event validates the sordid news she rubbed in my face earlier. Bai Hu proposed and she accepted. He's considering retirement to start their perfect life together. Kai asked for my departure so that her new position as mistress of this house may begin.

I'd promised to support Bai Hu with the stipulation that when I could no longer fill that role, then I would do the right thing for us both. There's only one right thing to do when he's determined to make a life for himself.

"Congratulations... on your engagement. I hope— know—I know that you'll be very happy. There's a small wooden chest in the drawer, you know the one. San An was very generous with my salary and then His Highness sent over another substantial sum, so... consider everything inside repayment for the pink robe and an early wedding present. A good start on that retirement fund too, huh?"

Why is it so difficult to keep from embarrassing myself? Congratulating someone for a momentous event in his life doesn't call for petty tears. He's happy. I should be happy for him.

"Well! I heard a few apartments near the clinic posted openings. Short walk to work sounds great! Maybe, I won't be late for once! Just have to pack a few things before running over there. Drop by the clinic if you need anything! See you around!"

Oh, geez. That was excessively perky. Slightly less embarrassing than crying but still embarrassing.

Everything I own in this house could easily fit inside these two pockets on Dui's shirt. The pink robe, Handsome Husband Hu's gift to Wife, doesn't seem appropriate to wear anymore. I'll take it as a keepsake along with the blue robe from my cross-dressing days. That about sums up my entire life for the past six months.

I have everything I sought in hand and yet my feet won't move. How can I possibly part from this room where we shared our first kiss, our first moments of intimacy, our secrets and joy? How can I accept anyone else replacing the one part of his heart that was mine? It hurts. I thought I could be an adult and do the right thing but I can't!

Chapter 39: Odd Happenings

"Why are you crying?"

"*Ahh*! Don't sneak up on me!"

"I waited in the living room but you were taking your sweet time mouthing a soliloquy."

"I did it again?! Ugh. Sorry. Left your house key in the drawer. Don't forget to lock the door. Thanks for everything and... congratulations."

Sharp piercing eyes suddenly emerge over his calm expression, followed by an exasperated sigh. He's agitated again; the common theme of our relationship, ending exactly where it first started.

"Bye."

I slip around Hu's broad figure and somehow fall against his chest. Something warm unexpectedly touches my lips. By the time I realize he's kissed me, Hu's already moved away.

"Didn't I say it's only polite when someone's kissing you, to kiss back?"

"That's... terrible logic?"

"Should have known. You're still the most unromantic person in the world."

He scoffs at my incoherent stammers and leans in for another kiss. This time, I'm prepared.

"Hu, don't! This is inappropriate! You're engaged to Kai!"

"Do you hear yourself? How can I be engaged to Kai when I already have a wife?" Strong arms pull our bodies closer. For the first time in a long while, he's actually smiling. "Don't give me that look. You want to ask who my wife is, don't you? Think about it. I better not hear a wrong answer."

"M-Me?"

"It's about time, Wife."

"But—"

"Quiet. Don't make a fuss, Wife."

He sweeps my body off the floor and starts for the bed. Leaning over me, Hu plants kiss after kiss as though it were only natural. I've a million things to shout at him, a thousand grievances, and a hundred confessions. And yet, the moment his passion begins to overtake me, I lose my mind and throw caution to the wind. The warmth I've missed so much, the tender touch from his rough hands, the sound of his soft sigh draping over my lips, and everything that is Bai Hu—the man I've loved all my life—is mine in this moment. Whatever comes next is inconsequential. I simply want to stay in this time with him forever.

"Handsome Husband Hu."

"What is it, Wife?"

Chapter 39: Odd Happenings

"Welcome back."

"I'm still me. You're the only woman who can make me fall under your spell three times without fail."

"Three, including Xiao Meow?"

"Do you really have to ask? And don't call me that anymore."

"Why didn't you tell me the truth? You knew it was me that day on the road. Why did you keep pretenses?"

"Until your attitude surfaced, I wasn't certain. I didn't admit the truth because, well, I was a shrimp who couldn't win one fight against Little Hung. Not exactly the manly image I thought you should perceive."

"Ha! You were a shrimp. Half my height, as I recall."

"That's some exaggeration, Wife."

"What was it you said? I'd never find a man if I kept cross-dressing and I'd probably end up married to some random loser? That makes you the random loser."

"All right, already! How do you always manage to ruin the mood, unromantic woman?"

"Gripe all you want. I don't see you stopping."

His kiss silences my lips. His fingers thread through mine. The immense heat rising from his body thoroughly warms my former lonely soul. Darkness of night casts a shrouded net over the heated room, giving new boldness to express my love and desire for the man I'll never again let go.

We've lived two lives together and as they say, third time's the charm. He's finally become whole and through his love, so have I.

Chapter 40: Husband and Wife

"You're awfully late, Wife. The fish were filleted and the radishes were peeled an hour ago."

"Sorry! Sorry! I was having too much fun chatting with a new friend at the market."

"Oh? Should I be jealous?"

"Not sure. I know I am. Feng You couldn't stop gushing about a certain *romantic* lover of hers and I just had to know *every* detail."

Hu spits out the tea he'd just drank, splattering the mouthful over the pristine carved wooden table. I wonder why he's surprised. We were bound to run into his former paramour now that our life is in Bi Xi. Hu retired from Nan Rong's imperial army and I left the clinic after Master Yu hired a new assistant. Aside from taking part in Bi Xi's security, Hu opened a martial arts school near the markets, adjacent to my small apothecary shop. Students tend to injure each other and there aren't ever enough balms and salves. We're also by the foothill of Mount Chou where rare herbs are plentiful, along with some not so rare, like wormwood.

"Wh-What did she say?" He runs a kerchief over the table, smearing the mess about more so than cleaning anything.

"You're on pins and needles, Bai Hu. Don't worry. She's still very pretty and single."

"Wh-Wh-What are you talking about? I-I have you."

"Uh-huh. You sound so happy about it."

"I-I am! You're the only woman for me!"

"Funny. Sometimes I wonder if you even love me."

"That's ridiculous! You should know by now!"

"How's a girl to know that? The most I've ever received in exchange for professing my love is a smile. You can't say it, can you?"

"Ah!" He sighs, scratching his head hurriedly. "Why do I have to say it? I'm not good at that sort of thing."

He's on his feet with back turned from me. Hu's embarrassed; it makes me smile. Too bad I'm not that forgiving.

"Really? Feng You remembers you fondly as the most romantic person she'd ever met. How was it you admitted to her your worship? A hundred paper cranes inside a glass jar, each one a confession? Under a starry summer night, atop a firefly-lit hill, you pledged your immortal love through a composed poem. How did it go? Oh, that's right. Feng You, Feng—"

"That was a long, *long* time ago! I was a stupid, stupid teenage boy! Besides, you don't like sappy things anyway, unromantic woman."

"Is a short admission, conveyed through words and not your busy hands, that much to ask?"

Chapter 40: Husband and Wife

"No. It's just... difficult. You're... you're special... to me."

"Why? Because for two years of our young lives, you and I caused troubles for the monks and beat each other senseless on the training fields? She told me, you know, how close you two were. If it hadn't been for your nightmares, a future together was certain."

I will never give Hu away to anyone but a part of me wonders whether he loves me half as much as I love him. Half of his heart is all I need. I just doubt he has half left to give after Feng You, Kai, and who knows how many other women.

"You're insecure, hmm? That's kind of cute."

"Wh—?! Don't turn this on me!"

A rough hand gently tousles my hair. I bat it away and move back, overwhelmed by the same confusion experienced that first day when I entered his house in An. Despite the playful gesture, his gaze couldn't be more serious.

"What is this really about, huh? You're not sour over a few sweet things I said to another woman ten years ago, are you? She never left Bi Xi. Our romance could have easily resumed. I didn't love her. I've never said those words to her either, so don't misunderstand. Before meeting you, I was a runaway orphan who never felt that I belonged anywhere. You were my first friend. When we weren't fighting over nothing, and even when we fought, I had fun. We raised hell at Tian Mao Yi and for those short years, you were all mine. You made me feel accepted and needed. We shared our thoughts and dreams without fear. That meant more to me than anything."

"Same. I feel the same and I know it's petty considering the sacrifices you've made for me but I... how can I possibly feel assured after..."

"After?"

There's a knot in my stomach and an insatiable itch wreaking havoc across both hands. Talk about being petty, bringing this subject to light is even pettier than asking for three simple words. This feeling of resentment I thought was buried away is clawing at my throat, forcing its way out.

"Tell me." A warm hand touches my cheek and draws my attention into golden eyes peering worriedly. More than my lover and beloved, this man is my best friend. We never kept secrets back then and that's why we trusted one other indiscriminately. I want that trust again, to fully appreciate that he's finally mine.

"How can I feel assured after seeing you make love to Kai? I'm happy that you're with me but you were happy with her too. What's keeping you from changing your mind for Feng You?"

"Hey, now! I did *not* make love to Kai! What gave you *that* idea?"

Chapter 40: Husband and Wife

"Right. Two consenting adults lying naked in bed together is the norm for carrying on civil conversations. I might have been raised in a temple but I'm not *that* gullible!"

"We weren't *naked* and I didn't... Tsk, damn it! Should have known that would come back to bite me in the ass!"

"So, you admit it. You cheated."

"I did not! It was a stupid idea devised by a stupid man because he was driven to jealousy by stupidity! What was I supposed to do? You ran off every day and maybe... I just wanted a bit of attention."

"The more I doted, the farther I was pushed away. You didn't want my attention, so I turned to my job. Don't tell me your private amorous sessions with Kai were all an act because you clearly enjoyed yourself!"

"At first... I liked her and I was mad at you. And then, I don't know, I realized everything was a mistake but I was afraid to hurt Kai. You wouldn't fight for me. I thought you didn't care so I figured pushing you over the edge was the answer. How would I have known you'd turn submissive?"

"I was trying to be an adult by being there for you and not throw tantrums. How would I have known you just wanted me to break all your fingers?!"

He wasn't himself. He hated me for causing his misery. He didn't remember one speck of our time together.   These are reasons I could overlook his intimacy with Kai. Simply because he was attracted to another and angry with me is not good enough. From now until the rest of our lives, there will be angrier spats. Am I expected to give chase each time he feels attraction for another and our relationship happens to become strained? That's hardly healthy for either of us.

"Excuse me. I need some air."

Chapter 40 – 2

I didn't want to run away but apparently, this is our immature relationship, as it has been for twenty years. We always have a reason to argue but we always need one another. Being an adult is hard. I miss the days when we could just beat each other silly and then become friends again before dinner.

"Stop walking so fast!"

"Hu?"

"Were you expecting someone else?"

Our arms are suddenly linked. He's taken the lead of this stroll.

"At least let me explain."

"Sure you want to make a scene, Bai Hu? People will talk and I mean all fifty people in Bi Xi. You won't hear the end of it."

"Let them. Look, after my two halves joined, I felt like a child growing up again, but I was inside a man's body so I hurt you as an adult would. Recently, I've caught up to you. I finally understood why you *just didn't break all my fingers* and... I'm sorry. You loved me, we were living together and I intentionally kissed someone else. I cheated. I'm so sorry."

That's a much better answer; though, I wonder if I'd mouthed it to him by mistake. However, his countenance couldn't be more serious. The rigid jaw line, furrowed brows, and tightening grip around my arm make me believe he won't ever let go. Of late, there has been a mature air about him that was lacking during our time in An which validates his claims. He has grown. The fact that we are in Bi Xi starting a new life together is proof of that. Past experiences won't permit doubt from leaving my mind but my heart believes him. Hu may have trouble expressing affections in words but he's right, I should know better.

"Anything else bothering you? Once this stroll comes to a halt, I won't put up with anymore interrogations."

"Maybe one more. When did things officially end with Kai?"

"The night she came by while I was sick. Maybe you didn't notice but I asked you to stay when I heard her walked through the door."

"So, you did say, 'Wife.' I thought you said, 'Kai.'"

"I said both. The latter was a warning, the first was a request. I'm flattered she liked me so much but taking credit for your kindness and then lying... your conversation made me realized I was jealous over nothing. She twisted the truth. Everything she told me about you and Dui were false. I made you feel terrible for no reason at all. The farce ended that morning."

666

"No wonder she left and didn't come back. You could have sent for me. I came home and you were shriveled up in bed!"

"I'm fine now because of you. You shouldn't have run home from work six times a day after that to coddle me. Did I mention how sweet you are?" The amorous tint in his eyes forces my feet back a step. His arms draw my entirety forward into a longing embrace.

"Listen, Hu. Since we're being honest, things between Dui and me weren't entirely innocent. He kissed me, aside from that time in the clinic. That really was an accident but um... later, he wasn't joking, and I... liked him too; but I love you so... I'm sorry."

"For liking him? I knew that much twenty years ago. Why else would I have goaded you into giving him a hard time at Tian Mao Yi?"

"You did? I don't remember that."

"Of course you don't. You were too busy ogling Tai Hung's tall, lanky apprentice, so your short friend might have suggested a few mean pranks to capture his attention."

"That's just... downright manipulative! Poor Dui!"

"Are you complaining? As I recall, my mere suggestions were taken overboard by an overzealous girl who confused attraction for dislike. Maybe now you'll understand my overreaction when it comes to Dui."

667

Chapter 40 – 3

"Little Hung and Xiao Mao bickering. How nostalgic!"

Hu's arms constrict when that smooth tone makes an entrance, mashing his chest against my face.

"Hu, I can't breathe!"

"Don't fall for temptation, Bao Lai! Resist looking at that charming face. This man is a snake!"

"You're overreacting again, Bai Hu! Lo Han helped the Western Alliance! We reunited in Ye!"

"Is that so? Come to take my Bao Lai, have you, monk? Over my dead body!"

"I think you said the exact thing the last time, Xiao Mao, to me and every other man at Tian Mao Yi." Lo Han's melodious chuckle makes Hu's growling deepens, which in turn tightens his grip around my shoulders. "Back then, you were a child and I was bounded by faith. It seems as free men we share the same ambition but I've come too late. Still, I'm unconvinced. Are you really his wife, Bao Lai?"

We reply in union; our answers are complete opposites. Lo Han laughs at our awkward outburst as though having succeeded a mean prank. This was his intention, fueling humor at the expense of our amity. My mentor had his vengeance after all.

Chapter 40: Husband and Wife

"W-Well, we're not actually married." My explanation is more so to a distancing Bai Hu, whose arms have relaxed from my shoulders, than the pleased Lo Han. I've spoken the truth which, apparently, is more difficult to take back than a lie. "Hu and I are together, Lo Han. I'm practically his wife, I mean, I would never consider anyone else and... and, um... What are you doing away from Feng Jia? How's Diao?"

"Diao is doing as well as can be expected. She needed time alone. Don't glower, Xiao Mao, I didn't expect this trip down memory lane. Master Zhuang and I have unfinished business which I suppose I best tend to. It's getting late."

"Yes, you're right. Please send Diao my regards."

"Sure. Oh, before I forget, Ma Tai Tou asked about you. Do visit her when you have a spare moment."

"I will. Certainly! Thank you for telling me. I'm glad we could meet again."

"It's never truly good-bye between us, Bao Lai. I'll always see you in the stars. You too, Xiao Mao. I apologize for the troubles at Tian Mao Yi."

Lo Han leisurely moves down the road toward Master Zhuang's abode, whistling a familiar tune to himself. His easy-going nature is back; seemingly as carefree as ever on the outside. His real self is still buried under that smile.

Chapter 40 – 4

The trek home was quiet, as was the house once we stepped inside. He's mad again. This time, I'm not certain how many months will pass until he forgoes the silent treatment. Still, I'm glad for our chance meeting with Lo Han. Through him, I've come to realize the reason for my doubt: the link missing between Hu and me. I've been afraid that this relationship is a mere fling until Hu's next romance. Fear, another childish aspect that still conquers me. I'm insecure, as he'd said. Marriage would make this dream become real, make me feel assured, but also serves as bondage to force his loyalty. I don't want him to feel obligated and trapped. Marriage is pointless if he's unhappy.

Contrarily, I am happy. Until today, I never knew just how much Bai Hu has accomplished to keep me for himself. All of the men he's intimidated and all of the ways he has manipulated me to keep my attention, which I can't say was a good thing, were somehow strangely sweet. His obsession for me borders Kai's obsession for him. Slightly frightening but again, perplexingly adorable. From this awkward revelation, I've concluded that Hu will never let me go. I am his favorite. If that isn't marriage, I don't know what is.

A few more firewood sticks are shoved into the pit. We're having grilled sardines, Hu's favorite, because despite having become Bai Hu (White Tiger), he's still Xiao Mao (Little Cat). The crackling flame brightens when a sharp sweep of wind passes by, a warmer wind than usual. It's almost summer again. Time sure flies. Not long ago, the thought of having another day by each other's side was but a wish during the midst of Nan Rong's conflict with Bei Ling. I've made many friends and lost many allies. In the face of distress, people often come to appreciate the preciousness of life and in time of peace, often forget. We've walked a long road, Bai Hu and I, to find this place called home. Despite our differences, every moment with Bai Hu will be special to me.

How wondrous! The man with the worst timing in the world finally makes a proper appearance, exiting through the backdoor just when I long to see his face. He comes closer, pouting.

"Hey, Hu."

"Hey, who?"

"Hey, you. Still mad?"

His face is as red as the surrounding sunset. I'll take that as a yes.

Rising up, my tired back arches, and then I move from around the cooking pit to meet my glowering lover. He's cute when he's angry.

"H—"

"*Marry me!*" Right after the unexpected, excessively loud shout, the uptight posture and tense shoulders finally loosen. In contrast, his face turns redder.

"Are you asking me or telling me?"

"Both."

"Uh... huh. Thank you but, no."

"Why not?" And now he's panicking. That's even more adorable.

"Indisputably, I am your wife and I'll never say otherwise again. A ceremony proves nothing. Let's save the money for that trip you wanted to Northern Jing."

"You are just... *unbelievable!*"

Instantly, I'm swept off the ground and rushed into the house. Everything happened so quickly, I don't recall when his body first pinned mine to the bed or when his rough fingers stretched my cheeks flat. They're still being stretched.

"Quit acting like a man! Don't you dare refuse marriage after *thoroughly* enjoying my body!"

"What about you? You're such a woman, bullying me into marriage! That hurts! Knock it off!"

"No. Agree!"

Chapter 40: Husband and Wife

"Ack! I can't feel my face! Don't ask if you don't want to!"

"I want to that's why I'm asking! Say it!"

"You're just overreacting because of Lo Han!"

"I'm not! And don't say other men's name in bed! I love you, unromantic woman, and I'm not taking no for an answer! You might as well agree!"

"Then isn't it pointless to ask?"

"Say it!"

"*Okay*! Fine! I'll marry you!"

"It's about time! Why do you have to make everything so difficult?"

"Because... Wait, did you just say you love me?"

"You know I do."

The sharp pains disperse, replaced by a numbing reminder of his assault. Soft lips caress my sore cheeks until I'm filled entirely by another rising emotion.

"Hu! The fish!"

"How can you think of food at a time like this?"

"They'll burn!"

Silence is his answer, coupled with joining our hands and lips. He didn't need to push himself this way but I'm happy to be so spoiled. His love, gentle and sweet as always, pull me under. I never cease to lose my mind in his loving embrace. The fever growing inside burns hotter each time we are together, eventually consuming our souls and melding our two beings into one.

From the first moment we met, he has been a part of my heart and soul. Time has only made that attachment grow stronger, into an undeniable love I can never again be without. I love him and he loves me, making the long road that came before worth walking and this life we share now, well worth the wait. For the rest of our days, we shall remain inseparable. This I know in my heart and entrust in my soul.

The End.